PROVIDENCE
AND
HARD WORK

PROVIDENCE AND HARD WORK

The Story of Caleb Morgan VOL II

James F. Hunt

TATE PUBLISHING
AND ENTERPRISES, LLC

Providence and Hard Work Series; You Shall Know the Truth
Copyright © 2014 by James F. Hunt. All rights reserved.

No part of this publication may be reproduced, stored in a retrieval system or transmitted in any way by any means, electronic, mechanical, photocopy, recording or otherwise without the prior permission of the author except as provided by USA copyright law.

Unless otherwise indicated, all scripture quotations are from New Revised Standard Version Bible, copyright © 1989 National Council of the Churches of Christ in the United States of America. Used by permission. All rights reserved.

Scripture quotations marked (kjv) are taken from the Holy Bible, King James Version, Cambridge, 1769. Used by permission. All rights reserved.

The opinions expressed by the author are not necessarily those of Tate Publishing, LLC.

This novel is a work of fiction. Names, descriptions, entities, and incidents included in the story are products of the author's imagination. Any resemblance to actual persons, events, and entities is entirely coincidental.

Published by Tate Publishing & Enterprises, LLC
127 E. Trade Center Terrace | Mustang, Oklahoma 73064 USA
1.888.361.9473 | www.tatepublishing.com

Tate Publishing is committed to excellence in the publishing industry. The company reflects the philosophy established by the founders, based on Psalm 68:11,
"The Lord gave the word and great was the company of those who published it."

Book design copyright © 2014 by Tate Publishing, LLC. All rights reserved.
Cover design by Allen Jomoc
Interior design by Joana Quilantang

Published in the United States of America

ISBN: 978-1-62902-507-0
Fiction / General
14.02.24

DEDICATION

This book is dedicated to the loving memory of my late father and mother, J. Max Hunt and Mary M. Hunt. Their love and devotion to their family, friends, and Lord has been my guide and inspiration throughout my life.

ACKNOWLEDGMENTS

I am deeply indebted to the following people:

Ann Obrien, teacher, friend, for her encouragement and guidance; Jamie Hunt, my son, Beth Fudge, the late Anita McKnight, and Julie Bryant, my three daughters, and Leon Franklin, for their help in the development of the manuscript; Dawn Taylor, my computer wizard who kept things moving; Ginger Andrews Hunt, my wife of fifty-three years who thinks anything is possible with hard work and perseverance and who gave me the courage to move forward; Andy Ash, Adele Goldsby, and Andy Dreher, editing assistance; Dr. Thomas Trihan M.D., medical adviser.

ABOUT BOOK ONE

Providence and Hard Work is a journey back to the golden era of the fifties as seen through the eyes of Caleb Morgan, a strikingly handsome poor farm boy from rural Mississippi.

Caleb arrived at the exclusive Marston College in 1955 driving a '23 Model T pickup. He soon became the brunt of everyone's jokes, appearing somewhat slow because of his deep, southern drawl and naivety. Caleb's dream was to play football at Marston College and become a teacher, although he had never played before. He soon fell in love with the campus beauty; however, she wore an engagement ring. There was sadness in her gorgeous, brown eyes, and a shroud of mystery concerning her past.

Caleb secured employment at the local country club, tried out for football, attended class, and made a fool out of himself at every turn. He was ready to forsake his dreams and return to the cotton fields after he and his roommate were the victims of a cruel prank that landed his roommate in the hospital near death.

Dr. Marston, the most affluent man in Mississippi, and owner of the Marston Memorial Hospital and prestigious country club where Caleb worked, was so impressed with Caleb's humility and integrity that he took Caleb under his wing, convinced him to stay in school, and began making secret plans for Caleb's future.

Caleb's fortune began to change after that day, and in time the campus goat became the campus' "Golden Boy." The education he received was a far cry from the one he expected.

Providence and Hard Work will tug at ones heartstrings, yet it is filled with wry humor.

CHAPTER ONE

The staff arrived at the coaches' office early Friday morning and had coffee. They began to talk about the game plan to make sure they had covered all the bases. Coach Stan commented, "Coach Shook, did you read the Memphis sports page this morning?"

"You know I don't read that crap, Stan. I read the front page and Metro section, and then it hits the trash can."

Stan handed Coach Shook the sports page, saying, "I think you need to read it this morning."

Coach Shook raised his head, widened his eyes, and looked at Stan. "I told you I don't read that crap!"

"I read it," Coach Billy Ray said. "Coach Stan's right, you need to know what Norris Beckham wrote. He said the alumni plan to storm the administration building Monday and demand your resignation. Otherwise, there will be a boycott of the games, and all alumni financial support will cease until you're fired. He further stated that as an alumnus, he would be leading the brigade. He said you had nothing to do with Caleb Morgan coming to Marston. He said he knew for a fact that you and the staff tried to discourage him from playing football. Further, that Morgan was forced to run the gauntlet in an effort to injure him and force him to—"

Coach Shook slammed his fist down on the desk and yelled, "Enough! That low life son-of-a— Hell, he's right. Do y'all want me to resign? You men know that I respect each of you. If you tell me that it's my fault we're not winning, I promise you I won't hold it against you. I'll go to President Parker and tender my resignation right now."

Stan walked over to Coach Shook, put his arm around him, and said, "I've been here through thick and thin with you. I swear by all that's good and pure that no mortal could have had those kids any more prepared than you and this coaching staff has. To answer your question truthfully, hell no, it's not your fault, and I'll fight anyone who says it is."

Billy Ray added, "You know my feelings, Coach. I wouldn't be here if I felt that way." The other coaches echoed similar responses.

"I pride myself in having a thick hide, men, but I don't know how much more of this I can endure, or ask Mavis to take. Can we win this game tomorrow?" Coach Shook asked.

"You bet your rear, we can," Stan said.

"You can bet the farm on it," Billy Ray said.

Coach Shook forced a smile and said, "I love you guys. I would have walked away. You know, sometimes those outside looking in can get a better view than those inside."

"Answer me this," Billy Ray said, "why does Norris have it in for you? I've been out of state since I graduated. I don't understand what the problem is."

"It's simple," Coach Shook said. "It's vindictive. Norris was a hotshot running back from a small school in West Tennessee. The alumni from that area kept hounding me to go watch him play. I did, and against my better judgment, I gave him a scholarship. He had all the tools to be a great running back, except one, no guts. Give him a hole and he would look like an all-American. But if he had to bow his neck and fight for a yard, he'd crumble rather than take a hit. He rode the pine here for four years, and he never forgave me for that."

After lunch, Caleb went to the stadium to see Will and the team off. They had had a good week of practice, and their confidence had returned. Caleb walked Will to the bus. "I'll be listening to every play, Will. You're the captain of this team. You've got to get up in their faces and make them play as hard as you do."

"I got the situation covered, kid. I just wish you were not a freshman and could play with the varsity. We'd kick their rears for sure if you could play with us."

"Will, I heard some talk at the club that if we lose this game, the alumni are going to demand Coach Shook's resignation immediately. You don't think it's his fault that we can't win any games, do you?"

"If I did, I wouldn't have come here, Corn Shuck. We need a few 'blue chippers' on this team. When we win a few games, we'll be able to recruit some studs. We're going to turn this program around starting tomorrow night. I guarantee it. I'm going to call a team meeting tonight, no coaches, and we're going to do some soul searching. If anyone is not willing to pay the price, we're going to send him packing. These kids need to know what's at stake."

"I pray you're right, Will, because I like our coaching staff. I want to play for all of them."

A few hundred fans, students, and well wishers gathered to see the team off. Caleb waved at Will and the team as the Greyhound bus pulled away.

Coach Parrish, a graduate assistant, was in charge of freshman practice that afternoon. The team worked on polishing their offense and defense and special teams, and concluded the practice with a short and spirited scrimmage. Caleb alternated with Cliff at the running back position. He tripped once when he ran up the heels of his lead blocker and was mobbed by the defense. It was the only time in six carries that he didn't score. He was equally as proficient on defense, using his quickness and his keen sense of precognition as he smelled out the ball carriers and receivers. There was nothing timid about his hits either, but he always helped the ball carrier up after he drove him into the turf. His teammates were in awe of his athletic prowess. After sprints, the team walked back to the dressing room. Cliff eased up by Caleb and extended his hand. Caleb took it and they shook. "I need to apologize because I acted like a fool earlier," Cliff said. "It'll be a pleasure to back you up."

"We'll back each other up," Caleb said with a nod. Cliff smiled, nodded, and winked.

Coach Parrish eased up beside Caleb and said, "I want you to know how proud the staff is of you. I'm sure they haven't told you because you might get the big head. You did it the hard way, kid, and you did it with dignity. A lot of kids would be strutting around like a turkey gobbler with a flock of hens, after the show you put on last week."

"I was very fortunate to score the way I did. I don't have anything to be proud about. When I play an entire ballgame and can help the team win, that's when I'll feel like I've accomplished something."

"Some people have to work hard for greatness, for others it just seems to come natural. You've had to work hard for what comes natural. Now, you need to enjoy it. It's supposed to be fun."

"I won't lie, it did feel good when I crossed the goal line. It felt so good that I was a little ashamed of myself. You know they say pride comes before a fall. I probably shouldn't say this but—Will told me that scoring is the only thing that feels as good as sex." Caleb snickered, somewhat embarrassed. "I don't know about sex, but if it feels that good, I can't wait to get married."

"Will has a point, but he might get an argument from most folks. His problem is that he hasn't found the right girl yet. If he doesn't learn to keep his wang-dang in his pants he's going to get into more trouble than his father can buy him out of next time. I'd hoped he learned his lesson last year."

"I know." Caleb nodded. "He doesn't listen to me." He wondered what Coach Parrish meant about last year, but he didn't ask.

Caleb walked into the dining hall at the Marston Country Club where he worked and greeted everyone as he went to the back. He put on his waiter's jacket and began setting the tables. A few minutes later, the dinner crowd began to arrive. The staff was very busy the next few hours. Around eight, Doc and Edith came in. Caleb rushed over to seat Mrs. Edith and greet them.

"Did you forget something today?" Doc asked coolly.

"I don't know," Caleb responded, somewhat surprised by Doc's tone. Doc slipped his hand into his coat pocket and flashed a syringe filled with penicillin.

"Oh, Doc, I'm sorry. I went over to see the team off after class and then to practice. I clean forgot."

"If you get blood poisoning, it'll be too late to remember," Doc scolded.

"Ease up on the boy, James," Edith chided. "His schedule is tighter than your shorts are getting. He can't be expected to remember everything. How many kids have you known who can work forty hours a week, play football, attend class, and study at night, and manage to get enough sleep to stay awake in the daytime?"

"Go ahead, Edith, reprimand me in front of everyone. They all know who wears the pants in our family."

Edith smiled, patted Doc on the cheek, and said tenderly, "I'm sorry, sweetheart. I didn't mean to scold. No one is big enough to wear your pants. I know you're only concerned about Caleb's health."

Doc looked up at Caleb, winked, and said, "It's okay, honey, I know he's burning the candle at both ends. If his mother would allow him to accept the scholarship, he'd have more time to relax—and play golf."

Caleb took their order and went to the kitchen. Doc's order always took priority over all others because he owned the country club. In only a few minutes, Caleb was serving them. As he placed their dinner plates on the table, a strange, almost frightened expression came across his face as he stared at the front door. Doc and Edith turned to see what his concern was. Chris Black and a very attractive young lady were walking in. Doc nodded and mumbled, "That's what I thought." Doc looked at Caleb and said, "Go take their order, and don't let him intimidate you. You're a damn site better man than him."

"James!" Edith gasped.

"Calm yourself, sweetheart. Sometimes there's only one way to articulate the truth."

Caleb eased over to their table, held the chair for the pretty young lady, and handed them menus. "May I get ya'll something to drink?" Caleb asked.

"I'll have branch water and bourbon," Chris said curtly.

"I don't think I'm allowed to serve you that, sir," Caleb responded as politely as possible.

Looking up, the young lady smiled and said, "Don't mind him, he's just being facetious. Oh my heavens!" She gasped in amazement, her eyes widening. "You're Caleb Morgan, aren't you?"

Caleb gave her a timid smile and nodded.

"I recognized you from your picture in the paper this week. There was one close up of you crossing the goal line to win the game. I could see the smile on your face. I'm Peggy McNeal, a sophomore at Ole Miss." She stood up and shook Caleb's hand. Chris was sitting there, fuming with jealousy. "Is it really true that you've never played football before?"

"Yes ma'am." Caleb nodded, cutting his eyes down at Chris.

"You're the talk of the campus at Ole Miss. The girls all think you're gorgeous. After seeing you, I'm inclined to agree with them. Is there any chance you might transfer to Ole Miss, you know, because of the losing streak Marston is having over here?"

"Are you going to order, or sit here all night passing pleasantries with that plow boy?" Chris snapped.

"What's your problem?" Peggy responded. "I think it's an honor to get to talk to a real live hero like Caleb Morgan. All the girls at school are going to be jealous when I tell them I got to meet him and talk to him."

"The seafood platter is quite excellent tonight," Caleb said, praying for a quick exit.

"If you recommend it, that's good enough for me," Peggy said, "and a coke." Caleb glanced reluctantly at Chris.

"The same!" He sneered. Caleb grabbed their menus and rushed into the kitchen.

Abe, the black head waiter for thirty years, walked up to Caleb and said, "Your ears are red, and your face is flushed. Is something wrong?"

"Yes, sir. It's Chris Black. He makes me so angry I'd like to——"

"Son, remember this, anger is your enemy, fear can sometimes be your friend. Remember what the Bible says about kindness. It heaps burning coals upon a person's head. I do know how you feel. I fight those same feelings about his father, Doctor Black. He hates me, and I've never shown him anything but respect."

"Would you help me, Mr. Abe? Would you serve Chris and his date?"

"There you go with that mister stuff again. You gonna get me and you in trouble sayin' that. Son, I'm disappointed in you. You have to stand up to him. He's spoiled and rotten, and everybody knows it. Just stand your ground and don't let him intimidate you, and he'll leave you alone."

"I don't understand why he hates me. After what he did, I thought he might, well, I just thought maybe…"

"His kind doesn't change, son. Don't let him change you. Look, Doc's waving for you."

Caleb rushed over to Doc's table. "Meet me in the ballroom in five minutes," Doc said. "I need to get this penicillin in you before it gets warm."

"Oh, Doc, do you have to? It doesn't hurt anymore."

Doc patted the syringe in his pocket and said, "This is the reason it doesn't hurt anymore. Did you know more people died from infection in the Civil War than from all other causes?"

Caleb frowned and shook his head as if he was about to swallow a bitter dose of castor oil. "Okay, let's get it over with now." They walked back to the ballroom and closed the door behind them. Doc took the syringe and wiped Caleb's arm with an alcohol pad. He popped the needle in quickly, and Caleb almost fainted. Doc chuckled.

"I saw your ears turn red when you took that rotten snot's order. You looked really nervous. Why do you let him intimidate you so?"

"His snide remarks get to me, Doc. I wanted to knock his block off, but that ain't right. I mean that *isn't* right."

"I'm glad you didn't. His attitude will make it all the more sweet when we kick their rears in the tournament. Dr. Black wants that trophy more than all his concubines, but I want it more than him. That may be childish, but I can't help it."

"I think I want it as much as you, Doc. Maybe he'll respect me if we—when we win."

"No," Doc said. "He and his father respect nothing but power and prestige. You and I will have to work hard and get blisters on our hands and toes to whip them. If you're willing, so am I. I'll pick up another hundred balls for you, so you won't have to stop to pick them up until you finish practicing. We're on a mission, and nothing is going to hinder us. There's only one trophy for first place. What do you want to do with it?"

Caleb smiled and said, "I'd like to put it on the stand in your office by the other, Doc." Doc's lips began to quiver as he put his arms around Caleb and hugged him.

Edith stuck her head in the door and said, "What are you two men still doing in here? Don't tell me—talking golf?"

"I told you she had ESP," Doc said, "and it's not contagious. Oh, by the way," he continued, "can you come at eight tomorrow morning? I have you signed up for a thirty-minute lesson. Don't worry about missing work. I'm covering that with Burt. He thinks it's time you learned how to shape your shots."

"Who wouldn't rather play golf than work, especially when you get paid for it," Caleb remarked.

"I'll make rounds at the hospital early. I should be here by eight-thirty, and we can get in a quick nine."

After the dining hall emptied and the tables and floor had been cleaned, Caleb went to the driving range and turned on the lights. It was a glorious sight with the dew sparkling on the freshly cut grass. The only sound to be heard was the crickets and an occasional horn from US 51. Caleb relaxed and began to hit the balls. The time flew by. The only thing that broke his concentration was a glorious shooting star that lit up the north sky. Around midnight, he felt a blister forming on his hand, so he decided it was time to quit for the night. He quickly picked up the balls and drove back to the dorm and climbed in bed.

Caleb opened his eyes next morning and looked out the window across the campus. During the early morning hours, a brief and welcomed refreshing shower had passed, followed by the first cool front of the season. The world seemed new and fresh. Summer had tried to keep its oppressive heat and humidity, but nature had finally won the battle. It was a glorious day. Excited about Will's game and the coming day's activities, he dressed quickly and rushed to the cafeteria for an extra large "Will's special breakfast."

Twenty minutes later, Caleb pulled up to the pro-shop, grabbed his clubs and balls, and went to the range. Burt was on the range working on his game, so he stepped over and began Caleb's instructions. Burt discussed the physics involved in the flight of a golf ball, and he demonstrated the proper swing plane, grip, and stance, which affected its flight. Then he let Caleb work on the swing, primarily the fade. Caleb had become fairly proficient at the draw; however, his swing sometimes produced a dreaded duck hook that even caused professionals to use unsavory words occasionally. Before the lesson was over, Caleb had learned to move the ball left to right occasionally, but with much difficulty.

When the lesson was over, Burt said, "Go with the draw unless you absolutely have to hit a fade to get to a hidden pin tucked on the extreme right side of the green. If the match is tight and you can't afford a bogie or worse, just hit the ball onto the green somewhere and try to make a long putt." Burt became serious and said, "Son, you have more coordination and natural ability than anyone I've ever worked with. If you're willing to commit yourself to this game, you could play on the golf team next year. Who knows, you might be the next Sam Snead, or Ben Hogan, or another young Arnold Palmer? I think the sky is the limit if you want it. It's an addictive game. The better you play, the better you want to be. Everyone who loves the game strives for perfection, but it's an impossible goal. I love to practice. Most people hate practice and love to play, and those never improve much. Doc knew that when he put the lights up on the practice range. He did it for you."

"I know, and you're making my head swell. I think I'll just take it one day at a time. For now, I'll try to make Doc's impossible dream come true." Burt patted him on the back, nodded, and headed to the pro-shop. Caleb continued to practice fading the ball as he waited for Doc.

A big, black Cadillac pulled into the parking lot, followed closely by a '98 Oldsmobile. Dr. Black and his son Chris stepped out of their automobiles, grabbed their clubs from the trunks, and proceeded into the pro-shop. Caleb hadn't noticed their arrival, but he heard the unmistakable sound of Doc's Plymouth a few minutes later as it pulled into the parking lot. He looked up, grabbed his bag, and rushed over to Doc's car. He grabbed Doc's clubs from the trunk, and they walked into the pro-shop.

Doc, with a sheepish look on his face, walked over to the counter where Burt was standing. "I have surgery at eleven-thirty today," Doc said. "I can manage only nine holes. I was hoping you might be able to join young Caleb and I for a quick nine and work with him on the course."

A disgusting, yet familiar voice from behind the merchandise racks responded, "You know Burt can't play on Saturday morning, Doc, but Chris and I are going to try to get a quick nine in before I fly to Little Rock for the game. We'll be happy to accommodate you and make it a foursome."

Dr. Black and Chris appeared from behind the merchandise racks with two light sweaters in their hands. "It's a little chilly this morning after the cool snap, and we didn't dress appropriately," Dr. Black said, gesturing for Burt to put the sweaters on his account. Then he reached for Caleb's hand, saying, "I'd like to shake your hand, young man, and congratulate you for making the team and for your remarkable performance last Thursday night. I listened to the game on the radio. I'd say the odds were stacked against you, and you hit the jackpot. The press is making you out to be quite the hero. How are you handling all the accolades?"

"I'm not sure what that word means, Dr. Black, but I don't feel any different," Caleb said.

"He might not feel anything," Chris smirked, "after those animals from Tulane get through with him next Thursday. They have some high school all-Americans on their team, and they won't get surprised like Memphis did at the end of the game when everyone was spent."

Doc glanced at Caleb then responded, "I'm trying to teach young Caleb the game. I fear we'd slow you two accomplished golfers down."

Chris laughed and said, "You're actually going to try to teach that hayseed how to play golf. Good luck! I thought golf was a gentleman's game."

Doc bristled and said, "I don't suppose you ever heard of Sam Sneed? He wasn't born into affluence, and yet he is one of the most revered champions on the tour."

"And by the way," Doc continued, "what's this I heard about you having a taste for stolen watermelons and watermelon parties late at night, Chris?"

Chris shot Caleb a look of revulsion, but didn't respond.

Caleb, shocked and embarrassed by Doc's comment, gave Chris a very surprised look and shook his head, wanting to say I never told Doc that.

"I don't know where you got that bogus information," Dr. Black retorted. "Chris has always despised watermelon. He said the seeds were repulsive to him. Has your taste changed, son?" He smiled and said to him, "Maybe you've been entertaining some young lady late at night that has a taste for melons—and other things. We can't fault the boy for doing what comes natural, can we, Doc?" Dr. Black laughed again, while Chris's fiery eyes continued to pierce Caleb.

"Nine holes are about all I can manage anyway," Christian said. "I have to drive back to Memphis and pick up Annie. I hear rumors that this might be Coach Shook's last game. I want to be able to say I was there at the end, which I might add, is coming about five years too late. Now, about this game," Dr. Black said, "slow play won't hurt our game. Possibly young Caleb can learn a few things while watching Chris swing. What time do we tee-off?"

"Now," Doc growled, and they started out the door.

Caleb said, "I'll be out in a second. I need to run to the restroom first." Caleb eased around behind the clothes rack to hide until they were out the door. "Mr. Burt, please tell me there is something really, really urgent that I need to do on the course this morning. Just get me out of this game. Chris and Dr. Black make me so nervous that I know I'm going to embarrass Doc. Please help me out of this predicament."

"Nope!" Burt answered. "This will be the best lesson you could have today. You'll learn how to play under pressure. You have to conquer your nerves to be a good golfer—or a good football player. Play your game and block out all distractions. That means all their cute, snide remarks. Concentrate on your shot. Don't worry about the last shot, or what your opponent is doing. You have no control over their game. Focus on each shot and don't worry about the next one. This ain't football, son. You can't depend on your teammates to save your butt when you screw up. Relax and concentrate, and just play the game. If you get too quick with your swing and start screwing up, just count one on the takeaway and two on the downswing. That'll get your tempo back. If you play really badly, it could work in your favor. They may be so overconfident that they won't even practice for the tournament. There's always a bright side to most every situation. Now scoot."

"I really do have to go to the restroom, now," Caleb said, streaking away. Burt laughed.

CHAPTER TWO

The four players gathered on the first tee. Dr. Black remarked, "We have to play for something, Doc. I can't play just to be playing. I realize you don't have much of a partner so we can play best ball. We'll give you guys, say, four holes and play for ten bucks. Surely you can manage to tie us on half the holes. Who knows? You might even win one."

Doc bristled and said, "How 'bout giving us, say, two holes for twenty bucks?"

Dr. Black and Chris laughed. Dr. Black said, "If you're going to be that generous with your money, we'll give you gentlemen the honor on the first tee." He laughed again. "It'll probably be your last one."

"Don't get too cocky," Doc said. "Remember what happened to Goliath."

"You're right," Dr. Black said, "but I've heard David had a little better partner than you."

As Doc motioned for Caleb to go first, he joked, "Try not to miss the ball, Caleb."

"This ought to be a fiasco," Chris mumbled. Dr. Black grinned and nodded.

Caleb nervously placed the ball on the tee and eased it into the ground. He stood up, waggled the club, and knocked the ball off the tee. He looked up at Doc. Doc smiled and nodded. He placed the ball on the tee again, waggled the club, and knocked the ball off the tee again.

"Is this going to take all day?" Chris muttered.

Caleb went through the routine again. His hands were shaking so badly he could hardly hold the club steady. His mind went blank as he began his backswing. When the club reached the top of his backswing, he lunged at the ball. The club head stuck the turf eight inches behind the ball and laid sod over the ball, barely advancing it to the end of the tee. Chris burst out in hysterical laughter. Dr. Black snickered, turned away, and tried to hold a straight face. He said, "Hit another one, Caleb. You can't do any worse."

"Thank you, Christian," Doc said, "however, I don't think that's permitted under the rules of golf. He'll play the next shot as it lies." Dr. Black smiled and shrugged. Doc set up, addressed the ball, and hit a nice drive down the right side of the fairway.

"Nice shot," Dr. Black said. "I feel really bad about our bet. Why don't you take four holes so we can at least have a respectable contest?"

"The wager is firm!" Doc responded curtly.

Dr. Black took his turn and hit a high banana ball to the right, which landed in deep rough. "Damn it," he barked, slamming his club-head to the ground. "I spent half a day with my pro working on that damn slice last week. I think we may need a new pro at my club in Memphis."

"What he really needs," Doc whispered to Caleb, "is to take two weeks off and then quit. He hasn't improved his golf game in twenty years. Chris wins the tournament every year, and Christian struts around like a peacock."

Chris swaggered up to the tee and readied himself, giving Caleb a quick smirk. He was tall, lean, and very athletic-looking. He was handsome, and his long, golden hair sparkled in the bright sunlight. He began his swing. It was smooth, long and extremely rhythmic. The club head traveled so fast through the hitting area that the eyes could hardly follow it. He finished in perfect balance and held the pose until the ball landed almost 300 yards down the center of the fairway. Caleb's mouth gaped open, and his eyes widened as he watched the ball rocket down the fairway. "We're in trouble, Doc," Caleb whispered.

"Drive for show, putt for dough," Doc whispered.

"Beg your pardon?" Caleb said.

"It means he doesn't putt as well as he strikes the ball. It's his Achilles heel."

"His what?" Caleb asked.

"It means it is the weakest part of his game. You'll learn about the Achilles tendon in anatomy and physiology and again in history."

"I don't think that is in my academic program."

"Then, we'll get it into your program." Doc nodded. "You can hit the ball that far, son," Doc encouraged.

"Yes, sir, but I don't know where it's going. Do I need to hit my ball?" Caleb asked, standing over the ball at the end of the tee.

"Certainly," Doc said. "Your third shot might land on the green, then you could still par the hole. Take your four-iron and try to hit it into the fairway. Just try to relax." Caleb took the club and thought, *What did Burt say? Relax and concentrate. Block out everything. Huh! That's easier said than done.* The Blacks had walked a hundred yards ahead, so they were not close enough to intimidate Caleb. He looked at the ball, took a deep breath, and let it out slowly. His swing was smoother this time, and he caught the ball cleanly. It flew 200 yards down the fairway, leaving him about 150 yards from the green. He breathed a little sigh of relief and managed to smile at Doc.

"Blind hog found an acorn," Dr. Black jested. "I'm picking up my ball, Chris. You should birdie this hole and not require my assistance."

"That's my plan," Chris said smugly.

Doc walked up to his ball and commented, "I'm one-seventy-five from the pin. I think I can reach the green with a four iron."

He settled over the ball and made a smooth swing. The ball flew toward the green, tailing right as it landed on the right side of the green, leaving him a long twenty-foot side-hill putt. Caleb walked up to his ball and selected an eight iron. He tried to relax and concentrate on a smooth swing. The Blacks were eyeing him from the side. His nervousness returned. He took the club back, and then rushed his down-swing again. The ball duck-hooked left into a deep bunker short of the green.

The Blacks snickered. Chris was only seventy-five yards from the flag. He addressed the ball, cutting his eyes up at Caleb, and laughed as he swung the club back confidently, contacting the ball perfectly. It landed three feet past the pin, hopped up, and shot backward stopping ten feet from the pin.

"How'd he make the ball do that?" Caleb asked.

"Practice," Doc said.

"I'm picking up," Caleb said. "I can't help you now." Doc nodded. Doc and Chris studied their putts. Then Doc stood over his ball and made a smooth stroke. The ball rolled smoothly and began to break left toward the hole as it lost speed. It continued to slow and began to die a yard from the hole. It rolled up to the edge of the hole, rocking forward, then back, stopping with half the ball appearing to hang over the edge of the hole, seeming to defy gravity. Doc wilted after the ball stopped.

"Tough break!" Christian yelled and laughed. "I'll concede that one." He reached out with his putter to tap the ball back to Doc. Miraculously, before his putter head reached the ball, it caved into the hole.

"That won't be necessary now," Doc said. "Birdie, gentlemen. The blind hog got new glasses." And he wagged his head, smiling.

"You make that putt, son," Christian demanded. Chris set up over his ball, taking a long time. He made a smooth stroke, and the ball rolled into the center of the hole.

As the four men strolled to the second tee, Caleb whispered, "Look at my hands, Doc, they're shaking. I'm so nervous, I'll never help you."

"Pretend you're playing a practice round. The nerves will ease up after a few holes. This is not life or death. I deal with that every day. So they kick our rear? That's what they're supposed to do. There's no accomplishment in that. But, what if we keep their feet to the fire and let them know they've been in a scuffle?"

"I'll do better," Caleb said.

"Never doubted it," Doc said. Doc cleared his throat and said, "I think we still have the honor. Caleb, you do realize as long as we have the honor, we're still in this match against the club four-ball champions, six years running, don't you?"

Caleb nodded and said, "Yes, sir."

"I'll hit first this time, " Doc said facetiously, looking at Dr. Black. "It might be our last honor." He made a smooth swing and hit his best drive in months. It drew slightly and landed in the fairway over 250 yards away.

"I see you've been working with Burt on your drives," Christian said.

"Nope! Blind hog just found another acorn," Doc said.

Caleb glanced at Chris and his father. They were whispering and smiling. *I'm not going to let Doc down,* he thought. *I have to swing smoothly. Burt said to count one, two, and be smooth.* He quickly placed his ball on the tee, took one waggle, and thought, *one,* on his backswing and, *two,* as he started down. The ball exploded off the club head, the length of the drive equaling Chris's on the previous hole. It landed in the center of the fairway.

"Nice shot," Christian said, then whispered, "Don't let that hick out-drive you, son." After Christian hit his usual fade into the rough, Chris stood up to his ball. He was angry, and he rushed his routine. He snatched the club back and tried to overpower the swing, almost falling backward on the follow-through. The ball went high and left, landing in the deep Bermuda rough, some fifty yards behind Caleb's ball. He slammed his club-head to the turf. His mouth erupted with profanity and vulgarity like Caleb had never heard.

"Calm yourself!" Christian shouted. "This is not a construction site. You need to clean a few of those words out of your vocabulary. This is a gentleman's game, in case you've forgotten. Get control of yourself, and swing as you've been taught. There's no need for that kind of roguish language."

They walked to their balls on the par five hole. The two doctors hit their shots down the fairway. Chris tromped into the deep rough and was forced to hit a nine iron to extricate the ball from the deep, matted Bermuda grass. He managed to advance the ball about one hundred yards. Caleb's turn came next. He took his three-wood out and decided to go for the green in two. He blocked out everything, except making a smooth swing. He stepped up to his ball and said, "Don't jump at it, smooth and slow." Caleb made a perfect swing. The ball flew high and long and began to draw toward the flag. It landed on the front of the green and rolled to within twelve feet of the pin.

Doc went wild, jumping up and down yelling, "That's my boy!" as he applauded him. Caleb felt a strange sensation of calmness and confidence come over him as the fear disappeared.

Chris and Christian had their heads together now, and they were chattering, but the laughter and smirks were gone. They were in a battle, and they had just realized it. Christian said, "We're in a game, son. Doc has pulled a fast one on me. This kid can play the game."

"I'm telling you, Father, he'd never seen a golf course or ball before Doc gave him the job. It's just blind ass luck," Chris insisted.

"I hope you're right, boy. Doc would never let me live this down if they win."

"Not one chance in a million," Chris reassured him. "I'll guarantee you he can't putt. He may not be able to keep the ball on that slick green with the putter."

Each player went to their ball. The doctors managed to get their balls on the putting surface in positions that would require long putts. Chris addressed his ball, confidently hitting a nine iron. His ball ended up five feet from the pin. "That should get us a half," Christian said confidently.

"I'm betting the plow-boy'll take three or four putts," Chris said. "We're going to win this hole and the rest. I'm pissed off, and I'm going for the juggler now."

"That's what I want to hear," Christian said.

The doctors putted and both missed their birdie putts. Next came Caleb's turn. He studied the putt from all sides, then walked behind the ball and lined it up. *I have to make this putt,* Caleb thought. He addressed the ball, but just as he began his backswing, Chris let his putter fall. The noise as it plopped on the ground broke Caleb's concentration; however, he was able to stop his putter stroke.

Doc, aghast at Chris' dubious gamesmanship, looked at Christian with searing eyes and said, "Is this the way you taught your son to win? If so, this game is over."

"Hold on!" Chris protested. "I accidentally dropped my putter. You want to make a federal case of it?"

"Hush, son!" Christian said. "If he said it was an accident, I believe him. He doesn't have to I resort to gamesmanship to win. He's an all-American in case you've forgotten. It'll not happen again."

Doc, forcing himself to bite his tongue, looked at Caleb and said, "You can make that putt." Caleb bent over, picked his line again, and wasted no time striking the ball. It tracked like a magnet was pulling it toward the hole. As it lost speed, it curved very slightly and fell into the center of the hole.

"Your birdie is good now, Chris," Doc said, as he tapped the ball back to Chris, smiling again. "Let me see, that puts us up by three holes with seven to go. How many more do we need to tie to win this match, Caleb?"

"I have no idea," Caleb said. "I don't understand anything about this game."

"Oh well, let's just keep trying to tie them and see what happens," Doc whispered just loud enough for Christian to hear him. Christian and Chris were fuming as they stormed off to the next tee.

Chris began to press, and after another halved hole, he tried to drive the short par-four fifth hole. He hooked two balls out of bounds, and Christian could manage only a bogie. They lost that hole, too, and the match was in jeopardy. Dr. Black pulled Chris off to the side and said, "It's time to get serious and stop screwing around. I refuse to be humiliated by a novice and a pompous old fart. Now get your act together."

"I'm not screwing around," Chris snapped. "This crap was your idea anyway. You knew I didn't want to play with that hick." He gritted his teeth, doubled up a fist, and pounded his palm. "I despise that country hick so much that I can't keep my mind on the game."

Christian said sternly, "I'm telling you—no, I'm ordering you to get your act straightened out and birdie these last few holes." Chris's jaw tightened, and he looked at Caleb with fiery contempt.

Burt looked out the window anxiously at ten a.m. as he awaited their arrival on the number nine hole. He planned to walk out and watch the finish. His wait was short as he saw them rounding the dogleg hole almost 200 yards from the green. The ninth hole was the number one handicap hole, and par was a premium score. He locked the door and rushed out beside the green. The road paralleled the fairway on the right with out-of-bounds stakes close to the road. Thick rough and trees lined the left side of the fairway with half a dozen traps lining both sides of the fairway. A giant sand trap was located on the right side of the green. The hole was 430 yards long with a slight dogleg right. The green was elevated almost eight feet on the right, and the right side of the green was three feet higher than the left. A ball hit from the right bunker would not stay on the green unless hit by the most accomplished golfer. Even then, the ball would run to the extreme left side of the green. On this day, the pin was in the center of the green.

Doc's ball was in the short rough on the right side of the fairway, 200 yards away. Christian's ball was in the same rough, ten yards short of Doc's ball. Caleb's ball was in the fairway, 170 yards from the green. Doc and Caleb had found some trouble down the stretch, and the Blacks had made a comeback. Chris needed only to win the hole to claim the victory. He had hammered a drive down the left side of the fairway and had only 160 yards to the green.

Christian hit first, but his ball came up short of the green and bunker on the right. Doc hit a good shot, but it faded right and landed in the deep bunker on the right side of the green, an impossible up and down.

Caleb steadied himself and hit a solid ball. It hooked slightly and landed on the left side of the green some twenty-five feet behind the pin. A few members saw Burt watching from the back of the green. They knew it must be a hotly contested match, so they all gathered by him to watch the finish.

Chris looked at his father, grinned, nodded confidently, stepped up to his ball, and made a perfect swing. The ball flew past the pin ten feet, hopped up, and backed up to within a foot of the cup. "Well done, son!" Christian shouted, rushing over to congratulate him as he put his arm around Chris's shoulder, and they strutted to the green.

Doc, somewhat dejected, looked at Caleb, shook his head and commented, "I can't help you, son. You know what you have to do. If you one-putt, we win. If you two-putt, we lose. Chris has a kick in."

"I'll do my best."

Christian hit his shot onto the green. It rolled to the back of the green, some forty feet from the hole. He said, "I'll pick up, Chris, because you have the birdie for sure."

Doc trod into the sand and set his feet. He took a wild swing and bladed the ball into the side of the bunker, and it plugged. He slammed his wedge into the sand in disgust. Then he looked up, somewhat embarrassed, and raked the trap before walking up on the green.

Caleb circled the green, studying the break from all sides. He walked around behind his ball and knelt down for a last look. "You don't know what the hell you're looking at. Just putt the damn ball and get your twenty bucks out," Chris said, gloating. Caleb didn't respond but continued to study the break.

Doc couldn't restrain his disgust at Chris' arrogance and insolence. He said, "I'll tell you what he's looking at. He's looking for a way to kick your smart ass."

"James!" Christian protested, "that kind of talk is beneath your dignity. I'm shocked at you."

"Hell, Christian, he's been trying to intimidate and humiliate the boy all morning. Caleb is too much of a gentleman to retaliate, but I'm not. I don't know what your son has against Caleb, but I think you should teach him some manners."

"I'm capable of raising my son," Christian said, "and you raise your—country boy. Now let's get this match over because I have a ballgame to attend."

Caleb cleared his mind and concentrated on a smooth stroke. He played the ball to break right about a foot, and then he hit the putt. It held a good line until it was about ten feet from the hole. Then it started to break to the right. The ball appeared to be a little too high as it approached the hole; however, as it began to die it hit a spike mark and kicked right slightly and caved into the high side of the hole.

"Nice putt!" Doc shouted in disbelief, and the small gallery clapped for Caleb.

"Nice putt, my ass! Chris screamed. "It was pure luck. He missed the putt three inches, and that spike mark kicked it in."

Christian, angry and humiliated, barked, "Just tap your damn birdie in and let's get out of here. You've embarrassed and humiliated me enough today."

Chris slammed his putter to the ground and yelled, "Just how in hell did I humiliate you today, Father? When I make this putt,

I'll have shot a sixty-eight, and you didn't help one damn stroke. Don't try to lay a guilt trip on me because of your ineptness."

Doc, in a calming voice, was quick to say, "That putt's good, Chris." Chris grabbed the ball, tossed it up, swung his putter at it, and hit it into the grove of trees next to the green.

Christian snatched his wallet out and slapped a twenty-dollar bill into Doc's hand. He looked at Chris, saying, "You pay your own debts, smart ass!" Chris snatched his wallet out, grabbed two ten dollar bills, and wadded them up.

"I don't want your money, Chris," Caleb said, shaking his head. "I play golf for fun. I don't believe in gambling. I think it's a sin." Chris, tight-jawed and almost trembling with anger, threw the money in Caleb's face, turned, and stormed off the green.

"Get yourself back here this instant and apologize to Caleb!" Christian shouted.

Chris turned and said, "I'd sooner kiss a goat's ass, Father." He ran to his car, threw his clubs into the back seat, and peeled rubber for half a block.

Christian threw his hands up, shaking his head and said, "I'm sorry for his conduct, gentlemen, but you do understand he's not used to losing? Caleb, you probably didn't know that he advanced to the quarterfinals of the National Amateur Championship last year. His mother and I will have a talk with him next weekend." Christian grabbed his clubs, rushed over to his car, and drove away quickly.

The other members present began to laugh. Burt said, "I wouldn't have missed that for a million dollars. Did ya'll actually beat them?"

"I reckon we done it," Doc said with a head bobble. "They gave us two holes, but the win was still sweet. Here's the twenty to prove it. Caleb, you take it. You won it for us."

"No, sir, Doc. I don't want that money Chris gave me." He picked it up and handed it to Doc.

"Caleb thinks it's sin money," Doc said, "so the best thing I can think of is to give it to charity. Or we could give it to Burt and let him take his family out for dinner and a movie." Caleb nodded and smiled.

"If you two clowns think I'm going to turn it down, you're nuts. I wasn't the one gambling. It's not sin money to me."

Doc took the money and put it in Burt's hands. "Compliments of next year's four-ball tournament champions."

"I'll buy you two the best dinner you ever had if you pull that one off," Burt said. They walked inside and opened sodas. Doc and Burt began to laugh, joke, and act ridiculous, like two kids who had accidentally found their Santa Claus. Doc recounted every shot and how they might have humiliated the Blacks even more, had their game held together down the stretch. Caleb sat there with a somber face.

Doc noticed Caleb's expression and asked, "Is something bothering you?"

"Yes, sir. I felt sorry for Chris because of the way his father was pressuring him to win. He was riding him so hard that he didn't shoot as well as he can. He missed three birdie putts less than eight feet. Those would have wiped us out. We were fortunate to win."

"You listen to me, Caleb. Your providence and hard work might have had something to do with our winning. Those two needed a lesson in humility. Yes, I felt a little sorry for him, too, but that kid is rotten to the core. Have you so soon forgotten that he took you to a watermelon patch, and shot at you with no regard for your life or Emil's? His father wasn't encouraging him then. They've both been beaten before, but never by—what did Chris call you, Barnyard Barney or something derogatory like that? It wasn't that they were beaten, but who beat them. Any time you get to feeling sorry for Chris, just remember the boy that nearly died in your arms and that bullet hole in your rear that was two inches from paralyzing you."

"What are you saying?" Burt gasped. "Chris shot Caleb and another boy in a watermelon patch!"

"Quiet down," Doc whispered. "Caleb didn't report it to the authorities. I treated them and charted it as an accident. Let's just leave it at that."

"What about the other kid?" Burt asked.

"He almost died from barbed wire cuts to the abdomen. He was just released to go home to Memphis. His mother didn't press charges because of Caleb's heroic action."

"I'd like to hear the whole story, please," Burt said.

"Okay," Doc said, "but it's strictly on the QT. Chris and a couple of his buddies came by the dorm on Wednesday night before the Memphis game on the pretense of having a watermelon party to make friends and bury the hatchet with Caleb. And you know how gullible Caleb can be sometimes. Caleb insisted that his roommate go with him. But Chris didn't take Caleb to his apartment like Caleb had thought they were going to do. Instead he took them to Mr. Turnipseed's watermelon patch and planned to pull the old watermelon patch prank on them. Caleb and his roommate went into the field to get a melon, because Chris said the farmer let the town folk pick them for free after the Fourth of July. It was a dark night, and Chris and his buddies hid and shouted in a disguised voice, 'I told you kids I was going to shoot you if you stole another melon.' Chris started shooting indiscriminately in their direction, and he hit Caleb in the butt, and Emile ran wildly into a barbed wire fence and ripped his abdomen open. Then Chris and his buddies sped away, leaving Caleb and Emil in the field. Caleb thinks they didn't realize that they were injured. Caleb ran all the way back to my house with the boy in his arms in shock and bleeding to death. Miraculously, we were able to save the boy's life. Caleb didn't want Chris to go to jail, so he didn't tell anyone who did the shooting. Chris got off Scott free. That's the story in a nutshell."

"Did Chris apologize?" Burt asked.

"He will one day," Caleb said. Doc and Burt looked at each other and shook their heads.

"Doc, can I possibly get off this afternoon to listen to the game in the dorm with the freshmen team?" Caleb asked.

"Son," Doc said, "with an extra hole in your gluteus maximus, you weren't supposed to be working this week anyway." Burt burst out laughing, and they both motioned for him to go.

"I'll be back as soon as the game's over, and thank you," Caleb said as he rushed out the door.

CHAPTER THREE

Caleb hurried back to the lounge in the dorm. The team had placed a radio on the table in the center of the room. The couches and chairs were pulled up close around the table. Someone had iced down sodas in a cooler. Chips and cookies were on the table.

"Go Cats!" echoed around the room as Caleb entered. Everyone jumped up to greet him and gave him a whack on the back. "Glad you could make it!" Cliff yelled, and everyone echoed his sentiments. "The star has reappeared!" Carl Ingram, a big guard, yelled.

"That's enough of that foolishness!" Caleb yelled. "I ain't no star. I came to listen to the game with y'all."

"Kickoff time!" someone yelled. "Be quiet." Everyone stopped talking, and the game was underway. Marston had come to play football, and play they did. Will was all over the field, and Clancy Young's passes were right on target. Every time Arkansas would score, Marston would counter with a score. Wally was screaming over the radio and praising the effort of the entire team, especially Clancy and Will. At halftime, the score was knotted at fourteen all. Everyone's hopes and dreams were that the three plus years of frustration—and the longest losing streak in the nation—was about to end. The second half was equally as exciting as the first. Both teams scored twice, but Arkansas missed an extra point, so Marston led 28 to 27 late in the fourth quarter. Marston mounted a late drive with four minutes left in the game. Then Clark Cunningham, the fullback, took a big hit and fumbled the ball on the Arkansas twenty. Arkansas recovered the fumble. The freshman football team was bouncing off the floor and walls, hugging and screaming with jubilation. The same excitement and tension was unbearable in farmhouses all across north Mississippi as all true Marston fans were at the point of near-cardiac arrest. Houston and a few friends were sitting on his porch in Choctaw County, screaming and yelling like a bunch of cowboys at a wild-west rodeo. Mary sat in her rocker, calmly knitting, rolling her eyes and shaking her head.

Luther and Buckie were draped over the radio at Buckie's bedside in Marston Memorial Hospital. Luther had been warned a half dozen times about disturbing the patients on the second floor with his screams and shouts. Buckie was smiling through his pain and thoroughly sharing his father's excitement and the game.

The razorbacks had no intentions of getting beat by the worst division one team in the nation. They decided that they would run the ball away from Will's side every play. They pounded the ball to the left on every play. Even though the Marston team knew where they were coming, the stronger Arkansas linemen were able to physically control the line. They were ripping off big chunks of real estate with every snap of the ball.

Coach Shook moved Will to the opposite end. Arkansas simply checked off the play at the line of scrimmage and continued to run away from Will's end. Arkansas crossed the fifty-yard-line with two minutes left in the game. It appeared that Marston was about to lose another game when Will backed up and moved behind his defensive tackle. When the ball was snapped, he sprinted down the line of scrimmage and made a crushing tackle for no gain at the other side of the field. Arkansas lined up again and ran the same play. Will played it the same way and made another tackle for no gain.

The Arkansas coaches called a timeout and discussed the situation with their quarterback. Coach Shook talked with Will on the sideline reminding him that it was third and ten. Coach Shook said, "They have to pass this down. Go huddle the team up, and tell them to tighten up the coverage. Get in their hip pockets when they release down field. Jam the tight end and blitz the weak side linebacker. We have to hold them two plays, and this nightmare will be over. I'm counting on you, my boy," Coach Shook said and slapped Will's huge rump as he sprinted back to the defensive huddle.

Will huddled the defense and said, "Coach Shook said that they're going to pass, so tighten up the coverage, and jam the tight end and don't let him release. Blitz the weak side linebacker. This is it, team, this is where we grow up and become winners. Play like your life is at stake, and let's get the monkey off Coach Shook's back." They clapped and lined up on defense. Arkansas broke the huddle and lined up with the wing left and the tight end left and split the right end out. Will lined up on the left side of his defense and backed up, moving over behind his tackle as before. Arkansas snapped the ball, and the quarterback tossed the ball to his tailback running left to Will's and everyone's surprise. It appeared to be the same play as before, so Will sprinted down the line of scrimmage as before; however, it was a reverse to the wingback. Will was totally out of position. The defensive backs were chasing receivers all over the field and out of position to cover the reverse. Will's adrenaline kicked in, and he seemed to cross the field in ten strides as the wingback headed down the right sidelines. The ball carrier had gained fifteen yards before Will cut him off at the thirty-five-yard line. Fearing for his life, the wingback attempted to step out of bounds to avoid Will's violent hit. Will laid out his huge frame and made a bone-crushing tackle at the same time the ball carrier stepped on the sideline chalk. The force drove them into the turf some five yards out-of-bounds. The wingback lay there moaning and groaning, unable to get up. The official closest to the sidelines grabbed for his red flag and tossed it into the air. The stands went wild. Will, seeing the official's call as he climbed to his feet, ran at the official, screaming his protest. "I couldn't stop!" he yelled at the official. "He was still in the field of play. What the hell did you expect me to do? This is football! If you were planning to give them the game, we might as well have stayed home. That call is nothing but home cooking." Will deliberately bumped the official chest as he stomped away.

Another official grabbed his flag, tossed it into the air again and yelled, "Number eighty-eight, you're out of the game!"

Will turned and started back at the official, yelling, "You no good son-of—"

Before he could finish, Coach Stan and Billy Ray grabbed him by the shoulders and jerked him around, escorting him off the field.

Coach Shook was screaming for the referee to come talk to him while another official walked off fifteen yards to the twenty and then half the distance to the goal for Will's un-sportsmanlike conduct. Arkansas was now poised to score from the ten-yard line. The referee jogged over to the sideline and explained the calls to Coach Shook. "That's bullshit!" Coach Shook yelled. "I could see the chalk fly at the same time Will hit the ball carrier. I know you did, too. You can overrule his call if you're man enough."

"You better calm down, Coach, or you're going to get another flag," the referee cautioned.

"Calm down! Calm down! That bogus call just cost us the ballgame. You're all an incompetent bunch of bastards!"

"That's it, Coach," the referee barked, throwing his flag into the air. He quickly picked it up and ran onto the field, stepping off half the distance to the goal. It was first and goal from the five-yard line now. Arkansas quickly ran two plays, pounding the middle of the Marston defense, leaving them with a third and goal from the one. Coach Shook called a timeout with less than thirty seconds on the clock and pleaded with the defense to stop them and force a field goal. "We can possibly block it," he encouraged.

Arkansas lined up in a strong right formation and tossed the ball to the fullback who swept the right end where Will's replacement was, and the ball carrier high-stepped it into the end zone un-accosted. The Arkansas fans erupted with jubilance. The victory was virtually assured. They kicked the extra point and led by six points with less than twenty seconds to play.

The game was over, and everyone knew it. The Arkansas team kicked the ball, and Marston was down to its last two plays. Clancy threw two long, incomplete passes to end the game. The dejected Marston team walked somberly to the dressing room.

"The party died in the dormitory, and everyone looked at each other in disbelief of the last minute of the game. Cliff commented, "I wonder who our new coach'll be?"

"Don't talk like that!" Caleb snapped. "Doc won't let that happen. They're friends."

―⁎―

Inside the dressing room, Coach Shook huddled the team and his staff around him. "Men, this may be of little consolation, but I want you to know that I couldn't be more proud of you if you had won by fifty points. I saw a real team out there tonight, and everyone else did, too. The Arkansas coach said that the referee blew the call on Will's tackle. It happened ten feet from him, and it should never have been called. He said for me to tell you guys to keep your heads up, and be proud of the way you played tonight. Further, he said that he knows you are going to win some games this year. I agree with him. Now we're not going home like losers. We're going home like valiant warriors who did ourselves and our school proud this afternoon, and—"

"Coach," Will interrupted, "I lost the game for us, and everyone knows it. It was a bonehead mistake to get that penalty for losing my temper. I don't like to admit a mistake, but I let you and the team down today. It won't happen again."

"It takes a real man to say that," Coach Shook said, "but it's not true, Will. There are dozens of plays that influence the outcome of a game. One play or penalty doesn't win or lose a game. It seems so when it comes at the end of the game. My penalty was more of a bonehead penalty than yours. I'm apologizing to the team, too. It won't happen again."

A ruckus broke out at the front entrance to the dressing room. The state trooper who accompanied the team from Marston was stationed at the door. He yelled, "I said no one can go into the room until Coach Shook says so!"

"I'm Bill James, you idiot, and I'm coming in if I have to walk over you to do it."

Coach Shook yelled, "It's okay, Trooper Jackson, let him in!"

Bill James stormed into the room and walked up to Will, staring at him scornfully with hard cold eyes, then shouted, "I hope you're proud of yourself, son!"

Will, startled, shocked, and embarrassed, responded, "No, sir, Father."

"And you should not be. That was the stupidest move I've ever seen you make. It cost us the game."

"Bill," Coach Shook said, stepping in front of him, "I don't think this is the right time for—"

"Begging your pardon, Coach, but he is my son. Anytime I feel the need to reprimand him is the right time. Please don't interrupt me again because I have an important engagement in Memphis at seven. I don't have time for pleasantries."

"I've already apologized to the team for the penalties, Father" Will said.

"For the penalty, you idiot!" he yelled. "The penalty was justified. The stupidity was for running yourself out of position and chasing the ball carrier to the right on that reverse. Any fool should have known they were not going to run the same play three times after gaining nothing on the first two attempts. I thought I had taught you better than that, or at least the coaches should have."

Will's eyes flashed with fire, and his jaw became rigid. His face became blood red. The veins in his neck began to bulge, almost bursting, as he began to shake all over.

"Mr. James, I'm going to have to insist that you leave, right now! This is not the way we do things around here," Coach Shook said firmly. "Your son played the best game I have ever seen anyone play, and I don't think this is justified."

"I demand perfection out of my son, Coach Shook, just as I demand it out of myself. It's obvious that you and I don't hold to the same standards."

Will stepped up nose-to-nose with his father, shaking more violently now, and screamed, "You'd better get out of here now because your important engagement in Memphis might not be waiting for you if you didn't pay her in advance—Father!"

Bill James raised his fist to strike Will, and then he froze for a few seconds. He slowly lowered his fist, turned, and started walking away. He stopped, turned, and said to Coach Shook, "I've supported you for many years when most of my friends said your time had passed but—"

"Father!" Will screamed. "Don't embarrass yourself anymore than you have already. Just get the hell out of here!" Mr. James paused a few seconds, then stormed out the door.

The team gathered around Will to console him, but he pushed them away and rushed out of the room. "Leave him alone," Coach Shook said. "He has to handle this in his own way." The team shucked off their uniforms and went to the shower. Coach Shook looked disparagingly at the staff. "Now, do you coaches understand why I cut him a little more slack than the others? How would you like to grow up with that as a role model?" The coaches lowered their heads, shaking them.

"Are we ready to get our bones picked by the vultures?" he asked.

"Might as well," Stan said, "it couldn't be any worse than that fiasco." Coach Shook motioned for Trooper Jackson to open the door. The reporters from Memphis, Jackson, and elsewhere in Mississippi stormed in.

"What do you have to say about the game?" Wes Kling from the Jackson Daily News asked.

"I'm very proud of these kids," Coach Shook responded. "We're improving every week." Then all the reporters began to bombard him with questions about the end of the game.

"It was very unfortunate," Coach Shook said. "It was a bad call on Will. Even I saw the chalk fly at the same time Will hit the ball carrier." After a dozen or more questions, a Tupelo writer asked about Will's lack of discipline and all the penalties and ejections he had received.

"I suppose," Coach Shook said, choosing his words carefully, "Will could be what some like to call a free spirit, and that's not all bad. He has more ability than anyone in this country. He plays with more heart, spirit, and passion than anyone I have ever known. We're working with him. He's making a supreme effort to control himself even under adverse conditions."

Norris Beckham from the largest newspaper in Memphis raised his hand. Coach Shook tried to ignore him, but he was persistent, and the other scribes let him have the floor. Coach Shook finally had to recognize him. He began his questioning. "Coach Shook, do you think you'll have a job after tonight?" A hush came over the room. Norris had asked the question that all the writers wanted to ask, but respect and professional ethics had prohibited their asking.

Coach Shook took a deep breath and responded, "I can be replaced at any time the administration wishes, but I don't think this is the time or place to discuss my job. Some of you have already done extensive writing on that topic during the past few weeks. These kids played their hearts out today. I think we need to be talking about them, and their efforts, and their improvements."

"Well, I don't agree," Norris said. "I played for you in the, quote, unquote, 'Good old days,' and you did an adequate job twenty-five years ago. But it's obvious to me that you haven't kept up with the times and the new trends in the game. It appears to me that you're still running the same old offense and defense we played when I was at Marston." He turned to his fellow reporters saying, "This is off the record, men." Then he looked at Coach Shook and said, "Why don't you resign and save the school and yourself the embarrassment of a firing. The alumni are tired of your lame excuses about not having the talent to compete with the other division one schools. There was no reason to lose that game today. You blew it, even when it was apparent that you had the best team. It pains me to say this, and it's still off the record, but you are totally incompetent."

Coach Shook, steel-eyed yet appearing very calm, stepped up to Norris. The tension was so thick in the room that no one dared breathe. "This is on the record, and it doesn't pain me to say it. I don't think the offense we played today resembled the single wing we played when I wasted a scholarship on your sorry ass. You were a cocky, yellow dog, son-of-a-bitch when you played for me fifteen years ago, and you're still a cowardly son-of-a-bitch, hiding behind a poison pen, and this doesn't pain me like it's going to pain you." As sudden as a flash of lightning, Coach Shook's right fist crashed into Norris's cheek, propelling him backward through the dozen reporters onto the floor.

Coach Shook yelled, "You bunch of vultures, drag that bastard out of here before I whip the whole lot of you." He stormed into the small office slamming the door so hard it broke the glass in the door. The reporters grabbed Norris off the floor and quickly dragged him outside.

Billy Ray, Stan, Toad, and Ollie stood there frozen, with shock, and disbelief, their mouths gaped open. A lifetime passed before Stan said, "Oh shit! What has he done! He finally cracked. He just ended his career, and he could spend some time in jail."

Billy Ray snapped angrily, "Well! You got your wish, Stan. It's too late to find another head coach, so I guess you're it!"

Stan bristled, responding, "I resent the hell out of out of that, Billy Ray. Certainly I'd like to have a head coaching job someday but not like this. I'll refuse it under these circumstances."

"If I had had any guts, it would have been my fist that punched him out instead of Coach Shook's." Billy Ray said. "He doesn't deserve to go out like this. I can't take this crap. I think I'll resign when he's fired. This ain't worth it, men. I'll find me a little high school in the sticks somewhere. The worst thing that could happen would be a mother spitting across the fence at me because her all-American son is playing third string center or some irate dad calling me a dumbass because his kid's playing guard instead of fullback."

"Thank the Lord the kids didn't see this," Ollie said. "Are we going in to see him?"

"There ain't enough gold in Fort Knox to get me in there before he cools off," Stan said. "Did you see that punch? I didn't know the old man had it in him."

"I'm going in," Billy Ray said. "He needs a friend."

"Me, too," Ollie and Toad echoed. They stepped over the broken glass and tapped on the door. Coach Shook looked up and motioned for them to come in. They eased in and stood there with long faces, not knowing what to say.

Billy Ray reached his hand out to him. Coach Shook took it with both his and said, "I hope I didn't mess things up too badly for you men. I knew I was gone the minute my fist hit his face. The truth is that I really have no regrets. I don't think my heart could have taken any more. I still have a few friends so I'll go to bat for y'all. It's too late to put a new staff together anyway. Did any of the kids see it?"

"No, I don't think so," Ollie said. "I was standing in front of the shower room door when it happened."

"Well," Coach Shook said, "I committed the unpardonable sin tonight. You don't hit a ref, and you never *ever* hit a sports writer. I'll tender my resignation tomorrow and save Dr. Parker the embarrassment. Let's not spoil it for the kids on the way home. I'm so proud of them."

Billy Ray and the other coaches said, "We're proud of you, too, Coach."

Stan walked into the room. "You'll always be the best in my book, Coach. I know I've been an ass in the past, but I think I became a coach this year because of you."

"Sit down a minute, men," Coach Shook said, "I want to tell you a few things. It'll be the last time I have to meet with you. Stan, you'll be a head coach soon even if you don't get this job right now. You have all the skills to do a good job. Billy Ray, you are an offensive genius. All of you men are the best at your profession, but that's not enough anymore. Fans don't love the game…they love winning the game. Winning is the name of the game, and winning starts with recruiting. That's a real crapshoot, at best. One in three recruits live up to your expectations. The reason some schools seem to stay on top is that they have the opportunity to select from the best kids in the country. The rest of us have to do a masterful job of coaching, or we're out. We didn't have three kids on our team who could have started for Arkansas today, and we almost pulled off the impossible. How did we do it? We did it by coaching. Our kids played at a higher level than they are capable, yet they did it. Coaching is not all about Xs and Os as Norris would have you believe. It's about heart and soul, and character. Football is a hard and brutal game, but we all love it because it reveals character like no other sport. You don't just coach skills…you must develop character. When you find a kid like Will or Caleb, you get down on your knees and thank the Lord for them because they come along once in a lifetime, if you're fortunate.

I have no regrets. I've spent over forty years doing what I love, and I'm going home now with my head up. I don't remember the last time I told my wife I love her, and that's about to change. Now, get out there and hold this team together, because things are about to look up at Marston. You're going to beat Tulane next week. They have a very good team this year with extremely intelligent and talented athletes, but our kids are hungry, and we're going to win with heart and character."

CHAPTER FOUR

Caleb left a dejected group of freshmen and drove to the club. The parking lot was virtually empty. Most of the members had driven to Little Rock early that morning for the game.

Abe was making last-minute preparations for the small crowd that was expected. Caleb apologized for being late and pitched in with the preparations. They served less than a dozen members, and by eight p.m., the hall was empty.

Doc and Edith had eaten at six and returned home. Doc didn't have much of an appetite and was visibly shaken over the fiasco at the end of the game; however, he tried not to show it.

Paul and Clotile cleaned the kitchen while Abe and Caleb cleaned the dining hall. Caleb was so upset by the loss he was nauseated and had refused to eat anything.

They walked to the door together a little after nine. Abe said, "Where is your providence, son? Don't you think the Lord is in this situation, too?"

"I think the Lord is in every situation, Mr. Abe. He may want Coach Shook out for a good reason. We'll never know, short of glory, but it still hurts. I think the team's ready to win some games, but it may be too late for Coach."

"That's a pretty good answer," Abe said as he locked the door, "but you have to learn to accept what you can't control." He put his arm around Caleb's shoulders as they walked out to the car.

Caleb raised his arms and said, "Feel that glorious cool breeze, Mr. Abe. You can stand here and look up toward God's Heaven and think that everything is wonderful in the world tonight, but it isn't."

"Son," Abe said, "you have too much heart and compassion for others. This college life might not be right for you."

"I'll be all right, sir, but there's something I've wondered about ever since I came to work here. How did you come by this job, Mr. Abe?"

"You just answered your own question, son." He laughed. "I'll explain. It was another one of God's miracles and your providence. When my mother died, it was during the great depression. Hard times were everywhere. I tried to get a job in Tupelo and everywhere else I could walk to, and nobody was hiring. When I ran out of money, they kicked me out of the little shotgun house we'd been renting. I was on the streets for weeks, going from door to door asking to do work for food. I almost starved that month. I hoped there might be some work in Memphis because I knew I'd die if I stayed where I was that winter. I set out walking toward Memphis. I caught an occasional ride with a farmer who took me a few miles, but I reckon I walked most of the way here. The soles of my old shoes tore loose, and the sharp rocks cut my feet and toes. They were a bloody, painful sight.

"Son, I ain't never told a living soul what I'm about to tell you… not even my wife…because I'm so ashamed. But I think you need to hear it. I hadn't eaten in five days when I passed the Marston city limit sign out on Fifty-one Highway. I had been sleeping under bridges with the frogs, mosquitoes, rats, and moccasins. I was at the point where I either wanted to die or get some relief. I didn't even care if I went to prison because my stomach felt like it was beginning to eat itself. I didn't intend to pass another house that didn't have smoke coming from the chimney. It weren't my intent to hurt anybody...I just wanted some food. I was prepared to go to prison. I came to that house near the entrance to the club, and I stopped and looked for smoke. It was freezing, and I didn't see any smoke from the chimney, and no car was parked outside. So I was ready to make my move when I heard a car coming up behind me. I lowered my head and looked away so they couldn't see my face. As it passed, a sound like a shotgun blasted about three feet from me. I dove into the ditch, head first, and covered my head. I figured it was some KKKers out to have a little fun getting their kicks shooting at a no-account Negro. I heard the brakes skid, and the car stopped up ahead. I was so scared I didn't know whether to run or crap on myself. Finally, I decided if it was my time to die, I might as well die like a man, because what I'd been doing wasn't really living anyway. So I eased up the ditch bank and peeped over the edge of the road. What I saw was a very handsome, distinguished-looking young gentleman in a beautiful, expensive gray suit walking around the new car shaking his head, disgusted. I knew he was rich. Then I saw the tire that had blown out. I took a deep breath for the first time since I had dived into the ditch. I saw the opportunity to make a dime, so I ran up to him and asked if I could change the tire. 'I know you don't want to get that beautiful new suit dirty,' I said. He looked at me with his hard, steel-gray eyes. I could tell he was disgusted about the tire. Then his eyes softened as he said he would appreciate it. In a flash, I had his tire changed. I stood there hoping and praying that he'd give me a dime. You know some rich folk are tighter than poor folk. I hoped he wasn't one of them because it was obvious he was rich.

He said, 'I can't thank you enough for helping me with that flat, mister,' and he gestured for my name. He called me *mister*. I would have changed the tire for nothing because no white man had ever called me mister before, but I needed a dime. 'My name is,' I said proudly, 'Abraham Lincoln Washington, sir, but everybody calls me Abe.'

"He gave me the queerest look. His eyes went downward, and he focused on my bloody feet for a few seconds. I saw compassion in a white man's eyes for the first time in my life. I knew I'd get my dime now, so I smiled like I was fat and fine. He said to me, 'Your parents gave you a name that's a hard act to follow, Mr. Washington.' I didn't know what he meant, but I said, 'Yessa.' I was gettin' more nervous as every second passed when he didn't reach in his pocket.

"'Where are you from, and where are you going, Mr. Washington?' he asked, glancing down at my feet again. I swear, as hungry as I was, he didn't have to give me a penny now. He made me feel like I was a man and not a homeless piece of trash on the side of the road. I told him my story…all except the part about the house I was intending to rob.

"He said, 'Have you ever worked in a kitchen or dining hall before?' I answered, 'shore I have.' I lied, except I convinced myself it was only a half lie. I figured helping my mother wash dishes at home had to count for something. He said, 'I just came from the funeral of a wonderful, old, black gentleman who worked for me in the kitchen and dining hall at the club. If you're interested, I'd like to try you at his job.'

"I swear my blood pressure shot so high my head almost exploded off my shoulders, and I bit my lips to keep from crying, I was so appreciative. He told me to get in the car, and he drove me back to his clinic. He washed my feet…did you hear me? He washed my dirty, bloody, filthy feet." Abe wiped a tear from his eye and continued, "and cleaned them and put ointment on them. He arranged for me to stay at a black friend's house. Then he called the department store up town and told them to fit me with presentable clothes and shoes. Plus he gave me twenty dollars and said it was an advance on my salary."

"Mr. Abe, he did the same thing for me."

"Not quite, son," Abe said with a wink. "You'd have to be a black man living in the thirties to realize what he did for me. Sometimes in the still of the night when I'm laying in bed, I relive those moments of my life, and I realize how blessed I am, and what that man did for me. I love him like no man I've ever known. I truly believe I'd give my life for him…Goodnight," Abe said, and drove away.

Caleb drove somberly back to the campus, still sick about the game, and concerned about what might happen the next day. He parked at the dorm and saw that most of the lights were still off. He knew that the team hadn't returned from Little Rock. He dreaded the thought of how Will would react to the loss. He glanced at his watch and looked up the hill that led to the girls' dorm. He felt a compulsion to walk in that direction. Knowing that curfew was extended on weekends, he wondered if Angelle had already returned to the dorm from the hospital, where she worked as an aide evenings and weekends while she got her degree in nursing. There was scarcely any activity on the campus because most students went home for the weekend when Marston played an away game. He walked up the hill to his favorite bench in front of the girls' dorm and sat down, wondering if he should be there, and how Angelle would respond to his presence after their last cold encounter.

Although he had known Angelle only a few months, he was deeply in love with her. He felt that she had some feelings for him, although she wore an engagement ring. She had tried to discourage him a few times, yet she always seemed excited to see him. She usually had sadness in her eyes, and Caleb couldn't understand how someone so beautiful and intelligent could ever be sad. Everyone on campus thought she was the most beautiful girl in the world. Caleb had vowed that he would marry her shortly after they first met.

Angelle had become angry with Caleb after he professed his love for her, because she thought he had lied to her. Unbeknownst to Caleb, Will had secretly made a date for him and Caleb to go dancing with two of the girls from the dorm after a varsity game. It was rumored that both girls were somewhat promiscuous. Caleb was shocked when Will stopped at the girls' dorm and picked up the girls. Angelle saw Caleb and Will pick up the girls, and she became angry with Caleb, and thought he was a liar and like all the other boys who wanted only one thing from her. Caleb didn't know how he would be received, or what to expect if Angelle returned from work.

As Caleb sat and considered leaving, he became fascinated with the couples who pulled up to the curb. He quickly observed a pattern in their exits from the car. If the young lady waited for her escort to come around and open the door, it was sure he would be rewarded with a goodnight kiss at the entrance to the dorm. If the car pulled up and the young lady flipped the door open for herself and rushed to the dorm, it was sure he would get no kiss.

Caleb was watching one couple almost devour each other at the door, and he couldn't restrain his laughter. He felt a firm finger poke into his back, and he jerked around. A neatly dressed, fairly attractive young lady was standing in front of him with her hands on her hips. "You're Caleb Morgan, aren't you?" she said curtly. Caleb, somewhat shocked, nodded politely. He detected a coolness in her voice, and her eyes were cold and tight. "Why are you sitting here looking into the girls' dorm? Do you get your kicks looking in windows?" Caleb, shaken by her remarks, and tone, didn't know how to respond. She waited.

After a few seconds, he eased his hands up and said, "Now hold on, Miss…whoever you are…You have this all wrong. I'm waiting for Angelle Noel to come back from the hospital."

"I realize that!" she snapped. "I'm Sarah Catherine, Angelle's roommate. I've wanted this opportunity to talk to you for weeks now."

"Then sit down and talk," Caleb said, somewhat irritated by her demeanor.

"I'll stand, if you don't mind," she said firmly. "There are a few things I need to tell you that you obviously don't realize or don't care about. Angelle is in love with a wonderful young man who's in the service. They plan to be married when he's discharged. Everyone knows what you want, and you're not going to get it. I know she's infatuated with you because you're very handsome and somewhat of a hero around here. You can have almost any girl on this campus, but you'll never have her. I know what you're after because Darlene talks, and I do mean *talks*."

Caleb bristled and said, "Just hold on a second, young lady. There are some things that you obviously don't understand about me. I don't know what Darlene said, but I'm not that kind of person. I'm in love with Angelle. When she tells me to leave her alone, that's when it will end, because I love her more than you will ever know."

"If that's true, I'm obliged to tell you something. Angelle has some serious emotional problems, and your persistent hounding is making things worse for her."

"I don't believe a word you're saying. Angelle is the picture of health. I believe you're lying to me to stop me from seeing her."

"God only knows I wish that was true," she said, her voice revealing sincerity. "Angelle hides her illness by living in her own busy world. She's done it so long that she's mastered it. I think what's best for her is to marry the boy she really loves and settle into a normal marriage and have children. Then she might find some peace and security. If you're sincere about loving her, you have to love her enough to give her up because you're killing her."

"I'm killing her! That's very strange talk, and I don't like it," Caleb said. "No one can love her any more than me. If she does have some kind of emotional problem, why do you think the boy she's engaged to would be better for her than me? Why do you think I can't make her just as happy? I can't stop loving her, but I'll leave her alone when she tells me to."

"You're a selfish bastard." Sarah Catherine snarled. "You didn't hear a word I said. Have you ever heard of depression or anxiety? Angelle suffers from both. She has horrible nightmares, screaming and crying half the night, and saying terrible things like, 'Please don't hurt me again' and 'don't take my baby. Please, don't take my baby.' I think she may be paranoid, too."

"I certainly have heard of depression, and people can get well. My mother had a couple of bad years after my father was killed in the war, but she got well."

"You should be proud of yourself because since you've been hounding her, her condition has worsened. She sits up half the night with her fiancé's picture in her arms and cries herself to sleep. She made her choice long ago. Why can't you accept that and leave her alone?"

"Have you ever been in love, Sarah Catherine? Some people have died for love. I would die for her. I can't stop loving her anymore than I can stop breathing. I won't hound her, as you put it, but I plan to be around for four years. If the time ever comes when she decides she loves me more than him, I'll be waiting. I'll wait forever if there is a glimmer of hope."

"I hope you break your neck when you play another game," she said, wheeling around and storming into the dorm.

Caleb, so shaken by her remarks, stood up to leave. He saw Angelle coming in the distance. Her sweet voice rang out, "Caleb, Caleb, wait, I'm coming." He stood there looking at her, his mind in a fog of confusion and dismay. Her beautiful hair sparkled in the moonlight as she drew near. She wore the biggest and brightest smile he had ever seen on her face. She walked up to him and said, "You weren't leaving, were you?"

"It's late," Caleb said. "I knew you'd be tired and the last person you'd want to see would be me, here…hounding you."

"I'm never too tired to talk to you, " she said, her face still beaming.

"You look particularly beautiful tonight," Caleb said. Then, realizing what he said, he quickly added, "I shouldn't have said that."

"It was very nice of you to say it. I certainly don't mind a compliment." Her smile became brighter. "Why are you so bright and bubbly tonight?" Caleb asked. "I've never seen you smile so beautifully before."

"It might be that I was happy to see you waiting for me. Can't I smile if I'm happy?"

"I'd love to see you smile all the time. But your smile is so bright, the sun might not come up tomorrow." Caleb jerked his head away again, frowning. "I didn't mean to say things like that. I say the stupidest things when I'm around you."

Angelle touched his hand softly, which she had never done before, and whispered, "You say the most beautiful things. Don't apologize for being kind."

Caleb shook his head as if to clear his mind. He said, "Angelle, we need to talk."

She laughed softly and said, "I thought that's what we were doing."

"No! We're not talking, Angelle, I'm acting like a lovesick fool as usual. Anyway, I thought you weren't talking to me anymore. You haven't said two words to me in class since…you know."

"Oh! I can explain that. It was childish of me. Darlene has been running all over the dorm bragging about what you and she did on the date. I thought you were like all other boys in the world who want just one thing from a girl. I thought you had been lying to me about the way you felt about me just to get me out on a date so you could…well, you know what I mean. But I heard Carol and Darlene get into a screaming fight across the hall last night. Carol was sacking Darlene out about the lies she'd been spreading about you and her and how it was ruining your reputation. She said that it wasn't even a date, that Will had contrived the scheme just to get you out on a date. I realized that you were a decent, honorable person. I felt ashamed about the way I've been treating you, and I need your forgiveness."

"No, Angelle, it's not you who needs forgiveness but me. I've been acting like a dumb, lovesick fool when I'm around you. Now I realize that there's no hope of you ever loving me. Will told me you were engaged, and that should have ended it. But no, dumb me had to keep on bothering you, trying to make you fall in love with me. I have no right to come between you and your fiancé. I can't control my feelings for you, but it's not right for me to try to steal you from someone you're obviously very much in love with."

Angelle looked at Caleb curiously and said, "What was that all about? I said I was glad to see you. I don't think marriage entered the conversation."

Caleb turned two shades of pink. "I just wanted you to know how I felt."

"Let's sit down a minute," Angelle said, "I have lots of time before curfew." They sat down on the concrete bench, and Angelle sat close to him. She turned and smiled, saying, "I don't feel like you're bothering me. I really enjoy your company. Why would you suddenly decide that it's wrong to be with me? Is it because I've treated you so unkindly? Or have you met someone else?"

"There'll never be anyone else. I told you I was in love with you. I'll always be in love with you, but I wish with all my heart that I wasn't. Answer me truthfully. If the young man you're engaged to was here, do you think we'd be having this conversation?"

Angelle's head lowered slowly, and she tried to answer, but a tear ran down her cheek.

"Now look what I've done," Caleb said contritely. "That's why we had to talk about it. I think I better go."

Angelle wiped away the tear and in a broken voice said, "We can still be friends and not sweethearts, can't we?"

"I don't think so. Every time I'm around you, I want to take you in my arms and hold you and kiss you. I've wanted to kiss your sweet lips since the first time I looked into your beautiful eyes. I'm leaving now, but always remember that I do love you. It's because I love you so much that I won't place you in this situation anymore." Caleb stood up to leave, but Angelle grasped his arm.

She stood up close to him and forced a painful smile. "I want you to kiss me before you go, Caleb."

Caleb looked at her, shock and disbelief in his eyes. After an eternity, he managed to say, "I can't do that." He shook his head. "If I kiss you, I'll never want to let you go. No, I won't hurt you anymore."

Angelle grasped his other arm, held it tightly, and moved closer to him. Her breath quickened as did his. He could feel her soft body press gently against his and her sweet breath caressing his face. He tried to turn away from her, but his resistance was gone. Her face began to move closer and closer to his. His heart pounded, and his resistance quelled, as the anticipation of what was about to happen was complete intoxication. The moment he had dreamed of was here—and yet, he prayed it would not happen.

Angelle leaned forward slowly and kissed him softly and tenderly on the left cheek. Her warm lips eased across his, scarcely touching them, and she kissed him softly on the other cheek. The kisses were so soft and tender he could scarcely feel their warmth. But his emotion was all consuming, and he began to tremble. She released his arms and placed her hands on his cheeks, looking longingly into his tormented eyes. Her eyes closed slowly as she leaned forward, and her soft, warm lips pressed gently against his. Then slowly and deliberately, her lips began to move over his. She pulled him closer to her. The moment became magical and mystical as Caleb's spirit was lifted to a place in his being that he had never before experienced.

Caleb's mind was clouded by a fog of ecstasy. His hands moved slowly around her tiny waist as her sweet lips continued to move over his. He drew her warm body so close to his, it was as if their bodies became one. She gasped and pushed him away. A look of panic and horror like Caleb had never witnessed before came over her face. She backed away, continuing to gasp and tremble.

"What's wrong?" Caleb shouted. "Did I do something wrong? Tell me what's wrong with you."

Finally with tear-filled eyes, Angelle gasped and managed to say, "I should not have done that. It was wrong. I'm so sorry. Forgive me." She turned and ran into the dorm as he stood and watched in shock and disbelief. From the pinnacle of ecstasy his soul had never known, it plunged to depths of despair like he had never experienced.

Providence and Hard Work Series
You Shall Know the Truth

Caleb looked up at the dorm and thought about everything Sarah Catherine had confided in him. He realized that she had told him the truth. With tear-filled eyes, he whispered, "Good bye, my love," and walked somberly away. As he walked down the steep hill in the shadows of the stately oaks, he could still feel her soft lips against his and her passion and warmth. He fought the tears as he began to pray. "Lord, what have I done? What have I done? Please don't let me destroy the life of the girl I truly love. I don't deserve your forgiveness because it was my selfish desires and lust of the flesh that made me want her so desperately. I need your strength to do what is right. I can't stop loving her, but I won't destroy her life because of my selfish love. Help me, please, to forget her, to forget that moment of bliss and how wonderful that kiss felt on my lips. There is so much I don't understand, Lord. If there is one true love in everyone's life, how can I love her so much and her be in love with someone else? There is no sense to that. Is Will right? Is marriage simply a commitment to someone that we don't truly love? Can we marry anyone if we are faithful and truly committed to them…even if we don't truly love them? Is Mother wrong? Can I love someone and not be loved in return? I know I have to do what's right. I have to put her out of my mind and try to stop loving her. I won't hurt her any more. I've never seen such fear and agony in someone's face before. Please, help me to do what's right, Lord."

From the bottom of the hill, Caleb could see the lights in the windows of the athletic dorm. After what he had just experienced, he dreaded the thought of facing Will. Inside the dorm, the atmosphere seemed more like a wake. No yelling or clowning, no grab-assing, or tussling. No loud music, singing, or vulgarity—just an eerie silence.

Caleb walked into Will's room. Will was sitting on the windowsill in his silk bikini briefs, starring out into space. Caleb eased up beside him and put his hand on his shoulder. Will flinched and knocked it away. "Still gazing out the window," he murmured. "I blew it, kid. I screwed up. I cost us the game and probably Coach Shook's job." Pain and anger was in his face and eyes.

Caleb, careful to choose his words, said, "Will, I'm going to remind you what Coach Shook preaches to us. No one play or player wins or loses a game. There are almost two hundred plays in a game. The final outcome is a culmination of the efforts that went into every single play."

Will jumped up and yelled, "You don't get it, do you? I'm Will James, the all-American. I don't make stupid mistakes, and I sure as hell don't when the game's on the line. My father was right, damn his soul. I chased a sucker play and ran myself out of position. That cost us the game. On top of that, I got a dumb penalty that sealed our fate."

Caleb threw his palms up, stepped back, and said, "Hey! I'm on your side. I have no idea what you're talking about. But I know this…you didn't lose the game. One day you're going to realize that there are ten more players on the field with you. They have the same responsibility that you have. You're never going to win or lose a game by yourself. Nobody's that good."

"There are things you don't know, pal. My father forced his way into the dressing room after the game just to humiliate me. Then he spewed his damn venom on Coach Shook. He actually raised his hand to strike me in front of the team. I hope he burns in hell, if there is a hell."

"Please sit down, Will, and calm down. What you're saying doesn't help anyone, especially you. Your father was wrong. Hopefully one day he'll realize it and apologize to you and Coach Shook."

Will plopped down on his cot and gave Caleb a dubious look, shaking his head. He mockingly laughed and said, "I wish I lived in your world, Corn Shuck. It must be a beautiful place."

"What do you mean?" Caleb asked.

"You know, love your neighbor as yourself. Honor your father and mother. Peace on earth and good will to men. I've read the black book. That's all a crock. There is no peace on earth and good will to men. It's a dog-eat-dog world. How do you be-bop around here with that silly, girlish grin when everyone here tried to kick your teeth in? How can you still preach that stuff?"

"You'll understand one day, Will. I'll pray for you every day."

"Save your prayers for someone who wants them, like Coach Shook…" Will calmed somewhat, and then he continued, "That's not all the story, kid. It seems there was some kind of altercation between Coach Shook and one of the sports writers after the game, Norris Beckham I assume. I heard that Coach Shook decked him. I'm sure he deserved it, but if he did, Coach Shook has coached his last game. A lot of people wanted his hide. Now they have a reason to get him. And you can thank your pal, Will, for that." Will doubled up his fists and shook them violently. He shouted, "We had them, Corn Shuck! The streak was over if I'd just stayed home and played my position. But I chased a sucker play around the other end. It was a reverse, and I had to chase it down from behind instead of making the tackle behind the line of scrimmage as I should." He pounded a forearm into the door followed by a knee into the door, and it sounded like a small thunderbolt hit the hall. Everyone in the dorm knew where it came from, and no doors were opened.

He lowered his head, letting his arms fall, saying, "I lost the game. I haven't made a mistake like that since junior high. My father was right…but he had no right to vent his anger on Coach Shook. We had the right plan, and we had the game won."

"Things will look better tomorrow. Try to get some rest. Things always look better in the morning sun."

Will's head hung low, yet he still managed a little chuckle at Caleb's eternal optimism. They didn't talk again that night.

Will had nightmares all night, and Caleb couldn't sleep for worrying about Coach Shook's fate. He did remember the kiss and how Angelle's warm body felt in his arms. He knew that feeling would remain deep in his heart forever. Completely exhausted, he finally fell into a deep sleep in the late hours of the night.

CHAPTER FIVE

At six o'clock the following morning, the phone rang at Dr. Marston's home. Doc sat his coffee down and picked up the receiver. "Hello," he said.

"Good morning, Doc. This is Dr. Parker. I hope I didn't wake you."

"No, just enjoying my first cup of coffee with Edith. Is something wrong?"

"Have you read the morning paper?"

"No. I haven't brought it in yet."

"Read the paper. You'll understand why I feel it necessary to call a special meeting of the Board of Trustees tonight at seven o'clock. As chairman of the board, I need your approval to do so. It seems as if Coach Shook lost all control last night and attacked Norris Beckham in the locker room after the game. Coach Shook continued on a tirade and ran everyone out of the dressing room. Norris had to be carried to the hospital. I was informed he might have a broken jaw."

"Have you discussed this with Coach Shook?" Doc asked, somewhat startled.

"I didn't feel that it was necessary. The incident was documented in all the papers. I know how you feel about Coach Shook, however, this kind of action can tarnish the Marston image, and there might be litigation. I wouldn't do this if I didn't think it was the appropriate action to take. Do you concur?"

"If you feel that strongly about the situation, I certainly don't object, however, I would remind you that you shouldn't believe everything you read in newspapers."

"Then I'll see you at seven tonight," Dr. Parker said and hung up the receiver.

"What now?" Edith asked.

"It seems Coach Shook finally had his fill of Norris Beckham and pasted him after the game. This is just what most of the board has waited for. This won't be easy to defuse. I haven't lost many battles in the boardroom, but that might come to an end tonight. Sweetheart, I'm tired of all this. I'm going to make you a promise, and you know I keep my promises. When Caleb graduates and goes to medical school, I'm severing all ties with the college. We're going to do some of the things we've dreamed about all our lives. When he takes over my practice, I'm devoting all my time to you, with an occasional game of golf just to give you a break."

"Dearest," Edith said, smiling, "you can't orchestrate that boy's life. What makes you so sure he's capable of handling that much responsibility? Or that he wants to?"

"You know I pride myself in judging character. This boy is truly a diamond in the rough. His talents and abilities are limitless. I've never known anyone with so much compassion and integrity. I know I have to proceed slowly in molding his future. I never thought I would ever get this opportunity again after we lost June. To use Caleb's favorite expression, providence and hard work has put him in my hands. I'm going to do all in my power to see my plans come to fruition. I love that boy, and I won't watch his talent and abilities go for naught…look up Coach Simpson's phone number, Edith."

"It's two, seven, nine," Edith responded. "I talk with Gail occasionally."

Doc rang the operator and gave her the number. Coach Simpson answered the phone. "Billy Ray, this is Doc Marston. I just had a call from Dr. Parker. He's called an emergency meeting of the Board of Trustees tonight. I'm sure I don't need to explain why. Do you think you could round up the coaching staff and meet me at my office around ten this morning? If I can possibly defuse this bomb, I'm going to need all the facts."

"We'll be there, Doc. The story in the papers didn't give an accurate account of the facts. We'll all be there."

Doc had no sooner hung up the phone when it rang again. He picked up the receiver. "Hello." He listened for a few minutes, and then said, "He probably took it off the hook, Coach Vaught." Again he listened for a couple of minutes, and then said, "I know how much he respects you, too, Coach, and how much he'll appreciate the things you've said. I'm going to fight for him. With your permission, I'd like to tell the board what you just told me." Then Doc said, "Thank you, Coach. True friends are a rare commodity in this life. I wish you another very successful season." He hung up the phone.

"He's a class act, isn't he?" Edith commented.

"Yes," Doc said, "and more important, a very good friend."

Caleb opened his eyes and looked at his watch. "Great Scott!" he yelled as he jumped up and began grabbing his dress clothes. "Ten o'clock, and I'm almost late for work." He looked at Will's unmade bed. Will never left his bed unmade since he was somewhat of a neat freak. Caleb knew he must still be upset, and now he had something else to worry about. He dressed quickly and rushed to the club.

Abe was setting the tables and appeared very troubled. "You read the paper yet, boy?"

"No, sir, I couldn't sleep because of some things that happened yesterday. I'm late because I didn't get much sleep."

"It's on the table in the kitchen. I think you need to read it," Abe insisted. Caleb went to the kitchen, and he could hear Abe mumbling, "Ain't nothin' but trouble around this place. Just something else to add more gray to Doc's head. He don't need no more worries with the load he carries."

Caleb returned in a couple of minutes. "Will told me something happened after the game. He wasn't sure about the details, but I hope this is not all true."

"It doesn't matter whether it's all true or not, they're going to fire the man, for sure."

"I prayed about it last night," Caleb said, "and I'm going to pray about it all day."

"Well son, there's one thing to remember about prayers. God answers all prayers, but the answer ain't always yes. But don't let that discourage you, because miracles still happen. If I know Doc, he'll fight for Coach Shook."

The lunch crowd started arriving around eleven. By two, the dining hall was empty again. Neither Edith nor Doc had come for lunch as they usually did. After the hall was cleaned, Abe locked up. Caleb, filled with fear and apprehension, went to the library to study.

⋯

At six-forty-five p.m., a procession of expensive, new cars began pulling into the parking lot of the administration building. Smartly-dressed, distinguished-looking gentlemen filed out of their cars and started up the steep flight of steps to the entrance of the president's office where the boardroom was located. A long, black Cadillac limousine pulled up to the steps. A chauffer hurried around the car and opened the door. Two large ostrich boots hit the pavement, followed by a pair of black satin western pants. Then a large, white Stetson cowboy hat that looked like it came off the set of the last Tom Mix film appeared. Bill James stood up, raised his long arms, and stretched himself for a few seconds. Then he proceeded up the steps at a double-time pace.

The last car to enter the parking lot was Doc's old blue Plymouth coupe. He and Judge Knight eased out and walked slowly up the steps. The lines in their faces revealed their deep concern. A half-dozen newspaper reporters stood at the top of the stairs. "Do you see that?" Judge Knight said. "Didn't they get their pound of flesh this morning in the papers? Why can't they leave it alone?"

"I can imagine who called them," Doc said.

Inside the boardroom, the members were shaking hands and patting each other on the back. Comments like, "How good you look," and "how pleased I am to see you again," were exchanged all over the room. There was no mention of the reason for the special meeting. Doc and Judge Knight joined in the masquerade, shaking hands with everyone and complimenting them on their appearance. Doc was quick to assess those who came for a quick lynching and those who were genuinely concerned about the fate of Coach Shook. He eased up to Judge Knight and whispered, "We have problems, Horace. I estimate two-to-one in favor of a lynching."

Horace responded, "I observe more like three-to-one."

"Say a little prayer for Coach Shook," Doc said. Judge Knight nodded.

The door to Dr. Parker's office opened, and his secretary appeared, followed closely by Dr. Parker. He moved quickly around the room, shaking hands with the board members. He greeted them and said, "I have seven sharp, gentlemen. Would you please take a seat at the table?" Doc sat at the head of the huge mahogany table that had been donated by his grandfather. Dr. Parker sat to his right, and his secretary sat next to Dr. Parker to record the minutes. As Chairman of the Board, Doc called the meeting to order followed by a roll call. Reverend Allen Blackwell from Jackson led the board in an opening prayer, as was their custom.

Doc nodded for Dr. Parker to begin the meeting. Dr. Parker began, "Gentlemen, my sincere apologies for calling this meeting on such short notice; however, the situation warranted immediate attention. I'm sure everyone has read the morning paper. The news about Coach Shook's inappropriate action after the game last night made every newspaper in this country. It was an embarrassment to the athletic program and did immutable damage to the image of this institution. I was up all night talking calls from alumni and a few board members. Thankfully the problem has resolved itself." He took a piece of paper out of his briefcase and held it up. "At eight o'clock this morning, Coach Shook's secretary hand-delivered his letter of resignation. It was short and to the point. I'll read it to you. 'I wish to tender my resignation as head football coach and athletic director effective immediately. I realize my conduct last evening was an embarrassment to the college and the athletic program. I offer no excuse. This college has been my life for the last thirty years. I will always cherish the memories of the good times and good friends I have made along the journey. I leave with no malice in my heart toward the college or anyone affiliated with it. I wish only success and glorious days in the future for Marston. Respectfully submitted, Calvin Shook.'

"Under the circumstances it appears that we simply need a motion to accept Coach Shook's resignation and then appoint an interim head coach. We will want to appoint a search committee to secure the finest coach available after the season is over." The majority of the board nodded their approval of Dr. Parker's recommendations.

William James stood up proudly to say, "I make the motion that we accept Coach Shook's resignation."

Shelby Johnson, a wealthy, sleazy ambulance-chasing lawyer from Memphis, was quick to second the motion.

Doc shot up from his chair, flinging his hands into the air, and barked, "Gentlemen, don't you think this drastic action warrants just a little discussion? After all, Coach Shook has given his life to this college with faithful and exemplary service. I think if you check his record, you will not find the slightest hint of any misconduct or impropriety in his past. Are we so quick to say one mistake warrants such extreme punitive action? As a new board member, some thirty years ago I was on the search committee that was appointed to find a coach to start the football program here at Marston. Coach Shook was a young, promising, energetic coach with a brilliant football mind, and he was my choice. He proved himself year-in and year-out. Gentlemen, before we do something we may regret, I would like you to read this document. This is an accurate account of the events that precipitated the unfortunate event of last evening." Doc passed out the document, and each member of the board read it intently. After all the eyes were focused on Doc again, he continued, "We all know Coach Shook is under extreme pressure at this juncture. I certainly don't condone this kind of behavior…however, I can see how one might react like that under the circumstances. After all, he's just a man. Every man has his breaking point. We need to remember that he's no different than you and I. As my pastor once told me during a personal crisis, the best of men are men at best."

William James stood up, saying, "Doc, we all know how you feel about Coach Shook. I respect him as a man but no longer as a coach, I played for him. He was a terrific coach in those days, but his time has passed. Thankfully, he's recognized that fact and has given us a golden opportunity to find a great, young coach who'll get this program back to the glory days of old. I didn't send my son here to play for a loser. If he stays, I'll consider transferring my son in January." The board members began to whisper among themselves after his threat.

Dr. Parker, anxious to get the board and alumni off his back, said, "Are we ready to vote, gentlemen?"

Doc, red-faced and irritated by Bill James's comment, stood up again and threw his arms into the air, palms up. "Gentlemen!" he began, "we're talking about retiring a legend in his profession. There are a few things you need to consider before you make a rash decision. I had a call from one of the most successful and respected coaches in the nation this morning, Coach John Vaught. He said he's been trying to reach Coach Shook all morning, but the phone was apparently off the hook. He said that after reading the article, he feared things might come to this. He said there was no coach in the nation that he had more respect for than Coach Shook. He also said that he had done more with less talent in the last ten years than anyone else could possibly have done. He further said that we have only two football players on our team that he tried to recruit. The first is John David. We all know who the other one is.

"With only two kids on our team who are major college prospects, we expect the impossible. When we don't get it, we are quick to point fingers and place blame." Doc looked around the table and into every board member's eyes. He said, "Now, let us be true to ourselves. This is not about Coach Shook losing control and decking Norris Beckham, is it? Every true Marston fan who has read his articles during the last few years would like to have done the same as Coach Shook. No, gentlemen, this is about finding a scapegoat and getting the alumni off our backs, isn't it?" Doc's cold, gray eyes looked straight at Dr. Parker. Dr. Parker looked up at Doc, slowly lowered his head, and nodded.

Doc continued, "I'm probably the last person in this room who should be quoting the Scripture, after my relationship with the Lord the last ten years, but I think it is appropriate at this time." He paused and looked the board members in the eyes, one-by-one, and said slowly, "'He that is without sin, let him cast the first stone.' However, in this case I'll substitute vote for stone."

William James shot up again and shouted, "If I wanted to hear a sermon, Doc, I'd be in church tonight! I'm not concerned with sin…I'm concerned with winning football games. My motion stands. My time is valuable, and I call for the vote."

Judge Knight stood up. "I offer a substitute motion to refuse to accept the resignation and to have Dr. Parker send Coach Shook a letter of reprimand." Five board members seconded the motion at the same time.

Doc said, "We'll vote on the substitute motion first, gentlemen. All in favor of the substitute motion, please raise your right hand." There was silence for a few seconds, and then Judge Knight and the five men that had seconded the motion raised their hands. The other board members looked at each other. Slowly, one-by-one, they raised their hands. Only two hands didn't rise. William James jumped up and stormed out of the room, mumbling profanity.

Dr. Parker stood up and said, "Again, I wish to apologize to you gentlemen for the inconvenience. This matter is closed. I'll send the letter tomorrow. I'll see you gentlemen at our semi-annual meeting in January. Have a safe trip home."

Doc walked around the table, shaking everyone's hand and saying, "We did the right thing, gentlemen. Thank you." He and Judge Knight walked slowly out of the room and down the steps. A half-dozen news reporters had followed William James down the steps. They were crowded around him at the bottom. They could hear him railing at the top of his voice about the board's decision.

One of the newsmen recognized Doc and ran up the steps stopping in front of Doc. "Doctor Marston, I'd like to get some information about the meeting. Why didn't the board take more punitive action against Coach Shook?"

"No comment," Doc said.

The young reporter didn't move, blocking Doc's exit, and asked, "Is it true that you preached a sermon inside the board room?"

"No comment," Doc said, becoming irritated. Doc tried to get around him, but he kept stepping in front of Doc.

"William James says you run the board like a tyrant. The board is composed of a bunch of cowards who won't buck you."

Doc bristled. "Young man, I'm not going to stand here and get insulted by you or anyone. I'm going to ask you to step out of my way just one time. If you don't, one of us is going to get an ass-whipping right here." The young newsman jumped out of Doc's way.

Doc and Judge Knight crawled inside the car. The judge slapped Doc on the back and burst out laughing. Doc grinned and said, "I thought we had lost the battle when William James threatened us."

"They all knew it was a bluff," Judge Knight shrugged. "This is the only place where that egotistical SOB ever gets his ego massaged."

"I need to go by Coach Shook's house and give him the news. I'm sure he's upset. He and his staff need to be preparing for Tulane."

"Drop me off first. I need to get back and do a little work tonight. I have a heavy case load tomorrow." Doc hurried home, and the judge jumped into his Cadillac and started back to Jackson. Doc rushed inside and grabbed Edith, picked her up, and swung her around, then kissed her.

"I never doubted that your golden tongue wouldn't sooth the savage board," Edith said.

"Well, I didn't have your confidence, sweetheart. I want to go over and tell Coach Shook the news. I'll be back soon."

Doc rushed out, hopped into his car, and hurried across town to Coach Shook's modest home on the outskirts of town. He parked on the road outside his house. When he knocked on the door, Mavis, Coach Shook's wife, let him in, red-eyed from a million tears shed. She hugged Doc. "I'm glad you came, Doc. I'm worried sick about Calvin. He sat up all night, drinking three pots of coffee. Then before daylight, he went out on the patio. He's been out there all day with a strange look on his face. He did come in once to call Claire and tell her what to write in the resignation letter. She came over crying and had him sign it. That didn't help. Our lives haven't always been a bed of roses, but I've never seen him act like this."

"You just relax, Mavis," Doc reassured her, giving her a hug. "Everything is going to be all right. I need to see him." Mavis pointed to the back door. Doc walked through the house and out the back door. Coach Shook's head was slumped down. He appeared to be sleeping. Doc eased up beside him and put his hand on his shoulder. Coach Shook turned his head slowly and looked up at Doc.

"I hope I didn't wake you, Coach."

"No. Actually I was praying. Doc, I've read about coaches being fired, and I've had to let a few go. Until you've experienced it yourself, you'll never know how it tears your guts out. Those are my kids, Doc. They are not the best athletes in this country, but they have heart. You can't coach heart." He put his thumbs and fingers together, leaving a small space between. "We came this close to winning that game and breaking the streak. Do you know what it would have meant to those kids to have won?"

"Well, there are eight more games," Doc said. "Who knows, next week might be the one? Don't you think you need to be looking at the films and putting a game plan together for Tulane?"

Coach Shook, startled by Doc's words, looked at him in shock and disbelief.

"Yeah," Doc said, smiling and nodding, "the Board refused to accept your resignation; however, there will be a letter of reprimand in your file."

Coach Shook lowered his head, his jaw tightened, and big tears welled up in his eyes. He reached out for Doc's hand and gave it a hard squeeze. Then he took a deep breath and let it out slowly, wiped his eyes, and stood up. He looked Doc in the eyes and said, "How do you do it, Doc? How do you carry the world on your shoulders without collapsing?"

"The same way you do," Doc said. "'To him who has been given much, much will be required.' I just try to give back a little that has been given to me."

Coach Shook put his arms around Doc and hugged him. Mavis was standing at the back door crying. Coach Shook said, "You are one special man, Doctor James Marston."

Doc laughed and said, "Why doesn't someone tell Edith that?"

"I'll tell her!" Mavis yelled, and ran out to embrace Doc and then her husband.

"Now, don't get mushy on us, Mavis," Coach Shook said. "I'm heading for the office. Call the coaches and tell them to get their rumps over there PDQ. Make us a few dozen sandwiches, and bring them over to my office, honey. I'm already hungry. I'll be back…when you see me coming. Don't wait up for me. We're going to win a dang ball game. My kids are primed and ready to win." Coach Shook put his arm around Doc's shoulders and walked him to his car. Coach Shook asked Doc if he wouldn't mind running by the dorm and telling Will and Caleb that he's still around. "They'll get the message to the rest of the kids."

"I'm way ahead of you, Coach. You know those boys love you."

"I know. No coach has ever been blessed with two kids like those two on the same team except possibly, Red Blake at Army when he had Glen Davis and Doc Blanchard. I know I'm thinking big, but it's possible that we could have two Heisman trophy winners on our team at the same time. Now, wouldn't that be a hoot! To be honest with you, it was killing me to think I wouldn't be a part of it."

"I'm no coach," Doc said, "but I know talent when I see it. Everyone knows you're playing with a half deck, but you need to break this losing streak somehow. I know your kids played their hearts out last night, and they almost pulled off the impossible. What concerns me is can they continue to play with that same intensity without winning. Human nature says sooner or later, they'll give up."

"That's where we as a coaching staff have to earn our keep by making sure they don't. If we can't, then it's time to find someone who can. If they quit on us, I will retire. That's my promise to you."

CHAPTER SIX

Doc went to the dorm and found Caleb studying at a small desk in his room.

"Doc!" Caleb said, somewhat surprised as he sprang up. "What are you doing here? Is something wrong?"

"No, my boy, actually something is very right. The Board has decided not to take any punitive action against Coach Shook. I'm sure the team would like to know that."

"Thank you, Lord!" Caleb said, looking up. "I'll tell everyone."

"Get a good night's rest," Doc said as he walked away.

Caleb ran into the hall and yelled, "Coach Shook will be at practice tomorrow, boys! Doc Marston just told me." A roar could be heard from the rooms, and everyone ran into the hall cheering and clapping their hands.

Caleb's thoughts immediately turned to Will. *Where is he? Is he all right? I need to find him before he gets into trouble and puts Coach Shook on the hot seat again, but I don't know where to start.* He paced the floor until midnight, then walked downstairs and outside to the bench in front of the dorm. There was a gentle, cooling breeze. Caleb ran his fingers through his soft hair as he looked at the road leading to the parking lot. He fought thoughts of Angelle and the kiss that still remained on his lips and in his heart. He shook his head violently and bumped his forehead with the palm of his hand. *No. I won't allow myself to think about it again.* Even as he was saying the words, he could feel her soft, tender lips press gently against his. He cried out, "She's not mine. She never will be! Stop acting like a fool!"

A voice from the second floor window called out, "Are you all right, Caleb! Why are you shouting?"

Caleb answered, "I'm okay, John David. I was just battling with myself and doing some soul-searching. I'm all right. Go back to sleep. I won't yell again."

"Do you want to talk about anything?" John David asked.

"No," Caleb said. "It's kinda personal."

"Well, if you ever need a friend to talk to, I'm a good listener."

He's a nice person, Caleb thought. *He'll make a wonderful preacher.* His thoughts went on. *If Coach Shook loses again next week, they'll be yelling for his resignation again. This'll start all over again. We have to win a game soon. If Will had just stayed in place and not chased the play, I know we would have won. I just know it. I wish he could be on both ends of the line…then we'd never lose a game unless the offense couldn't score.* Caleb eyes widened, and his mouth flew open. He put his palm to his forehead bumping it lightly. *Why not? Will is a superman on the field. Why not?* He looked over at the coaches' offices. All their cars were parked in front of the coach's office, and the lights were still on. He jumped up and ran there. The door was unlocked so he walked in. He went back to Coach Shook's office and opened the door. The cigar smoke was boiling up as usual, and the coaches were at the chalkboard working. They all turned and looked surprised to see him there.

"What's the problem, son?" Coach asked. "Is something bothering you?"

"The team's happy about…you know, but that's not why I came over here. I apologize for interrupting you work, Coach Shook, but I was just thinking…"

"It's all right, son. Just tell us what's on your mind," Coach Shook said.

"I know you'll think I'm a stupid country hick for coming in here and disturbing you, but—"

"But what?" Coach Shook said, getting a little impatient.

"I know you coaches are a thousand times smarter than me but—"

"Son," Coach Shook said, "tell us what's on your mind because we are kinda busy. But never too busy to listen."

"Y'all are probably going to laugh at what I'm going to say, but I think it's worth saying. I know how we can win a game, lots of games."

The coaches snickered under their breath, and Coach Shook grinned. "Tell your trick play, son, and if it has merit, we'll consider it."

"I don't have any trick play, Coach. There's nothing wrong with our plays. I just have two suggestions. If Will was playing middle linebacker, I don't think anybody could run the ball on us, and when we get in a position to score and we have short yardage, Will could play fullback. He'd block any end or linebacker in the country and clear the way for our running back. Now you can laugh at me," Caleb said. "I promise never to disturb y'all again or make any more suggestions." He backed out of the door and closed it quickly. He walked slowly down the hall and paused at Claire's desk. The coaches waited until they were sure he was out of the building, and then burst out laughing. "I guess it wasn't such a good idea," Caleb mumbled.

They looked at each other, shook their heads, and continued to laugh. Then the laughter stopped abruptly, their eyes widened, and they all looked at each other again. "Do y'all think?" Coach Shook said. "No! He's never played linebacker. Plus, he's an all-American end. They would crucify me, and Bill James would break me in two pieces."

Billy Ray smiled, his eyes brightened, and he said, "That marvelous, young, country boy might have just given us the key to the treasury. Why not? What do we have to lose? Why didn't we think of that?"

Stan, somewhat skeptical, questioned, "How do you teach someone to play linebacker in five days if he's never played the position before? I think we may be asking too much out of Will."

Toad, the offensive line coach, stood up and said, "Will James could play quarterback with three days practice. My only question is why didn't *we* think of this?"

Coach Shook's face brightened, and he commented, "Out of the mouth of babes, gentlemen. Sometimes you have to be on the outside looking in to get the picture." He ran his fingers through his thinning gray hair and asked, "What do you think, men? This is the kind of move that can get me fired for sure if it backfires. But if it works, we'll be called geniuses. I'm ashamed to admit it, but I think that kid hit on something brilliant. What do y'all think?"

Toad and Billy Ray nodded their agreement. "When you own the longest losing streak in the nation, what's to lose? I say go for it," Billy Ray said.

"Stan?" Coach Shook queried, wide-eyed.

"I'm with the rest of you guys," Stan said. "What do we have to lose?"

"We are agreed then," Coach Shook said. "Now we really have to get to work to decide on the best defense that'll protect Will and allow him to roam free down the line of scrimmage. I think we need to close practice to the public and news media this week. This needs to be a surprise right up to kickoff." Everyone nodded in agreement.

Stan said, "I think we need to look at the five-three first. It's a middle linebacker defense. The guard is the only player that can block the middle linebacker, and Will will take his head off when he tries."

"That sounds good," Coach Shook said. "We also need to look at personnel to beef up the interior line. What do y'all think about working Will at fullback some?"

"I'm buying the whole package," Billy Ray said. The coaching staff went back to work with a renewed sense of jubilant optimism.

Caleb walked slowly back to the concrete bench, embarrassed and feeling like a fool. *When am I going to learn to keep my mouth shut?* he thought. *The Bible says, 'Be quick to listen, slow to speak, and slow to anger.' I blew it on two out of three.* As he sat down, he saw headlights flash in the distance, and he jumped up in anticipation. As the car drew closer, Caleb could see it was Will's Chevrolet. He ran to the parking lot, certain he would need to help Will into the dorm.

Will stopped and opened the door at the same time Caleb reached the car.

"Is that you, Corn Shuck?" Will asked. "Why are you still up?"

"No, it's not me, I'm the ghost of Christmas past. Where have you been all day, and night? You about worried me sick."

"Now, Mommy," Will said, "I've asked you not to wait up for me. You know nice boys don't talk about their escapades."

"Be serious for once in your life, Will. I was very concerned about you."

"I know you were. I guess I should appreciate it. To be truthful, I would have been back hours ago, but I made a little unscheduled stop at the city slammer in Memphis. It so happened that the Chief of Police was a former Marston football player who luckily played on the team with my father, and he was at the game last night. He handled the problem."

"What problem, Will? What did you do to get thrown in jail?"

"Actually, it wasn't my fault this time. I was sitting quietly at a table in this semi-high class joint on Beale Street with a cute little trick that I had just met. Well, I'm getting ahead of myself. Before the trouble started and before I picked up this cute chick, I was listening to this kid up on the stage singing. He was a good-looking sucker, coal black hair, long sideburns, and a voice you wouldn't believe. The place was going wild listening to him sing and watching him gyrate all over the small stage. He was singing 'Blue Moon of Kentucky.' I was sitting there minding my own business, patting my foot, keeping time to the music, and wondering if some black family had raised this kid because I never saw a white man with dance moves like that before. The women and girls were screaming and acting like fools. When he finished singing, he took out a handkerchief and wiped his face, then tossed the handkerchief on the dance floor. I swear, there was scrambling and screaming and hair-pulling like you wouldn't believe. I've never seen anything like it before, not even at some of the dives I frequent. Finally, this big, husky heifer managed to wrestle it away from the others, and she tore out of the pile. The kid didn't look any older than me. The band took a break, and he walked off the stage and walked right up to my table. Half the women in the place was drooling after him.

"He said, in this deep, harmonious voice, 'Mind if I sit here?' I shrugged and nodded. 'You're Will James, aren't you?' he commented. 'That's what's on my birth certificate,' I said, kind of cocky. 'I'm Elvis Presley,' he said. 'I recognized you from all your pictures in the sports pages and magazines. I like sports, and I've kept up with your career so far. I'd like to run down to Marston and catch a game, but our weekends are booked solid through December.' I said to him, 'now, I remember who you are. You sang on the Louisiana Hayride in Shreveport last year. I caught you on the radio a few times. Hell of a voice.'

"'I confess,' he said, with a cockeyed smile. 'I managed to get out of that contract this year. How did you like that last song?' he queried. Fan-damn-tastic, I replied. 'Good,' he said with a big sideways smile. 'I hope everyone likes it. We just cut the record. It's my first.' He stood up and said, 'I better get back to work.' I stood up to shake hands with him. His eyes widened, and he looked me up and down and said, 'I see why you're an all-American.' He reached in his coat pocket and took two tickets out and handed them to me. 'I have a concert scheduled here in the coliseum in a few weeks. If you happen to have an open date that week you might like to attend, if not give them to a friend. They are hard to come by,' he said. I thanked him and we shook hands.

"He returned and sang until after midnight then they packed up and left. After he left my table, I could have had any woman in the joint because they thought we were friends. Now back to my story. I was planning to get a few more drinks down the cute little trick and then find a hotel for the night. Suddenly the bartender who was listening to the radio yelled, 'They didn't fire Coach Shook, just gave him a reprimand!' Half the bar flies stood up and cheered. The other half began to boo. I took offense at their boos. A few drunken locals took offense at my offense. I had to kick some ass, so the bartender called the Law. I was still sober, so I didn't resist arrest. I didn't want to put Coach Shook on the spot after what he'd been through."

"That was commendable, but you shouldn't have been there in the first place. Why do you do things like that? Why can't you be satisfied just being a great athlete and one of the most intelligent people in the world?"

"It's who I am, kid. Now, shut up and let's get upstairs and get some shut-eye. We've got to get ready to win two games this week. I have confidence that we're ready to get that monkey off our backs and start kicking some ass, because the alternative stinks."

"We agree on that, Will." They walked up to their room. Will undressed and hopped in bed. He was asleep in seconds. Caleb looked at the back of his eyelids for the longest time. Finally, he gave up and opened his eyes. His thoughts returned to the events that had occurred earlier. He could feel Angelle's soft lips against his cheeks and the exhilaration of her lips pressing against his and the warmth of her body in his arms. He tried to block that memory from his mind, but it was impossible. He tossed and turned until nearly dawn, finally falling asleep.

Caleb went to class and then to work for a few hours. As he was leaving work for football practice, Doc pulled in and flagged him down. Caleb stepped out of his old truck as Doc said, "I need a special favor if you have time."

"I'll always have time for you, Doc."

"There's a special kid in the hospital, room two-twelve, and he's dying. He's special to me. He wants to meet you and shake your hand. His name's Buckie. He's Luther Cummings's son. Do you think you could run by and say hello to him soon? I say soon because he won't be with us long."

"Buckie Cummings?" Caleb asked quickly.

"You know him?" Doc replied, somewhat surprised.

"I know Mr. Luther. He hitched a ride with me when I came to school. I really liked him. I should've visited Buckie already because Luther asked me to. But I've been so wrapped up with myself, I kinda forgot about him. I'll go right after practice."

"It'll mean the world to him. He's quite a football fan. He knows everybody on the roster. I took him a program, and he memorized all the names and numbers."

"I have to go now. I don't want to run laps for being late. The team appreciates what you did for Coach Shook. It ain't his fault…I mean it isn't his fault that we're losing, and the team knows that."

"A one-eyed baboon would know that. Now scoot off to practice."

After the team dressed, Coach Shook made an announcement: "We will be practicing in the stadium this week, team." Everyone looked at each other, wondering what this was all about. The team never went on the field until Friday. All the gates were locked, and campus security stood at the tunnel leading to the stadium.

Duck whispered, "He's going to line us up and shoot us, and he doesn't want any witnesses." Some uneasy snickers could be heard.

After calisthenics and stretching exercises were completed, Coach Shook said, "Men, I think you grew up Saturday afternoon and became a team. I saw a supreme effort out of everyone like I've never seen before. We were the best team on that field that day. You deserved to win. We want to make a few changes that we think will give us the best chance to win and make your parents and the Marston community proud of you."

Coach Shook looked at Will. "Will, you're our leader and a true all-American. Are you willing to sacrifice and do what's best for the team to give us a better chance to win?"

"I'd tear my heart out and give it to you, Coach, if it would make us winners," Will said.

"I believe you would," Coach Shook said. Every player held his breath in anticipation of what was about to be revealed.

"The coaches want you to work at middle linebacker in the five-three defense this week. We're going to look at the six-three also, but we feel that the five-three might be the best for us." Will's jaw dropped. He had never played linebacker before. He had only dreamed of being a two or three-time all-American at defensive end to out-class his father.

"Do you think I can play that position?" Will asked, a slight tremor in his voice.

"Son," Coach Shook said, "I know you can play that position better than anyone in the country…if you put your heart into it. I know you had your heart set on being an all-American end like your father, but all-American is all-American. You'll probably be a defensive end in the pros. But I know you can be the best linebacker in the country for the next three years. Are you willing to try?"

Will lowered his head, shaking it slowly. After a brief pause, he raised it and said, "I want to win, Coach, and if that gives us a better chance, then I'm game."

"Also, I'd like to put in a few plays with you at fullback, particularly on short yardage."

"Now, you're talking my jive!" Will blurted, flexing his biceps muscles. "I always wanted to make a touchdown."

"I was thinking more on the line of a bulldozer clearing a path for the running backs on short yardage and goal line plays. I know no one can play both ways and be effective, but, when the game is on the line and we need someone to clear out a linebacker or end, that's when we may call on you."

Caleb was standing there swelling with pride, then he reminded himself that pride comes before a fall. However, he couldn't help but feel good about his suggestion.

"Now I'm not going to stand here and take credit for all these changes," Coach said.

Caleb blurted out quickly before Coach could say another word. "We all know who to give credit to, Coach Shook. You and the best coaching staff in this wonderful country of ours." The team clapped and yelled their agreement.

Coach Shook looked at Caleb. Caleb returned a subtle headshake and lowered his brows. Coach Shook received his message and said, "We have a lot of work to do in the next four days to get this new defense ready, but we're going to do it, men. Let's get to work. Also," he yelled, "this is all on the QT, men. Surprise is the essential element in most victories."

"That means keep your traps shut!" Will yelled.

After a few hours of intense practice, the varsity jogged to the dressing room for showers. Coach Stan and Coach Simpson held the freshmen team for a spirited practice to get them ready for the Thursday game with Tulane in New Orleans. Caleb and Cliff alternated at tailback. A few new plays were added, and then they worked on special teams. Spirits were high. After another hour, the coaches dismissed practice.

Caleb showered, dressed quickly, and walked into the equipment room. Ira was just starting to wash the sweaty practice jerseys. Caleb asked, "Will you give me one of the game balls that we played with in the freshman game? I'll pay for it, and it needs to be the cleanest one in the bag."

Ira informed him that he didn't know which ones were used in the freshmen game. "We throw all the game balls into the practice bag after a game. You must want to give it to your gal, huh?"

"No. I want to give it to a child in the hospital who's dying."

Ira looked at Caleb with a warm smile and shook his head. He scrounged around in the bag of balls until he found one that looked new. "No charge," he said. "It was paid for with your sweat, blood, and kindness. I'm not just the equipment manager around here. I know how they treated you at first."

Caleb walked by the coaches' office and noticed Will and the coaches talking and diagramming plays on the chalkboard. Caleb stuck his head in and inquired if he might speak to Will for a second.

Will walked outside, and Caleb informed him that he was going to the hospital to visit a sick kid, and he knew the young boy would be thrilled to meet him.

"How sick?" Will asked.

"Dying."

"I'll have to pass on that. I'm not much on sick and dying. Death scares the hell out of me. I don't go to funerals either."

"There might be a good reason it scares you."

"Oh! You're into psychology now, Corn Shuck?" Will scowled. "I suppose sick and dying doesn't bother you."

"You miss the point," Caleb snapped.

"I have lots to learn," Will said, turning to return to the office. Opening the door, he paused, looked back, and said, "I admire you for going. I wish I could, but that's not my thing."

"Then will you sign this ball for him? His name's Buckie." Will took out a pen and wrote, 'For a very special boy. Get well quickly, Buckie,' and he signed it, 'Will James, all-American.' Caleb flipped out his pen and wrote, 'To my good friend, Buckie,' as he signed the ball, too.

As Caleb hurried to the hospital, he had an uneasy feeling about what he had to do. This was a new experience for him. He took the elevator to the third floor, wanting to avoid the second floor nurses' station. As the elevator door opened, Caleb was surprised to see Angelle standing at the nurses' station with an older nurse. Caleb walked up to the station and said, "I thought you worked on the second floor."

Angelle looked steadily at a chart, commenting, "I work where I'm needed."

"I'd like to visit Buckie Cummings, if it's okay."

The other nurse asked, "Are you Caleb Morgan?" Caleb nodded. "Doc said you'd be coming. Buckie'll be thrilled to meet you. He worships you. He's constantly talking about you and how much he wants to be a football player like you. Is that ball for him?" Caleb nodded again. "That's very, very kind of you. He's on the second floor, room two-twelve." Angelle appeared very nervous and never raised her eyes. Caleb walked back to the elevators to go down to the second floor. The nurse whispered, "That's a very special young man, and I might add, he's not just handsome, he's absolutely beautiful."

Angelle's head shot up quickly, and she said, "I think I should go in with him. I don't want him to upset Buckie. He may not know the situation, and there is no telling what he might say to him."

"I wouldn't worry about that," the nurse said. "He appears to be quite intelligent, but if you wish, go down with him. If I was thirty years younger, I'd go in with him myself."

"That's certainly not my reason," Angelle replied, somewhat defensively.

"Wait, Caleb!" Angelle called out. "I'd like to go with you, please. I don't want Buckie to get too excited."

"Good," Caleb nodded, "because I don't know what I should say."

Angelle walked over to Caleb, smiled, and said, "You won't have to say much. He'll do most of the talking. He loves visitors, and he's ecstatic about meeting you."

Caleb paused at the elevator, lowering his head, and said, "I feel a little...embarrassed about last night."

Angelle looked away and said, "Last night never happened as far as I'm concerned. It wasn't your fault. It won't happen again."

As the elevator eased down, Caleb remarked, "If it's a problem, my sitting by you in class, I'll drop the course and take it next semester."

"You'll do no such thing!" Angelle snapped, looking up at him. "We'll just pretend it never happened."

Caleb forced a smile and nodded. He tapped on the door of room 212. A weak, childish voice responded, "Come in." Caleb and Angelle eased in. Caleb stopped just inside the door, while Angelle walked over to the bed and took Buckie's hand in hers.

Buckie was lying there with Curley, Caleb's beloved teddy bear, nestled in his arm. Caleb had given Luther the teddy bear after Luther caught a ride with Caleb when Caleb first arrived at Marston. He had loved his teddy bear, but he was embarrassed to take it to the dorm. Buckie's appearance was ashen and gaunt, so thin the skin appeared draped from his bones. The tumors on his neck and chest were very large and grotesque. The sight sickened Caleb.

Buckie's eyes were glued to the football in Caleb's hand as Caleb slowly walked toward his bed. He looked up at Caleb and asked, "Is that your football, mister?"

"Yes," Caleb responded, forcing a painful smile. "I'm bringing it to a friend. This is the game ball that the freshmen team used to win the game a couple of weeks ago."

"I wish I had a friend like you, mister. I always wanted a leather football like that. Poppa bought me a football for Christmas when I was seven. I took it to school after Christmas. One of the big boys took it away from me and kicked it. It burst wide open. They laughed at me when I cried. It weren't no good leather ball like that one. When I get well, I'm gonna get big and strong like Caleb Morgan and Will James. I'm gonna play football at Marston College."

Caleb turned away from the bed quickly and faced the window. Every muscle tightened in his body, and he bit his lip so hard to keep from crying he tasted salty blood. Snatching his handkerchief from his back pocket, he pressed it to his mouth. Angelle, observing Caleb's reaction, stepped between them to block Buckie's view as she said, "I've heard that Caleb Morgan is your hero."

"You know he is, Miss Angelle. I done told you that. He's everybody's hero. Will James is real great, but Caleb is everybody's favorite player now. Doc brought me a football program, and I've memorized all the player's names and numbers, but Caleb's name and picture ain't in the program. Now, when I listen to them games on the radio with poppa, I can look at their pitcher. I wish I had a pitcher of Caleb Morgan.

We listened to the game on the radio last Thursday when Caleb made the last touchdown to win the game. I heard the crowd roar through that window over yonder. I know it must be pert near a mile to that stadium. Poppa went crazy when Caleb scored because he knowed it was Caleb. He said he just knowed it." Buckie grinned and said, "That's the way Poppa talks. Poppa knows Caleb Morgan. Caleb gave Poppa a ride to the hospital when he first come up to school in his old honeymoon truck. I wish I knew him. You know he's a country boy like me. He don't have no poppa, and I don't have no momma. I wish I had a brother like him."

Caleb took a deep breath, turned, and walked back to Buckie's bed. "People can be brothers without having the same parents, Buckie."

"You mean like them Indians when they cut themselves and hold their arms together."

"There's another way that's not so painful. You spit in your hand, and your friend does the same. Then you shake hands seven times as you both repeat, 'We are brothers.' Then you are brothers forever."

"I ain't never heard that," Buckie said, managing a grin. "Ain't that a little…nasty?"

"Both spit and blood are mostly water." Caleb said. "If they both come from the body, what's the difference?"

"Are you a football player?" Buckie asked.

"Yes," Caleb said. "I heard some boy on this floor wanted to meet me."

"So you brought that football to him?" Caleb smiled and nodded. "There're lots of sick kids on this floor. Who did you bring it to?" Buckie asked.

"I brought it to you. I'm Caleb Morgan. I'd like to be your friend, and your brother."

Buckie's eyes widened, his face brightened, and he looked at Angelle and asked, "He ain't funning me, is he?"

Angelle smiled, and said, "No. He really is Caleb Morgan, and he brought you that football." Buckie's lips began to quiver. He would start to smile, then almost cry. Caleb handed him the football. Buckie held it up and turned it around, reading the two inscriptions on it. He couldn't restrain his emotions any longer. He began to cry. Angelle embraced him as she kissed his cheeks and wiped his tears. "I'll leave you two alone to get acquainted," she said, "but I'll be back with a cup of ice cream later."

Buckie sniffed the leather ball. "It has the sweetest smell, don't it, Caleb?"

Caleb leaned over and smelled the ball. "There's no smell like a new leather football," he agreed. "It makes goose bumps pop up on my arms."

"Mine, too," Buckie said. "Show me how to hold it so I can practice."

Caleb snuggled it against his chest with his arm, and his muscles bulged. "This is the right way. No one can knock it out of your arm when you run with it like this."

"Let me feel your arm," Buckie said, wide-eyed. He squeezed Caleb's forearm. "Oh my goodness, your arm feels like steel. If your legs are that hard, somebody might get hurt trying to tackle you."

"I hope not," Caleb said, smiling. "Do you want to be my brother, Buckie?" Buckie's eyes brightened, and his hand shot up, and he spit into it quickly. Caleb did the same. They shook hands seven times as they both said, "We are brothers."

"Now we're brothers forever," Caleb said. "You can never take it back."

"I don't wanna take it back. You're the only brother I have. I bet I got the most famous brother in the world."

"I have a pretty famous brother, too," Caleb said. "Everybody in the hospital knows you and loves you a lot more than they love me."

"That's 'cause they don't know you like I do," Buckie said proudly. "I can't wait 'til Friday to tell Poppa that you come to see me, and brought me this ball." They talked for a long time until Caleb said, "I need to get back to the dorm and do some studying tonight, but I promise I'll be back tomorrow."

"What time?" Buckie asked excitedly.

"I'm not sure, but before the day's over, I'll be back to see you." Caleb walked out into the hall and strolled by the nurses' station. Angelle wasn't in sight. He started walking back to the dorm feeling guilty about not visiting Buckie sooner as he had promised Luther.

Caleb saw Sarah Catherine walking toward the hospital. He paused when she came near. Her eyes were ablaze. She stopped abruptly and began to admonish Caleb. "I saw what you did to her last night. You, you sadistic…You could go to jail for less."

"Just what do you think you saw!" Caleb snapped, appalled by her unfounded accusation.

"Don't play dumb with me, you country hick!" she replied curtly. "I looked out the window and saw her tearing herself away from your grasp in tears."

"I can explain that!" Caleb snapped.

"How can you explain that after what I told you last night? You might be interested to know that she sat on her bed with Maurice's and her mother's picture in her arms and cried half the night. I begged her to call campus security and have you arrested, but she said it was none of my concern."

"Is that his name…Maurice?"

"You never quit!" she yelled. "Why would you care what his name is? You are trying to break up their engagement and steal her from him. I suppose you've been at the hospital stalking her again tonight."

"I've heard about enough from you!" Caleb barked. "You're probably right, I am trying to steal her love from him, but it's obvious you've never been in love. Angelle is right. This is none of your concern." He rushed away as Sarah Catherine stood and watched. He could feel her cold, angry eyes piercing his back. Caleb hurried to the dorm, racked with guilt about Buckie and his hopeless love for Angelle. He still needed to review the notes from his classes and read the next chapter in two other classes, but his heart wasn't in it.

When Caleb walked into his room, Will was pacing like a caged tiger. He didn't ask why—he knew.

CHAPTER SEVEN

Will erupted as soon as Caleb sat down. "I'd like to know what idiot dreamed up this hair-brain idea about my playing middle linebacker! It's a ridiculous idea! I'm going to make a fool out of myself! I'll have to learn new keys and how to read the offense. Besides, I've never played that dang position in my life!"

"I think it's a great idea. You were very, very good today in practice," Caleb said, hoping to appease Will.

"What the hell do you know, Corn Shuck!" Will shouted. "You didn't know how to put on a jock strap three weeks ago. Now you're evaluating my performance." Will's harshness pierced Caleb, and he lowered his head.

Will, quickly realizing how cruel and heartless his curt response had been, eased over by Caleb, put his hand on his shoulder and said, "I'm sorry for venting my frustration on you, my friend. I didn't mean it. But I know you had to see me miss the read and start the wrong way a half-dozen times when they ran Tulane's cross bucks and counters…and reverse. The reverse was a catastrophe. I looked like a damn fool again chasing the ball carrier on the wrong end of the field…but I have to admit when I learned a few keys, I did do a little better job, didn't I?"

Caleb responded quickly, "I saw you take a step in the wrong direction a couple of times, but with your quickness, you recovered and still met the ball carrier in the hole each time except for the reverse."

Will wrinkled his face, scowled, and whispered, "That was the scout squad, Corn Shuck. Hell, they're about as fast as a herd of turtles with boots on. We're talking Tulane. They've already won two games and they have speed to burn. That bunch of Cajuns may not be as big as some others on our schedule, but they're quick as cats. One wrong step and they'll shoot by me like I'm in quicksand."

"Well, you're pretty darned quick, too. If anyone can do it, you can. You're going to be great at that position."

Will, being the egotist that he was, loved Caleb's encouragement. He shrugged, saying, "I've mastered the position of defensive end. It might be a nice challenge to master another position. I'm going to give it my best shot. I have to admit, I like the idea of leading the ball carrier into the hole on offense. Who knows, they might let me run one before I graduate."

"I know they will. They want to win more than we do. Now, I need to do some studying. I'll go down the hall to the lounge and let you get some sleep."

"No need. You can study in here. I'll be asleep in ten minutes anyway. If you hit a snag, wake me and I'll help you."

"I don't think so," Caleb quipped. "I value my teeth."

After one a.m., Caleb took a shower and turned in. He remembered Buckie and Luther in his prayer, but he couldn't shake the guilty feeling about his love for Angelle. Sarah Catherine had struck a nerve, but he knew in his heart that she was right, and it gave him a sick feeling.

They rolled out early the next morning and went to breakfast. Caleb became uneasy about attending history class. He tried to convince himself that it would be better if he skipped it, but he had been taught to face his fears and act like a man. He reluctantly went to the classroom, sticking his head in slowly. When she wasn't in her seat, he breathed a sigh of relief. *She must have been too embarrassed to come to class,* he thought. As he walked down the aisle, some boys slapped him on the back as he passed. They commented, "We can't wait for the Tulane game Thursday. We have a dorm party planned to listen to the game together. How many touchdowns are you going to make?"

Caleb grinned, shrugged, and said, "I may never make another touchdown."

Two other boys ran up to him to say, "We're going to skip class Thursday and Friday to drive down to New Orleans just to see you play again, Caleb."

Caleb shook his head, frowning. "I don't think that's such a good idea, fellows."

"Our parents gave us permission," they said, smiling excitedly. "They live in Biloxi, and they're going to meet us at the game. I think Dad's more excited about the game than we are. He even thinks you're going to be better than Will James."

"Please don't go just to see me play. I may never make another touchdown. I was very fortunate in the first game."

They patted him on the back. "You are too modest, Caleb. You're going to be great."

"He's not going to be great, he's already great," the other boy said. "Some kids in the dorm want to charter a Greyhound bus and go to the game, but I don't think the administration would look favorably on that."

Caleb took his seat and flipped up the desktop. He saw Angelle out of the corner of his eye. She slipped down the aisle and sat down by him. Caleb sniffed and thought, *Do I smell perfume?* He cut his eyes toward her. She looked at him and exclaimed, "It's scented soap. I would never use perfume." Caleb nodded and forced a smile. Dr. DeHaberman rushed in like her skirt was on fire and began the lecture almost before she reached the podium. They didn't talk again. When the bell rang, Angelle stood up and said, "Good luck at the game Thursday."

Caleb responded, "I don't believe in luck I—" Angelle didn't wait for his response. She scooted down the aisle and double-timed it out of the classroom. Caleb said, "Huh!" shrugged, and went to his next class. He managed a few hours work at the club before practice.

The team worked hard and long, trying to perfect the new defense and incorporate the new game plan for Tulane. Will had studied his keys all day. He looked sharp at linebacker. The practice was spirited because the team had bought into the new defensive scheme. They had a renewed confidence that had not been felt for three years.

After almost three hours of grueling practice, the team huddled around Coach Shook. "Men," he began, "you know I'm not much on pep talks. I've always believed that if you prepare a team to play, give them the tools to win, and they play to their potential, you should be victorious. We've put in a lot of changes this week, both on offensive and on defensive. Tulane hasn't prepared for them…our advantage. They will adjust at halftime and be ready for the second half. That's when we find out what kind of character we have. They'll test our home training, our real values, and if we truly love the game.

I've always asked you for one hundred percent for sixty minutes. You gave it to us last week. But if we're going to win our first game in three years this week, it's going to take more." He looked around and noticed the expressions on the team's faces. "I know what you're thinking, men. No one can give more than one hundred percent, and you are right. But one more thing is needed to make you a winner. It's called teamwork. You can give me one hundred percent blocking, tackling, and running the ball, but without teamwork you are no more than eleven individuals running around on the field.

"Come here, Will. I want you to pick Caleb up and throw him up into the air, and be sure to catch him." Everyone looked at Coach Shook and began to snicker. "I'm serious, Will, just do it!" he demanded.

Will walked over to Caleb, putting his arms around his legs and back, and gave a long look at Coach Shook. He nodded. Will squatted low, sprang up, and threw Caleb into the air. Caleb gasped as he fell, but Will caught him safely and stood him up. "Now give me the other ten starting defensive players. Men, all eleven of you put your hands under Caleb's rear. On the count of three, hoist him into the air with all your might."

Caleb's jaw dropped. His eyes widened as the team converged on him and lifted him up with their hands. "Ready," Coach Shook said. He counted, "One." The team lowered Caleb and brought him back up. "Two," Coach Shook said, and the team did the same thing. "Three!" Coach Shook yelled, and the team lowered Caleb. This time, a mighty heave sent him rocketing into the heavens. Caleb let out a bloody scream that could be heard across the campus as he fell toward the earth from what seemed like over two stories high. The team cradled their arms and gently broke his fall. Caleb wiped his brow with a big sigh. "I knew you wouldn't mind, Caleb," Coach Shook said with a big grin. "Seriously, team, did you get my point?"

John David answered, "Yes, sir! As a team, we have great strength, but as individuals, we're limited. Even Will, as strong as he is, couldn't do what the team did together."

"I'm going to make you a promise, men. If you play as a team, we are going to win the games, both Thursday and Saturday. Remember you're strong as a team. Here's our schedule. The freshmen team will be boarding the bus at one p.m. sharp tomorrow for New Orleans. Everyone will be listening to you on the radio. I want an undefeated season from you boys," Coach Shook said. "I can't spare any of my regular staff for the game because we have so much to do before Saturday. Coach Parrish, our graduate assistant, will be handling the coaching duties. Stan and Billy Ray have gone over the defense and offense with him very carefully. Remember, he played four years here, so he already knows most of the plays. I have every confidence that he'll be able to do the job. I expect you to give him the same respect as you would any of our regular staff members."

"Coach, may I say something to the team before we go to the locker room?" Caleb asked.

"Certainly," Coach Shook said.

"Team," Caleb said, "there's a young boy in the hospital by the name of Buckie Cummings. He's really sick with cancer, and probably has only a few weeks or days to live. He loves Marston football, and he's memorized every one of your names and numbers. He's never seen us play and never will, but he listens to all our games. I visited him last night, and I fell in love with him. It broke my heart to see his condition. I know everyone is busy and it's hard to find time, but if you have a minute, day or night, you can make him the happiest boy in the world by just sticking your head in room two-twelve and introducing yourself, and sign the ball I gave—" Caleb cut his eyes at the coaches. "Tell him who you are and that you want to sign the football that Will and I gave him. That's it, Coach."

Coach Shook pointed at the dressing room and the team yelled and sprinted away. Billy Ray looked at Stan and said, "What do you think of our boy now?"

"I'll pick up another carton of Havana's Best for all of you when the season's over," Stan answered. "I'm going to visit that kid in the hospital, myself."

"Likewise," Coach Shook said.

Caleb rushed to the club in time to prepare the tables. Abe was quick to notice Caleb's demeanor during the evening. Doc and Edith came for dinner. Doc thanked Caleb for visiting Buckie the evening before. He commented, "I'm driving down to Jackson early Thursday. I'll pick up Horace and Jennifer for the game. It seems Jennifer finally broke Horace's will, and he agreed to take her. He suspects that she has a full blown crush on you, but I'm sure you knew that." Caleb grinned and nodded, then shook his head and looked down.

"What's troubling you?" Doc asked.

"I hate for everyone to take off and spend money to go to the game thinking I'm going to do what I did at the last game. I don't know if I'll ever make another touchdown, and I'm worried sick about it."

"Sweetheart," Edith chimed in, "who cares if you ever make another touchdown? The important thing is that you made the team and you're having fun. Life is full of problems and disappointments. Don't create more by worrying about trivialities. Enjoy these four years. Now, give me a kiss and stop worrying." Caleb forced a smile and kissed Edith.

Doc patted him on the rump and added, "Relax, son. I've seen hundreds of college games, and I've never seen a boy with more God-given ability than you. You'll make dozens of touchdowns before you graduate. Remember, Doc ain't never wrong." Edith cut her eyes at Doc. "Don't say it, Edith."

The dining hall cleared early. After the cleaning was completed, Abe said, "Talk to me, boy. I know something is eating at you."

"Yes, sir, it is." Caleb told Abe about Buckie and how rotten he felt about not visiting him sooner. He told him about Angelle and how much he loved her. That she was engaged, but he thought she might have feelings for him, and how guilty all this was making him feel. Then he added his concern about everyone going to the ballgame and thinking he was going to be great.

"Son," Abe said, "you ain't got yo' wings yet. You're still a young man. You ain't perfect, even though you might come as close as anyone I've ever known who was wearing Adam's flesh. I don't know why you haven't had a nervous breakdown with the load you're packing. What's important is that you did go see that boy. What you did for him was worth more than silver and gold. Now, as for matters of the heart, I ain't no expert. Only time will settle that matter. But, if she loves you and you love her, it'll all fall into place in time. If not, remember providence. My advice to you is to slow down and catch your breath. Things have a way of working out, and worryin' doesn't help one smidgen. I used to worry about Doc before you came, but now I don't. He's the old Doc that we knew years ago. I believe the good Lord sent you here. I been able to relax lately, and you ain't going to be heaping another load on me. I'm just getting too old to start worrying again."

"Don't worry about me. I'll be fine." Caleb looked at his watch. "I'm going to try to see Buckie tonight if he hasn't gone to sleep." Abe pointed at the door.

Caleb rushed to the hospital and shot up the stairs by the nurses' station. Angelle and Mrs. Gladys were behind the counter. Mrs. Gladys flagged him down and came out of the nurses' station. "What's going on?" she asked, with an edge to her voice.

"I just wanted to see Buckie for a minute if he's awake," Caleb said.

"No…that's not what I mean. We've had a steady stream of football players in here since five o'clock, and the coaching staff just left."

"I hope I didn't mess up, Mrs. Gladys," Caleb said, shaking his head apologetically. "I asked the team to drop in and sign his football. I didn't realize they'd all come today."

"I didn't say you messed up," Gladys said. "I think it was a wonderful gesture. I just wish they'd spread their visits out a little better. You can go in. Buckie is so excited he may not be able to sleep tonight. I'll give him something to calm him so he can get to sleep when you leave." Caleb tapped on the door, and a happy voice called out, "Come in." Caleb opened the door and eased in. Buckie was laying there with Curley in one arm and the football in the other, beaming with excitement, and some color had returned to his face.

"I heard you had some visitors, little brother," Caleb said.

Buckie, still beaming, said, "I reckon most of the team come to see me and signed my ball. Why did they do that?" he asked.

"I told them at practice that I had a little brother in the hospital and that you were our number one fan and how much you loved football. They wanted to meet you."

"They're so big and strong!" Buckie said, wide-eyed. "I didn't know football players was that big. I hope they don't hurt you in practice."

Caleb doubled up his fist and held up his arm. His huge biceps bulged. "Look at this hammer. How do you think they can hurt me?" he replied.

Buckie grinned and said, "I look out the window every night to see the first star, and I make a wish. I've made three wishes and one's already come true," Buckie said.

"Tell me about your wishes," Caleb said.

"I wished that I could meet you before…you know, and I did."

"What are the other two?" Caleb asked.

Buckie smiled as he said, "You know you can't tell your wishes, or they won't come true. Did you ever make a wish on a star that came true?"

Caleb pulled the chair up next to the bed. "I had a big wish that I told your father about on the way up here. My wish was that I could make the team at Marston, and it came true."

"On a star?" Buckie said, brightly.

"Oh no! I prayed about it. The stars have no power. After all, God made the stars. He has the power to make any wish come true. Of course, if it's a selfish wish like asking for a pot of gold, He wouldn't bother to do it."

Buckie shook his head. "I ain't ask for no pot of gold, and I did pray, too, but God didn't answer my other prayers."

"It's not too late for him to answer unless it's not His will. Sometimes what we think is best for us is not really what God knows is best. You tell me what you wished for, then both of us can be praying for them. God wants us to acknowledge him by praying and asking often."

Buckie looked at Caleb a few seconds then said, "Okay. I been praying for a long time that I could see my mother before..." Buckie looked away and hugged the teddy bear.

There was silence for a long time as Caleb pondered Buckie's words and how he should respond. Finally, he said, " Why did you say *before* and then not finish your sentence?" Buckie didn't answer. "I'm your friend and brother, Buckie. You can tell me anything and be sure that what you say to me will be between you and me only. I don't gossip or tell secrets."

Buckie looked into Caleb's eyes for a few seconds, studying them. His eyes began to fill with tears, and he said, "I know I won't be going home no more, Caleb. Doc and Poppa thought I was asleep one night. They were standing outside that door whispering. I heard Doc tell Poppa that he had done all that was humanly possible and...but I knew it anyway."

"I'm going to pray for you. I'm going to pray hard, and I'm going to pray often. Doc is one of the best doctors in the world, but he's not God. Only God is in control of our living and dying. The Bible says there is a time for everything. He sets the time of our birth and death. Miracles still happen if it's God's will."

"Brother Rufus Branch, he's our preacher back home, said that everyone needs to be baptized so they can go to heaven. I was gonna get baptized, but I got sick and had to come back to the hospital. Do you think God will let me into heaven if I ain't never been baptized?"

"I'm not a preacher, but I know the Bible pretty well. My mother taught me to read it before I went to school. We read it every night. If that's what's worrying you, you can stop worrying. Do you know the story of Jesus when they nailed him to the cross?" Buckie nodded. "Then you know there were two wicked men who were crucified beside him. They both mocked Jesus at first, and one of the men said, 'If you are the Son of God, come down off the cross and get us down.' But the other man saw the way that Jesus acted on the cross and how he asked God to forgive those who were crucifying him. That man realized that only the Son of God could love and forgive like that, and he believed in Jesus. He asked Jesus to remember him to his Father in heaven. That means he had faith that Jesus was the Son of God. Do you know what Jesus said to the man?"

"No," Buckie said in a whisper.

"Jesus looked at him with compassion and love, and said, 'Today you will be with me in paradise.' This was a wicked man in this life, but the Lord saved him at the very end of his life. He wasn't baptized. Now, don't you think that if Jesus could love and save a wicked man like him because he had faith and had never been baptized that he wouldn't do the same for a wonderful boy like you?"

"I reckon he would," Buckie said, smiling. Caleb hugged and kissed Buckie.

"I really wanted to see my momma before I go to be with Jesus," Buckie said. "I know why she left Poppa and me. Mrs. Mattie said I was a sickly baby, and I cried all the time. She's our neighbor that helped Poppa raise me. She said she didn't think I'd live to see my first birthday. She loves me like Mrs. Gladys and Miss Angelle. I know it was my fault that Momma left Poppa and me."

"That's not true. Did you ever tell your poppa what you just told me?"

"Heck, no. Poppa don't even like to talk about her. All he ever said was that your momma left, and we're gonna be just fine."

" I don't feel right talking to you about all this. Mr. Luther might not like it."

"But you said we are brothers, and we could tell each other anything. You didn't really mean that?"

"Sure, I meant it. I just don't know if your poppa would want me to talk about something that's so personal."

"What's *personal* mean?"

"It means private, which means something that you might not want everyone to know." Buckie looked so disappointed that Caleb said, "We'll talk about anything that you want to."

"Why did you say it wasn't my fault that Momma left?"

Caleb looked away for a second, then turned back and began. "Your poppa told me why your mother left." Buckie's eyes opened wide. "He said your momma was like a wild rose, and she couldn't be cooped up in a small house with the responsibilities of a mother and wife. He said she was only sixteen and too young to marry. He said he should have never married her because he knew that she would leave one day. I believe that the right marriages are made in heaven. Sometimes people go out on their own and do foolish things such as marrying someone before they know if they can live together forever. After a while, they have problems because they don't have a real commitment to each other. Then the marriage ends in divorce. Your poppa said it was his mistake for marrying your mother. Your mother's leaving was not your fault. It was a mistake that both your parents made. You've been suffering for their mistake for a long time, and that's wrong."

"But they're still married," Buckie said. "Momma didn't get no divorce. She might still love Poppa. She might be ashamed to come back. I keep hopin' and prayin' that one day she'll walk through that door. Or maybe she'll go home and Mrs. Mattie'll tell her where I am."

Caleb leaned back in the chair and looked up at the ceiling. He prayed silently. *God, give me the right words to say to this blessed child.* He stroked Buckie's thinning hair and said, "Miracles still happen, if it's God will. Never quit praying or hoping. God works in mysterious ways and in his own time." Caleb took a deep breath and thought, *Lord, why did I say that? Why did I give that precious child false hope? But maybe false hope is better than no hope at all.*

CHAPTER EIGHT

Angelle walked into the room, sporting a gorgeous smile and carrying a cup of vanilla ice cream. "Are you ready for your treat, Prince Charming?"

"That's what she calls me," Buckie said to Caleb, grinning. Caleb eased back from the bed to let Angelle feed Buckie. He managed a few bites, then said, "It's making my head hurt."

"I'm leaving now, sweetheart," Angelle said, "but I'll be back tomorrow and visit with you." She leaned over and kissed Buckie's cheek, glanced at her watch, and looked at Caleb.

Caleb got the message. "I have to go, too, Buckie. I won't be able to see you tomorrow or Thursday. We're leaving for New Orleans right after lunch tomorrow, but I'll come back on Friday. That's a promise."

"Will you make a touchdown for me…please?" Buckie pleaded.

"If I make a touchdown, I promise that I'll be thinking about you when I cross the goal line. But I may never make another one."

"You know that ain't true. I know you'll be so excited when you score, you won't be thinking about me."

"How 'bout this, if I score I'll toss the ball into the stands and pretend I'm throwing it to you."

Buckie laughed. "You ain't going to do that after every touchdown, are you?" His eyes brightened.

"I wouldn't lie to you, Buckie." He bent over and kissed Buckie, then he and Angelle eased out.

Angelle punched her time card and followed Caleb down the stairs. Once outside, Caleb hopped into his old truck, and cranked it. Angelle walked down the sidewalk by the truck, paused, and began to laugh.

Caleb had never heard her laugh before. It was a beautiful laugh, mellow and soft like her voice. She smiled, and it was so beautiful it took his breath away.

"Are you laughing at me, or my old truck?" he asked.

She continued to smile, saying, "You do realize that everyone on campus laughs at your truck, don't you?"

"I've heard those rumors," Caleb said, "but it got me here, and it gets me to work. I'm not trying to impress anyone, so I suppose I can live with the humiliation."

"It's really quite a cute, little truck," Angelle said. "You're not really going to throw the ball into the stands, are you?"

"A promise made is a debt unpaid, Uncle Houston always says."

"But you know that's a fifteen yard penalty, don't you?" Angelle remarked.

"No! I didn't know that!" Caleb said, somewhat surprised. "How would you know that? I didn't know you went to football games."

"They used to take us to a few college games when I…I mean I used to go to a few college games when I was in high school. I saw someone do it before and get the penalty."

"Where did you go to school, and what college games did you see?"

"I have to go now," she said and began to walk briskly away.

"I don't suppose you would care to ride to the dorm in my cute little truck? The seat is actually very clean." Angelle paused, looked at him a second, smiled, then shook her head and started walking again.

"I didn't think so," Caleb said, pulling into the road, driving slowly beside her. "You don't mind if I ride along by you just to make sure you get to the dorm safely, do you?"

"It's a free country and a safe campus," Angelle said. They eased along for a while in silence. Then Angelle commented, "It's a kind thing you're doing for Buckie."

No words were spoken for a few hundred yards. Caleb was frantic to break the silence so he asked, "What did you do last weekend?"

"The usual," she said with a shrug.

A few seconds passed. "What's the usual?" Caleb asked.

"You know, girl things."

"No, I don't know what girl things are. Tell me."

"Why?"

"Because I'm interested."

"Why are you interested in girl things?"

"I'm not interested in girl things. I'm interested in how you spent the weekend."

"Why?"

Caleb became frustrated at her obvious attempt to evade the question. He explained, "Because I'm writing a book about how college girls spend their weekends." Angelle began to smile and then laughed at Caleb's ridiculous answer.

"You have a beautiful smile and a pleasant laugh. You should do it more often," he said. "I'd like to ask you something personal."

"Whether I answer or not depends on how personal it is."

"I'd like to know something about the young man who slipped that beautiful ring on your finger. I want to know what kind of man would be so blessed to be loved by you."

Angelle stopped walking, stepped over to the truck window, looked into Caleb's eyes, and whispered, "He's a lot like you."

Her response shocked Caleb, and he said, "What does that mean, *like me?*"

"The person that I love is very, very kind and handsome, but that's not why I love him. I love him because he has a pure heart and is very compassionate. He's soft spoken and…I could go on all night about his good qualities, but I have to get to the dorm and study."

Caleb managed a sick smile. "He sounds like a saint. It's no wonder I didn't have a chance with you. I'd like to meet him someday."

"That's not likely. He's in the service for three more years. He may not get home at all before he's discharged."

"His name is Maurice?" Caleb asked.

"Yes, Maurice Laurent…how did you know that?"

"I must have heard it somewhere. I'll see you in class next week." And he drove away.

Sweet mercy, he thought, *I never had a chance with her. There's no fool like a dumb, lovesick fool. Why did I ask her that? I didn't want to know. I feel like a thief.* He gritted his teeth and stomped the floorboard so hard that a few pieces of rust fell from the firewall. He shook his head and gave a disgusted laugh. *What else can I screw up tonight?* Suddenly, he remembered his promise to Buckie. *Sweet mercy! I wish she hadn't told me about the penalty for throwing a ball into the stands. Now I can't plead ignorance if it happens…I'm going to take Abe's advice. I'm not going to worry about that because I may never make another touchdown. If I do, I'll cross that bridge when I get to it. I have too much to worry about so I'm wiping that out of my mind.* As he drove on, he began to pray for Buckie's life, however, after what Doc said, deep in his heart he felt that his prayer was contrary to God's will.

Caleb parked the truck and jogged up the stairs to his room. Will had the radio on with a broom in his hands as he danced around singing a Faron Young song, Live Fast, Love Hard, Die Young, and Leave a Beautiful Memory. He stopped in mid-song to say, "Hello, Corn Shuck. How was your day?"

"Don't ask," Caleb mumbled.

"Mine was good, too," Will said. "Actually, mine was terrific. I mastered the keys to their offense. Now I love the position. We're going to kick some ass Saturday. Who knows, we may win the rest of our games. How about you guys? Are you going to win?"

"I don't know, Will. I'm going to do my best. That's all I can promise."

Will grabbed Caleb by the shoulders and began to shake him. He shouted, "Did you hear what Coach Shook said today? Didn't you get thrown up in the air? Teamwork! That's the key to victory."

"Stop, Will, you're 'bout to break my neck!"

"Corn Shuck, what's the matter with you? Where's your piss and vinegar? You almost got maimed trying to make the team. Now, you're a hero. What the heck's wrong with you?"

"I'm going to play hard, Will, and I'm going to play as a team member. But...but, I've realized there are more important things in life than winning football games."

"Well, shed a little light on me, sunshine," Will retorted. "Because I can't think of what that might be with a thirty-five game losing streak."

"It's about living and dying, Will. It's about a ten-year-old boy who suffers with every breath. He won't ever play football or see a football game, or even sleep in his own bed again. He's accepted his condition and never complains. It sickens me to see the condition he's in. How can he smile through his pain over a gift of a football that he'll never be able to throw or kick?" Caleb was in near tears as he plopped onto his bed.

Will sat down to think. After a brief time, he responded, "That's why I didn't go to see the kid, and you shouldn't have either. You have to separate yourself from that situation. I'm sorry the boy is dying, but it's not your problem. You've got yourself involved in something that's not good for you. You've worked hard and paid the price for glory. Your responsibility is to the team and not that kid." Will doubled up his fists and shook them as he barked, "You can't perform at your best with all that hanging over you. Now, as a friend, I'm telling you to back off."

Caleb walked to the window, gazed out for a while, and then walked back to the bed. "I can't back off, Will. I can't help what I am and the way I feel. I'm going to play my heart out Thursday, but I'm going to do it with a heavy heart because of a boy that stole my heart tonight."

Will looked at Caleb, feeling his pain, and said, "I suppose you have to be who you are…even though you're weird, but you're the best friend I ever had. Let's drop it. Remember this, I expect no less than five touchdowns out of you tomorrow."

Caleb managed a smile. "I was thinking more on the line of… six."

"Now, you're talking, pal!" Will shouted, slapping Caleb on the back. They went to bed. Caleb fought his pillow half the night, managing a few hours of hard sleep. He ate a big breakfast at Will's insistence and attended his Wednesday morning classes. After another hearty lunch, the team went to the dressing room and packed for the long bus ride to New Orleans. Outside, most of the student body had gathered to give the team a rousing send-off. The team boarded the bus, waved to the well wishers, and headed south down US 51 for New Orleans.

Cliff sat with Caleb. They talked about the game and how great it was to be going to the famous historic old city of New Orleans. Caleb fought the negative thoughts that had consumed him the last few days. He tried to get into the same spirit that had pervaded the team all week. As they passed the sawmill north of Grenada, he remembered the two young Negro boys. He looked out the window, hoping to see one of them working on the grounds. A few minutes later, they passed the café where Sula worked. Caleb laughed aloud and shook his head.

Cliff said, "What's so funny, Caleb?" He shook his head but didn't answer.

After another couple of hours, they passed the Durant exit. Caleb grabbed Cliff's arm and said excitedly, "If we turned here, I could be home in less than an hour. I know Uncle Houston's sweatin' buck-shots in the field pulling corn or picking cotton today." Cliff said something to him, but Caleb was oblivious of his comment. His mind had returned to another time and place where his world had seemed small and innocent, a place where warmth, kindness, and love surrounded him. "I should have never left," he murmured.

"Beg your pardon?" Cliff said.

"I was just reminiscing," Caleb said. As they went through Jackson, Caleb's thoughts turned to the free-spirited, bright eyed, outspoken Jennifer. He remembered some of the beautiful moments they had shared together and of her hopes and dreams of walking again. Caleb said a little prayer for her and Buckie. A few hours later, the swamps began appearing alongside the highway. He noticed an occasional pickup parked on the side of the road. Men were throwing wire traps into the sloughs alongside the road. Others were pulling them out and dumping their catch into buckets. "What are they doing?" Caleb asked Cliff.

"I think they're catching crawfish," Cliff said.

"They do make darn good catfish bait," Caleb commented.

"No," Cliff said, laughing, "they eat them."

"How in tarnation do you eat a hard-shelled crawfish?" Caleb asked.

"They don't eat the shell, silly. They peel the shell off the tail and eat the meat inside it." Cliff snickered as he added, "I've heard it said that they eat the tail and suck the head."

"You'd have to eat a hundred to get enough meat to fill up a cup," Caleb said.

"That's right. They claim they're very tasty crustaceans."

"It's for sure I'll never find out, but I guess that's better than eating snails. I've heard the French eat those slimy little suckers. Just the thought nauseates me."

"They say these Cajuns will eat anything that crawls, walks, or flies. I've heard they eat giant rats that live in the swamps and bayous. Those suckers have tails about two feet long."

"No way!" Caleb said. "That's foolishness."

"Yeah. They call them nutria rats. They eat alligators, too."

They rode a while longer, and soon they passed the airport. After that, one business after another lined both sides of the road.

Caleb was fascinated with all the new sights. Eventually, the bus turned down Canal Street. Towering skyscrapers lined the streets. The sight was so awe-inspiring that it took Caleb's breath. Most of the team members had never seen such a sight. They let the windows down, stuck their heads out, and marveled at the sights.

Coach Parrish turned and yelled, "Get your heads back in the bus. We don't want to look like country-come-to-town!"

"Is that a trolley car up there?" Caleb asked.

"That's what it is," Cliff said.

"Wait until I tell Uncle Houston what I've seen. I don't know how to describe all this."

The bus turned off Canal Street and stopped in front of the Roosevelt Hotel. It was nearly dusk. Coach Parrish said, "Get your overnight bags. We'll go in and check into our rooms. Take a few minutes to get settled in. We have dinner reservations in the Blue Room at the restaurant here, so meet me in the lobby at seven sharp. I'm sure that I don't need to remind you that you're representing Marston College, and I won't tolerate any foolishness. If you get in trouble, I'll put you on the next bus home, or you'll spend the night in jail." The team nodded and piled out of the bus.

Inside the hotel, the décor was elegant and quite breathtaking. Caleb feasted on the grandeur of his surroundings. They were given their room assignments so they went to their rooms to rest a few minutes before dinner. Caleb felt a case of nerves creeping in. He could hardly sit still. He said to Cliff, who was rooming with him, "Let's go down to the lobby. It's a quarter to seven. I'm so nervous my skin is stinging."

Cliff laughed. "If I had your talent, nothing would make me nervous." They slipped on their Marston blazers, straightened their ties, and rode the elevator down to the lobby. Caleb paced back and forth a few minutes, and then said he needed to go back upstairs to the bathroom.

"No need," Cliff said, "I'm sure there's a restroom in the lobby." They walked down the elaborate corridor until they saw a sign on the door. "Here it is," Cliff said. "I'll wait outside." Caleb rushed in, hurried toward the line of urinals on the wall, and started to unzip his pants. He was totally shocked to see three tall, well-dressed, supposedly ladies in high heels, beautiful dresses, and heavy makeup standing in front of the urinals with their dresses pulled up. He gasped, threw his hands up, and started apologizing as he began his retreat.

One of the supposed ladies said, "Come on in, kid, we're for real." Their faces and figures looked like beautiful ladies; however, their voices were definitely male. Caleb's jaw dropped, and he froze in his tracks. They laughed at him as they took care of business and walked out smiling at him. One winked. After they left, he stood at the urinal a few seconds before he could relieve himself. "I ain't telling Cliff about this," he murmured. "I ain't telling nobody. Uncle Houston would never believe me anyway."

Caleb walked out of the restroom still white-faced and breathing hard. Cliff was leaning against the wall laughing so hard there were tears in his eyes. "Welcome to New Orleans," Cliff said. "You might see anything here. That's why they call it the Big Easy, or as the Baptist call it, Sin City. I wish we could slip down to Bourbon Street tonight, but I know Coach Parrish would send us home if we did."

"I think I lost my appetite," Caleb said as they walked into the elegant Blue Room Restaurant and Ballroom. A man in a tuxedo sat at the piano on the stage, while a very attractive lady in a gorgeous evening gown sang. The maitre de seated them at one of the tables reserved for the team. After one of the best meals Caleb had ever experienced, Coach Parrish gathered up the team, and they walked a few blocks from the hotel to the Saenger Theater. "Picnic" was playing. Caleb smiled as he walked in, thinking, *I'll get to watch it this time.* His nerves calmed somewhat, and he enjoyed the wonderful movie.

Caleb spent a restless night of sleep. The team had a hardy breakfast next morning. They walked the streets of New Orleans for a while. After a brief pre-game meal, they returned to their rooms to rest before heading for the Tulane stadium. When they arrived at the stadium, the nerves returned. Caleb stuttered during casual conservation with his teammates. He was more nervous than he had been when Coach Stan yelled, "Get your ass into the game." All thoughts were negative as they walked out on to the plush, beautiful grass of the Sugar Bowl stadium. He looked up at the massive structure and thought, *This place must hold a million people. I'm going to make a fool out of myself. I'm going to disappoint Buckie. I'm going to forget the plays and run the wrong way. What have I got myself into? I could have picked a hundred pounds of cotton or a wagonload of corn today if I was still on the farm.*

Coach Parrish put his arm around Caleb and said, "Nervous, huh?"

"That's not the right word for it," Caleb said. "I'm so...I'm so scared that I feel like I might faint."

Coach Parrish said, "What if I told you that it's perfectly natural? Everyone who's worth his salt feels that way before a big game. I used to throw up several times before big games. Now, here's what's going to happen. Pay attention to me because I've been there. You've never started a game, so it's a new experience for you. Everyone is nervous, but when the ball is kicked off and the action starts, your training and instincts take over. After someone has knocked the crap out of you, the nerves are gone. All that matters is the game. You'll get caught up in the moment. Hopefully, you'll be half as good as everyone thinks you're going to be. Now, take some deep breaths, and think about something pleasant."

Caleb nodded and continued to walk around the field until the Tulane players joined them on the field. His blood pressure shot up as he looked at their size and stature. He went back to the dressing room and sat until Coach Parrish yelled, "It's time to saddle up, men." He felt faint at that moment, but he took a few deep breaths and got dressed.

Doc had left Marston earlier that day and had driven to Jackson. He pulled into Judge Knight's driveway. He was greeted at the door by Judge Knight, Lillian, Jennifer, and a handsome, distinguished-looking gentleman. "Doc," Judge Knight said, "I'd like you to meet my banker, Mr. Travis Hodges. He's an Ole Miss graduate…however, we'll forgive him." The judge laughed. "He listens to the Marston games and was fascinated, to say the least, over young Caleb Morgan's performance and everything that's been written about him. He called me early this morning and asked if I'd like to ride down to New Orleans and watch the game. I knew Edith wasn't coming, so I took the liberty of inviting him to ride with us."

Doc extended his hand, saying, "It would be my pleasure to have you accompany us."

Mr. Hodges replied, "You wouldn't believe the number of my friends that said they were going to the game. I don't think there's been this much excitement about Marston football since Coach Shook recruited Will James. Now, there's possibly more."

Lillian kissed Doc. "Y'all be careful driving."

The judge informed her that they should be back by two a.m., and he kissed her.

Lillian shook her finger in Jennifer's face and chided, "Don't make a fool out of yourself and embarrass your father like you did at the last game, sweetheart."

"Mother, please!" Jennifer snapped, then wheeled the chair around and steered it near the car.

As they pulled away from the house, Mr. Hodges said, "Doctor Marston, I'm curious about the Morgan boy. Wally Stewart said that he was from Choctaw County. I was president of the bank at Ackerman before I accepted the position in Jackson. At that time, I knew most everyone in Choctaw County. I might know the boy's parents. Actually, there are more Morgan's in that neck of the woods than boll weevils." They all laughed at his humor.

He continued, "You wouldn't happen to know his parents' names, would you?"

The wheels began to spin in Doc's head as he realized that he was talking to Caleb's grandfather. Doc was slow to respond, but quick to contrive a scheme. It could backfire; however, he felt that it was worth the gamble. "Oh, oh," Doc stammered, not at all comfortable telling a lie. "I, I…I should remember their names but…you know, in my profession I meet many new people every day. This gray matter in my head isn't quite what it used to be. It'll probably come to me later." He continued, "Mr. Hodges, you're not going to believe that a boy who never played football could have so much natural ability. You know he works for me at the club. All the publicity and accolades haven't gone to his head. He's humble and kind. One can tell he was brought up by caring and loving Christian parents because he exhibits their values. Anyone would be proud to say that he was their son. I know I would."

"That's why I'm going to marry him," Jennifer added.

"I'd like to invite you and your wife to come up to the game next Thursday evening. You can have dinner with Horace and Lillian and my wife, Edith, at the club. Afterwards, we can go to the game. I have four bedrooms in my home. Everyone can spend the night or the weekend, if you like. We might even work a game of golf into the visit if you have time."

The judge looked curiously at Doc, knowing Doc had never forgotten a name in his life. He certainly wouldn't forget the names of the parents of someone that was so dear to his heart. Doc returned his stare with a grim, subtle headshake.

"That's very hospitable of you, Doctor Marston. I've always wanted to drive up and look at your beautiful college and country club. I've been told it's one of the most beautiful in the south. I'll check my calendar. If it's possible, I'll call and let you know."

The judge knew Doc better than anyone except Edith. He realized that Doc had devious plans, so he quickly changed the subject. "I just love to visit historic old New Orleans and observe the vast diversity of cultures within such a short distance."

"Mother said you loved to visit New Orleans because of the strip joints in the French Quarter," Jennifer retorted.

Judge Knight shook his finger at her and said, "I've warned you about such talk. Your mother never said such a thing because she didn't know."

"I think you're right, Father…it was grandmother who said that." Everyone had a good laugh at the judge's expense.

"The truth doesn't make a good joke, does it Horace," Doc said, laughing.

A few minutes before game time, Luther rushed into Buckie's room. Angelle was sitting next to the bed, desperately trying to get Buckie to eat a few bites of his dinner. Luther strode to his bedside and kissed Buckie and gave him a gentle hug.

Buckie's eyes brightened, and he said, "I didn't know you were coming until tomorrow, Pop."

"I couldn't wait no longer to see you, son. I knowed you'd be a listening to that game. I wanted to be wit' you, and I gest made it here in time."

Angelle put an arm around Luther's shoulder and hugged him saying, "This is going to be a good weekend with you here."

"Pop, I got something to tell you that you ain't gonna believe. But Miss Angelle's gonna back me up." He held up the football.

Luther took it in his hands and said, "It's pert near the nicest fooball I ever seen."

"Look at all them names, Pop. I think every one of the football players at Marston has signed it. I got to shake hands with them, too, even the coaches. Look at these two," and he pointed at Caleb's and Will's names. "That's Caleb Morgan's and Will James's names. Me and Caleb Morgan are brothers now. Tell him I ain't lying, Miss Angelle." Buckie became so excited he began to tremble and gasp for breath.

"Just relax, Buckie," Angelle said, grabbing the oxygen mask and putting it to his face. "It's the truth, Mr. Luther. They all visited him. Caleb and Buckie are—" she grinned, wrinkled her face and said, "spit brothers."

"I hear'd 'bout spit brothers," Luther said. "It's gest like them Indians who are blood brothers."

Buckie pulled the mask from his face and said, "Caleb's going to make a touchdown for me tonight, Pop. He promised to throw the ball up in the stands when he scores to prove to me that he made it for me."

"No, Buckie, he can't do that! They might kick him out of the game if'n he done that. I 'spect them balls costs twenty dollar or more."

"I just know he's going to do it, Pop, 'cause he promised. He wouldn't ever break no promise to me. It's almost time for the game," Buckie said. "Will you turn on the radio, Miss Angelle?"

Angelle put the radio on the bedside stand. "Do you mind if I listen a few minutes? It's time for my break anyway."

"I reckon you like him, too, huh, Miss Angelle?" Buckie said, forcing a smile through his pain and nausea.

"I do like him, Buckie. I think he's about the kindest and most humble boy I've ever known," she answered, smiling and nodding.

"I know'd he were like that," Luther said, "and I can't wait to see him again." They turned on the radio, and Wally Stewart was wound up tighter than a top, raving about the feats of Caleb's last game.

CHAPTER NINE

About six o'clock on Thursday evening in Choctaw County, Houston set a chair next to the swing. He pulled an extension cord out to the porch. Then he went back inside to get the radio and plugged it into the extension cord.

Mary walked out the door. "What are you doing, Houston?"

"A few friends asked if they could come over to listen to the game," Houston said, sheepishly. "We ain't goin' to be in the house. No need to get huffed up."

"I don't believe you did that without informing me," Mary scolded. "I haven't prepared anything for them. Besides, look at me. I've been working all day in the field with you, and I look like a common field hand. I look awful. Look at me, Houston!" she demanded.

Houston cut his eyes up at her, looked her up and down slowly and carefully, and then commented, "I reckon I'm looking at the most beautiful and desirable woman in the world." He reached up, quickly grabbing her around her waist and pulled her onto his lap and planted a Saturday night special kiss on her lips.

When the prolonged kiss ended, she sat up slapping and kicking, while she fought the urge to laugh and savor the beautiful compliment. Managing to get off his lap and to her feet, she said,

"I knew you'd say something foolish like that. Don't expect me to join you looking like this."

"Mary," Houston said, "we ain't holdin' no beauty contest out here tonight." She jerked around and went inside, snatched off her dress to take a quick bath. Then she went to the closet, frantic to find something more appropriate. After she'd dressed, brushed her hair, and put on a little make-up, she went to the kitchen to make a cake for their friends.

The sun began to set around 6:30 p.m., and the trucks and cars began to roll in. By six-forty-five p.m., the yard was so full of vehicles that some had to park by the road. Mary heard all the commotion outside and went to the window to see what was happening. It looked like a Fourth of July celebration in progress outside. Half the county had come to listen to the game with Houston.

Mary mumbled, "Is everyone in this county insane? What's so wonderful about football?" She picked up the cake batter and went out the back door and gave it to old Homer, Houston's bird dog, who was lying by the back steps.

Outside, Houston was yelling, "The game's about to start, fellows. We have to quiet down so everyone can hear." Instead, the noise seemed to increase. He spotted a few quart fruit jars obviously filled with white lightning being passed around. He shook his head in resignation, sat back in his rocker, and turned up the volume as loud as it would go.

Inside, Mary eased over to the mantle over the fireplace and turned on the other radio. After several minutes, she found the station that was broadcasting the game and sat down. The team had finished their pre-game warm ups and had returned to the dressing room for final instructions and a restroom break.

Wally said, "It's about that time, folks. In my twenty-five years of announcing Marston's games, I've never witnessed this much excitement and anticipation about any football game, much less a freshman game. The world wants to know, and I'll quote Norris Beckham, Coach Shook's good friend and number one fan, 'Is

Caleb Morgan an aberration or is this kid the real deal?' Now, if some of you good, country folk are like me, and you didn't know what in the Sam Hill aberration means, I'm gonna tell you. I dusted off my ol' Webster's and looked up the word. It means an act or condition that ain't normal. Hell! I knew that. Oops! I can't say that word on the radio, so 'skuse my French, folks. I get carried away sometimes. What I was about to say is that a one-eyed baboon would know that Caleb Morgan's performance a couple of weeks ago was not a normal occurrence. I reckon it ain't ever been done before. Now, I hate to bust your bubble, but if you think it's going to happen again tonight, you're going to be very disappointed. What I think is that we've found a very special young man with tremendous talent, and he's going to do great things at Marston. But no one can repeat the feats of the last game.

Now, I need to clear up one other little matter that my boss down at the station suggested that I do. Actually he ordered me to do it. It seems that he's been gettin' lots of mail and calls from some sweet ol' English teachers around this here state, as well as some real smart EdD's and PhD's…" Wally put his hand over the microphone and whispered as if he were telling a secret, "and some SOB's. Clifton Haynes, Wally's sidekick and color man, cracked up at Wally's comment. He had to rush out of the room until he could quit laughing. "They seem to think my use of the King's English ain't appropriate over the airways. Okay, boss, I apologize if I've offended anyone, but this here's the way I talk, folks. If the truth be known, ninety-eight percent of the folk listening to these games talk just like me. I'll try to do better folks, but it ain't gonna be easy," he said, grinning at Clifton.

"I don't know how many fans are in this here stadium 'cause it's so dang huge. But, I'd swear there must be fifteen thousand head or more out there. I believe most of them are our fans. We'll know soon enough 'cause I see those beautiful blue and orange uniforms coming out of the tunnel." A big roar went up from the stands. Wally said, "That noise you just heard confirms my guess. We actually have more fans in the stands than Tulane has.

There'll be some bloodshot eyes at work tomorrow if this crowd plans to drive back home tonight. And if they stay here tonight, I know there'll be some blood shot eyes tomorrow. I think I'm in enough trouble already, so I'm going to turn the mike over to Clifton Haynes, my good buddy, for his comments and to give the starting lineups."

Caleb jogged across the field to the sidelines and looked up to the stands and saw thousands of faithful Marston fans standing and cheering. His heart leaped into his throat. Then came the unmistakable voice screaming out his name. He turned, spotting Jennifer screaming and waving at him, while the judge tried to calm her. Caleb smiled and gave a quick wave.

"Was that the Morgan kid that just waved at Jennifer?" Mr. Hodges asked.

"That's our boy," Doc said proudly, smiling at the judge.

"I'm going to marry him someday when I can walk," Jennifer said confidently.

The judge commented, "She has a crush on him. She'll get over it."

"You don't get over true love, Father," Jennifer said.

"There is no such thing as true love at sixteen," the judge said. "This discussion is over."

The captains went to the center of the field, the coin was tossed, and Marston won and elected to receive. The band played the National Anthem. The teams huddled around their coaches for final instructions.

Coach Parrish asked, "What are the two things that Coach Shook stressed this week?" The team shouted, "Teamwork and one-hundred percent for sixty minutes!" They put their hands together, and then thrust them upward, yelling, "Go Cats!"

The receiving team jogged to their positions. Caleb set up on the five-yard line, flanked by Cliff and Russell Cox. Every nerve in his body was on fire, and he couldn't stand still. He felt numb, except for those burning nerves. He tried to relax, but it was impossible. The whistle blew, and the ball was propelled high and deep. It was coming down directly at Caleb. He didn't have to move an inch. He watched the ball, then glanced down field at the herd of green jerseys closing in on him. He looked up again as the ball fell toward his hands. He heard the thundering cleats and took his eyes off the ball and gave a quick glance at the defenders who were only yards from him. The ball shot through his outstretched arms and bounced on the ground. He scooped up the ball, but three green jerseys were in his face. He sidestepped two defenders and tried to run around the third. The defender was quick, and he put a shoulder into Caleb's ribs and knocked him backward behind the goal line. Somehow Caleb managed to regain his balance and dodged another defender. Most of the defenders were closing in on him, so he tried to run around them. The mob of green jerseys swallowed him up, and he was smothered a yard behind the goal line. The referee threw his hands up, signaling a safety. The Tulane fans went wild. There was silence and disbelief in the Marston stands and all over north Mississippi.

The defender who had put the shoulder in Caleb's ribs reached down and helped Caleb to his feet. He whispered, "You've been reading too many of your press clippings, country boy. Welcome to the big city." Then he laughed.

The team jogged off the field in disbelief and shock over Caleb's mishap. Caleb's head was down, and he was ashamed for disappointing the team. He wanted to climb under the bench and stay there until the game was over and then go home to Choctaw County. He sat on the bench with his head down as the punting team jogged out to kick to the Green Wave from their twenty-yard line.

Jennifer yelled, "That's all right, Caleb, you'll make a touchdown the next time you get the ball!" Caleb wanted to dig a hole under the bench and crawl in it after hearing her voice.

Coach Parrish walked over to Caleb and put his hands on his shoulders. "Did you think you were going to score every time you touched the ball? Get your head up. This game isn't over. The team looks up to you, and they need your leadership."

"I took my eyes off the ball," Caleb said. "I know better, but I made a mistake."

"You'll learn from your mistakes, Caleb. We all make them."

Caleb stood and said, "Yes, sir." He walked to the sidelines and cheered for the defense.

⁓∕ɪ∖⁓

Inside Coach Shook's office, the staff had been working on their strategy and game plan while listening to the game on the radio. They looked at each other, more shocked than the fans and team had been. Billy Ray said, "What did you expect? That's the fourth time the kid ever touched a football in a game."

Stan quipped, "Look on the bright side. Every time the kid touches the ball, somebody scores."

Ollie laughed, Billy Ray snickered, but Coach Shook growled, "I don't see the humor in your remark."

Stan said, "It ain't over, Coach. Lighten up."

⁓∕ɪ∖⁓

Luther said, "What you reckon's wrong wit' Caleb, Buckie?"

"Ain't nothing wrong!" Buckie snapped. "He made me a promise, and I know he's going to keep it. The game ain't over, Pop."

"I can't listen to anymore of this," Angelle said. "It makes me so nervous, I want to jump out of my skin. I'll check on you later, Buckie." And she left the room.

⁓∕ɪ∖⁓

The party died quickly at Houston's house. There were mumbles and whispers. Houston said, "The game ain't over. I know my boy, and the game ain't over."

Wally said, "All you good folk out there in radio land, don't get nervous. I ain't gonna say I told you so even though I told you so, but don't turn your radios off yet, 'cause this game ain't over. We had a temporary setback, but I believe our boys'll fight their way back into this game before the night's over."

Marston punted to the Green Wave. Their offense was too big and quick for the smaller Marston defense. They marched down the field and with only six minutes gone in the first quarter, the Wave was up by nine points.

Caleb met the defense as they jogged off the field. He yelled to them, "That nine points was my mistake. I'm not nervous anymore. I'm ready to play football. Now, get your heads up, and give us some support." Their heads rose, as did their spirits, and the offense sprinted onto the field as if they were leading by nine points. Caleb's nervous jitters were gone. He was focused and eager to prove he was a football player, not what Norris Beckham had written, 'Just a flash- in-the-pan.'

The whistle blew, and the ball was kicked high and deep again. Caleb backed up near the goal line and watched the ball as he cradled it in his arms. He shot up the field behind the wedge until it broke down near the twenty-five. Two green jerseys broke through, and they were taking a bead on him. He planted his foot and shot right through a small gap in the defense, then raced around two other defenders to the sidelines and turned downfield. The race was on. There was one defender left, the kicker, and he had the angle on Caleb. As the white stripes flew by, the defender moved in to make the hit near the visitors' sideline. He lowered his head and made a lunge at Caleb. Caleb hit his 'afterburner' stride and shot away from him as the defender went headfirst into the bench. The crowd roared. Caleb began to swell with pride as he crossed the goal line and ran under the goal posts. He held the ball up to throw it to the official when he remembered his promise to Buckie.

The teams jogged down for the extra point try. Caleb was still standing under the goal post. The referee gestured for Caleb to throw him the ball. Caleb froze for a second until Cliff yelled, "Give him the ball, Caleb. Snap out of it. What's the matter with you?" Caleb was torn inside. He couldn't decide what to do. He thought, *I'm about to get kicked out of the game, and if we lose, it will be my fault. But what about my promise to Buckie? What should I do? I can't break my promise to a dying boy.* The referee walked up to Caleb and said, "Give me the ball, number twenty-two."

Caleb looked at the referee and said, "I'm sorry, Mr. Ref, I can't do that," and he turned and threw the ball halfway up the bleachers of the massive Sugar Bowl Stadium. A dozen Tulane students were sitting in the end zone bleachers, and they all scrambled for the ball. One grabbed it and streaked for the nearest exit. Five red flags shot up in the air and floated to the ground.

Some of the spectators clapped while others booed. The referee warned Caleb after he stepped off the fifteen yards and said, "If that happens again, you're out of the game, number twenty-two."

"What the hell did he do that for?" Coach Shook yelled. "Please Lord, don't tell me we've got an all-American hot dog on our hands. I don't think I can take three more years of Will's antics, and now…now a hot dog on our hands."

"He's not a hot dog, Coach," Billy Ray said.

"How do you know that?" Coach Shook barked.

"That was a sign or signal to someone. Did you notice how long it took him to make up his mind to do it? A hot dog would have run into the end zones and just thrown it as far as he could. I'll bet it was a sign to the boy in the hospital that he was making a touchdown for him."

Stan said, "I think you're giving him too much credit. He probably didn't know any better and just got caught up in the hype and excitement."

"I think you're wrong, Stan. I'll bet he does it again and gets kicked out of the game."

"You're on," Stan said. "I'd like to get my carton of cigars back." They shook on it.

As Marston huddled for the extra point, Cliff asked, "Why did you do that, Caleb? Didn't you know it's against the rules?"

John David said, "Hush, Cliff, he must have had a good reason. Now, let's make this extra point." The kick was good, and Marston was down by two points.

Coach Parrish met Caleb at the sidelines and asked, "What was that all about? That's not teamwork. That's calling attention to yourself. I don't care how good you are, if you do it again, you'll ride the pine for the rest of the game."

Caleb nodded and said, "Yes, Coach."

Marston kicked off, and the defense stiffened. However, Tulane managed to march down to the Marston twenty-yard line where they kicked a field goal. They were up by five points. The wave lined up to kick. The kicker had received instructions to kick the ball away from Caleb. Cliff took the kick-off and managed to advance the ball to the twenty-yard-line. The wave changed their defense and went into a six-three. The linebackers were instructed to shadow Caleb and not to let him get to the corners. John David mixed up the plays, and Caleb carried the ball on every other down. He ripped off big chunks of yardage every time he touched the ball, so Marston drove quickly down to the wave forty-yard line. Caleb was in a quandary over what to do if he broke into the open and made another touchdown. John David called a quick trap up the middle, and Caleb hit the hole like lightning. He was past the safety before he could react. Caleb was flying down the field with the closest defender ten yards behind him. Caleb felt like a tornado was twisting in his head as he pondered his options. As he neared the goal, he deliberately looked back and allowed his feet to get tangled up. He tumbled to the ground at the one-yard line. The fans were screaming, but Caleb was relieved at his quick decision.

The team rushed down and patted him on the back. Some said, "Tough luck, Caleb, but you'll get it this time." John David huddled the team and called Caleb's number on a dive play.

"No," Caleb protested, "Let Cliff make this one. This is a team sport." John David changed the play, and Cliff dove in for the touchdown.

Back on the porch at Houston's house, Grover Mayfield complained, "That ain't fair, Houston, 'cause Caleb run it down there. He should oughta made the touchdown."

"My boy ain't selfish, Grover," Houston said. "Now, hush and listen to Wally."

"Well, folks, if you ain't a believer by now, you never will be. We just may have the best running back in this here nation," Wally said.

The Coaches had stopped working on the game plan and were huddled around the radio. After the score, they were jumping up and down and slapping each other on their backs like kids at a circus. "Tell it like it is, Wally!" Ollie yelled.

Coach Shook put his hands together, lifted them high, and yelled, "Thank you, Lord! Thank…you…Lord!" And he began to dance a jig.

Wally Stewart said, "Why don't they change that dang rule that won't let the freshmen play on the varsity team? We might win the rest of the games with that kid playing for the varsity."

The Green Wave managed a long drive that took most of the time off the clock before the half. They scored with two minutes left before halftime. They now led nineteen to fourteen. The Wave kicked away from Caleb again. Marston ran a few plays before the half ended, but Caleb wasn't able to break free for the big gain. The half ended with Marston on its own thirty-five yard line.

After a needed break and a spirited halftime talk by Coach Parrish, the team returned for the second half. Caleb's mind was still in a quandary over what to do if he broke loose again. He didn't want to look like a clumsy fool again. It was obvious the

Wave had a terrific offense. It seemed that they were too strong for the Marston defense. Caleb knew he had to score soon for the team to have a chance.

The Wave received the second half kickoff and began a time-consuming march that ended with another seven points. Things were beginning to look bleak for the Marston squad.

Again, the Wave kicked away from Caleb. Marston was once again starting the drive at their twenty-three yard line. Coach Shook's philosophy was like most of the great coaches of the era, three yards and a cloud of dust. The pass play was viewed as a dangerous way to get yards, and it was used as a last resort. Marston had thrown only one pass all night. Coach Parrish didn't intend to throw another one unless the situation was third down and more than five yards for a first. The team started to drive on the Wave. Caleb began to rip off big chunks of yardage, however, Cliff lost five yards on a sweep, and the drive seemed to stall with a third and six at the Tulane forty-five. Coach Parrish decided it was time to try a quick pass to the right end. He called the play. John David took the snap, stood up, and tried to hit his end on a quick look-in pass behind the linebacker and in front of the safeties. Unfortunately, the ball was tipped by one of the tall linemen. It went over the end's head and into the waiting arms of the Wave safety at the thirty-five yard line. He was smothered after gaining five yards. Tulane took over at their forty.

"That were a dumb call," Luther said.

That was a stupid call," Houston said.

"Has he lost his mind?" Coach Shook yelled. "It was only third down. Caleb could have gained five yards in two plays against any team."

"I thought it was a good call," Stan said. "It was just bad luck."

"I agree with Stan," Billy Ray said. "How often does a dumb lineman think to raise his hands up on a pass play?"

"I take offense to that comment," Ollie said. "I teach all our defensive linemen to get their hands up when the quarterback throws the ball."

"And how many have we knocked down the last few years?" Billy Ray retorted.

Ollie shrugged and said, "None."

"I rest my case," Billy Ray said, laughing.

Mary mumbled, "That doesn't seem very intelligent to throw the ball to the other team when our team has been running the ball so well. Oh, well, what do I know? I haven't seen a game since I was in college."

The wave began another one of their methodical drives. They burned most of the third quarter clock and were about to score again when the quarterback mishandled the snap. Marston recovered the fumble at their five-yard line. Down by nine, Marston started a drive with Caleb carrying most of the load. He made quick work of it, and the third quarter ended with Marston down to the Wave twenty-yard line. The teams changed ends. The Marston fans were as exuberant as they had been at the beginning of the game. Caleb could still hear Jennifer's piercing voice over the thousands of other screaming fans as she shouted for her hero. John David called Caleb's number for a power sweep around the right end. He called for the ball and tossed it to Caleb, running right following his blockers. They caved in the defensive left side, and the field opened wide. Caleb shot around the end like a flash. Again, the race was on down the sidelines. It was decision time again. The Wave safety had the angle on Caleb as they neared the end zone. Caleb made his decision as he neared the five-yard line. Caleb could have easily put a move on the safety and cut back to his left and walked into the end zone, however, he braced for the collision and took the full force of the safety's shoulder in his rib cage, allowing the defender to knock him out of bounds at the one. He was slow to get to his knees as if he was hurt. He held his side as most of the team and trainer ran to attend his injury. He faked a few gasps, and the referees called an injury timeout. That meant Caleb had to leave the game for at least one play. After his academy award performance, he stood up and jogged gingerly to the bench holding his side. Both stands gave him a standing ovation. Caleb felt like a hypocrite as he raised his hand to acknowledge their support. The team lined up for the next play. Cliff went into the line, and he was slammed down for a one-yard loss.

"How do you feel?" Coach Parrish asked nervously.

"Better," Caleb said, frowning and holding his side.

The team huddled and John David said, "We are not going to blow this touchdown." He called Cliff's number on a power sweep. The fullback missed his key block on the defensive end and Cliff was horse-collared for a four-yard loss.

"How do you feel now?" Coach Parrish asked again.

"A little better," Caleb said, feeling like a traitor.

The ball was back on the six-yard line now, and John David looked toward the sidelines at Caleb. Caleb dropped his head quickly. John David called a wingback reverse, but the play was a disaster. Marston faced a fourth and eleven.

Caleb jumped up and said, "I feel better now, Coach." Coach Parrish slapped him on the butt, and Caleb sprinted on to the field to the cheers of the Marston fans.

"What play did Coach call?" John David asked nervously.

Caleb didn't answer. He said, "Now listen to me team, we're going to fake a power sweep to the right. Make it look good. Linemen do not go down field. John David, you're going to toss me the ball. Everyone is going to block to the right except you. You're going to make a half-ass attempt to block the left end.

Then you turn on the speed and head down the left sideline to the end zone. I'll get the ball to you. You just make the catch."

"We never practiced that," John David said. "Are you sure?"

"Just make the catch!" Caleb demanded.

They broke the huddle. John David took the ball, tossed it to Caleb, and continued to jog toward the defensive end. He saw the outside linebacker and the safety take the fake and race across the field toward Caleb; however, the left defensive end broke free of the first block and made penetration. Caleb had to run backward to avoid getting hit. The linebacker and safety came up fast, and they had Caleb cornered near the sidelines. He reversed field and started running left. He gathered himself and looked down field. He saw John David standing alone in the end zones with his arms outstretched, the closest green jersey was fifteen yards back up the field, giving chase to Caleb. Caleb planted his feet and threw a perfect spiral into the waiting arms of John David. A roar went up from the Marston faithful that could be heard on Bourbon Street.

"That was brilliant," Coach Shook shouted. "When did you put that play in, Stan?"

"I didn't," Stan said. "We do have that play in our play book, but we never practiced it."

Coach Shook looked at Billy Ray. "I didn't either," he said, shaking his head.

"I suppose Coach Parrish just improvised," Stan said.

"We need to put him on the staff when he graduates," Coach Shook said.

The party was on again at Houston's house. Mary fought back a smile with glassy eyes.

"That's my brother," Buckie said as the tears ran down his cheeks.

Coach Parrish huddled the defense and said, "Give me everything you have, team. Keep them off the board, and we'll win this game and have a wonderful ride home tonight."

The team jogged out for the kickoff. Coach Parrish slapped Caleb on the back, saying, "That was a great pass, Caleb, and a brilliant call, John David. I didn't realize Coach Stan had put that play in. It's not on my play sheet."

Caleb gave John David a hard look and shook his head.

John David eased over by Caleb and whispered, "What if the end had hit you behind the line, or the safety hadn't bit on the fake and intercepted the ball?"

"Then it would have been providence, I suppose," Caleb said nonchalantly.

John David laughed, nodded, and said, "I can't argue with that, you brilliant Corn Shuck."

Marston kicked deep, and the ball carrier was tackled at the twenty-five yard line. The Wave went to work and began to hammer the smaller Marston defense. They were marching down the field again, and there seemed to be no stopping them. Coach Parrish made the decision to substitute six of his best offensive players to stop the drive. Caleb went to the outside linebacker while Cliff and John David went to the two safety positions. The two big offensive tackles went to the defensive line, and the center went to middle guard. The move proved effective, and Marston held the Wave at the Marston thirty-eight yard line. They decided to punt on fourth down and five. They had no intention of kicking to Caleb, so their punter kicked the ball out of bounds at the ten. The clock was moving, and everyone knew it was now or never for Marston. The Wave coach sent in his best eleven players on defense, knowing that a stop meant victory.

With four minutes to play, Marston went to work with Caleb right, Caleb left, Caleb up the middle. It was Caleb against the Wave's best defenders now. He was working as hard as he could and managing to drag the Wave defenders for two and three extra yards after first contact. He became totally exhausted. He ran around the right end for five yards. Half the Wave defense cornered him on the sidelines and crushed him. He tried to get up, but his legs gave out, and he fell to the ground.

Coach Parrish signaled for a timeout, rushed over to Caleb, and said, "Have you had it? Is the tank empty?"

Caleb gasped, "Call another timeout when this one's over, and I'll be ready."

Coach Shook yelled, "Call another timeout and give him a little more rest."

"It's just a freshman game," Stan argued. "Get him out of the game before he gets seriously injured."

"I agree," Billy Ray said. "He's not in shape for all that pounding."

Mary gritted her teeth and shouted, "Get my boy off that field now!" Houston heard her shout and realized she was listening to the game inside. He shook his head and said, "That ain't good."

Angelle had returned to Buckie's room and was listening to the game. She was in near tears as Wally described Caleb's condition. She prayed out loud. "Lord, make him leave the game, please."

Coach Parrish called his last timeout as Caleb's respiration began to ease. "If you don't think you can help the team in your condition, I want you to come out of the game…immediately."

"I've got a few more good runs in me," Caleb said. Coach Parrish helped him to his feet, and he jogged slowly to the huddle.

"We don't have much time," John David said. "Hustle back to the line of scrimmage, and I'll call the plays from there. Ten is the hot number." John David called a crossing play with a fake to Caleb. The defense took the fake, and Cliff ripped off nine yards for a first down. John David called for a power play off right tackle with Caleb running the ball. He gained ten more yards and another first down. The clock went to one minute, and they were only at the Wave forty-yard line. They hustled to the line and ran a quick trap up the middle. Cliff gained two yards. John David called a draw play to Caleb. The defense smothered him for a five-yard loss.

—⁂—

Coach Shook barked, "That was a stupid call. Who are you going to fool with a draw play when you've only thrown two passes all night? He's going to get Caleb killed."

—⁂—

The clock was running inside thirty seconds, and Coach Parrish motioned for a pass play. Marston rushed to the line of scrimmage. John David called for a long desperation pass to the two ends. He took the ball and dropped back. The Wave defense broke through the line and smothered him for a six-yard loss. The clock was ticking inside ten seconds as his two ends ran back toward the Marston line of scrimmage.

Coach Parrish signaled for another long desperation pass. John David motioned for Cliff to split out wide.

—⁂—

"This is it," Billy Ray said. "We have two chances to win the game, slim…and none."

"What would you call, Mister Genius?" Stan asked Billy Ray.

Billy Ray and Coach Shook said simultaneously, "A draw to Caleb."

"You just called Coach Parrish an idiot for running the draw," Stan exclaimed.

"The situation's changed," Coach Shook said. "Everyone knows it's a desperation pass now. We have the element of surprise. Who would you want to have their hands on the ball in a situation like this?"

As the ends neared the line of scrimmage, Caleb whispered to John David, "Run the draw now, and I'll score."

"But Coach called a pass."

"I'll take the blame, or you'll take the credit," Caleb said.

"I can't defy the coach," John David whispered.

John David screamed the signals calling for the desperation pass to the end zones. He reached under the center and received the snap a fraction of a second before the horn sounded to end the game. The stronger Green Wave defense bowled over the smaller Marston line as John David retreated. They were in his face before he could set up to throw the ball. He turned to run backward and saw Caleb setting up to block one of the big linemen. As John David passed Caleb, he slammed the ball into his gut. The defensive linemen flew by Caleb, and the center of the field opened up for him. He shot forward, fueled by pure adrenaline now, as he flew down the field. Five defenders were down field chasing the three receivers. When they realized it was a draw, they all converged on Caleb. He ran like the wind at the first two putting a fake on them and shot around them. The other three were moving in on him like a closing umbrella. He ran at them as he liked to do before he made his cut. The defenders were almost shoulder-to-shoulder as they neared Caleb. Caleb made a quick cut to his right, then to his left. They didn't take either fake, and he realized he was going to be hit. He was quick to select the one he was going to try to run over. The smallest of the three was on his right. He gave a quick juke left to freeze the two on his left, then with all his might, planted his left leg, and shot right into the waiting arms of the smaller defender. It was a violent head-to-head collision that could be heard over the screaming fans on both sides of the stadium. The defender flew backward, burying himself into the plush, green grass. Caleb's forward momentum carried him five yards down the field and over the defender. He stumbled forward with one hand down and the ball still securely locked into his other arm. He pushed himself up, regained his balance, and jogged the last fifteen yards into the end zone. When he reached the goal posts, he continued to the stands, took the ball, and flipped it into the first row of the stands. Then he quickly jumped over the retaining wall, retrieved the ball, and tossed it to the referee. The team rushed down and mobbed him as he entered the field again. The fans went wild; another victory, and their hero was for real.

The referee walked over to Caleb and said, "Son, you're the best-looking freshman ball player I've ever seen. I don't know what all this crap is with the ball into the stands, but it has to end tonight. You're too good to be a grand-stander."

"It won't ever happen again," Caleb assured him.

The two teams shook hands and went to the dressing room to shower and prepare for their long ride back to Marston.

Back at Marston, the coaches were lighting up another round of stogies to celebrate. Billy Ray said, "Forget the cigars, Stan. I'm in a charitable mood tonight."

CHAPTER TEN

Coach Shook and his staff had just finished discussing the freshman game when Coach Shook asked, "Have y'all seen that hunk of junk Caleb rides around in? It's a disgrace. I'd buy him some decent transportation if it wasn't against the rules."

"I wouldn't feel too sorry for the kid," Stan said. "After he graduates, he'll be able to buy all of us a new car if he wants to. It sickens me when I think I tried to run him off."

"We ain't runnin' that dog again," Coach Shook said. "We need to get our minds back on the game at hand. I'd like to hang around here long enough to see Will and Caleb play on the same field together. I might let Coach Parrish stand by us to help with the play calling Saturday. The young man shows a lot of potential. I'm going to offer him a job next year…if I'm still here. If one of you is running the show, you could do a lot worse."

"We ain't running that dog tonight either, Coach," Billy Ray said. "Let's get ready to win a game. I feel good about the changes we've made and what we've accomplished this week."

The other coaches agreed, so they went back to work.

Alvin Chalmer had brought moonshine from his small private still to the porch at Houston's house. He had consumed most of it himself. He staggered over to Houston and offered him the last swig from the fruit jar. "Not tonight, Alvin," Houston said, "I couldn't be higher if I had drunk the whole jar." The rowdy crowd began to break up and head for home.

Houston waved goodbye to the last friend, unplugged the radio, and hesitantly walked inside. Mary had already gone to bed, but she whispered, the tone of her voice held a special nuance. "Are you coming to bed, sweetheart, or staying up all night?"

Houston's eyes twinkled, and a mischievous grin came over his ruddy face. He answered, "Don't go to sleep, sweetheart. I'll be there before the cat can blink its eyes."

―⁂―

"Caleb does love me, don't he, Pop," Buckie said as he lay in his hospital bed, gasping for breath and forcing a smile.

"I reckon he loves you 'bout as much as me, son," Luther responded.

Angelle kissed Buckie goodnight and gave Luther a hug. "I have to go now, but I'll see both of you tomorrow evening. Sleep well, my handsome prince."

―⁂―

The team, dressed in their sharp blue blazers, grabbed their gear and walked out of the stadium dressing room. Hundreds of adoring fans and relatives were outside to greet them. Jennifer and her party were closest to the door as Caleb walked out to the cheers of his fans. Jennifer held out her arms, and Caleb went straight to her. She hugged him tightly and tried to kiss him. Caleb backed away and said, "I didn't know you were coming, princess."

Doc managed to push through the crowd that had gathered around Caleb. He gave Caleb a brief hug and then asked about his physical condition.

"I feel great, now," Caleb responded. The judge and Mr. Hodges also wanted to congratulate Caleb, but they weren't willing or able to fight through the boisterous crowd that had surrounded

Caleb and the other athletes. Many fans wanted to touch Caleb or get his autograph.

Coach Parrish walked outside and yelled, "Load up, team, we've got several hours of hard driving tonight." Caleb had to tear his way through his adoring fans to get to the bus. He sat by a window. He could still see Jennifer waving and yelling his name. He gave her a quick wave and blew her a kiss as the bus pulled away.

The hotel had prepared sandwiches for the trip home. Everyone ate and drank sodas as the bus weaved its way through the beautiful, historic, old city. Soon they reached US 51 and headed north for the long drive to Marston.

Most of the team was exhausted after the extremely physical game. Soon, the celebration ended and everyone was snoring. An occasional pothole roused Caleb for a second, but he quickly drifted back into a restless sleep.

Caleb was startled by the sound of air brakes. He opened his eyes to see the sun rise just over the stately oaks as the bus drove down the street leading to the stadium.

"Wake up, sleeping beauties!" Coach Parrish yelled as the bus turned into the stadium parking lot. Everyone was surprised to see that over a thousand students and fans were standing in front of the dressing room awaiting their arrival. "Grab your bags and take them inside. Class attendance is optional today," Coach Parrish announced. A few boys laughed from the back of the bus as they whispered, "We weren't going anyway."

Caleb was shocked to see Will standing there, his head towering above the crowd. The team staggered out of the bus, grabbed their bags from the cargo hatch, and began milling around with their adoring fans. Caleb scanned the crowd, hoping to see Angelle, although he knew she wouldn't be there.

The students and fans rushed over to Caleb, bombarding him with accolades and questions. Six reporters were standing at the entrance to the dressing room waiting for Caleb and Coach

Parrish. After a few minutes of cheering and backslapping, the team began to ease toward the dressing room. Will walked up behind Caleb and slapped him on the back so hard that his knees almost buckled. He put his arm around Caleb to say, "I was proud of you, Corn Shuck. I truly wish that this year could end today. Then when we wake up tomorrow, it would be August 1956. I don't know how I can wait another year to play with you. Do you realize how great we're going to be together?"

"I wish I was as confident as you, Will. I don't think I played that good last night. They almost killed me…and that was their freshman team."

"Damn it!" Will barked. "When are you going to realize how good you are? Do you think you should score every time you touch the ball? Are you that naive?"

Caleb didn't answer. They walked to the dressing room door. The reporters swarmed around Caleb. One commented, "Morgan, it's easier to get an interview with the Pope than you. Tell us how you learned to play football so quickly. Did it really come that easy to you?"

"Nothing comes easy, sir," Caleb said. "I give all the credit to the coaching staff and to Will who worked with me at night to teach me the plays and drills."

Another writer said, "What's your opinion of Coach Shook? Do you want to play for him for three more years? Do you think it's time for a coaching change in lieu of what happened last week?"

Caleb answered promptly. "I chose Marston because of Coach Shook, and I don't want to play for anyone else. He and the other coaches have worked with me and taught me everything I know. They gave me a chance to play, even though I had no background and experience. I think they are the greatest coaching staff in this country."

One of the other writers commented, "Will, why all this secrecy over the Tulane game? The Green Wave has a great team this year, and they're undefeated. Doesn't Coach Shook realize that Marston doesn't have a chance against their size and speed?"

Will bristled and barked, "Don't bet the farm on it, mister." He grabbed Caleb's arm, and they went into the dressing room together.

The sports writers laughed. One quipped, "If Morgan could play, they might stay within thirty points of Tulane." They closed their note pads and left.

Caleb took his equipment bag inside and dumped the sweaty uniform in the wash basket, hung up his pads to dry, and turned in his blazer. He joined Will for breakfast. After a hardy meal, Caleb went to his English class. His classmates greeted him with praise and accolades.

"I didn't expect you this morning, Caleb," Professor Sutton said. "You must be exhausted after the game you played and the long ride back. Why don't you go to the dorm and get some rest?"

"Thank you, sir, but I can't afford to get behind in my class work. You know I'm not the brightest star in the heavens."

"You actually are quite intelligent, son. Don't sell yourself short." Then turning back to his podium, Professor Sutton began class. "Today's assignment is this. Take a paper and pen out of your book sack and write your autobiography. You must finish and turn it in before the bell rings. You may begin now."

Everyone began to write. Caleb took out his paper and pen and sat there embarrassed and puzzled over the assignment. After a few minutes, he stood and walked slowly to the professor's desk. Somewhat embarrassed, he whispered, "I don't know what an autobiography is."

Professor Sutton smiled and whispered in his ear, "It's the story of your life."

Caleb whispered, "That'll be hard to write in an hour."

"Just the highlights, son," Professor Sutton whispered and winked.

"Yes, sir," Caleb said as he walked back to his chair. He sat down and thought, *I must be the dumbest country hick who ever attended this college. I was the only person who didn't know what an autobiography is.* He began to write frantically.

Caleb finished in time, went to all his other classes, and then rushed to work. He and Abe served lunch, and then he went to help Burt on the golf course.

When Caleb walked into the pro-shop, Burt tossed him a cap and said, "Try it on."

"Why?" Caleb asked.

"I want to see how much your head swelled after last night."

"I didn't hurt my head," Caleb said. "I just got pooped out at the end of the game."

"Big head," Burt said, holding his hands apart.

"I don't understand what you're trying to say," Caleb said, somewhat perplexed.

"Why did you throw the ball into the stands?" Burt asked. "That's something show-offs do. You're the last person in the world I would have expected to do that."

"I wasn't showing off, Mr. Burt. It was a promise I made to Buckie to let him know I made the touchdown for him. I didn't know it was illegal when I promised him I'd do that."

"Who's Buckie?" Burt asked.

"He's the sweetest little boy in the world. He's in the hospital dying with cancer. Doc asked me to go see him."

Burt looked away, feeling like a first class heel for questioning Caleb's integrity. "Let me extract my foot from my mouth," he said. "I'm sorry for chastising you, son. I should have had more faith in you. You should let everyone know why you did it. You've become everyone's hero and a role model for the kids all over this state. Everything you do'll be scrutinized and emulated from now on. I don't envy you that."

Caleb said, "Mr. Burt, sometimes I want to pack up, ease out of town, and just go home. I didn't expect any of this. My mind stays in a whirlwind most of the time. It seems I don't know right from wrong anymore."

"I can understand that, Caleb. What's happened to you doesn't happen to many people. If you don't mind, I'd like to give you some advice. I know advice is cheap and sometimes not worth much, so you can do with it as you please. What you have to do is to establish your priorities and limit yourself to accomplishing them. You're here for an education first and foremost. You obviously love football, but it has to be your second priority. You need this job because your mother…I don't know her, and I won't judge her. Everything else has to be placed on the back burner for a while. Now, to accomplish all this will be an arduous task. Most young people would crumble under the pressure, but I have faith in you and your commitment. The important question is one that only you can answer. Is it worth it to you?"

Caleb thought for a second then answered, "I may wind up in Whitfield, but, yes, it's worth it to me. It was my father's dream, and now it's my dream to graduate from Marston. Even if I have to give up football, I plan to graduate."

"Caleb, you know Doc wants to help, and if you'll let him, you won't have to give up anything."

"No, sir," Caleb said, shaking his head. "I won't accept his charity. I have to work for my education. You have to work for something before it has any value to you."

Burt reached behind the counter to get the tractor keys. As he tossed it to Caleb, he said, "We had a little blow last night. Police the fairways and pick up any fallen limbs. If you get tired, go back to the dorm and rest. I can tell you didn't get much rest last night."

As Caleb headed out the back door, Burt yelled to him, "Do you think we have a chance Saturday night? There have been whispers that Coach Shook has a little surprise for Tulane, you know, because of the closed practices."

"Will thinks we're going to win," Caleb said, "and I believe in Will." Then he disappeared out the door.

"Huh!" Burt said. "Will believes in Will, too, but he ain't Superman, close maybe, but he can't fly. At least, I've never seen him fly."

Caleb worked on the course until dinner then helped Abe until nine-thirty p.m. before going to the hospital. He walked into Buckie's room; Angelle was trying to get Buckie to drink some juice. He gagged with every sip. "Please try to drink a little more," Angelle pleaded. "You didn't eat a bite of your dinner, and you're going to get dehydrated."

Caleb took the glass and said, "Let me try. Where's Luther?"

"Doc made him go over to his office and lay down on the couch to get a little rest. He hadn't slept in two days. I'll come back before I go to the dorm, Buckie." And she brushed his cheek with her hand.

"Are you hurtin' bad, little brother?" Caleb asked.

"Sometimes I hurt bad, then they give me a shot, and I sleep awhile. But the hurtin' don't ever go away. I'm so tired all the time now, I can't hardly sit up no more." Buckie was holding a stack of letters in his hand. He said, "Would you put my letters on that table over yonder?"

Caleb nodded, took the letters, and did as Buckie asked. "You must have a sweet little girl back home to get so many letters," Caleb said, trying to get Buckie to smile.

"Nah," Buckie grinned. "Them ain't from no girl. They're from my Sunday school class. I got some good friends in my class. They write me a letter every week. Brother Branch brings them to me when he comes to visit."

Caleb bent over to kiss him on the cheek, hugged him gently, then put his hand to his mouth and looked into his eyes. No words of comfort came to his mind as he ran his fingers through Buckie's hair. He whispered, "It will get better soon, little brother. The Lord won't let you hurt like this much longer." Buckie understood what Caleb meant. But Caleb wondered if he had said the wrong thing.

"Will I see you in heaven?" Buckie asked. "Will you still be my brother in heaven?"

"I promise you I'll see you in heaven. Everyone will be brothers and sisters in heaven."

"You mean like real brothers?"

"I mean better than real brothers, better than we can ever imagine."

"I'll see my momma in heaven, won't I, and she'll love me, too, won't she?"

Caleb put his hands over his eyes to conceal the pain in his face.

"Please don't cry," Buckie said. "You make me sad when you cry."

Caleb wiped his eyes and forced a smile. "Everyone in heaven will love you. That's what heaven is, a place where everyone loves everyone. You won't hurt anymore."

"I won't be sick no more, will I?"

"Buckie, I promise you that you'll have no pain, sickness, or sorrow in heaven. Imagine the happiest day of your life. Then know that heaven will be a thousand times more wonderful than that day."

"The happiest day I ever had was when you first come to see me," Buckie said. Then an agonizing look fell across his face. He started to moan and rock, holding his side saying, "Oh, ooh, oooh."

Caleb ran out of the room to the nurses' station and yelled, "Somebody please come see what's wrong with Buckie. He's in terrible pain!"

Gladys knew what was happening. She grabbed a syringe, went to the locked cabinet, and drew up pain medication. She rushed to Buckie's side and gave him a shot in the fleshy part of the hip. The pain eased almost immediately. Angelle rushed in a few seconds later and said, "He'll sleep now, Caleb. You might as well go back to the dormitory."

Buckie's eyes began to close as Caleb knelt down and kissed his forehead. "I'll see you tomorrow, little brother. May God watch over you through this night." Angelle pulled the covers up and walked out with Caleb.

"What happened?" Caleb asked.

"The cancer has metastasized to his liver, and who knows where else," she said, in near tears. "We have to do this every few hours. Doc said for us to keep him as comfortable as possible."

"Metastasized means spread?" Caleb asked. "How long does he have to live?"

"Any day now. Any minute," Angelle said, trying to fight back the tears. "His fever could spike, or he could get pneumonia, and it would be over in minutes. He can't eat anymore. Everything nauseates him. He has no resistance to infection."

"I might as well go," Caleb said, lowering his head and walking away.

"Let me check out, and I'll ride with you if you don't mind," Angelle said.

"I'll wait," Caleb said, somewhat surprised.

As they walked to the truck, Caleb said, "I'll walk you back and come back and get my truck later, if you'd rather. I'm kind of ashamed for you to ride in this old hunk of junk."

"I thought you were proud of this truck," Angelle said. "Everyone knows the story that you told the class about your life and the history of this truck. All the kids call it the honeymoon truck now when you drive by."

"I'm ashamed of what I just said, Angelle. I do love this old truck because it was a part of my father's life. He loved it, and it makes me feel close to him when I drive it. What I really was trying to say is that you deserve better. You're very special. You should be riding in a beautiful carriage like Cinderella."

"I don't know why you think I'm special. There's nothing special about me. What you're doing for Buckie is very special. You're the special one."

Her kind words made Caleb smile again. He cranked the truck, and they drove slowly toward the campus. Caleb wanted to put his arm around her and hold her close for an eternity. *No one could be so wonderful and kind,* he thought. *What have I done to be cursed by loving someone so wonderful and knowing that I will never be able to hold her and kiss her again?* As they neared the gates to the campus, Angelle said, "I'm hungry, Caleb. Have you eaten tonight?"

"No," he responded.

"Do you have time to run by the drive-in on fifty-one and let me get a hamburger and coke?" Caleb smiled and nodded. They pulled up to the drive-in. The carhop ran out to the car and both ordered burgers and cokes. The drive-in was packed because the downtown movie, as well as the drive-in movie, had just ended. Many of the college kids were there. They all recognized Caleb's truck and hopped out of their cars and ran over to speak to him. When they spotted Angelle sitting next to him, the ooohs, aaahs, and catcalls rang out. They pointed to Caleb and Angelle, laughing and clapping.

One boy yelled, "I told y'all so! We all knew they were going to get together! The hero and the beauty queen."

Angelle turned three shades of pink, and Caleb wanted to slide down to the floorboard. One girl, obviously a little jealous, yelled, "She's engaged, too! I wonder if she has her ring on?"

"Do you want to leave?" Caleb asked.

"We've done nothing wrong," Angelle said. "No. I don't want to leave. I'm hungry." Hands started shooting through the window to slap Caleb on the back.

A carload of freshmen football players pulled up beside his truck. They noticed all the commotion. One of the football players spotted Angelle in the car. He said, "Do y'all see who Caleb's with?"

Another one said, "That old hound dog. I can't believe it." He stuck his head out the window and began to sing, "You got to be a football hero to get along with the beautiful girls."

Tilly, short for Tillman, was the center on the freshman team. He climbed out of the back seat and said, "I think Caleb's probably had enough of all this crap. He's trying to make time with someone else's gal, and I'm going to help him." He yelled, "Okay, all you riff-raff, get away from that truck. Let Caleb make some time with that gorgeous Cajun queen!" They scattered like a covey of quail at Tilly's gruff command. Tilly stuck his head in their window, inches from Angelle's face and said, "Don't thank me, Caleb. I'd do that for my worst enemy if he had a beautiful girl like Angelle in the car. How long has this romance been going on? Let me see your left hand, Angelle."

"Tilly!" Caleb said sternly, "If you don't get your face out of my truck and stop embarrassing Angelle, I'm not going to look for a hole next practice. I'm going to put cleat marks up your back."

Tilly jerked back from the window and said, "Don't get huffy, Mr. Superstar. I was just trying to do you and your gal a favor."

"She's not my gal, Tilly, and you can tell the rest of those bums that I was just giving her a ride to the campus."

"Sure you were," Tilly said, grinning as he eased back to the car.

"You don't have to defend my honor," Angelle said. "It's really none of their business." The kids from the college settled down, and Caleb and Angelle enjoyed their burgers. Caleb started back to the campus. Angelle said, "I have almost an hour before curfew. Can we drive around and talk a little longer?"

Caleb's eyes widened, and he asked nervously, "Where shall we drive?" His heart pounded, amazed and startled at her suggestion.

"Just around town. We can ride and talk like good friends do." Caleb smiled and nodded.

"Good friends confide in each other, don't they?" Caleb said, as they drove past the gate to the college. "I don't know anything about you. It's like you never existed before you came here. No one knows anything about you or your past. Is it some big secret?" he said, jokingly. "Are you an escaped convict in hiding? Why don't you want to talk about it?"

"Caleb, it's not that I don't want to talk about myself. I just think that a person's private life is just that, private and personal. There's no reason for everyone to know about my life before I came here. I'm the same person now as I was then."

"Tell me about your father. What's his occupation?"

Angelle smiled and replied laughingly, "You don't give up, do you?" Caleb returned her smile and shook his head.

"I…I don't like talking about the past. Some things are painful, but if you insist, I suppose I'll tell you about my father. It's no big secret. He was a wonderful father, but he's no longer alive. He was a policeman in New Orleans many years ago. He and his partner responded to a robbery in progress at a liquor store. They rushed in to break up the holdup, but there was someone outside working with the robber inside. The rotten thief ran in behind them and shot my father and his partner. My father's partner lived, but my father died on the way to the hospital where my mother worked in the emergency room. You can't imagine how it affected her when they pronounced him dead in her presence. They never caught those rotten…" Her soft, brown eyes hardened, and tears formed in her eyes as she lowered her head. Caleb reached over and gently put his arm around her shoulder, giving her a gentle squeeze to comfort her. She gasped, jerked away from his grasp, and the same frozen look of horror as before came across her face.

She gasped again and in a broken voice asked that he take her to the dormitory as she continued to tremble with labored breath. Caleb turned around quickly and started back to the college. Angelle gazed out the window, trembling and sobbing.

"I'm sorry," Caleb said, as they turned into the campus. "It seems that all I ever do is bring you pain. You know how I feel about you. I think you have some feelings for me, but I don't want to ever hurt you again like this."

Angelle's respiration eased somewhat as they neared the dorm. She wiped her eyes, looked at Caleb, and said, "It's not your fault. Don't feel guilty. There are things that you don't know about me. I can't talk about them, and I do care for you. I just can't fall in love with you. It would be wrong." A minute later, Caleb pulled over in front of the dorm. Angelle stepped out and said, "Forgive me," and rushed into the dorm.

Caleb drove slowly down the hill to the dorm, confused and heartsick. He slowly walked up the stairs to his room. Will was lying in bed reading a novel. "Where have you been?" he growled. "It's after eleven!"

His comment and tone of voice angered Caleb like never before, and he shot back, "Who made you my keeper?"

"Let me enlighten you about a few things, Mr. Hot Shot. These PhDs don't give a damn about your athletic prowess. Half of them resent the money spent on athletics. You drop below a 3.0 and you're out of here. You've let down yourself, the team, the coaches, and, not least of all, me. In six months no one will remember your name. Then everything you've busted your ass for will be out the window. I'm not anybody's keeper but mine, but you need a little guidance even though you seem to think you have all the answers. When was the last time you opened a book?"

"I'll stay up every night and cram, if that's what it takes. You worry about you, and let me worry about me."

"Now when did you get so independent, Corn Shuck? If I leave you alone, you'll last about as long as a snowball in hell. Now, climb down off that high horse and tell me what's got you so jacked up?"

Caleb paused a few seconds, took a couple of deep breaths, and said, "It's that boy in the hospital, Buckie. I can't stop thinking about him and the pain and agony he's going through."

"I know you think I'm cold hearted and even sadistic at times. The world is a cruel place, and you won't change that. My philosophy of life is simple. You have to take care of number one, and let the rest of the world take care of itself."

"Will, I don't understand a philosophy like that. I don't think I would want to live in a world where everyone felt that way."

"What happens when the boy dies? Are you going to crawl in the grave with him? Don't you understand that boys die every day, and the sun still rises the next morning? Life goes on and everyone forgets. That's the way life is. At best, it's just a crap-shoot."

"I'll remember," Caleb said. "I'll remember him for the rest of my life. I love that boy like he was my own brother."

"Then you're a chump and setting yourself up for a heartbreak. I'm going to bed and get ready to win a ball game. That's what I have on my mind. I thought you might feel the same way, but no, you drag in here three hours after work, carrying the woes of the world on your shoulders and give no thought to the most important game of my life."

Caleb showered and went to bed. He prayed long into the night for Buckie, then Angelle, even for Will. He fell asleep while he was still praying. He awakened before dawn and went to the club and worked until eleven. He helped Abe in the dining hall, and then returned to work on the golf course.

Since Caleb had permission to go to all home games, he left for the campus at six p.m. The traffic was bumper-to-bumper on Hwy. 51. After a five-minute drive turned into a thirty-minute drive, he arrived at the dorm late and hurriedly dressed for the game. Knowing it would start at 7:30 p.m., he decided to wait for the kickoff before entering the stadium. The last thing he wanted was to endure the embarrassment of the last game and steal the thunder from the varsity team. He didn't want the complimentary tickets after the fiasco at the last game. He waited outside the student gate until he heard the roar of the kickoff. He ran into the stadium and up the bleachers. Thankfully, no one noticed him running up the stands. The seats all seemed to be taken. He saw a long, slim arm waving at him toward the top, so he rushed up the steps. He realized it was Rachel waving for him to come and sit by her. "I saved a seat for you," she said, smiling.

Caleb sat down, and then looked over at her. "Thank you, Rachel. That was very thoughtful of you."

Rachel gave him an impish look. "Don't get any funny ideas, Shorty. I had a feeling you'd come late after the last game."

"Who said red heads are dumb?" Caleb joked.

"Get it right, Shorty," Rachel quipped. "Blondes are dumb, red heads are fiery spirited, brilliant, and beautiful. I added the last two adjectives."

"They are correct in your case," Caleb said, extending his hand. She grasped his hand and gave it a big firm shake.

She said, very matter-of-factly, "We're about to get our butts kicked, again, aren't we?"

"I don't think so," Caleb said, shaking his head. "We may lose the game, but it won't be a butt kicking, as you called it. We have a few surprises for Tulane."

"The only surprise we could possibly have for Tulane would be if your hero, lecherous Will James, had a twin brother to play the other end. That coach isn't stupid. Everyone knows that all you have to do to beat Marston is to run away from Will's side. I don't know didley-squat about coaching, but I know that. My little brother, Jacob, knows that."

"Where is Jacob?"

"He's in the stands with our parents over there somewhere." She pointed at the center of the home bleachers. "Now, hush and let me watch the massacre." Caleb gave her a curious look, and then laughed.

Marston had received the kickoff and returned the ball to the twenty-yard line. Marston lined up, snapped the ball, and gained three yards off tackle on the first play. The next two plays gained a total of five yards. Then the team lined up to punt. Will went in on the punting team. The ball was kicked high and traveled forty yards. Will made the stop at the Tulane thirty-two yard line. The Wildcats defense rushed onto the field and lined up in a five-three defense with Will at middle linebacker. The Greenies broke the huddle. The quarterback looked for Will planning to call an audible at the line of scrimmage. He spotted Will at middle linebacker and with a puzzled look turned and gave the coach a palms up and shrug. The coach screamed, "Hurry up and call a play." It was obvious to everyone that the quarterback had been instructed to call the play at the line of scrimmage and to run the ball away from Will. The quarterback took too long, and the whistle blew for a delay of game penalty. The whispers began in the stands. They soon turned to a roar as the faithful realized what Coach Shook had done. Some shouted, "Brilliant!" while others screamed, "stupidity!"

Three plays later, everyone was screaming, "Brilliant." Will had made three straight tackles, and the Wave was faced with a fourth and seven. The fans smelled victory. They began to scream and voice their praise of the fabulous defensive stand.

"What do you think now, Amazon woman?" Caleb asked.

"I think the game ain't over yet, munchkin," Rachel replied, slapping Caleb on the leg.

"We haven't stopped anyone on their first drive in years," Caleb said. "I think our chances look pretty darn good."

"Well, as repulsive as Will's conduct is off the field, I have to admit that he's a tremendous football player. That was a brilliant idea to put him at linebacker. His head may get so big that they can't find a helmet to fit it. Jacob thinks Will's Superman, and he calls you Jimmy. Sorry about your second billing. I'll never understand how you can be such good friends with him! You're a modern day Don Quixote, and he's a modern day Don Juan."

"Who?" Caleb asked. "Never mind."

Bill James was standing up in the box seats in total shock and disbelief and railing at Coach Shook's decision to put Will at linebacker. He said to one of his ex-teammates who was sitting in the box seat next to his, "Who in the hell gave Coach Shook permission to move my son to linebacker? He's an all-American end…like me. Has he totally lost his mind?"

The teammate commented, "You better sit down and shut your mouth, Bill. I never heard of an all-American coming from a zero and ten team. I think it was the most brilliant move Shook has ever made. Who knows, you might have been all-American for three years if you'd played linebacker."

Bill stood there a few seconds, digesting the comment, and then said, "You're probably right, but he should have conferred with me before he made the move."

"After what you said in the paper last week, Bill, I'd be surprised if he ever speaks to you again," the old teammate remarked.

"Actually," William said, "I gave the move some thought myself, but I knew Will had his heart set on playing end like me." His friend nodded, then looked at another friend with raised brows.

The rest of the first half was a defensive struggle with neither team gaining much yardage. The ball was punted every fourth down. Wally was almost in cardiac arrest from excitement, yelling the praise of the Marston defense and the brilliant move of Will to linebacker. He stressed how confusing it appeared to the Wave offense. As always, the eternal optimist continued to say, "If we can get one break on offense and make a few points, we're going to win this game."

Marston had managed to stay close in the first half in a few games the last three years, but a lack of depth and talent always seem to cause their demise in the second half. But this team had something that had been lacking the last few years. It had heart and Will James, so the hopes grew brighter. When the horn blew to end the first half, the fans stood and roared their approval of the team's Herculean effort.

Caleb was so into the game, he forgot the pain of the last few days. His excitement was equally shared by Rachel. She had stood and screamed, "Kill them, knock their heads off, crush the bums, and bury them," and many other colorful verbs and adjectives during the first half. As the team jogged off the field, Caleb and Rachel turned and embraced each other, screaming and jumping up and down. Every time Rachel jumped up, her bosoms knocked Caleb's head backward. She slapped him on the back so hard it almost knocked out his breath. As the roar subsided, she realized what she had been doing. She turned him loose and giggled, commenting, "Sorry, munchkin, I didn't mean to get so physical. I'm usually very docile and reserved."

"Yeah!" Caleb said. "I've noticed. What do you think now? Have we got a chance?"

"Sixty-forty their way," she said. "They have a good team and a good record. We'll have to play the best second half we've ever played to keep them off the scoreboard. Without much offense, I don't know if we can score. They're bigger and quicker than our boys."

"You sound like a coach," Caleb said, amazed at her knowledge of the game.

"I haven't missed a home game since I was two years old. My father goes nuts over these games, and my brother's going to play for Marston in seven or eight years. I'll tell you something else. If I were a male, Will James wouldn't be the only all-American on that field tonight. The only thing I regret about being a girl is not being able to play football."

"I believe you, Rachel. I absolutely believe you."

"Do you want a dog and Coke?" Rachel asked.

"Sounds good to me," Caleb said. "How 'bout you?"

She nodded and said, "I'd like two."

"I'll run get them," he said and rushed down the stands.

Luther said, "I believe we gonna win this here game, Buckie."

Buckie nodded. "I know Caleb's jumping up and down, Pop. I hope we win. I know how happy it'll make Caleb if we do."

Caleb returned with the food, and they devoured it in seconds. The roar from the stands had never ceased throughout the half. The fans smelled victory—sweet victory. It was hard for most to remember that feeling.

Shortly before the teams returned to the field, Rachel turned to Caleb and said, "I want to ask you something, and I don't want you to feel that you're obligated to say yes if you don't want to. You know homecoming is in two weeks. The court hasn't been announced yet, but my faculty adviser is on the selection committee. She whispered to me that I might need to buy a nice gown for the Homecoming Ball. Then she winked. I'm assuming that meant I've been selected to represent the Education Department on the Homecoming Court. I have to have an escort at the Homecoming Ball at the Marston Student Union after the game. I'm not asking you for a date, I'm simply asking you to escort me. That is, if you don't already have a date. There'll be no hard feelings if you say no."

"I thought you were a nursing student?"

"I am. I have a double major. I like to be prepared."

Caleb pondered the question briefly before responding with a soft smile, "I don't have a date. I don't date anyone here, or anywhere. It would be an honor to escort you."

Rachel gave a big sigh of relief and said, "Thank goodness. I didn't think I'd get anyone to escort me. I'm taller than most of the boys here, and all the ones that are my height look like Ichabod Crane. You don't know how much I appreciate this."

"What do I wear?" Caleb asked.

"You have to wear a tuxedo. Don't worry, I'll pay for it."

"I'd die before I'd let a girl pay for something like that," Caleb said, somewhat insulted by her kind gesture. *Sweet mercy*, Caleb thought, *what have I gotten myself into? I don't know if I have enough money for an expensive tuxedo. I don't know what one costs. Oh well, I guess its providence. If I have to work overtime to pay for it, I will. But I'm not going to worry about it now. We have a game to win.* The teams took the field for the second half. The tension was so electric through the second half that a man had a heart attack. He was carried out of the stadium on a stretcher.

Three plays and punt was the norm through the third quarter. When the fourth quarter began, the Wave finally abandoned the running game and began an aerial assault and managed to get to the Marston twenty-yard line midway through the fourth quarter. The defense stiffened, and they were able to manage only a field goal. It appeared that the game might end with Marston going down by three points.

The Wave kicked to Marston. They were unable to move the ball, and they had to punt. The clock became their enemy as it seemed to speed up. The Wave was very conservative with their play calling and tried to run the clock out. As the clock began to wind down, Marston got the first big break of the game. The Wave had a third and four. They ran a sweep to their right. Will broke through the line and hit the ball carrier with such force that the ball shot out of his grasp and hit the ground. Will scooped it up and sprinted toward the Marston goal line. He was finally dragged down at the eight-yard line by two Wave defenders.

The offense sprinted onto the field with less than one minute on the game clock. They tried to run up the middle on two consecutive plays, however, they only advanced the ball to the five-yard line. With only one timeout left and realizing that the wave's goal line defense was too stiff to make five yards, Coach Shook decided his only chance was to pass the ball as the clock neared twenty seconds. He grabbed Wendell Sanders, a reserve end who was the tallest man on the team, but not very physical; however, Wendell had the best hands on the team. Coach Shook instructed him to tell Clancy to fake thirty blast and then try a jump pass to him over the middle. Wendell sprinted onto the field as the clock neared ten seconds. Clancy made a good fake up the middle before jumping high and flipping the ball toward Wendell who was alone in the end zone. A linebacker jumped high in the air and barely tipped the ball, and it flew a few inches over Wendell's outstretched arms. Coach shook and the other coaches kicked the ground, realizing what might have been. It was now decision time. Coach Shook called his last timeout and huddled his coaches around him. "We're down to the nut-cuttin' boys," he said. "Do y'all want to tie the game or try to win?"

"It's your call," Toad said.

"Let's get the monkey off our backs," Stan said. "These fans deserve a victory, and as they say, a tie is like kissin' your sister."

"Go for it," Ollie said.

Billy Ray added, "These seniors have never tasted victory. Go for it, Coach!"

Will stuck his head in their huddle, pleading, "Give me the ball, and I swear I'll get those five yards, Coach." The coaches looked at each other for a few seconds, and then began to nod.

The fans were in agreement to go for it as they all stood screaming, "Go for it, Coach."

"Okay, Will, it's yours to win or lose," Coach Shook responded nervously. "Run thirty blast, and wedge it right up the gut. You line up a yard deeper at tailback and tell Clancy to raise up and fake a quick pass to the right end then give you the ball up the gut. Tell the line to block like hell or get their asses out of your way, because you're heading for the goal line. Split both ends wide and put Willis in motion. Hopefully they'll think it's another desperation pass."

"I'm way ahead of you, Coach," Will said, "and you won't be disappointed." He sprinted onto the field. Coach Shook wiped the perspiration form his face, trembling, and almost in tears.

Wally Stewart said, "Folks, Will James is going into the game. What do you reckon Coach Shook has up his sleeve? I 'spect Clancy's going to throw a pass to him. Well, we'll know soon enough because it all comes down to this play. I swear, folks, my heart's skipping like a old two-cylinder John Deere tractor motor. If you're faint of heart, take a glycerin tablet and lay down, because we ain't come this close to winning a game in thirty-five tries. There ain't nothing to do now but sit and wait." The crowd noise became so loud that the radio audience couldn't hear half of what Wally was saying. "Don't tell me this is just another game," he declared, "'cause it don't get no better'n this."

Will ran into the huddle, saying, "Thirty blast, men." He sent Allen Freeman, the starting fullback, to the bench. "Now listen to me carefully, team, 'cause I ain't gonna say this but once. You block like your life depends on it. If anyone breaks through the line, I'm going to personally kill all of you." Will grabbed Clark, the other running back, in the collar and said, "Clark, you move over to left halfback and cheat up a few feet. I expect you to bust that linebacker so damn hard it knocks his tit up 'side his ear. I'll be right up your ass. Both ends split out about ten yards. Willis, go in motion right. We're five yards from winning the biggest game in Marston history. Clancy, Coach said for you to stand up quickly and fake a pass to the split end on the right then hand the ball to me up the gut."

Clancy became concerned, saying, "Will, we ain't never practiced that play. Are you sure?"

"Improvise," Will barked. "Just call the play and get out of my way."

Clancy said, "Motion right, thirty blast with a fake jump pass on one, and nobody jump off sides. Let's win one for Coach." They clapped their hands loudly, broke the huddle, and sprinted up to the line of scrimmage like gallant warriors. The noise from the stands was so deafening the team couldn't hear Clancy bark the signals. He backed away from the center and held his hands out for quiet, but the noise level seemed to rise. The referee didn't step in and allow him more time to quiet the crowd.

Will yelled, "Snap the ball before we get a penalty!" Clancy stepped back under center and barked the snap count as loudly as he could. The ball was snapped, and Clark dove into the zero hole ahead of Will and put a crushing blow on the huge middle linebacker. Clancy made a quick fake jump pass before handing Will the ball at full speed. Will lowered his shoulders and lumbered through the hole behind Clark's key block. Two linebackers converged on Will, landing crushing blows to his thigh and midsection. Will absorbed their blows, tearing away from them. He continued to churn his huge, muscular legs toward the goal line. The last two remaining defensive backs dove at Will's ankles and knees, causing him to stumble at the three-yard line. Will fell forward like a giant oak, and as he neared the turf, he extended the ball as far as his long arms could stretch. The tip of the ball touched the chalk line just before his huge body crashed to the turf. The officials' arms shot up, signifying a touchdown. An end to the longest losing streak in the nation had just occurred.

A roar like never before heard in that small town vibrated windows as far as the outskirts of Marston. The team ran onto the field, and the fans began to boil out of the stands. William the Conqueror stood screaming and jumping up and down like a child, shouting, "That's my boy! That's my boy! Did y'all see that? He's a chip off the ole block!"

Wally lost his voice screaming into the microphone. He could barely whisper. In a raspy voice, he managed to say, "That was the greatest performance by a varsity player in the history of Marston football. I might add, the greatest coaching job I've ever witnessed. All those folks that were screaming for Coach Shook's head a week ago might want to give him a raise after this game. It don't get no better than this, folks. Just imagine how good this team'll be next year when Caleb Morgan lines up in the backfield."

The coaches hugged each other, and then rushed onto the field to congratulate the team. Coach Shook walked out to meet the Wave coach. They shook hands. Then the Wave coach said, "Everyone was pulling for you to get a win, but why did you have to do it this week?" Then he patted Coach Shook on the back and continued, "Great game plan, Coach. I congratulate you on a well-deserved victory. I hope you win the rest."

"You're too kind," Coach Shook said. "It's hard to imagine what this win means to our kids."

William James had jumped over the hedges onto the field and rushed out to Coach Shook. After Coach Shook and the Wave coach had finished their conversation, he grabbed Coach Shook's hand. As they shook hands, he said, "That was brilliant what you did tonight. I hope we can let bygones be bygones and be good friends. After all I am one of your boys."

"We have no problems as far as I'm concerned," Coach Shook said, "as long as you let me do my job the way I think best."

"Good, good," William said. "I think Will showed great potential running the ball tonight. Keep up the good work."

Coach Shook turned to walk away. Will rushed up behind him, grabbed him under the arms, and hoisted him on his shoulder as if he were a child. The rest of the team rushed over to walk Coach Shook to the sidelines. Will eased him down and said, "That one was for you, Coach."

After an extended celebration, the team went to the dressing room, and the coaches walked into Coach Shook's office and lit up cigars, compliments of Stan again. Coach Shook said, "They all say we're geniuses now, men. The truth is we would still be winless if that silly young country boy hadn't walked in here last weekend and offered a brilliant suggestion. And we can't even give him credit for it. Now ain't that a crock."

"Now, just wait a minute!" Stan said. "You ain't gonna rain on my parade tonight. I feel like celebrating. After all, how often do we win a game around here? Why don't we round up the gals and scoot up to Memphis. We can eat the biggest steak in town, listen to a little jazz, and enjoy a few compliments from our fans, if we have any left. You, most of all, Coach, need a little relaxation."

"I'm game," Billy Ray said.

"If it involves food and a little libation, I'm always on ready," Ollie said. "I haven't had an appetite in three weeks. My gut thinks I've been on a seven-day fast. What are we waitin' for?"

"What do you say, Coach?" Stan asked.

"I'd love to, but Mavis came to the game with Doc and Edith tonight. They invited us over after the game for one of Edith's special dinners. I don't have many friends left, and I can't afford to offend any of them. Maybe next time, but y'all go and enjoy yourselves. I'll even catch the tab. You earned it. Oh! By the way, I don't think we need to enforce curfew tonight."

"What curfew?" Stan barked. "Nobody would be back before noon tomorrow…except John David and Caleb."

"Let the press in, Billy Ray," Coach Shook said, "if any want in," and they all had a big laugh.

———

Caleb went to the dorm to wait for Will. His wait was short. Will ran up the stairs before anyone else, shot into the room, and grabbed Caleb. He picked him up and slung him around, and yelled, "Did you see me bulldoze my way into the end zone, Corn Shuck? Did you? Did you?"

"I saw every play. You must have had forty tackles, too."

"Yeah, I was great on defense, wasn't I? But I never imagined how exhilarating it would feel to score a touchdown, especially with the game on the line. I'm high as a kite. Let's go to Memphis and celebrate. I need to unwind."

"When will we get back?" Caleb asked.

"Who cares!" Will yelled. "We just broke the longest losing streak in the nation, and we're now on a one-game winning streak. Don't sweat the small stuff. I'll get you back for class Monday if we don't wind up in jail." And he laughed.

"Will, you know I have to work tomorrow."

"Screw work! You have the rest of your life to work. Now, let's go. I need a beer. I'm parched."

"Will, why don't we go get a barbecue from Mr. Pigg's place? He stays open late on game nights, and I know most of the team'll be there and most of the students, too. We can sit around and talk about how great you played. It'll be fun."

"That's kid's stuff," Will scowled. "We're going to have a few drinks, eat the biggest steak in Memphis, and make out with a couple of hot chicks tonight. When those cute, little honeys in the club find out who we are, we'll have the pick of the litter. I'll find a cute one for you. Let's live a little, Corn Shuck. Like the saying goes, life is short, and you only make the trip once."

"I'm sorry, Will," Caleb said, shaking his head, "but you know I can't do that. I have a job and responsibilities. If I don't go to work, Abe won't be able to take care of the big crowd tomorrow.

We always have a huge crowd after church, especially with all those from out of town who came for the game."

Will slumped, and then cocked his head sideways, and said, "Hey, buddy, I'm your pal. I just won a ballgame. I want to celebrate, and you're turning me down. What the hell's come over you? Are we pals or not?"

"I can't do it! I live by a set of rules, and I can't change them. My word is my bond. I'd do anything for you, but you can't ask me to abandon my responsibilities. That's what keeps me in school."

"That's your final word!" Will barked.

"No. I have a few other words to say because I care for you. 'Let him who thinks he stands take heed lest he falls.'"

Caleb lowered his head, and Will yelled, "Okay, buddy, pal, friend, screw you!" He stormed out of the room, slammed the door mumbling, "I'm Will James, and I don't need you. I don't need anyone."

John David had walked up the stairs and overheard most of the conversation. After Will stormed by him, he walked across the hall and stuck his head into Caleb's room. "Don't worry about him. You're the only friend he has, and he'll get over it in a day or so. Do you want to go get that barbecue with me?"

"He just spoiled my appetite, but I'll go with you. I don't want to sit up here by myself. All I ate today was a cold hot dog at the game."

As they drove to Mr. Pigg's place in John David's car, John David asked, "Do you and Rachel have something simmering? I've noticed y'all together at the ballgames. She's a beautiful girl. Just think how big and strong your kids would be." He laughed and quipped, "But I wouldn't want to get her upset."

"I ain't going to marry any girl that can beat me up," Caleb said, laughing. "No. Actually we're just good friends. She has a great personality, although she can be a little…salty for a preacher's kid."

"Some of the boys said you were at the drive-in with Angelle. Is that serious?"

"I wish," Caleb said, grinning, "but, no, we're just friends, too."

"I think she's the most beautiful girl I've ever seen," John David added. "But she doesn't appear to be very happy. I've never seen her smile. Of course, I wouldn't want this conversation to get back to Cindy."

"Cindy's beautiful, too," Caleb said. "How long have you two been dating?"

"I fell in love with her in the third grade. I've always known that she was the one I wanted to marry. I do believe there's one true love in everyone's life, and the right marriages are made in heaven. Of course I think a person can love again, if they lose their first love. How about you, do you have a special girl at home?"

Caleb laughed again. "I've never had a real date in my life. Will fooled me into going with him and two girls a few weeks ago, but it wasn't a real date. I was miserable, and it almost cost me a week's pay before we got back after two a.m. We should have wound up in jail."

John David burst out laughing. "You watch your pennies pretty close, don't you?"

"I have to because I don't have much, and I have to pay for school."

"Your scholarship should pay most of your expenses. How much money do you need?"

"I'm not on a scholarship," Caleb responded.

John David's jaw dropped. He peered at Caleb and said, "You've got to be kidding!"

"It's a long story," Caleb said. "My mother wouldn't let me accept the scholarship. She thinks it's like charity. She doesn't believe in charity unless you're unable to work."

"Have mercy," John David said. "I had lots of respect for you before, but now I…"

"I don't mind working. I've worked all my life. It's really pretty easy compared to farming in the hot summer."

They pulled into Mr. Pigg's Place, hopped out, and walked in. Mr. Pigg commented, "I thought you and Will were boycotting me. Come over here behind the counter and let me shake your hand, son. You're truly an amazing, young man. Wally's going to have a heart attack if you don't quit making those big plays. Where's Will?"

"Chasing skirts," John David remarked.

"That boy'll never change, I fear," Mr. Pigg said.

"Yes he will," Caleb said. "I have him almost three more years. He's going to change before I finish with him."

"If anybody can do it," John David nodded, "you can, because you're a miracle worker."

"What's your pleasure, men?" Mr. Pigg asked.

"I'll have one of Will's special po-boys with pork," Caleb said. John David nodded, likewise. A few minutes later, the crowd began pouring in. Soon, dozens of fans and football players crowed into the place. For the next hour and a half, the team and fans had a rowdy and spirited pep rally. The party was still in full swing at one a.m. when Mr. Pigg began to hurry everyone up. The party moved outside in the moonlight, under the streetlight, and continued for another hour before the last of the revelers pulled away.

John David and Caleb arrived back at the dorm shortly after two a.m. As they strolled to the dorm, Caleb commented, "I can't believe Will wouldn't come with me. I don't know when I've had so much fun. That's what I imagined college life would be like. I don't know when I've enjoyed myself so much."

"I never heard you talk that much before," John David said. "But when you're the center attraction, you have to talk or look like a snob. Will doesn't know how to have fun. He's an angry young man, and I don't know him well enough to know what he's angry about. If you can get inside his head and find out why he's so angry with life, you might be able to help him."

"I already know. He despises his father, and he had no home life. He thinks the only way he can please his father is by excelling at athletics. He said that athletic events were the only time he ever saw his father while he was growing up. And he knows his father is unfaithful to his mother. He thinks the only reason he married her was to get her money to start his own businesses. Will's mother's family is very wealthy. So is his dad now."

"He told you all that?"

"Yes, and I had no right repeating it. You're the only person I would ever tell that. I believe you're a person of integrity."

"Man!" John David said, "I didn't know it was that deep. He needs psychiatric counseling, but that's not likely with his ego. So, the next best thing is to have a friend that he can confide in and one who sets a good example for him. I can't think of anyone better suited to the task."

As they walked down the hall to their rooms, Caleb put his arm around John David's shoulder and said, "You're a good friend, and I admire you a lot. You'll make a wonderful pastor. I wish Will was like you. I pray for him all the time."

John David nodded and said, "So do I." They said good night and went to their rooms.

CHAPTER ELEVEN

The bright, early morning sun awakened Caleb at seven o'clock on Sunday morning. He jumped up, dressed quickly, and rushed to the hospital. Angelle was already behind the nurses' station when he arrived. As he passed, he commented, "Do you work here all the time, young lady?"

Her eyes brightened, and she smiled with a subtle headshake.

"It appears that you do," Caleb said and continued to Buckie's room. He eased in and saw Luther sitting in a chair next to the wall, his head resting against the wall, his mouth gaped open as he snored lightly. Buckie opened his eyes and saw Caleb.

"I reckon you're pretty happy today," Buckie said slowly and softly.

"I reckon you're right," Caleb replied as he walked over to the bed to give Buckie a tender and loving hug.

"Doc tried to get Pop to go to the hotel and rest last night, but he wouldn't go."

Luther snored so loudly he woke himself. He shook his head and looked up at Caleb.

"You up mighty early today," Luther commented. "I 'spect you walkin' on clouds this morn'."

"I 'spect you're right," Caleb said as he walked over to embrace Luther.

"My boy told me you been a comin' to see him. You know how much I 'preciats it."

"I suppose he told you we're brothers now. I have to come see my brother every day."

Luther stood up and walked over by Buckie. "Me and Buckie been a talkin', Caleb, and he told me he's been prayin' on sumpin. You know y'all a playin' Kentuck' next Thursday, and Buckie is wantin' bad to go to that there game and see you play. I ain't asked Doc yet 'cause I knows what he'll be a sayin'. Now, you needs to know sumpin' else. Buckie done told me he knows he ain't gonna be wit' us much longer." Luther wiped his eyes. "I ain't nary lied to my boy, and if'n he knows that—ain't no need o' me a startin' now. He said this is the lastest thing he's ever gonna ask me fer. Now Caleb, I wants my boy to see that there game. I know Doc ain't gonna want to let him go, but I'm a askin' you to talk to him. I'm a saying he can go, and I'm his poppa. But Doc's been so good to me and Buckie fer me to be a goin' 'gainst his thinkin'. But it's gonna break his heart if'n he can't see his brother play before... I'm a askin' you to help me."

Caleb nodded. "I'll do all I can to convince him how important it is to Buckie."

"Now I'm gonna go and git me a bite to eat if'n it's all right wit' you and Buckie?"

"Take your time," Caleb said. "I don't have to be at work for a couple of hours. Buckie and I can visit for a while."

Luther eased out the door. Buckie was beaming and said, "I'm so happy 'cause I may get my second wish, Caleb...I reckon I won't get my third wish...I mean *prayer*. I've been praying hard every time I think about it. But sometimes my thinking don't come so good no more. I reckon it's that fever that's making me feel kinda strange. Sometimes I don't see so good neither. You was a blur when you walked in, and I thought I was still dreamin'. Don't let them give me no sleeping medicine this morning. I want to stay awake and talk to you and Pop before he has to go back home."

"I won't let them give you a shot unless you get to hurting and ask for one."

"Pop and me listened to the game. I reckon Will James is pert near as good as you, Caleb. He's the only boy on the program that didn't come to see me. I'd like to see him 'cause Mr. Wally said he looks like a giant amongst boys when he's on the field. Is he nice like you?"

"I think so," Caleb nodded. "He's nice to me, and he helped me get a chance to play football. He's my best friend except for you."

"I been thinking. I been praying, too. I been asking God to let me see my momma when we get to heaven. That ain't wrong is it?"

"No. It's never wrong to pour out you heart to the Lord. It pleases him. I pray that God will let me see my father when I get to Heaven and I believe with all my heart that He's going to answer my prayer. The Bible says that God loves it when we pray, and the prayers of a good man accomplishes much."

"Miss Angelle is going to be sad when I'm gone. She loves me. I wish my mother loved me like Miss Angelle."

"I'm sure she loved you, and I'll pray that you see her in Heaven. If your mother knew you were sick, I believe with all my heart that she'd be here with you."

"You really mean that?"

"With all my heart I believe that." A big smile broke across Buckie's face.

"It don't really matter if I don't see her now, if I can be with her in Heaven."

"Now, you're talking like the bright young man that I knew you were. Life is so short, and eternity is so long, there's no way to compare a few years of happiness, or pain in your case, to an eternity of bliss in Heaven."

"You always know what to say to make me happy," and he reached out and touched Caleb's face. "We're going to be together in heaven, ain't we?"

"For eternity, and that's a promise I'm making you, and I don't break my promises."

Buckie took a couple of deep breaths as if to relax and smiled at Caleb saying, "Did Curley ever talk to you?"

"I can't say I ever heard him speak out loud, but I always felt that he was more than a stuffed animal made of cotton and cloth."

"Sometimes, late at night, I almost think I can hear him talking to me."

"What does he say to you?"

"I ain't sure if it's him talking or just a dream, but he says if I go away, he wants to live with Angelle. He says he loves Angelle, too. Don't you tell nobody I said that 'cause they might think I'm crazy. You don't think I'm crazy, do you? When I wake up in the morning I know what I heard."

"You're not crazy. When I was young like you, I often walked and talked with my father as I slept. Believe it or not, I had Curley in my arms at those times. That just shows that we're really like brothers. I guess that's why I love you so much. Providence brought us together, little brother, and whether we are together or apart, we'll always be a part of each other." They talked until Luther returned and began bombarding Caleb with questions about the game. After they talked football for a while, Caleb had to go to work.

❦

Abe and Caleb expected and prepared for a large crowd. The dining hall was filled to capacity by twelve-thirty. They had to hustle to keep up with the overflow. Caleb's work was hindered because all the guests and members wanted to talk about the two unbelievable games that week. By two o'clock, the only members remaining in the dining hall were Doc and Edith. They had arrived late because Doc had an emergency at the hospital.

Doc told Abe to begin cleaning up and not to worry about disturbing them. They were busy sweeping and moping when the phone rang. Abe answered it and motioned for Doc.

"Gracious!" Edith cried out, scowling. "There are a dozen doctors at the hospital, and you can't get an hour to eat lunch, even on Sunday!"

"It must be important, or they wouldn't have called me," Doc said, thinking of Buckie as he hurried to the phone. He held the receiver to his ear and responded, "Oh my Lord!" He listened intently, and then said, "I'm on my way. Start the I.V." He motioned for Edith to head for the door.

Edith grabbed her saucer with the lemon pie, saying, "I'll return the plate tomorrow, Abe."

"Come with me, Caleb!" Doc called out.

"But, I...yes, sir!" He handed his mop to Abe, shucked off his jacket, and said, "I'll come back and finish." Abe shook his head and motioned for him to go. The three rushed across the parking lot, jumped into Edith's Cadillac, and Doc sped away. "What's the matter?" Caleb asked nervously. "Is it Buckie?"

"It might be better if it was, with his pain and suffering. But no, it's our all-American...again. The state troopers just rushed him into the emergency room, unconscious. They picked him up in the ditch on the side of the road just across the state line, with blows to the head, cuts, and who knows what else. They said to hurry because it's critical. Looks like someone took a tire tool to his head."

"Oh, my Lord!" Caleb gasped, turning pale, then beginning to tremble. "He asked me to go with him, Doc, and I refused. This is all my fault."

"Hush!" Doc snapped. "Don't be ridiculous. You made a wise decision. You might be dead on the side of the road if you'd gone with him. That young man has a death wish. I fear he may get his wish this time."

As Doc flew by his house, he said, "I'll get someone to run you home, Edith, when we get to the hospital. Seconds might be the difference in life or death."

Doc flew through town, and to the hospital, skidding into his reserved parking place. They jumped out of the car and ran into the emergency room. The nurse pointed at the room where Will lay motionless and pale on the gurney. Bright blood stained his head, cheeks, and his filthy, torn shirt.

Caleb eased into the room and looked down at the gory bloody sight. He began to gag, grabbing his mouth with both hands, and ran across the emergency room to the restroom. He fell to his knees and threw up in the commode. After a few minutes, he stood, washed his face, and rushed back to the emergency room. Another resident physician had arrived. He and Doc were examining Will. "He has a concussion," Doc concluded, after having pried his eyelids open. He listened to his heart and checked his blood pressure. Doc cleaned the wound, bandaged his bleeding head tightly, and then called the orderly to roll him to x-ray.

Caleb stuck his head into the room as they wheeled Will across the hall to x-ray. He asked Doc nervously two or three times, "What do you think, is he going to be all right?"

Doc was standing there with his head down, staring blankly at the floor. Again Caleb asked, "What do you think, is he going to be all right?"

Anger at Will's persistent self-destructive nature had welled up inside Doc, and he responded harshly, "How the hell do I know? I'm not God!" Then quickly realizing what he had said, he looked up at the fear and pain in Caleb's eyes—eyes of a young man that he loved as a son. He was ashamed of his outburst. He walked over to Caleb and put his arm around him. In a calming voice, he said, "His vital signs are fair, but we have to wait and see if there has been any permanent brain damage or internal bleeding. The x-ray should tell us more."

Caleb broke down in Doc's arms and began to sob. "What's wrong with me," he said in a broken voice. "Everyone I love gets hurt or dies. I believe I'm a curse to those I love. I wish I'd never come here. I hate this place. I can't take it anymore. I'm going home."

Doc held him tightly, saying, "Oh, no, no, no, son. You don't hate this place. You hate pain and suffering. You can't run from it…it's everywhere. I deal with life and death every day, and I know how you feel. Sometimes I want to grab Edith and run to a deserted island and forget that they're any other people in the world. But that's not God's plan for my life. That's not God's plan for your life either. I know this is hard for you to understand, but as I looked back at Emil's situation, I realized that as terrible as it seemed at the time, it was a blessing that he was hurt. He's where he needs to be, with his mother in the security of his home. He would never have survived here. Remember this, son: what Chris Black meant for evil, God used for good. 'His eyes are on the sparrow,' son, and He cares for you and sent you here for a purpose.

"Now, you go sit down. Better yet, go talk a walk outside and try to relax. Will is strong, and I think he'll make it. The only complication that I can foresee would be if a clot has formed in his brain. We'll cross that bridge if and when we have to." Doc walked out of the small room and over to Edith. He told her, "When you get home, call Coach Shook and tell him he needs to come. Tell him to get in touch with Will's father because he needs to come immediately." Doc looked at Caleb and said, "Better yet, why don't you take the car, and run Edith home? When you return, we'll know more about Will's condition."

As they drove, Edith stroked Caleb's hair as she said, "He's in good hands, son. You need to relax and pray for the best."

"I've been doing that. I've been doing that ever since I met him. I don't think it's helped him at all."

"You don't realize what you've done here. You've been sowing seeds of kindness and humility ever since you arrived. You're so much like June. That's why James loves you so dearly. I suspect that's why Will has befriended you. He sees your kind heart and deep compassion. He wants to be like you, but he hasn't been able to scale off that hardness and rebellion that consumes him. Just keep trying. Never give up on him. You may be the instrument the Lord uses to change his heart. Just don't give up."

"But what if he dies? I'm so scared."

"He'll be at the mercy of the Lord," Edith whispered.

"Yes, ma'am, I know that, and it scares me even worse."

Caleb let Mrs. Edith out at her house and jumped into Doc's Plymouth and rushed back to the hospital and ran back inside. Doc was standing over Will, checking his vital signs again. "Is his skull busted?" Caleb asked.

"I'm afraid so, and there seems to be swelling of the brain, not to mention a few broken ribs."

"When will he come to?" Caleb asked.

"It's not when, son, it's *if* he comes to. Hopefully, when he sobers up. He has a blood alcohol content that would kill a small elephant."

Caleb walked around Doc, bent over, and whispered in Will's ear. "Can you hear me, Will? Wake up 'cause…you're scaring me."

Will's bloodshot eyes began to open slowly, and he tried to focus.

"Look, Doc! He's trying to open his eyes. It's me, Will! Talk to me."

Will tried to speak, but he was only able to babble. After a few moans, he eased back into a deep unconsciousness. Doc pushed Caleb aside, bent over, and looked into his eyes with a small flashlight. Doc grabbed his handkerchief and put it to his nose. "Gracious," he gasped, "his breath reeks of rotten spirits. He has a severe concussion, but the fact that he opened his eyes and tried to speak is encouraging."

Doc called for a local anesthetic, a suture kit, a razor, and scissors. "I have to stop this bleeding. You hold his head steady while I do a little knitting."

"I'll try," Caleb said reluctantly. "You know blood makes me kinda woozy."

"Grow up!" Doc barked.

Caleb nodded nervously and whispered in Will's ear. "You have to behave, buddy. Now, promise me you won't hit me or Doc when he starts sewing you up."

"Hold his head steady!" Doc ordered. Caleb put a vice grip on Will's head. "Not that tight, son, I don't want you to strangle him. I'd like to reserve that honor for myself." Caleb eased off slightly, and Doc stuck the syringe into Will's scalp. He began to shoot the anesthetic into his scalp. Will never flinched from his drunken slumber. Doc took the scissors and cut the hair around the lacerations and shaved the area close to the wound. He quickly began to do his stitching. In minutes, he had sutured the three huge lacerations on Will's head. After the ordeal ended, Caleb and Doc looked at Will's head, then at each other. Both grinned because his head looked like the game rooster that hadn't survived the fight. "I hope he doesn't have a date for the homecoming ball," Doc quipped.

Doc walked over to the nurse's station and instructed the attendant to have Will admitted and to call a private duty nurse for him. Doc wrote the admitting orders.

"I'm going to stay with him tonight," Caleb said.

"You have school tomorrow," Doc said. "I want you to get your rest. I won't hear of it."

"Yes, sir."

Coach Shook came running into the emergency room as they were rolling Will to the elevator. "Was he in a wreck?" Coach Shook shouted.

"It might have been better if he had," Doc retorted. "He was dumped on the side of the road. It appears that he was beaten with some kind of blunt metal instrument. Possibly a piece of pipe or tire tool from the appearance of the lacerations and contusions."

"Is he going to be all right?" Coach Shook asked.

"Possibly, if the edema resolves." Coach Shook didn't have a clue what Doc had said and gave him a befuddled look.

"He has swelling of the brain, and it has to go away," Doc clarified.

"What!" Coach Shook blurted. "It's that serious?"

"Serious!" Doc snapped. "An ordinary man would be dead after the beating he took."

"What do you know about this, Caleb?" Coach Shook asked, with a cool stare.

"He asked me to go to Memphis to celebrate with him last night, but I told him I had to work. That's all I know."

Coach Shook lowered his head, shaking it slowly. "What's to become of him, Doc? Such ability, such talent, such intellect... and look at him now. If this doesn't kill him, something else will. I've never known such a self-destructive person as him...Did anyone call Bill?"

"I told Edith to tell you to call him."

"I believe she did tell me, but I was so shaken, I just ran out the door. I'll call him now. What should I tell him?"

"Tell him the truth. Tell him I think his chances are fair, but he's not out of the woods yet."

"He's going to ask about football, Doc. You know that. What should I say?"

"Tell him to go to hell! No. That was foolish. Forgive me. Tell him we don't know yet. We're concerned only with his recovery. I'll have a specialist here in the morning. He'll be able to shed more light on Will's condition and the prognosis."

They followed Will to a room on the second floor. The nurses rolled him into the room two doors away from Buckie's room. The two nurses eased Will onto the bed. He was snoring lightly as they covered him. Caleb hadn't noticed if Angelle was at the nurses' station as they passed. For the first time since he met her she had not crossed his mind. Seconds later, she came rushing into the room.

"Let's go outside and talk," Doc said, gesturing to Coach Shook. Doc gave Angelle a kiss on the cheek as they passed. He and Coach Shook walked outside and closed the door. "I'm not a lecherous old man," Doc said, grinning, "although she could turn many a man's head. I know she has Caleb's head spinning. She's one of my special Marston Foundation Scholarship recipients. She brilliant. A perfect four point O GPA and works like a slave here every day."

"Good Lord, she's gorgeous," Coach Shook said. "At least something's beautiful in the world today."

"In her case, all things are not as they seem," Doc said. "As beautiful as she is, there is a darkness and pain inside that beautiful creature that I pray time will heal. Now, about Will, he could be out weeks, or more likely, for the season. It's impossible to diagnose the severity of this kind of injury immediately. The specialist will be able to tell us more tomorrow. Additionally, he has some cracked ribs, and that alone will keep him out of contact for at least a month."

"You might not believe me, but my only concern is for his life," Coach Shook said. "After all, we no longer have the longest losing streak in the nation," and he managed a smile.

"I realize this is a crushing blow to you and the team, but there'll be brighter days. Prayerfully, if Will recovers, this might be his salvation." Doc put his arm around Coach Shook and said, "Everyone is calling you a genius, after that victory."

Coach Shook laughed, shrugged, and said, "I need to set the record straight on that matter, too. I want to tell you what a genius I am." He continued, "Last Sunday night, we were working on the game plan for Tulane when this silly, young country boy from Choctaw County walked into my office well after midnight. He apologized for interrupting and said timidly, "Coach, I think I can tell you how to win a ballgame." We humored him, but to make a long story short, he said, 'Will needs to be playing middle linebacker, and he could really help you on short yardage plays and goal line offense, running or blocking.' We thanked him and had a good laugh when he left. Then the lights came on. The boy had a brilliant idea. You saw the results. It was his brainchild, and I got all the credit. I did try to give him credit, but he wouldn't let me. That's the kind of kid he is."

"You leave it that way," Doc said. "No matter who suggested it, it was ultimately your decision, and it was monumental."

"The irony of the situation is that I actually wanted to try Will at linebacker last year. But I was a coward and didn't want to fight with his father. I thought he might make him transfer. I never told a soul that before, not even my wife. What does that make me, Doc?"

"It makes you a human being," Doc responded. "No more, no less. We all do what we have to do to survive in this life. There's no shame in that. It's just the way life is."

―⁂―

"What happened to Will?" Angelle asked Caleb. "I just arrived, and they told me that he'd been admitted."

"I don't know," Caleb said. "It looks like someone tried to beat him to death. Nobody knows what happened."

Angelle put her hand to Caleb's cheek and whispered, "Are you all right?" Caleb shrugged, and then nodded.

"I have to get to work," Angelle said, "but I'll check on you…I mean Will, regularly."

―⁂―

Doc made afternoon rounds in the hospital, and Caleb sat and watched Will sleep.

The private nurse arrived at 6:00 p.m., and Caleb decided to get out and stretch his legs. He walked down to the main lobby and put a nickel in the soft drink machine. After drinking the soft drink, he put the empty bottle in the rack and walked slowly up to the second floor. Angelle was walking out of Buckie's room, and she motioned for him. Caleb rushed over. She whispered, "Luther had to go try to catch a ride home, and Buckie isn't feeling well. He's been asking about you."

"I'll go see him," Caleb said and eased into his room. Buckie was rocking back and forth, holding his stomach, obviously in severe pain. Caleb kissed and hugged him gently. "You're not feeling well, are you, little brother?"

Buckie shook his head. "I'm kinda feelin' sick. I feel like I might throw up."

"I'll get the pan," Caleb said. "If you need to throw up, I'll hold it for you." Later the nausea passed somewhat, and Buckie began to feel a little better. Buckie said, "I had a dream, Caleb. I dreamed my mother walked through that door. She said, 'I love you, Buckie,' but I couldn't make out her face. It was like she was in the shadows, kinda like late at night when the lights are all dim. Or when someone is standing outside the window at night and you can't make out their face. I don't know what my mother looks like, but I know it was her. I just know it was her. Poppa had to go make some hauls 'cause he promised a man he'd do it, but he's coming back Wednesday night. He said he ain't leavin' no more when he comes back. He said he'll sleep on that floor, 'cause he ain't leavin' no more."

"And he won't either," Caleb assured. "I'd have been here earlier, but Will got hurt pretty bad. He's in the room two doors down. Now, I have my best two buddies close together up here, and I'm going to spend as much time as possible visiting both of you."

"He's gonna be all right, ain't he?" Caleb smiled and nodded. "You're sayin' Will James is just down the hall from me?" Buckie said, becoming excited. "I may get to meet him before he leaves.

Did you ask Doc if I can go to the game Thursday?" Buckie questioned, getting more excited, with a slight tremor in his voice.

"No. I have to wait until the right time. I have to catch him in a good mood. You know how Doc is. Some days he seems less stressed out than others."

"He's always nice to me," Buckie said.

Caleb smiled and said, "He's always nice to me, too." Caleb stayed until almost midnight, shuffling back and forth between the two rooms. Will had not awakened when Caleb finally walked across the campus to the dorm.

―・)|(・―

The news about Will's injury had reached the dorm, and the team was milling around in the halls mumbling and dejected when Caleb returned. He spent the next hour telling everyone about Will's situation. Caleb heard one of the defensive tackles say, "We might as well forfeit the rest of the games and wait until next year, 'cause we ain't shit without Will."

Everything said was negative. Finally, Caleb had heard enough. He called everyone together. "Team," he began, "Will is a great football player, and we're going to miss him next Saturday. But Will is not the team. All of you make the team. Will might be back in a few weeks, nobody knows for sure. If there is anyway under heaven for him to come back, I have every confidence he'll be back. But we all have a responsibility to our team, parents, school, coaches, and fans to go out and play harder than we've ever played. If we lose, it's providence. But our greatest responsibility is to ourselves to be the best that we can be. You became a team the last couple of weeks, and we're going to be a team when we finish this season, with or without Will. Now, get your heads up and be proud of what you've accomplished so far. Let's be better than anyone thinks we can be."

"Yeah!" John David yelled. "What about it, seniors? What about it, team? Are we going to bury our heads in the sand or come out fighting like men?"

The team all yelled, "Yeah! We're going to act like men and fight like men. One- hundred percent for sixty minutes! Teamwork!"

―✶―

Earlier that afternoon, Coach Shook had walked into his office with a hangdog look and said, "I have bad news, men. Will was almost beaten to death last night. He has broken ribs and serious complications with brain swelling. Doc thinks he'll be all right eventually, but it's for sure he's out for a long time, probably the rest of the season."

"Well that's a fine, how-do-you-do!" Stan said, kicking at the wall.

"I can be a little more explicit," Ollie added.

"Winning was too easy with Will," Billy Ray said facetiously, shaking his head. "I suppose we'll have to earn our keep now."

Ollie joined in again and said, "The old expression 'one monkey don't stop no show' surely doesn't apply to us, but I've learned one thing in my years of coaching. You can be sure that nothing is for sure." He looked despairingly at Coach Shook and said, "Coach, we all knew this could happen, especially with Will. I've heard you say we'll be very fortunate if we don't have to attend his funeral before graduation. We have a big game in six days, and I'm ready to go to work." Everyone chimed in and said likewise.

Around one a.m. William James ran up the stairs and over to the nurses' station. "Where's my son?" he bellowed to the night duty nurse.

"And who is your son?" the nurse asked, somewhat irritated by his demeanor.

"Will James. I want you to get Dr. Marston on the phone immediately."

"He's in room two-ten right over there." And she pointed. "I don't think it's a good idea to call Dr. Marston at this hour. He didn't leave the hospital until after midnight, and he's not on call tonight."

"Just do it," he demanded, pounding the desk with his fist and then rushing to the room. The private duty nurse was sitting in the chair nodding when he stormed in and rushed to the bed. She sat upright quickly, somewhat startled.

"Who are you?" Mr. James demanded, as he leaned forward to get a closer look at Will, "And how is my son?"

"I'm Miss Ellis, his private nurse, and he's resting comfortably. Who are you, sir?"

"Doesn't anybody know anything in this place? I'm his father, of course."

"I check his blood pressure and temperature every thirty minutes," Miss Ellis said. "He has a slight fever, but his blood pressure is good and stable."

The night duty nurse tapped on the door and stuck her head inside, saying, "Doctor Marston is on the phone."

Mr. James rushed out and grabbed the phone, "What's the situation with Will, Doc? This is Bill James. I'm at the hospital."

"Bill, your son almost died this morning. A lesser man would have. He was beaten within an inch of his life. No one knows who did it. He was found dumped on the side of the road just inside the Mississippi state line. He has a fractured skull, swelling of the brain, severe lacerations of his head, multiple bruises on his body, and some broken ribs. He was totally inebriated when they brought him in. He opened his eyes and babbled a few times, then fell asleep. So we know he still has some control of his speech. That's a good sign. I've called Cyrus Allbriton, a renowned neurologist and brain surgeon from Nashville. He'll arrive here in a few hours and make a professional diagnosis. That's about all I can tell you at this time."

"Don't you think you or another doctor should be by his side until Dr. Allbriton arrives?"

"I do not," Doc said firmly. "If he has a clot, God forbid, and it moves, he could die in his sleep. I could have the best team of neurosurgeons in the nation standing by his side, and they could do nothing. Now, I've prayed that won't happen. I suggest that you be patient and wait for the specialist to arrive. It might be helpful to pray."

"That's a hell of an attitude for a physician to have. You scare the hell out of me with your diagnosis, then tell me to pray. That's not some redneck hillbilly lying there. He's my son, an all-American. I demand some action around here, and I want it now. I want to be assured that my son will be all right."

"The only one that could assure you of that hasn't spoken verbally in over two thousand years. I do think Will is strong enough to whip this, but to guarantee you that a clot hasn't formed and he's out of danger would be a guess at best and totally uncorroborated. You need to calm down and try to relax for a few hours until Dr. Allbriton arrives, and we can get a professional and reliable diagnosis."

There was a long pause, then Mr. James' voice softened, and he said, "I suppose you're right. You know your profession better than I. Sorry that I snapped at you. I know you're doing all that's humanly possible for my son."

"That's all right. I'm sure I might have reacted the same way if my son was in his condition."

Caleb prayed until he fell asleep, then slept restlessly a few hours. At daybreak, he jumped out of bed, ran to the hospital and up the stairs. In front of Will's room, Doc, Mr. James, and the specialist were having a conference. Caleb eased over close enough to hear their conversation. Dr. Allbriton explained, "If the swelling persists, we'll have to relieve the pressure."

"What does that mean?" William James asked. "Are you saying you might have to cut his skull open?"

"I suppose you could say that," Dr. Allbriton nodded.

"What about football?" William asked grimly. "Does that mean his football is over this year?"

Dr. Allbriton lowered his head slightly, raised his brows, glanced at Doc, and said in a tone often used with a small child. "Mr. James, you don't comprehend the gravity of his condition. Football should be the least of your concerns at present. It doesn't appear that he has permanent brain damage, although I do not know why. I've never observed such trauma to the brain where the victim lived."

A strange look came across Mr. James's face, and he looked away amiss, shaking his head and said, "Where did I go wrong, Doc? I thought I raised him...I thought I did what was best for him. Where does all his rebellion come from? I've always feared that someday it might kill him."

"I'll wait until noon, then we'll x-ray again and make our decision," Dr. Allbriton said.

Caleb eased over by Doc and whispered, "May I go in, Doc?" Doc nodded. Caleb eased in. A different nurse was sitting by Will's bed. "How is he?" Caleb asked.

"I just arrived, but he appears to be resting comfortably." They shook hands and introduced themselves. Caleb stood by the bed for a long while.

Around nine o'clock, Will opened his eyes and looked up at Caleb. He raised his long arms to stretch and let out a painful groan.

"Easy, Will, don't move. I'll call Doc." Caleb ran out to the nurses' station and said, "He's come to, nurse. I know Doc will want to know." Mr. James had stretched out on a couch in the waiting room to catch a nap. The nurse rushed over to the room to tell him that Will had awakened. When Caleb ran back to the room, Will was trying to sit up. The nurse was having difficulty restraining him. "Lie down, Will!" Caleb yelled as he entered the room. "You have a bad concussion, and you have to lie still."

Will moaned and grabbed his head, saying, "Where am I?"

"You don't remember anything?" Caleb asked.

Mr. James rushed in, followed by Doc and Dr. Allbriton.

"I don't remember diddley-squat," Will said. He gave a big moan and grabbed his side, then let out a deeper moan, grabbing his head.

"Get him something strong for pain," Dr. Allbriton instructed the nurse.

Will looked strange. His eyes seemed to cross and moved from person to person.

"Do you know who I am?" Caleb asked.

Will studied him a moment, then mumbled, "My mind is cloudy, and my head is splitting." Then his eyes closed slowly.

"That's it," Dr. Allbriton said. "Get him to x-ray, and let's make our decision. I don't like what I saw and heard."

An hour later, Will was in surgery. He stayed in recovery another two hours. Caleb and Mr. James were frantic to receive information by then. Finally, the team of doctors walked out. Dr. Allbriton said, "We had no complications. I feel sure the pressure has been relieved. We'll give him something to hopefully dissolve any clot that might be present. He'll need to lie quietly for a few days. If there are any clots, we pray they will dissolve. Do you have any questions?"

"That's it, Doctor? We still don't know any more now than we did this morning," Bill James exclaimed.

"Mr. James," Dr. Allbriton replied, "the fact that your son is alive and breathing today is a miracle in itself. It's the best news you could have. Every minute that passes is critical to his well-being. I've done all that's humanly possible at this time. I leave Will in capable hands." He looked at Doc, commenting, "You can reach me any hour of the day or night if you need to consult. Now, I have to rush back to Nashville. I have a brain tumor waiting to be removed. It was scheduled for early this morning."

"I'm indebted to you, Dr. Allbriton," Doc said.

"Likewise," Mr. James said, extending his hand.

Dr. Allbriton left the hospital. Mr. James asked, "Where is Will's car?"

"The police didn't know," Doc responded.

"I'm going to Memphis and meet with the Chief of Police and the sheriff. We're going to find the car, and someone is going to pay dearly for this," Mr. James scowled.

"I called our local sheriff last night. He's already contacted the sheriff and Chief of Police in Memphis, and they are already on the case. The car will turn up. Hopefully, they'll have the thugs behind bars before the day's over," Doc said.

"If they drag their feet, I'll hire a dozen of the best private investigators in Tennessee. Those low-life bastards will curse the day they were born," Mr. James declared.

"You're welcome to stay at my home as long as you wish," Doc said.

"No. I'll get a room at the hotel. I have business to take care of on the phone. That's very thoughtful of you to offer. I don't know how to tell Elizabeth. She'll go to pieces. She doesn't fly, and I don't have time to go and drive her here."

"You don't have a close friend in Birmingham that might drive her here?" Doc asked.

"Close friend," Mr. James responded curtly. "I don't have time for close friends. I'm too busy for that luxury. I have business associates, none of which would I consider close friends. I suppose I can have Clovis drive to Birmingham and bring her here. She'll die if she reads the paper before someone can put her mind at ease. May I use the phone?" Doc nodded. Mr. James called his chauffer in Nashville and instructed him to go to Birmingham and drive Elizabeth to Marston. He cautioned him about discussing Will's condition with her. He turned to Doc and said, "She should arrive here by nine p.m. I'll make reservations at the hotel, then call her and tell her that Clovis will be coming to get her for a visit with Will. She'll be thrilled."

They rolled Will out of recovery and back up to the room. Caleb had stood at a distance and listened to their conversation. He thought, *Thank you Lord for my mother and father, and Uncle Houston. I could tell Mr. James a few things about being a parent and why Will acts like he does—but it's not my place.*

Doc, Mr. James, and Caleb walked back up to Will's room. Caleb looked at his watch. "Oh, Doc," he explained, "I missed lunch, and Abe is going to choke me."

"Son," Doc said, "this is Monday. We're not open today." Caleb grinned sheepishly. The nurses carefully eased Will onto the bed. Doc gave the private nurse instructions, and then he and Caleb walked outside.

"I think his odds just got better for a full recovery," Doc said. "The Lord is merciful. I do believe He watches over drunks and fools. It's for sure he watched over both today."

"I think He has great plans for Will," Caleb said, "because He wouldn't have given him so much intelligence and ability if he hadn't."

"I wish I shared your optimism," Doc said.

"This may not be the right time to ask you this Doc, but, Buckie and Mr. Luther aren't going to give me any peace until I do, so here goes." Doc turned and looked curiously at Caleb. "Buckie made a few last wishes a few weeks ago."

"What do you mean, *last wishes?*"

"Buckie told me and Mr. Luther that he knew he was going to die soon, and he had made three wishes. Actually he prayed for the three wishes. The first was that he would meet me, and you made that one come true. The second was that he could see me play a football game. The third and the most important, as he put it, was that he could see his mother before he dies. We both know that the third wish isn't going to come true. Luther said you had done so much for him and his boy that he was ashamed to ask you for the second one, so he asked me to ask it for him."

"That would be insane of me," Doc scowled. "Luther knows his condition. I tried to conceal the truth from the child, but he's obviously more discerning than I realized."

"Doc, It wasn't my idea. He asked me to talk to you about Buckie's wish."

"Caleb!" Doc snapped. "I can't believe either of you would ask if that's possible. I never know from one hour to the next if that child will be alive. Something greater than me has kept him alive these last few months. He has defied medical science. He should be in glory singing with the angels now." Doc held his palms out and said, "He would never survive a trip to the game and all the excitement there. He can't sit alone anymore. No…absolutely not! I can't believe Luther would even consider it."

"I reckon he figured Buckie has missed out on so much of the joy in life that if it was that important to him, it should be his decision, even if it—"

"No! No! You're not going to dump this on me. You're asking me to play God and set the time for this child to leave this world. I'm in the business of healing, not killing. I'm shocked that you'd even ask."

"Doc, it's not my request, it's Buckie's request."

Doc stood there a moment, gazing at nothing. "I'll discuss it with Luther and Buckie when Luther returns, but I'm totally against it."

"Luther's coming back Wednesday afternoon," Caleb said, "and he said he won't be leaving again until…"

"Can you handle this?" Doc said. "Suppose this happens. No, it's more than a supposition. You make a big run and score a touchdown. The crowd goes wild, and they will. Buckie gets so excited that his body can't take it, and he breathes his last. You jog off the field to give him a hug, and he just lays there lifeless. Would you feel somewhat responsible?"

"I don't know how I'd feel, Doc. I know I'd be heartsick. I'm sorry I asked. Buckie has to understand why you won't allow him go. It's for his own good."

"Oh, don't hand me that crap!" Doc barked. "You knew I couldn't refuse a dying boy's last request. You knew that before you asked me."

"You're wrong, Doc. I was sure you wouldn't let him go. I might not have asked if I had known that you might."

"Son, have you ever heard the expression 'quality of life'?" Caleb shook his head. "It means the condition in which we are living at present. Buckie has no quality of life. But I don't want to play God either. I'll do everything possible to keep him alive. I do believe, as the Bible clearly states, there is a time to be born and a time to die, and God has numbered our days. If this ballgame is that important to that blessed child and his father agrees, it might give him just a little quality of life before he meets his maker, regardless of the outcome. You go tell our boy his second wish has been granted. There should be no guilt on your part, regardless of the outcome. I'll pray that the Lord'll watch over him Thursday night so there will be no guilt on anyone's part."

"Luther may change his mind," Caleb said as fear and doubt crept into his mind. "I hope he does, because I don't think I can take it if he dies that way."

"As you said, it's not your request. You're simply the messenger." Doc put his arm around Caleb and said, "Son, there is joy and hope at birth, and there is sorrow and regret at death. However, when someone is as ill as Buckie, with no hope of recovery, and we are assured by the scripture and his confession of faith that he will be with the Lord in a place more glorious than the mind can conceive, we can experience both hope and joy commingled with our sorrows and regrets. 'Eyes have not seen, nor ears heard, or the mind conceived all the wonderful things that God has in store for those who love him.' Those Biblical words give hope and solace to the sick and weary who are in Christ."

"You sound like my preacher. I'm sad for Buckie, but I know he'll be in a better place when his time comes."

"Hold on to that thought," Doc said, "because his time is near. I need to get to the clinic. There won't be standing room by now."

"Doc, you have a telephone call," Gladys said.

Doc took the call and listened intently a few minutes then said, "Good. That's good news, sheriff. I'll tell Mr. James."

Caleb walked up beside Doc as he hung up the receiver. "The police found Will's car outside a honky-tonk just across the state line. The owner of the place said Will had a heated argument with a local they call Tex. Tex had four or five thugs with him. They were all drunk. An argument ensued about a car race that they had a few weeks earlier. Tex and his friends left the bar a few minutes before Will. They must have waited outside for Will and then bushwhacked him. The sheriff's rounding up the thugs, and he'll try to get some evidence or a confession."

"I know Tex," Caleb said. "Will humiliated him after a car race a few weeks ago, then tried to take his girlfriend, and he burned the money Tex had lost in the race. Tex pulled a gun on Will, but Will called his bluff. As we drove away, Tex screamed, 'This ain't over. You're going to get yours.'"

"Let's hope you don't have to testify to that," Doc said.

Doc went to his office, and Caleb walked back to Buckie's room. Buckie was dozing, but he awoke when Caleb walked in. "Did you talk to Doc yet?" he asked excitedly.

"Doc said it's up to you and Mr. Luther." Buckie was so thrilled his body went into tremors. Caleb put his arms around him holding him snugly and said, "Breathe slowly and deeply, and calm down." Buckie hugged Caleb and began to breathe easier.

After he calmed, Caleb said, "You have to try to eat as much as you can for the next few days. You need to be strong to go the game. I want you to be able to yell 'Go Cats' when the team runs onto the field."

"I will." Buckie nodded. "I will. I might be able to eat a little of those mashed potatoes and beans over there if you'll get 'um." Caleb held the tray and spoonfed Buckie a few bites, but he became nauseous. "That's enough," Caleb said.

A few minutes later, Buckie said, "Give me a drink of that orange juice. Angelle said it'll make me strong." Caleb held the glass while Buckie took a few sips from the straw.

"You're going to be stronger by Thursday if you keep this up," Caleb encouraged.

"God answered my second prayer," Buckie said. "Do you think He'll answer my last prayer?"

"I don't know, Buckie. We can't always know God's will. But I'll keep praying, and you do the same. Who knows, she may walk through that door tomorrow. 'The prayer of a righteous man availeth much.'"

"You already said that. What does it mean?"

"It means that God listens to those who love him and try to live right, and He answers prayer. But sometimes His answer is not the one we want."

"I ain't always been good, Caleb. I got in a fight one time at school, and I really wanted to hurt that boy."

"Did you hurt him?"

"Heck no! He whipped my butt, but I bit a plug out of his arm before the teacher got him off me."

"Why did you fight him, Buckie?"

Buckie lowered his head a few seconds before responding. "He said my poppa weren't nothing but dumb white trash, and my momma weren't nothing but the town whore."

"Did you understand what he was saying?" Buckie lowered his head and nodded. "You knew that wasn't true, didn't you?"

"Pops said it weren't true, and I reckon he wouldn't lie to me."

"You better believe him because I know your father. I know he would never lie to you. I have to leave for practice now, but I'll be back as soon as it is over. You try to rest and get stronger. I'm going to try my best to make a touchdown for you Thursday night. But no more throwing the ball into the stands. If I do, they'll kick me out of the game."

Buckie forced a smile and said, "I'm sorry for getting you in trouble."

Caleb returned his smile. "I'd do it again for you if you asked."

CHAPTER TWELVE

Caleb rushed across the campus to the dressing room. It was like a wake in the room as the team gathered to watch the game film. The coaching staff walked out of Coach Shook's office.

Coach Shook called out: "Men, gather around me." After they were seated and quiet and he had their full attention, he began to speak, "I know you've all heard that Will was seriously injured yesterday. Actually, it's only by God's grace that he's still alive. A lesser man would have died from the beating he took. Am I disappointed? You cannot imagine how the coaching staff and I feel. But our disappointment is not for us…it's for Will and you. I know he's a ruffian and wild as a March hare sometimes. But I also know how much he loves this silly game that we play. Doc thinks his season is over, but your season isn't over. What you've accomplished the last few weeks has made everyone in this state proud of you. You should be proud of yourselves. We were very fortunate to have a player that most consider the best in the nation. But he's no longer on the team.

"Now we can do one of two things. We can hang our heads and give up. We can think that there's no use in trying because we're just going to keep losing. We can expect to be humiliated for the rest of the season. Or we can reach down inside ourselves and grasp that little extra, that little part of our heart and soul that we always hold in reserve. That little bit of extra will make up for not having that all-American on the field with us. I'll never lie to you. The remaining teams on our schedule will be bigger, faster, and, in most cases, stronger than us. The truth is that there is something intangible in everyone that can't be measured. It's called heart. I've seen it in the way you've played the last few games. If you are willing to play with your heart, the size and speed and strength of the opponent won't matter. We will be able to compete with any team on our schedule. Win or lose, we will be able to walk off the field at the end of the game and feel that same pride we've experienced the last few weeks.

"I want to tell you a true story. The moral is quite evident. It applies to each one of you. When I was fifteen and my brother, Clovis, was thirteen, we were walking home from school one brisk October day. I had just finished football practice and didn't have a care in the world. Suddenly we saw our mother running down the little lane that led to our house, screaming and stumbling toward us. 'The house is on fire,' she screamed, 'and the chest is upstairs.' That chest held everything valuable and precious to Mother and our family.

"We ran like the wind to the house. By then, it was totally engulfed in flames. We didn't slow down. We just ran up the flight of stairs leading to the attic. The flames were leaping up around us, singeing our clothes and hair. We grabbed the huge chest by the end straps and pulled it down the flight of stairs and managed to get the trunk out into the yard to safety. The house collapsed behind us as soon as we left the porch.

"Now our heroic feat, or ignorance, is not the moral of the story. My father was in town buying livestock feed when it happened. When he got home, we all sat and cried with mother as we watched the remains of the house smolder until dark. Then we went to my grandmother's house. The next day my father hitched up the wagon to move the chest to her house. He and our neighbor, a strong farmer like my father, grabbed the chest and tried to pick it up. They couldn't budge it. It took four big men to pick it up and put it into the wagon bed. Need I say more, team?

"We all have that extra in our hearts, but it's in reserve. We have to want to use it more than we value our lives. That's the kind of Herculean effort it's going to take out of every one of you if we are going to represent this school with pride and honor. Are you willing?"

The team screamed, "Yes, Coach!"

As the team watched the film, the coaches pointed out the changes that would need to be made to cover Will's absence. The changes in positions that were suggested seemed to be satisfactory to the team. The coaches were very pleased at their reception of the new responsibilities, and their willingness to step up to the plate in Will's absence.

After the practice was over, the team asked, "Should we go see Will?"

Caleb looked at Coach Shook. "He doesn't know anyone yet. I don't think he's allowed to have any visitors yet."

"Possibly tomorrow," Coach Shook said to the team. They walked out, somewhat optimistic about the future of the season.

Although Caleb was in a hurry to return to the hospital and check on Will's and Buckie's condition, he lagged behind everyone. When the room cleared and all the coaches had gone to Coach Shook's office, he eased back to the equipment room. Ira had already started washing the practice jerseys.

"What's on your mind, kid?" Ira asked. Caleb stood there, calf-eyed with a silly grin on his face, somewhat embarrassed about his request.

"I was wondering if...I mean would it be possible to—"

Ira smiled and said, "Just spit it out, Caleb."

"Could I borrow my orange jersey tonight? I'll bring it back tomorrow."

"You got a gal, huh," Ira said, "and you want to impress her? Absolutely not! Coach Shook would have my job if I let one of these game jerseys out."

"I don't have a girl," Caleb said, even more embarrassed now. "I wanted to show it to a dying boy in the hospital. I'm kind of his hero."

"You mean Buckie? I heard the coaches talking about him. Just really breaks your heart."

Caleb turned to walk away as Ira said, "Wait up." He went back into the equipment room and returned quickly. He tossed the jersey to Caleb. "Tuck it under your shirt," Ira said.

"I sure wish we had two of these," Caleb said. "I'd ask Coach Shook if I could buy one if we did."

"Actually, we do have two of them," Ira said. "After that performance you put on in the first game, Coach Shook told me to order you two sets of jerseys. He said the way you run he knew you'd probably get them ripped off before the season was over. What are you thinking, boy?"

"I'd like to have one of them altered and cut down to an extra small size. I think I'll go ask Coach Shook if I can buy this one."

"What if he says no? I have a better idea. Give me the jersey." Caleb handed Ira the jersey. He went back into the equipment room. Caleb wondered what he was doing. When he heard the jersey rip, he knew. Ten minutes later, Ira walked out of the equipment room and tossed the jersey to Caleb.

Caleb inspected it. The seams were straight and looked professionally sewn. "How did you do this?" Caleb asked in total amazement.

"Jack-of-all-trades," Ira said, smiling. "Now, tuck it under your shirt, and forget where it came from."

"But what if you get in trouble for this?"

Ira laughed as he said, "As the old saying goes, it's much easier to get forgiveness than permission."

"Thank you. Thank you. Thank you," Caleb said. Ira grinned and motioned for Caleb to go. He tucked the jersey under his belt, giving him the appearance of having a slight potbelly. He rushed by the Coach's office and out the door.

Caleb jogged across the campus to the hospital and up the stairs, giving Angelle a quick wave as he shot into Will's room. Mr. James was standing by Will's bed, the nurse by his side with a thermometer in her hand. "The fever seems to have broken," she said as she inspected it.

"Thank God," Mr. James said. "Elizabeth might have died if she thought he was in any more danger than he is." Turning toward the door, Mr. James said, "You're Caleb Morgan?"

"Yes sir, Mr. James. I room with Will, and he's my best friend."

"Some best friend you turned out to be if you let him go off alone and get in this condition. Why didn't you go with him or at least talk him out of it?"

"He asked me to go, but I had to work. I guess I'm not too good a friend. Has he spoken yet?"

"No. They're pumping that dope into him so he won't wake up and do something stupid. They're going to let him sleep tonight and ease him off of it tomorrow. We'll know more then."

"I'll stay with him if you'd like to go get some rest or sup—dinner."

"Young man, I have a private duty nurse here with him twenty-four hours a day. We're capable of taking care of him. We don't need your help…now! It's a little late for that."

"Yes, sir," Caleb said nervously as he backed out the door. *I suppose he has a right to be angry with me because we are supposed to be our brother's keeper. He did ask me to go with him,* Caleb thought. *Maybe this wouldn't have happened if I had gone with him. Doc was being kind when he said I did right by not going.* He began to mumble and felt a gentle tap on the shoulder. He jerked around. Angelle was looking at him very curiously.

"Why are you mumbling?" she asked. "Is something wrong?"

"It's more like, is anything right," Caleb said with a doleful look. "My best friend almost died because I wasn't there to help him. Plus, the most precious boy I've ever known is dying in there." He lowered his head with a subtle shake. Angelle placed her hand on his shoulder and started to embrace him. Caleb turned and looked into her sad eyes. She stepped back quickly.

Caleb reached under his shirt, pulled out the tiny jersey, and held it up for Angelle to see. They both smiled to fight back the tears. "I'd like to go in with you when you give it to him," she whispered in her soft, angelic voice.

"Let's go," Caleb whispered, and they eased down the hall. Caleb opened the door and peeped in. Buckie was half asleep with the football in one arm and Curley in the other. Caleb crept in with Angelle close behind. He put the jersey behind him and gave a fake cough. Buckie's eyes popped open and brightened at the sight of Caleb. Angelle looked over Caleb's shoulder and winked at Buckie. He blushed slightly.

"We brought you a present, Prince Charming," Caleb said. "We hope you like it."

"I don't want no present," Buckie said. "You ain't got no extra money to be spending on me. You done enough for me."

"Oh! Not quite," Caleb said with a bright smile. "Look what I have." And he jerked the jersey from behind him and held it up high.

Buckie's eyes almost popped out. He gasped. "It ain't really for me, is it ? Where did you get it? Can I put it on? It's beautiful!"

"Believe it or not, this is the very jersey that I wore in the last game," Caleb said.

"Ain't no way you could'a wore that jersey," Buckie questioned. "It's too small."

"Oh, yes, I did wear it. Ira did some alterations on it and cut it down to your size. It's beautiful, isn't it?"

"It's about the most beautiful thing I ever saw." And he began to weep.

"Now, now, no tears. This is my good fortune jersey. It's your good fortune jersey now."

"Help me put it on, Miss Angelle." He held up his arms. Angelle stripped off the nightshirt, exposing Buckie's chest. His ribs seemed to be bulging out of his side. The tumors were large, and the sight sent a piercing and nauseous pain through Caleb's stomach. He felt like throwing up. Angelle slid the jersey over Buckie's head and pulled it down. It was a perfect fit. He traced the numbers with his finger. "I wish I had a mirror," Buckie said. "I want to see what I look like in a real game jersey. Twenty-two, that's my favorite number."

"If you're going to be on the sidelines Thursday night, you have to look like you belong on the team. That's why I got it for you."

"What's today?" Buckie asked.

"Monday," Angelle replied.

Buckie held up his hand and counted the days on his fingers until Thursday. "It ain't but three days 'til Thursday. I don't think I can wait. I have to eat something," Buckie said.

Angelle laughed and looked at her watch. "Your dinner should be here any minute, sweetheart. I know Caleb will make sure you eat as much as you can. I have to get back to work, but I'll be back shortly."

After Angelle left the room, Buckie asked, "Why are you so good to me? Nobody but Poppa and Miss Angelle and Mrs. Gladys ever loved me like you. Oh, and Mrs. Mattie. She's like a momma to me."

"You're just easy to love. I don't know anyone who doesn't love you. Some people are easier to love than others." Mr. James popped into Caleb's mind. He thought, *Forgive me, Lord, because I have to work hard to love him.*

Buckie's meal was served, and Caleb fed Buckie all he could eat, which was barely enough to keep a mouse alive. "You're going to drink every drop of this milk before I leave, or,"—Caleb raised his muscular arm up, doubled up his fist, and said—"I going to put this hammer on you."

Buckie laughed and felt Caleb's arm. "You must be 'bout the strongest man in the world," he said.

"You ain't seen nothing yet," Caleb said, jokingly. "Wait until you get an eye full of Will James's arms and legs. They could hold up the bridge over the Mississippi River at Memphis, I imagine. He's just two doors down. When he gets to feeling better, I'm going to ask him to come by to see you. Now, he just might be the strongest man in the world."

"You really like him, don't you? You probably like him more'n me, huh?"

"I don't just like you and Will, I *love* both of you. There is no degree in love. I think I'd die for either of you." Caleb remembered dead man's curve and the ensuing blowout and realized that he almost did.

"You ain't like nobody I've ever known, Caleb. I reckon I love you as much as I love my poppa and my momma. I just wish I could tell her I love her, and it don't matter that she weren't cut out to be no momma. I don't want her to feel bad about leavin'."

Caleb took a deep breath and let it out slowly. He said, "You ain't like nobody I've ever known either. You are about as close to an angel as I'll ever see this side of heaven."

Around nine thirty, Caleb heard a commotion outside the door, and a lady began to wail in the hall. When Caleb stuck his head out the door to look, he knew it had to be Mrs. Elizabeth James. She was standing outside the door to Will's room with the nurse and Mr. James at her side, a handkerchief to her mouth. She was a petite lady in her middle forties with prematurely graying hair. Her dress was exquisitely tailored and obviously very expensive. She wore pearls, a gold bracelet, and a diamond ring so large it sparkled like the stars at midnight. They led her into the room, and she began to wail even louder. After a few minutes, the crying ceased.

At ten p.m., Gladys walked in with a syringe filled with happy medicine. She said, "Buckie needs his rest, Caleb. I'm giving him his sleeping medicine. He'll be asleep in seconds."

"Yes, ma'am. I'll see you tomorrow, pal." And he kissed Buckie.

"Brother," Buckie said.

"Brother," Caleb said, "but you know brothers can be best pals, too."

Caleb walked outside and down the hall to Will's room. He could hear Mrs. James sobbing while saying, "My baby. Oh God, help my baby."

Mr. James growled, "Hush, Elizabeth. Will's going to be fine. You need to get a grip on yourself. You're beginning to irritate me."

She continued to murmur, "My baby, oh my baby."

Caleb glanced at the nurse's station as he walked by. Angelle had apparently left for the night. He walked somberly down the stairs, remembering the things that Mr. James had said and how much it had hurt him. Then he remembered the precious words of the most wonderful child he had ever known. He walked out of the hospital and was surprised to see Angelle sitting at the bottom of the steps.

"Are you waiting for Sarah Catherine?" Caleb asked.

"No. I was waiting for you. I knew it was time for Buckie's shot and you'd be leaving. Want to walk me back to the dorm?"

I believe I'd walk into hell with you, Caleb thought. He was so astonished at her request that he didn't respond.

"You don't want to walk with me?" Angelle asked, seeming disappointed.

"Of course I do. My mind was kinda preoccupied for a second."

"With all you've endured the last few weeks, it's a wonder you have a mind at all," she replied. As they walked very slowly along the street into shadows of the massive oaks and then back into the moonlight, Caleb studied her face. It was celestial in the moonlight. He remembered the kiss and how it remained on his lips to this very moment. He was sure that he would never experience it again.

They turned into the campus and strolled slowly along the brick sidewalk. Caleb couldn't keep his eyes off her face. It was painful to see her beauty and have felt her warmth and love her so deeply, while realizing it was forbidden love. She eased her arm around his and snuggled it close to hers as they walked. It startled Caleb, and he stopped abruptly. "Why did you do that?" he asked.

"It's chilly and your arm's warm. Does it bother you?"

"Well…no. But after the other night…I didn't think…"

"Just don't hold me tightly, and it won't happen again. I…let me explain. I react strangely when someone grabs me or holds me tightly. You know, when I feel trapped. It's a phobia of mine. Nothing for you to be concerned about. Just one of my quirks."

"The look on your face the other night was frightening to me. I hope I never see it again. It scared the heck out of me."

"Just don't grab me and hold me tightly, and it won't happen again."

"That's a promise," Caleb said, and he started to walk. Angelle held his arm tightly but didn't move.

It frightened Caleb again, and he said, "What's the matter? Have I scared you again?"

"No. I'm not frightened tonight." She began tugged at his arm, backing away slowly from the sidewalk, and led him behind the thick azalea shrubs. They stood there looking into each other's eyes for a moment. The moonlight danced and sparkled off her silky brown hair. Her beautiful dark eyes pierced his. The sight was breathtaking and intoxicating.

"Did you enjoy kissing me the other night?" she whispered.

"I didn't kiss you," Caleb said, grinning. "If you remember, you kissed me. And yes, I enjoyed it more than anything I'd ever experienced."

"Have you thought about it much?"

"Only every minute of every day and most of the nights," Caleb said with a childish blush.

"I was embarrassed because of the way I acted when you held me tightly."

"You scared the blank out of me when I held you," Caleb said.

"Would you like to kiss me again? But you can't hold me. You can never hold me."

"I'd like to kiss you through all eternity," he murmured. "But what about that?" And he pointed at the ring. "Someone is about to get hurt here tonight, and I'm afraid it's going to be me."

"Suppose I take it off." And she slipped the ring off her finger and dropped it in her small purse.

"That doesn't change a thing if you put it back on. What are you saying, Angelle? What does this mean? Does it mean the engagement is off, and you don't love him anymore, or does it mean you're lonesome and need someone in your life until he returns?" He remembered what Will had said about having her until her fiancé returned. The thought was sickening. "I won't be a part of that. I'm in love with you, and I want to spend the rest of my life with you. But I have to know where I stand with you."

She looked away a few seconds, looked back and him and said, "I think I could fall in love with you, but it would be wrong. There are things about my life that you don't know, and I can't talk about it."

"If you loved me, you should be able to tell me anything. I'll understand and help you with your problem. I know you suffer with depression and anxiety. But if you want to get well, I know there's help. Doc loves you, and he can get help for you. You don't ever have to fear me. I'd die for you. But I'd rather live and love you for the rest of our lives. Do you understand that? I don't want to hide behind some bush and kiss you like a thief stealing kisses that are not mine. Why would you want to kiss me? Is it some sort of test to see if…I just don't understand."

She looked up at him. Her eyes were teary, yet there was a hunger and yearning in them, and Caleb had no resistance. He felt only desire and anticipation for what he knew was imminent. She moved closer to him, and he eased toward her. Their bodies touched, and slowly their lips met. Caleb fought the urge to reach around her tiny waist and pull her close to him as before. She put her hands to his face; her fingers ran through his soft hair as their lips moved faster over each other's. Her mouth opened slightly, and he felt her warm, moist tongue move slowly across his. They were lost in each other's souls. Their bodies pressed against each other's as their mouths continued a deep, devouring kiss. After a few minutes of bliss like Caleb had never experienced, he forced himself to move away. They stood looking at each other, breathless.

"I dreamed it would be like that," Caleb said. "It could be like that forever if—"

"Don't say anymore," Angelle whispered, leading him to the sidewalk. They walked slowly in silence to the dorm, looking into each other's eyes. At the concrete bench, Angelle stopped and said, "I never thought I could feel desire like that with anyone after…"

"After what? After what, Angelle? Tell me what happened to you to cause you so much fear and pain."

"I have to go now. It's late." She rushed to the door and walked in.

Caleb walked back to the dorm in a whirlwind of ecstasy, and confusion. *What did her kiss really mean?* he thought. *Was it simply that she's human after all? Does she just need love and passion? Is she really falling in love with me and it's causing a frightful conflict?*

Other questions crept into his mind. Would Buckie be alive tomorrow when he returned to the hospital? What kind of revenge-seeking monster might Will turn into when he recovered? A thousand questions with no answers flooded his mind as he walked somberly down the hill to the dorm. He had missed classes today, and he needed the assignments to keep up his coursework. Everything felt like a heavy load on his head. *I need rest*, he thought. *My mind doesn't want to slow down.* He saw his truck in the parking lot as he walked to the dorm. *Burt*, he thought and smiled. *Burt drove it here.*

Caleb bathed, shaved, and went to bed. He had another restless night. By morning, he was so tired he could hardly walk to the cafeteria. He couldn't remember eating the day before. After a hearty breakfast, his strength returned, and he jogged to class. *Would Angelle come to class?* he wondered as he took his seat. The bell rang, and Dr. DeHaberman began her lecture. His question was answered. Angelle would not come to class. *She would never come late and risk further humiliation at the hands of Dr. Doom.* Caleb's mind was in a quandary again over Angelle's absence. *She couldn't face me today,* he concluded. "I don't know what to think," he murmured. After going to his other morning classes, he rushed to the club. Doc pulled in for a quick lunch, and Caleb followed him into the dining hall. "Can I talk to you while you eat, Doc?" he asked.

"It'll be my pleasure," Doc said as he served himself from the buffet and sat down.

"I want to talk to you about Angelle."

Doc took a bite of the salad and said, "Go on."

"Doc, I'm in love with Angelle, and I'm worried about her."

Doc smiled, snickered, and said, "Every boy in this school is in love with Angelle, and most of the male professors, I've heard. You'll get over it. She's one of my special scholarship winners, doing outstanding work. I love that beautiful young lady as I love you, my boy."

"You don't understand. She has serious problems."

"I think you're imagining things. I work with that young lady every day. If she had serious problems, I certainly would be cognizant of that fact."

"She's suffering from anxiety and depression and has horrible nightmares, Doc. She hides her feelings from everyone. Her roommate told me that she wakes up suddenly screaming and then cries the rest of the night. She has these panic attacks regularly. I've witnessed them twice. Sarah Catherine thinks her emotional condition is worsening. She said it wasn't this bad last year. She said she thinks she's getting paranoid, whatever that means. She wakes up at night screaming strange things like 'please don't hurt me again' or 'please don't take my baby.'"

Doc's eyes tightened, and a strange look appeared on his face. "I find that difficult to believe. She's so wonderful with the patients and such a loving and caring person. I've not observed any bizarre behavior working with her. However, after what she experienced as a child, I could see where she might have some recurring problems. But I…I just find it hard to believe that they are that acute."

"What problems? What happened to her?"

"Son, that's privileged information, and I'm sure she doesn't wants people to know about her tragic past."

"I'm in love with her, and I believe she's falling in love with me."

"What?" Doc blurted, appearing shocked. "When did all this happen? I didn't know you were seeing her. You do know she's engaged, don't you, son?"

"Yes, sir, but she took her ring off last night, and she kissed me."

Doc shoved his salad plate aside, put his fork down, and sat back with an austere look. He gave Caleb a cool stare and asked, "How long has this been going on?"

"Almost since the first day of school," Caleb replied.

"Was that the first time she kissed you?"

"No. She kissed me one other time after I walked her to the dorm. That's when I first witnessed the panic attack."

Doc's cold, blue eyes pierced Caleb again, and in a tone Caleb had never heard, Doc said, "Now listen to me, young man. You're playing with fire here, and you don't realize it. Angelle is a very unstable young lady. I know her situation like no one else. I've worked hard to make her life as stress-free as possible while she gets an education and prayerfully finds some meaning to life again. She's engaged to a wonderful young soldier, I've been told, but her wounds are deep, and they appeared to be healing slowly. The last thing she needs in her life at this time is discord. Whatever is going on between you and her has to cease immediately, for her wellbeing and sanity. I suspect that her recurred depression and anxiety was precipitated because you introduced a new conflict into her life. You are that conflict. Now, she doesn't know who she loves. She's very vulnerable and unstable being here alone with no family. This could be very destructive to her. It might push her over the edge."

"I love you like a father, and I'd do anything for you, but you just asked me to stop loving someone that I can never stop loving."

Doc shook his head, tightened his jaw and cried out, "Why the hell does life have to be so complicated? All right, son, I'm going to tell you about Angelle's past. If what I tell you ever leaves your mouth, our friendship ceases. That's how serious her condition is. She tried to commit suicide when she was in junior high. Notice the scar on her left wrist the next time you see her. I'm compromising my principles by even telling you this much. I'm going to leave out the filthy details, but you'll have the general picture when I finish."

"Angelle's family lived in New Orleans. Her mother was a nurse, and her father a policeman. Her father survived the war, but a year after he returned he was killed in the line of duty. Angelle's mother was a beautiful lady of French descent. A few years after the death of her husband, she began dating one of the police officers that had been a friend of her husband. She married him the next year. Angelle was as beautiful as a child as she is now. The stepfather began to sexually abuse her at night when her mother was on the three-to-eleven shift at the hospital. Angelle was a frightened child. She was threatened by her stepfather. She was so terrified that she wouldn't tell her mother. She began to lose weight and throw up every time she ate. She was wasting away in fear and dread. That was the onset of the fear, depression, and anxiety.

"Angelle's mother took her to many doctors, but they found nothing physically wrong. Finally, she took her to a psychiatrist, but Angelle wouldn't tell the doctor anything. Fortunately, he recognized the symptoms of sexual abuse. He asked Angelle's mother if it were possible that she was being sexually abused. That same night, Angelle's mother waited outside their home until the radio went off and the light went out in the living room.

The police report determined that she crept silently back into the house and eased into Angelle's room. What she saw was the naked bastard draped over Angelle as she sobbed and pleaded with him to stop. Angelle's mother ran back to the living room and grabbed his thirty-eight from its holster, ran back to the bedroom, but the sorry pervert had heard her running. He jumped up to leave Angelle's room. She met him in the doorway and pumped three thirty-eight slugs into his chest. He managed to wrestle the gun from her hand and slammed the butt of the pistol against her temple. They both fell dead in Angelle's presence.

"Angelle ran into the street, naked and screaming. The Child Protection Agency took her to safety, but she didn't speak a word for over a year. She was barely twelve years old when all of this happened. She spent the next year in the State Mental Institution in Jackson, Louisiana. After a series of shock treatments, she came out of the catatonic state. Shortly after, she was sent to a children's home in Monroe, Louisiana, where she stayed until she graduated and came here to enroll last year. I imagine she met the young man she's engaged to while she was in the children's home. I've never asked. I personally don't know him. Now, do you understand why I'm so concerned and protective of her?"

Caleb looked down, horrified at the thought of what she had endured. He looked at Doc and said, "God have mercy on my wretched soul for the pain I must have caused her."

"You didn't know, son. I'm glad you told me because now I can get her into treatment with Dr. Wellington. He's retired, but he still sees a few patients. If I can get her to agree, I know he'll see her as a favor to me. After what she experienced, there's no guarantee that she'll ever recover completely."

"Thank you for telling me that. I'll honor your request." Totally heartbroken, Caleb worked at the club until time for practice.

CHAPTER THIRTEEN

The varsity football practice went well that afternoon. Afterwards, Coach Billy Ray and Stan held the freshman team over to prepare for the Thursday game with Kentucky. Caleb went through the motions with a heavy heart, his mind totally in a fog. It was apparent by his performance. He ran the wrong way a number of times and collided with the other backs, a mistake he'd never made before. He hadn't spoken a word to anyone. His demeanor was very obvious to the coaches. After the team ran enough plays to get their timing, they worked on special teams. The team was dismissed, and Coach Simpson said to Stan, "I need to talk to Caleb. He's not himself today." Everyone realized something was troubling Caleb, but none asked. The team jogged away, and Coach Simpson stopped Caleb and asked, "What's troubling you ?"

"I kinda feel like the sun might never shine again," he responded.

Coach Simpson glanced up at the blazing sun, then back at Caleb. "Is it Will? Is that what has you in the dumps?"

"That's part of it, along with a few other problems."

"It's not your grades, is it?" Billy Ray questioned.

"Not yet," Caleb responded.

"It's Buckie, isn't it? We're all heartbroken about his condition."

"That's a big part of it. I never watched a child that I love die before."

Billy Ray put his arm around Caleb as they walked together. "One day at a time," Billy Ray said. "That's how we get through life. One day at a time. Remember the old saying, 'There ain't no horse that can't be rode, and there ain't no cowboy that can't be throwed.' You feel like you just got thrown, but you'll get up one day and ride that horse. That's who you are. The sun will rise tomorrow. This is a tough time for all of us, but there'll be brighter days. You can bank on that."

Caleb showered, dressed, and went to the club. Abe was quick to spot the wrinkles in Caleb's face and pain in his eyes. They were very busy, so Abe had no time to talk to Caleb. At closing time, after everything was cleaned up, Abe walked out with Caleb. "You want to talk about it, boy?" Abe asked.

"No need," Caleb said with a headshake. "It's like Coach Simpson said, 'Life is hard, and we have to take it one day at a time.'"

"I don't know Coach Simpson, but he gave you some good advice. He might have added one other thing, though. Un-strap that burden and give it to the Lord. You'll feel the relief."

"Mr. Abe, sometimes you just can't find those straps."

"Yeah, son, you can find um if you believe in the sovereignty of the Lord."

"I'm going to try. I'm really going to try."

Caleb drove to the hospital, fearful of what he might find. He walked slowly to Will's room and stopped at the door, very apprehensive about entering.

Angelle came rushing over to him, excited and trembling. She whispered, "You missed all the excitement. Will woke up this afternoon. He and Mr. James had a cursing, screaming fight that could be heard all over the hospital. We were all frightened to go in and ask them to quiet down. Mr. James called Will a spoiled rotten bastard and a first class F-up. He even said that he deserved to die.

Will yelled, "Who the hell are you to criticize anyone? You're a GD rotten, womanizing SOB and the sorriest excuse for a father and husband in the world. The filthy language and screaming insults continued to rage for another five minutes before Mr. James stormed out of the building. Thankfully, Mrs. James had gone to the hotel to rest. I've never heard talk like that in my life. They used filthy words like you can't imagine. I've never witnessed anything like that before, and I pray I never will again. I'm still trembling."

"I'm sure they got it out of their systems. It won't happen again," Caleb said in a calming voice.

"Are you going to walk me back to the dorm tonight?" Angelle whispered.

"I suppose so, if I'm still here. My grades are going to drop if I don't hit the books."

"You certainly don't want to get in academic trouble. I don't want you to get kicked out of school. I'd be glad to help you study in the library if you need help," she said, showing deep concern in her face.

"Just when do you think you'd have time to help me study?" Caleb said, forcing a smile.

"Sunday morning. I don't usually work on Sunday morning, just when we're short- handed."

"But I do," Caleb said, nodding, "and that's very kind of you to offer."

"I could give up a little time here at the hospital. I work just to keep busy. I don't need all the money I make here because of my scholarship."

"I can't let you do that, Angelle. Anyway it's not that I need help with my studies, it's that I don't have time to do them. But again, I'll never forget that you offered. That's one of the most unselfish things anyone ever offered to do for me."

"It's no more than you'd do for me."

"I'm going in now," Caleb said. "I hope Will's calmed down." He eased the door open and stuck his head in. Will was looking out into space with a scowl on his face. Mrs. James was reading a novel. "Hey, buddy," Caleb said brightly. "How's my best pal doin' today?"

"That's a stupid question!" Will snapped. "How do you think I'm doing?"

Will's curt answer pierced Caleb like never before, and he bristled and shot back, saying, "You're doin' a hell of a lot better than you were yesterday when they brought you in here bloody and almost dead. You should be on your knees thanking God for sparing your life you ungrateful—"

Mrs. James gasped, dropping the book on the floor, and Will was shocked speechless at his retort.

"Young man!" Mrs. James cried out, "Please leave this room immediately. You can't talk to my son in that manner!"

"Let him alone, Mother," Will said evenly. "That's my roommate. I imagine that's the first time in his life that he ever showed any real grit. You know my football's over this year, don't you, Corn Shuck?" Will said, with a calmness that usually preceded a storm.

"I was here through it all." Caleb nodded. "I know everything."

"Do you know who did this to me?" Will continued, a slight trimmer in his voice. Caleb nodded. Will exploded. "That cowardly weasel, SOB, Tex, and his no-account buddies cost me a year of football and—"

Mrs. James shot up from the chair, rushing to his bedside, and pleaded with him to calm down. "You know the doctor cautioned you about getting too excited," she exclaimed.

"I'm fine now, Mother," Will responded in a calmer voice. "Would you walk downstairs and get me a coke?"

"Certainly, son. I'll check at the nurse's station and see if it's permissible."

"Don't ask, Mother, just do it! Please!"

"All right, son, just calm yourself," and Mrs. James eased out of the room.

"They want me to go and identify those redneck bastards when I get out. I'm not identifying anyone. When my ribs and skull heals, I'm going to look 'em up and settle this my way. If I identify them, what'll they get, six months in the jug with free meals and a warm place to sleep! Hell, that'll be a free vacation! I know every one of them. Oh no! Those cowardly dogs are going to feel pain like they have never experienced. That's Will's justice."

"You can't do that, Will. They're going to be expecting you, and they'll be packing guns next time. Someone is going to get killed, and it'll probably be you. Will, I can't bury my two best friends. I love you, and I can't do that." He held his hand up, and it was shaking like a leaf in a whirlwind. "I'm about to the end of my road," Caleb murmured in near tears. "I'm not strong like you. Please quit talking like that."

"What do you want me to do, just ship them off to the slammer? Don't you realize they've torn my heart out? They robbed me of my, my god. Yeah, my god! Football is my god. I love it more than life. I live for it. What am I going to do for the next ten months? I'll be a raving lunatic before next fall. The thought of it is killin' me."

"I know it is, Will, and we'll get through this together, one day at a time. When the season is over, we'll lift weights and run together. We'll get in the best condition of our lives. We can look forward to playing together next year. You have to hold on to that and not jeopardize your future. We're going to be great together. Think about that and not—"

Mrs. James walked in with the coke. "Here, baby, now drink it slowly. I don't want the gas to build up in your stomach and put pressure on your heart."

Will raised his brows and commented, "Mother has a degree in nursing, although she never nursed a day in her life except to nurse me when I was a child. She also has degrees in political science and English literature. She took the full load while my father was here playing that William the Conqueror crap. Mother, this is Caleb Morgan, the young country boy that I told you about. He's my best friend and a real pal."

Caleb extended his hand and said, "It's a pleasure to finally meet you, Mrs. James. Will speaks of you often, and with much affection."

"That's so sweet of you to say, Caleb. Will wants everyone to think he's a tough guy like his father, but actually he's just a pussy cat at heart."

"Yes, ma'am, I've observed that," Caleb feigned, unable to bridle his laughter.

"Will, your father had to fly back to Nashville to close a big deal. He said Doc assured him that you were out of danger now, so he won't be back for a while. I told him I was sure you'd understand."

"Certainly I understand, Mother. You and I always understood about those big deals. Those big deals are what he lives for. I'm surprised he found time to come at all."

They talked a while then Caleb said, "I have to go see Buckie now. The end is near for him. He said he hoped to meet you before you leave the hospital, Will. He's just two doors down the hall in room two-twelve, but he's too weak to come see you."

Will looked away and said, "Thanks for coming, Corn Shuck."

Doc and Edith were sitting in their den at nine-thirty watching TV. Doc was very fidgety. "Is something bothering you, James?" Edith asked. "Why do you keep looking at your watch?"

"Sweetheart, I've been debating with myself over a situation that's absolutely none of my concern. I haven't mentioned it to you because I didn't want to worry you."

"I've heard enough," Edith said. "Spill it, buster."

"Caleb told us a story about his maternal grandparents when we drove to Choctaw County." Doc told Edith the story of how Caleb's father and mother were married. Doc continued, "I met his grandfather last week by chance or fate or, as Caleb would say, providence, when we went to New Orleans. It seems his grandfather is president of the largest bank in Jackson. He's a very handsome and distinguished gentleman. He had no idea that Caleb was his grandchild. I invited him and his wife to come and have lunch with us and attend the game Thursday night. He said if he could adjust his schedule, he'd love to come. He's an Ole Miss graduate, and a big fan of the Rebels. But he was captivated by Caleb's performance and even asked if I knew his parents' names."

"And you lied to him?"

"Well, no, kinda, yes. I said I couldn't remember their names."

"Oh, James! What have you gotten yourself into? This could get embarrassing or worse. It might get ugly if it doesn't work out."

"I've thought of nothing else since I contrived the scheme," Doc said. "But how could they not love Caleb when they meet him?"

"That's not your only problem," Edith commented. "You've already told me that Houston and Mary were coming to the game. How are you going to orchestrate that situation?"

"That's why I haven't slept too well the last few nights. I could put them on opposite sides of the stadium. They would never see each other."

"You can't invite guests to a game and not sit with them, James. You know that!"

"I know, but now it's done. It could be a disaster, but I hope—no, I pray that this situation might have a beautiful ending."

"Well, thank you, James. Now there'll be two of us that can't sleep."

Doc glanced at his watch again and said, "I don't think it's too late to call Horace and see if they're coming." He called long distance, and Judge Knight answered the phone.

"Horace, this is Doc, and I hope I didn't get you out of bed."

"Bed!" the judge barked. "Who gets to bed before eleven p.m. with a teenager in the house? The phone rings 'til midnight or the walls vibrate with rock and roll music. There might be a dozen half-naked girls running around the house squealing and giggling all night. I knew I should've never let Lillian talk me into going on that Caribbean cruise seventeen years ago."

Doc could hear Lillian in the background chiding, "Now you know that's a lie, Horace Knight. It was all your idea."

"I didn't call to start a rift," Doc said, snickering. "I was wondering if Mr. Hodges and his wife had made a decision about coming for lunch and the game on Thursday."

"So happened I was in the bank this afternoon, Doc. Travis and Iris are very excited about the trip. Travis said Iris doesn't care much about football, but she was thrilled about dining at the club and seeing all the beautiful homes and gardens. She said she'd never been to Marston and she was looking forward to the trip. We'll be driving back after the game. Neither of us could get off Friday. Iris must be like all women, always on go."

"I heard that," Lillian blurted. "The only place you ever want to go is to the golf course or to bed."

"She has no defense for her argument," the judge said to Doc. "Lillian, didn't I take you to Augusta last April?"

"Yes!" Lillian snapped. "And I shopped and went to the movies for four days—alone, I might add, while you went to that silly golf tournament."

Doc laughed. "I better hang up and let y'all settle this one. Oh! By the way, Horace, I'd like the Hodges to think this little excursion was their idea. I'd rather you didn't mention my calling you about it. I have my reasons. If things work out, you'll understand what this is all about."

"Doc—give me a little credit. After twenty-five years on the bench, I've learned a little about estrangement and domestic conflicts."

"You sly old buzzard," Doc said. "Pray that my meddling doesn't backfire. I'll see y'all at lunch Thursday."

The judge hung up the phone. Lillian commented, "That was a strange conversation, Horace. What was it all about?"

"I think Doc was impressed with Travis last week. Who knows, he might be looking for a place to invest a few million dollars."

"It's for sure we don't have that problem," Lillian remarked.

"I don't think money is a problem with us," the judge said. Then he murmured, "If I could get that checkbook out of your purse, I know it wouldn't be. Darn it!" the judge barked. "She's turned it up again." He yelled up the staircase, "Jennifer, turn that confounded radio down, or we'll all be deaf!" Turning back to his wife, he said, "That Caribbean cruise will be the death of me yet, Lillian."

"Shame on you, Horace Knight. I can't believe you said that."

"Oh, Lillian! You have no sense of humor. I wouldn't trade that cute little redheaded, freckled-face heifer for a million dollars. Two might be tempting."

Lillian doubled up her fists, giving Horace an impish grin and said, "I ought to sock you, old man."

"Oh! You're feeling frisky tonight, huh!" Horace said with a big grin as he started toward her.

"Get away from me you nasty old man," she said, laughing and running behind the sofa. "Ah-ha," he said, rubbing his hands together as he began to chase her.

"I'll scream if you don't quit acting like a maniac."

The judge continued to chase her saying, "You can run, but you can't hide."

"Who ever heard of a judge acting like this!"

"Sweetheart, where do you think little judges come from?" He reached over the sofa, pulled her to him, and they kissed passionately for a long time. When they parted, Lillian said, "I swear, Horace, you're an over-sexed old man."

"Yeah!" he said, nodding. "How could you be so lucky?"

Caleb walked into Buckie's room, and he was wide awake, waiting excitedly for Caleb's nightly visit. He snatched the sheet down and tried to throw his chest out. "How do I look in this beautiful game jersey? Everyone says I look terrific. But I got mad at Mrs. Gladys today. They came in to bathe me, and I wouldn't let them take my new jersey off. Mrs. Gladys said she was going to hold me up by my feet and skin it off if I didn't let them bathe me. I told her I'd let Angelle take it off because I knew she wouldn't let anyone steal it. Mrs. Gladys said I had to have it washed if I was going to wear it all the time. I let Angelle bathe me when she came to work. It ain't dirty, is it?"

"No, but if you wear it all the time, it might get a little rank after a few days. It really needs to be washed every now and then. If someone steals it, I'll give you another one just like it."

"All right, I'll let them wash it tomorrow so it'll be clean for the game."

"You really look stronger tonight. Have you been eating better?"

Buckie got excited as he said, "I ate almost a whole egg this morning. I had a few bites of buttered rice, too. The biscuit was so hard and cold I couldn't eat it. But I feel real strong. I know pop's going to let me go to the game when he sees how strong I am."

"I'm sure he will."

Gladys came in waving a syringe. "It's nighty-night time, little prince."

"Oh, can't I stay up a little longer? Caleb just got here, and I ain't hurtin' much tonight."

"If you want to go to that ballgame, you need a good night's sleep," Gladys said.

He rolled over, pulling the jersey up to expose his rear, saying. "Hit me then." Gladys and Caleb looked at each other and laughed.

"Where did you pick up that slang?" Gladys asked.

"That nice man down the hall sticks his head in every couple of days and we talk. He said they hit him with a ten-penny nail every few hours. He ain't been by for a while. Did he get to go home?"

"I'm not sure which man you're referring to, sweetie. Maybe he's been discharged."

"Well, that's good," Buckie said, "'cause he said he had cancer of the, the pancreas or some word like that." She took the syringe and eased it into his rear. Buckie was out before they could get out of the room.

Once outside the door, Caleb asked, "Was the man discharged?"

"Let's just say he checked out, and leave it at that."

"I don't know how you and Doc and the nurses here handle this every day."

"We have to look at it this way, Caleb. It's not all about dying. We see people admitted every day dying, but some get to leave here upright. That's how we manage to keep our sanity. But I'll tell you this, when that sweet child checks out, there'll be a lot of broken hearts and tears around here. He's been with us so long he's like one of our children. I think Luther is one of the kindest men I've ever known. He may not survive this tribulation. That boy's his life."

"That scares me, too, Mrs. Gladys." He turned and walked by Will's room, peeped in the door, and Will was snoring, and Mrs. James was asleep in the chair. *That's a sweet sight,* Caleb thought as he walked downstairs. Angelle was waiting at the bottom of the steps.

Sweet mercy, Caleb thought, *I hope Doc doesn't drive by.*

"Walk me back to the dorm," Angelle said, smiling.

"I have my truck over there, but I'd rather walk and try to get rid of these heebie-jeebies." Angelle snickered. Caleb said, "I'll come back for it tomorrow after class."

They hadn't walked far into the pleasant night before Angelle eased her arm around Caleb's, and snuggled close to him. At her touch, a feeling like none he had ever experienced rushed through his entire being. It was a cataclysm of fear, panic, sadness, and guilt. His heart raced, and he became frightened and started to perspire. *Oh Lord,* he thought, *is this what she experiences? Is this depression or panic?* He felt the urge to run. He began to tremble and breathe rapidly. He stopped and pulled his arm away from hers. "Maybe you shouldn't hold me so close. We both seem to have forgotten that you're engaged to be married."

She held her hand up and said, "Do you see a ring? It's still in my purse." Caleb looked at her hand, and the ring was no longer there, but what he saw frightened him more than anything imaginable. He saw the scar on her wrist, visible in the moonlight. Doc's warning resounded in his mind. A torrent of emotions overwhelmed him, and he turned away from Angelle for a moment, trembling. After he calmed somewhat, he turned and said, "Let's walk." Angelle studied his face as they strolled slowly toward the campus. She seemed wounded by his comment and strange behavior, yet she didn't speak.

As they entered the campus, she grasped his arm and stopped, asking, "Why are you so cold to me tonight? Are you upset? I don't understand you, Caleb Morgan. You said you'd love me forever so I took the ring off. Now you act as if I've committed a crime. I thought this was what you wanted. Do you love me?"

A thousand answers ran through his mind, but he knew he had to guard his words. He loved her too much to put her life in jeopardy.

"Now it's your time to talk to me," she said as she pulled him into the shadows away from the sidewalk.

"All right, I'll talk to you," Caleb said. "I'm here and he's not. I think it's as simple as that. I love you more than life itself. I know if you told Maurice you loved him and wanted to marry him, you had to mean it because you're not one to give your heart easily. Now I'm here, and he's far away. It's easy to confuse infatuation with love, especially when someone is lonely and away from the one they truly love. I have one question for you? Did you allow him to hold you when you kissed?"

Angelle stood there teary-eyed for a few seconds before she spoke. "There are things I would like to tell you, but I—I just can't."

"You won't answer a simple question?"

"I—I just can't talk about him and my past with you or anyone. I can't explain it. Just be patient with me, and one day I might be able to talk about it."

"Angelle—put the ring back on your finger. I'll be your friend, but I'll never kiss you again until I can put my arms around you and hold you and know that you love only me. I can't continue to hurt you and cause you pain."

"Don't say anymore," she said teary-eyed. "I want you to kiss me once more, and you may put your arms around me and hold me. Hold me gently, very gently—gently. You have to promise to hold me very gently."

Caleb shook his head, saying, "No. I can't put you through that pain again. I don't ever want to see that horrified look in your eyes and know that I caused it. I do love you. I wish I didn't, but I can't help loving you. I always will."

"I took the ring off for you, and you won't do this for me. I have to know if I…"

Caleb's mind went into a spin. *What if I kiss her and the fear is gone? I can't lose Doc's friendship. He's like a father to me. I promised. I don't know what to do.* Then that strange feeling of panic came over him again. He backed away a few steps.

Angelle followed him, placing her arms around his neck and began to pull him to her. Caleb tried to resist, but he had no control as he looked at her gorgeous face and sparkling eyes in the moonlight. The temptation overpowered him as the panic subsided. He felt her warm, moist lips move over his. They kissed passionately for a few moments, then he couldn't resist her invitation to hold her warm body close to his. He eased his hands around her tiny waist and up her back and gently pulled her close to him. Instantly, he felt her body tense, then tremble, and her lips tighten as she tremble in his arms. She fought her demon as long as possible before she tore away from his embrace, gasping with that same look of panic in her eyes as before. She stood in front of him, rigid, trembling, and the tears began to stream down her cheeks.

"Calm down," Caleb pleaded. "I'll never do that again. Just don't cry, please. I'm not going to hurt you. I'll never hurt you." They walked back to the dorm in silence. Angelle seemed to calm herself as they approached the concrete bench under the giant oak. She paused, teary-eyed, still trembling somewhat, and said, "This is not your fault, Caleb. I don't want you to feel any guilt. I can't help the way I am. I pray that one day this will all be over. I do trust you. One day I might be able to prove it to you, but I won't ask you to wait."

"You don't need to explain," Caleb said. "I—"

"You're so kind and pure. I don't deserve your love," Angelle whispered. "You need someone who'll cherish you, someone you can hold and love and will love you in return. I don't know if I'll ever be able to do that." The tears began to stream down her cheeks. She turned and ran into the dorm.

Caleb turned and walked away heartbroken. The tears began to stream down his cheeks.

Sarah Catherine had walked to the window to watch for Angelle. She had witnessed her tears and her flight. Angelle ran into the room wiping the tears from her eyes. She sat on her bed and fell on her pillow, fighting the tears.

Sarah Catherine walked over to Angelle's bed, sat down and began stroking her hair. "Why do you punish yourself like this, sweetheart? Why don't you go to the police and report that son-of-a-bitch. They'll stop him from stalking you like this. He's destroying you. It has to stop now. If I was a man, I'd beat the hell out of him and dare him to speak to you again."

"Stop!" Angelle blurted. "Don't talk about him like that. He's done nothing wrong. I asked him to walk me home. He's a kind and wonderful person, and … I could fall in love with him. I may be in love with him."

Sarah Catherine threw her hands up. "Look at yourself. Does someone in love act like you're acting? He comes on like a dumb country hick, but he's cast a spell over you with that pretty face and innocent country boy act, and you're too naive to realize it. How can you be in love with two boys? Think about what are you saying."

"Stop it!" Angelle cried out. "I'm not going to listen to anymore. Leave me alone. It's my life."

"I won't leave you alone. I love you too much to leave you alone. It's killing me to see you this way."

Angelle sat up and wiped her eyes and said, "I'll tell you something if you'll promise never, never, never, to repeat it."

"You know I won't tell."

"No," Angelle said, "swear to it."

"I swear," Sarah Catherine said.

"I'm going to tell you this because you're the one who's killing me because of the way you talk about Caleb. The reason I'm crying is because I suffer from depression and panic attacks. I don't know if I can ever marry because I can't allow anyone to hold me. I was sexually abused by my stepfather when I was only a child. He held me down and forced me to do unspeakable things. Then my mother realized what he was doing and they killed each other. I'm responsible for my mother's death." Angelle began to cry uncontrollably. She managed to say, "If I had just run away, she would still be alive."

Sarah Catherine leaned back in disbelief, and said, "What!"

"I don't think I'll ever be able to make love. Can you understand that? I don't even understand it."

Sarah Catherine shook her head. "I understand more than you think. My father is a doctor so I've heard stories about married women who won't make love to their husbands. I know the problem always goes deeper than what shows on the surface. I've suspicion that you were abused as a child for a long time. I prayed that I was wrong." Angelle buried her face in the pillow, weeping uncontrollably.

"Don't you know there's help for you if you'll accept it? Don't you understand that you don't have to live with this pain and guilt for the rest of your life? I know Doc loves you like a daughter. Why don't you ask him for help? You owe it to yourself to get help."

Angelle turned and said, "I don't want Caleb to know the truth. I'm too ashamed to tell him or anyone. I can't let myself think about it because if I do, I want to die. How could I ever let anyone help me?"

"I'm going to make you a promise," Sarah Catherine said. "I'll never give you any peace until you get into treatment. You can't live with this guilt the rest of your life. You're all wrong about your being responsible. It's all in your confused mind. None of it was your fault. Promise me you'll think about it. Please promise me you'll just think about it—please."

Angelle wiped the tears from her eyes as she answered, "I promise I'll think about it."

"And I'll keep my mouth shut about Caleb. It's your decision about who you truly love."

CHAPTER FOURTEEN

Caleb climbed the stairs to his room, mentally and physically spent. He opened his door and collapsed on the bed. A torrent of emotions ran through his mind. The ecstasy of her kiss that had consumed his every thought before this night was now like a dagger piercing his heart. Realizing the pain he had surely caused the one true love of his life seemed unbearable. The very thought of the pain and heartache that she had endured in her young life sickened him.

His door opened slowly and John David stuck his head in and asked, "How are Will and Buckie?"

Caleb wiped his eyes with his pillowcase and brushed his hair back. "Buckie seemed stronger today, and Will is back to his usual disagreeable self."

"Have you been crying, Caleb?" John David asked, with deep concern in his voice.

Caleb shrugged, forcing a smile. "You know... that's the way life is. Sometimes you need a good cry to get focused again."

"Yes, I know," John David said, nodding. "The truth is that sometimes life is the shits. But it's the only one we have, and the only one we'll ever have. We have to wipe off the shit and keep going. I might preach a sermon one day and entitle it 'life is sometimes the shits.' I can back that up with scripture, but I don't think it'll be received very well. I'll preach that one when I begin a prison ministry. You're a good person, Caleb Morgan, a lot better man than me. I don't know how you did what you did, and I don't know how you do what you do. You weep and pray for the sick and delight in truth. You lead by example and work your ass off. I love you, pal, and I know the load must be getting heavy. I love your spirit and your heart—and I'm worried sick about you. I'm afraid your candle is going to burn out too soon."

"I know my limit, I think," Caleb said. "If it gets unbearable, I'll go home. I almost did, you know, a dozen times, but something or someone didn't let me go. I like to think it was the spirit of my father whispering to me, 'Don't give up, son. Don't ever give up. Follow your dream.' When I think about my father and how proud he'd be of me in Marston College, I know he would swell with pride. I hope the Lord tells him I made it here. I don't care if he doesn't tell him that I made the team. That's kinda egotistical, and I don't think the Lord tolerates much ego."

"You have a gift, Caleb. Anyone who can make a friend out of Will is either a heathen or a saint. Everyone who knows you loves you. You have the rare gift of humility. I don't like to see you down like this." John David doubled up his fist and tapped on his heart. "It tears my heart out."

"You just stop worrying," Caleb said, "because I'm going to be all right. With friends like you and Doc and Mrs. Edith and the team praying for me, I have to be all right. I just haven't ever buried anyone close to me before."

"Sometimes we have to give up our friends and loved ones to the Lord. It's not easy, but whoever said life was easy?"

Caleb stood up. "Thank you for being my friend, John David."

John David put his hands on Caleb's shoulders. "It's easy to be your friend. Good night."

Caleb took his books and read a few chapters before falling asleep reading. In what seemed only a few minutes, the bright sun came radiating through the window. Caleb was so exhausted he pulled the sheet over his head and tried to go back to sleep. The events of the previous day began to roll across his mind. He snatched the cover off in disgust, jumped up, and took a quick shower. He felt better after he dressed and ate breakfast. He dreaded going to history class, but he had no choice. He entered the large auditorium and saw Angelle in her seat. He eased down the aisle and sat by her. Neither spoke. They sat looking straight ahead as if they were strangers. Dr. DeHaberman stormed in and began her lecture. Caleb tried to take notes, but he wanted to turn and look at Angelle. After a while he put his arm on the arm rest. It touched hers. She turned and whispered, "Did you want to say something?"

Caleb put his syllabus over his mouth and whispered, "No. Did you want to say something?"

Angelle whispered, "I thought you nudged me on the arm."

The girl to Angelle right whispered, "You two love birds better shut up or you're going to be kicked out of here—permanently this time."

The bell rang and they walked out of the auditorium together. Outside, Angelle said, "I need to ask you something." Caleb nodded and waited.

"I've been selected to be on the homecoming court as the nursing school representative. I don't know whether to accept or not."

"Don't be ridiculous. That's an honor. Why wouldn't you?"

"I'll have to go to the homecoming ball and dance the first dance with my escort."

A pain hit Caleb in the stomach. He didn't know what to say. "Uh, uh, are you asking me to escort you?"

"I certainly wouldn't think of going with anyone else. You don't want to escort me?" she said with a sinking look.

"You know I do, but I need to tell you something. Do you know Rachel McDaniel?"

"Yes. We have classes together. She's a real character. She makes everyone laugh. Why?"

"Rachel and I sit together at the varsity games. We're good friends. At the last game, she asked me to escort her to the ball. She's just a friend, and that's all. I did it as a favor to her because she said she was too tall to go with any of the boys here."

"Then I won't accept," Angelle said, disappointment written all over her face.

"Certainly you will. I'll work out something. Will doesn't have a date. I'll get him to escort Rachel. Don't worry anymore. Just let me handle it, alright?"

"You're so wonderful," Angelle said, reaching out and touching his cheek.

─❊─

Doc was seeing patients when Vivian, his nurse, said, "Doc, you have a phone call from a Mr. Houston Morgan. Can you take the call?"

Doc walked over to take the phone. "Hello, Mr. Morgan, it's so good to hear from you."

"Dr. Marston," Houston said, "I bought the new used car so we can drive up to Marston Thursday to see the game. Coach Shook said he was going to send tickets, but he must have forgotten. Is it too late to buy tickets?"

"You don't need tickets, Mr. Morgan. You're my guests. I'll leave you an envelope at the ticket office at the south end of the stadium. Just tell them who you are and you'll have seats beside us."

"Just don't tell Mary that you gave the tickets to us. She has some strange notion about accepting gifts."

"So I've heard," Doc said, "and it rubbed off on her son. That'll be no problem. I'm really looking forward to seeing you two again. Edith is equally excited about meeting you and Mary."

"I'm so excited that I can't get to sleep at night. If you can't get to sleep after picking cotton all day, you're pretty excited."

"I can promise you this, it's going to be a night that will long be remembered."

"It's been good talking to you, Dr. Marston, but I have to hit the cotton patch, and I know you're a very busy man. Thank you for all you've done for Caleb."

"You don't realize it, Mr. Morgan, but your boy has done a lot more for me than I have for him. Goodbye, sir."

Caleb went to the club and helped Abe with lunch. Doc rushed out of his office early to tell Caleb that he had talked to Houston and that they were coming to the game.

Doc arrived just as Caleb was walking over to the pro-shop to get his instructions from Burt. Doc blew his horn, and Caleb jogged over to meet him. "Good news, son," Doc said. "Mary and Houston are coming to the game."

"He got the car!" Caleb said, excitedly.

"Yes, he got the car," Doc said, "and he's so excited he can't sleep."

"If he can't sleep in cotton picking season, he must really be excited. I wish Mother was that excited."

"She will be when she sees you play," Doc said confidently.

Doc ate a quick lunch and returned to his office. Vivian greeted him as he walked in and informed him that one of his girls was in his office to see him. "I put her in there. She seemed very nervous and troubled, and I thought you might want to see her first."

"Who is it?" Doc asked.

"Angelle Noel."

"I'll be back in a few minutes," Doc said and walked back to his office. Angelle was sitting nervously on the edge of the couch, wrenching her hands.

"Good afternoon," Doc said brightly. "I didn't expect to see you until afternoon rounds. Is something troubling you?"

"Not really," she said almost trembling as she stood up. "It's really nothing. I shouldn't have come here and bothered you. I'll just leave now."

"Not so fast, young lady. I have a big investment in your future, and I know something is troubling you. We're going to sit here until you calm down and we can talk about it."

They sat silently for a moment. Then Angelle said, "I'm having some problems with—with depression and—anxiety attacks. I have horrible nightmares, too. I—I was hoping you might know where I might go to get some help. I have some money in savings, but I know how expensive that kind of treatment can be. I really shouldn't have come here bothering you with my problems, Doc. I'll be all right. I'll go now."

"No, you're not going to leave, Angelle. You've asked for help, and I'm going to get you some help. I didn't know you were having problems. You seem so happy at work. I should have been more cognizant. Have you ever been in treatment before?" Angelle didn't answer. She just lowered her head.

"Sweetheart," Doc said, "we have no secrets. I know what happened to you. I make it my business to get a complete report on any student that applies for a Marston scholarship."

Angelle was shocked at Doc's revelation. "Do you mean you know—everything?"

"Everything," Doc said.

"You know about my mother?"

"Everything," Doc responded. "How long has this condition persisted?"

"Ever since my mother married that—that monster."

"And you've never had any psychiatric counseling?"

"Some, before I left the…"

"At present, do you ever have thoughts of suicide, Angelle?"

"Constantly, but I don't want to die. I want to live and be normal. I want to get well." She put her hand over her eyes began to cry.

Doc sat down by her and whispered, "Calm yourself, you are going to get well. Half the battle is admitting that you have a problem and seeking treatment. Why did you wait so long to ask for help, sweetheart?"

"It's so shameful, Doc. I'm ashamed when I think about it. I can't talk about it. I'm afraid the memories will come back, and the nightmares won't go away. They frighten me. But there's another reason I want to get well now. I'm in love with the most wonderful boy in the world. I know I can never marry him with this illness. I can't allow anyone to hold me. I can't even shake hands with anyone." She began to weep again.

"Now, now," Doc said, "there's no need for tears. I just happen to be best friends with one of the most renowned psychiatrists in this nation. His office is only two door down from mine, and he's retired, but he still sees a few patients as long as it doesn't interfere with his golf game." Doc grinned. Angelle didn't. "That was a joke, sweetheart. He's really top drawer. I'll speak to him. He owes me a favor or two since I referred most of his patients to him the last twenty-five years. There'll be no charge. When would you like to begin?"

"As soon as possible," Angelle said. "If I wait, I may change my mind."

Doc put his hand on her shoulder. "Sweetheart, you've been living in a dark world too long. We are going to put some sunshine back into your life. That young soldier who gave you that beautiful ring is going to be the happiest person in the world very soon. But you need to understand that this is not going to be painless. It may take months or even years before you are completely cured. You have to be willing to face a little pain before the healing begins."

"I love him so much that I would do anything for him."

"You're doing this for yourself, my dear. You're the one suffering. He's the lucky one. I'll call Dr. Wellington and set up your first appointment. He's a wonderful man. You're going to love him, and feel at ease with him. What would be the best time for you?"

"Twelve or one would be perfect, but if that's not possible, anytime he'll see me will be fine."

"I know he doesn't work after twelve, so that should be perfect. His office is just two doors down. You can make plans for your first visit tomorrow. Take courage, sweetheart, because everything is going to be wonderful in time."

After Angelle went to work, Doc stuck his head out the door and told Vivian that he would be out a couple of minutes and to hold the next patient until he returned. He rushed down to Wellington's office. Fortunately, he was still in his office, and Doc walked straight back to his office. Wellington was filing some papers. "Hello, old pal," Doc said, brightly.

"What do you want?" Wellington said dryly.

"Now, why would you think I want something, ole buddy?" Doc said, still grinning.

"What?" Wellington asked.

"How did you know I wanted something, Wellington?"

"I'm a psychiatrist, dodo bird. In twenty-five years, you've never come in my office during working hours."

"Well, I know you're retired and not taking any new patients; however, there is this one special young lady who's on a Marston scholarship for nursing students. She's very special to me. She's suffering from depression and anxiety. Since you are an expert in that field, I was hoping, as a favor to me, you might consider seeing her a few times."

"I think you made your point. How serious is her condition?"

"Critical," Doc said. "I could take her to Memphis, but I don't know if she'd agree. She's ashamed of her condition, and the reason for it."

"You know the reason for her condition?" Wellington asked, looking up with raised brows.

"I know a little, but I don't want to discuss it with you. I want you to get it out of her. That's what you do best, isn't it?"

"You know that means I'll have to cancel my trip to Hawaii in a few weeks."

"You know I'd never ask if I didn't think the situation was critical, don't you?"

"Is our game still on tomorrow?" Wellington asked.

"Of course."

"Then I'll see you tomorrow."

Doc threw his palms up and said, "What about…"

"Noon tomorrow," Wellington said. "Tell her not to be late because I am retired."

Doc grabbed Wellington's hand, shaking it with appreciation. "I owe you a big one."

Caleb jumped on the rough mower and started cutting. The 'what ifs' began to roll through his mind. *What if I get hurt and Mother makes me quit football? What if Buckie dies and never gets to see a ballgame or his mother? What if Will gets well and tries to get revenge and gets killed or winds up in jail for life? What if I can't stay away from Angelle and she gets worse? What if I lose Doc's friendship? What if I don't make my grades and have to give up school? Sweet mercy, what if the sun doesn't rise tomorrow?"* He raised his fist and pounded his head, screaming, "Stop it! Where is your faith?" Then he heard a loud crash. The tractor jerked sideways and he heard the clanging sound of metal on metal. He slammed on the brakes, jerked his head around and saw the outside gang mower wrapped around a twelve-inch pine tree. "Ohhh! Ohhh! Ohhh! S-h-i-t! Ohhh! What have I done!" He wilted into the seat for a few seconds, then jumped off the tractor and inspected the mangled piece of steel. "Oh shit!" he said. "Oh shit! What have I done?" He glanced into the sky and said, "I didn't mean to say that, nasty word—three times. It just came out." *That's it,* he thought. *There goes my next three month's pay, if Burt doesn't fire me.* He jumped back on the tractor, raised the gangs, and drove slowly back toward the equipment shed with a sick feeling. *There's no telling what it will cost to repair that gang if it can be repaired at all.* He broke out into a cold sweat as he pulled up beside the pro-shop. Burt heard the tractor coming. He stood by the window and watched as Caleb drove by. He walked outside.

Caleb barked, "I screwed up, Mr. Burt. It was all my fault. I wasn't paying attention and drove to close to the pine tree on number one and ... well, you can see what happened. I'll pay for the damage out of my paycheck, if it takes six months, if that's all right," he said, wide-eyed.

"Do you have five hundred bucks?" Burt asked sternly.

"Five hundred dollars!" Caleb gasped. "Maybe I could pay for it over the next few years."

Burt laughed. "If you'll look behind the equipment shed, you'll see a half dozen gangs that look just like that one. Accidents happen occasionally, and we're prepared for them. Just put one of the rebuilt ones on and try to be a little more careful in the future. I'm not going to make you pay for it. Heck, a couple of those broken ones are my mishaps."

"Thank you, Mr. Burt. It won't happen again, I promise."

"Oh yes it will, if you stay here long enough. We all tend to get overconfident and careless sometimes."

"Yes, sir." Caleb thought, *This won't happen to me again.*

The afternoon practice was spirited. When it ended, the coaches voiced their approval. The freshmen team stayed over for a last workout before their Thursday game. Caleb forced his mind to stay focused on the task at hand. He didn't make any silly mistakes as he had the day before. When the practice ended, Coach Simpson said, "You must have resolved some of your conflicts, Caleb. You looked really sharp today."

"I have to be sharp, Coach Simpson, because my folks are coming to see the game. I don't want to disappoint them."

"I wouldn't worry about that. I don't think you could possibly disappoint them."

Caleb jogged back to the dressing room, showered, and rushed back to the club to help Abe. The crowd was slim, and they were out before nine. Caleb and Abe finished early, and he rushed to the hospital. He went to Will's room first. Will was staring out the window. He didn't acknowledge Caleb's presence.

Caleb touched him on the shoulder lightly, whispering, "How are you, buddy?"

Will turned slowly with a dazed look and said, "I have problems, kid. I have real problems. I can't handle this crap. This can't be happening to me. I'm Superman. What am I supposed to do the next ten months? I'll be crazy lying around here not being able to workout and play ball. That's what I live for. Why me? Why the hell me? Why not you or your preacher buddy? You two might be able to handle this crap, with all your providence and bullshit, but I can't handle it."

Caleb backed out of Will's reach and took a deep breath. His nostrils flared and he said, "Will, you don't have any problems. You don't know what a real problem is. What you have is an I.Q. off the charts, more ability than anyone imaginable, and you can be and do anything that you heart desires. You're filthy rich. Even though you won't admit it, you have two parents that love you and want the best for you. So you miss seven games? So what? Most kids never get to play one college game. You have two more years to be a great all-American. Even though you'll never admit it, you brought all this on yourself by your arrogance and insolence. If you had gone with me, you'd have had a great time and you'd be playing this Saturday night."

"I've heard about enough out of your country ass!" Will yelled. "Now, truck it out of my room. While you're at it, clear out of my dorm room. I don't want you around me anymore."

"I don't intend to go anywhere," Caleb said firmly. "If you want to get rid of me, you'll have to be the one that moves." Will's hard, cold eyes peered at Caleb. He looked as if he might bound at Caleb any second. He yelled, "I said get your sorry ass out of my room!"

Caleb casually strolled to the door, turned, and said, "I'm leaving and I'm going down the hall two doors to visit a kid who has real problems, not imaginary ones. He won't be leaving this place … alive, as you will. He won't have two more years to make All-American. He won't be driving a new red convertible when he leaves. He'll be leaving in a long black hearse. Give that a little thought while you're lying there wallowing in self-pity."

"You have all the answers, don't you, Corn Shuck? How the hell did you get so smart in three weeks?"

"I don't have all the answers, Will. I don't have half the answers. But I do have this little black book that has all the answers. I suggest you read it with all the spare time you're going to have on your hands." Caleb closed the door quickly before Will could respond.

Caleb walked down the hall and eased into Buckie's room. Luther turned, saw Caleb in the door, and jumped up. He rushed over and gave him a big hug. "I can't tell you how much I 'preciates what you done fer Buckie, Caleb. He's been throwin' the ball 'cross the room to me. He got more energy than he had in months. He said he been eatin' everthin' on his plate. I shore believes he be strong 'nuff to go to the game. Oh! Oh! Caleb, you ain't gonna believe what Doc gone and done fer me and Buckie. Come 'ere and take a gander at this." He led Caleb to the closet. "Look a here. You ever seen anythin' any more beautimus than this. I ain't never had no store-bought suit in my life." Luther's eyes glassed over. "Why you reckon he done this fer me and Buckie?"

Caleb, touched deeply by Doc's humanity, managed to say, "I reckon it's because he loves you and Buckie, Mr. Luther. I reckon that's the reason."

"He ain't nuttin' but a saint, Caleb. He knowed I couldn't 'ford no suit to go to that there game. That ain't all he done. He went and got me a room at the Marston hotel and told me I could stay there long as I needed to be wit' my boy. Ain't nobody woulda done that 'cept Doc." Luther shook his head and wiped his eyes. He paused for a few seconds, then asked. "You think you gonna play good tomor' night, Caleb. I ain't narry seen no big college game, and I'm 'bout as 'cited as Buckie ur."

"I promise you this, Mr. Luther, I'll do my best. That's all I can guarantee."

"I want to see you run down that field like the wind," Buckie said, "and I want to watch you score a touchdown more than … well, almost more than anything in the world." Caleb knew what he meant.

"I'm a gonna git you a chair, Caleb, 'cause we got lots o' talkin' to do 'fore Buckie has to go to sleep." He stepped out of the room to get another chair.

"How do you feel, Buckie?" Caleb asked.

"I reckon I ain't never felt so good in my whole life, Caleb. But I'm afraid I ain't going to be able to sleep tonight. Doc might not let me go to the game if I ain't up to it tomorrow night."

"Let me assure you that you'll get a good night's sleep, and Doc'll let you go to the game tomorrow night. He promised me that he would."

"Tell me what it feels like to be in that big ol' stadium with all those people screamin' and jumpin' up and down and cheerin' for you." Buckie asked.

"It's hard to put in words, Buckie. It's kinda like you're in another world with those bright lights shining down on you, and you have goosebumps all over you. You feel like you can run faster than the wind and jump higher than the sky. There's something they call adrenaline that runs through your entire body, and it makes you feel as strong as Hercules. You feel like you can fly and run through a brick wall. But sometimes, the other team is stronger than you. Even with all those emotions running though your body. You still can't win or make a touchdown."

"I been praying that y'all will win the game, Caleb, and you'll make five touchdowns."

"Oh! Buckie, I wish you wouldn't do that. I'd never pray that we win a game. I pray that the Lord will protect everyone on both teams from injury and help us to do our best, but never to win. Everyone loves to win, but if we win, I want it to be because we played our hearts out, and we were the better team. I think it might be selfish to ask the Lord to let us win. I don't think that would be fair to the other team, do you?"

"I ain't thought of it that way, but I reckon you're right. I'll change my prayer and ask that you don't get hurt 'cause I know you're going to win and make five touchdowns."

Caleb laughed and said, "I think that'll please the Lord."

Luther came in dragging a big cushioned chair. "There weren't no empty chairs in that there waiting room so I found an empty room and kinda borrowed this here one."

"Much obliged," Caleb said. He sat down and Luther bombarded him with hundreds of questions for the next hour.

Later that night Gladys came in with a syringe. "I hate to break up this little social gathering, gentlemen, however, if Prince Charming is going out on the town tomorrow night, he has to get a good night's sleep. I'd think you might want to do the same, Caleb, if you are going to make five touchdowns tomorrow night like I've heard. That's what Buckie told me."

Caleb grinned and shook his finger in Buckie's face. "Have you been running your mouth to everyone in this hospital today?"

"I ain't said a word to no one except Mrs. Gladys and Miss Angelle. I swear that's the truth. Oh! I might have mentioned to Pop that I had a dream about the game. In my dream, you made five touchdowns."

"Now both of you promise me that you won't be disappointed if I don't make even one touchdown. Those kids from Kentucky are big and fast, and real strong."

"They ain't no stronger'n you, Caleb," Luther said, "'cause you had to be real tough to make the team with no sperience."

"The jury's still out on that one," Caleb said. Luther tilted his head, looking puzzled at Caleb's response.

"It means he ain't real sure he's tough, Pop," Buckie said, "but we know, don't we?"

"I have to run now, Buckie," Caleb said as he hugged him gently. "I don't know if I'll see you until game time tomorrow, but

I'll be praying that you feel really good when they bring you to the game."

"Do you know Angelle is going to be my nurse at the game?" Buckie said.

"No, I didn't know that," Caleb said. "I thought she hated football."

"There's obviously a lot you don't know about Angelle," Gladys said with a silly grin. "I think she's waiting downstairs for you right now to take her to the dormitory."

"I have a little extra sleeping medicine for you tonight," Gladys said to Buckie. "I want you fresh and rested tomorrow night. My husband and I will be in the stands watching the game, and I'll keep an eye on you in case Angelle needs any help. My husband hasn't been to a game in fifteen years, but he said he had to see Caleb play. He wants to see if Wally is just exaggerating or if Caleb is as good as he says. Now both of you get out of here and let this boy get some rest."

"I'll be a'goin' to the hotel to take them new clothes, Buckie. I'll catch a short nap, then I'll come back here and be here when you wake up in the morn'." Caleb and Luther walked out and Luther said, "You ain't nuttin' but a saint gest like Doc. Ain't no way you'll ever know what you meant to my boy these last few weeks."

"Mr. Luther, your boy's done more for me than I could ever do for him. He's brought me back to reality. I know now there is more to life than making touchdowns and getting high on the applause and cheers of the crowd. We have to live life one day at a time, and be thankful for every minute. There's a lot of pain in this life that I never knew anything about when I was on the farm. I'm learning to be grateful for everything this life has to offer. I love your boy. I would give anything in this world if he could get better and walk out of this hospital. But we know that isn't going to happen. We have to accept that and love him every minute we have him with us. We're not ready to give him up to the Lord, but that isn't our decision. We have to accept the Lord's will."

"I knows what you a'sayin' is right, Caleb, but it ain't easy."

Caleb hugged Luther. "Just try to get some rest, Mr. Luther. You have to be strong through this. Now, you go get some rest."

Caleb walked downstairs and saw Angelle waiting outside for him. Her eyes were bright. And there was no sign of pain or sorrow in them. She smiled as Caleb walked up to her. "Why the bright smile?" he asked.

"I'll never tell," she answered, continuing to smile more brightly than he had ever seen.

"So you're going to the game tomorrow," he commented. "I thought you hated violence."

"I have to take care of my baby."

"That's the only reason you're going?"

"I'll never tell," she said, continuing to smile. "Are you hungry?"

"As a bear in spring," Caleb responded. "Do you like barbecue?"

"I like anything at ten p.m."

"What about curfew?" Caleb asked.

"They don't check my curfew because I have to work late when someone is out sick."

"Well, hop in my honeymoon truck and let's get rolling. I know this place about five miles out of town. It makes the best Memphis barbecue in Mississippi."

As they drove out of town, Angelle eased over by Caleb and slid her arm under his. She wrapped her hand around his arm and leaned her head over on his shoulder and snuggled close to him. After a few minutes, she said, "I feel better tonight than I have—than I remember in my entire life. I've never seen Buckie or Mr. Luther so excited and joyful. You would think they had just received news that his cancer was in remission. I suppose I've finally resolved the fact that we're going to lose him. But to see him so happy makes me happy too." Angelle took her hand and gently patted Caleb's cheek. "Do you really love me, Caleb Morgan? I mean—really, really love me. Am I the only one that you'll ever love?"

"You don't have to ask me that, Angelle. That's not the real question that has to be answered. The real question is, do you really love me and are you willing to take that ring off and honestly mean it?"

There was a long pause before she answered. "I love you more than my own life. That's all I can say right now. I hope soon I'll be able to say that you are the only one that I'll love for the rest of my life. I beg you to be patient and give me a little more time."

"Your answer tells me that there is still some doubt in your mind about whether you love Maurice more than me. You can't imagine how that hurts."

"I know. I'd give anything to be able to say that I'll marry you right now, tonight. That we can raise a family and be happy for the rest of our lives. But I have to ask you to wait just a little longer before I can be sure. I don't want to hurt you. I love you too much to do that to you."

"If there's the slightest chance that you'll marry me, I'll wait forever for you... Well, we're here. We're lucky he's still open. Let's hurry in." They rushed in and Mr. Pigg greeted them at the door. "I was about to shut the door, Caleb. I'm glad I didn't. I've never seen a girl as pretty as this little beauty. I see you two are engaged. Congratulations, my boy. That's a beautiful ring. I'd say you got the pick of the litter."

"This is Angelle Noel, Mr. Pigg. We're not engaged. I'm trying to get that ring off her finger, but so far I haven't had any luck," Caleb said, smiling.

"Miss Angelle, let me put a good word in for this handsome, young celebrity. He's one of the nicest and most mannerly young men I have had the privilege of serving. You could do a lot worse." Angelle blushed and nodded.

"I love his pork po-boys," Caleb said, "But he has beef or sausage."

"I'll have what you have," she said, continuing to smile.

"I like that," Mr. Pigg said. "You already have her trained."

He fixed two po-boys. Caleb commented, "We'll take them with us. I know it's late."

"You'll do no such thing. Sit right there and enjoy your meal. I'm in no hurry. I'll just sit here and admire Miss Noel's beauty. You kids take your time. I have some cleaning up to do. Oh! Would you like something to drink? I think I have a couple of beers in the refrigerator."

"No thanks, Mr. Pigg, we don't drink beer."

"See, Miss Noel, I rest my case. I've done all I can for you, Caleb. You'll have to handle the rest." They hurriedly ate the delicious barbecue. When Caleb tried to pay, Mr. Pigg said, "Not tonight, my boy. Save your money and buy Miss Noel a bigger ring. I've heard that works."

"If I thought that would work, I'd go to Alaska and dig for gold," Caleb replied. They thanked him and started back to the campus.

As they drove back toward Marston, Angelle snuggled close to him and casually remarked, "Would you like to go somewhere and park?"

Caleb jaw dropped and he was totally caught off guard by her question. "You mean— park, like in some dark secluded place?"

"That's what the girls in the dormitory say they do on dates."

"You consider this a date?" Caleb said wide-eyed and still in shock over her suggestion.

"I don't really know. I've never had a date before. I mean I've never parked on a date before."

"How could you be engaged without ever parking, or sitting in some quiet secluded place?"

Angelle shrugged and said, "I'm not the kind of girl that parks with anyone."

"But you just said—"

"Well, I'm in college now. I don't know what harm it can do. You are an honorable boy, aren't you?"

Caleb smiled and said, "There's a little gravel road that turns off to the right about a mile ahead. It's quiet and secluded with a watermelon patch about a half-mile down the road on the left."

"Is that yours and Emil's watermelon patch?"

"One and the same. I have some bad memories about that patch."

"Let's see if we can change your memories," Angelle said as she snuggled closer to him.

Caleb turned down the narrow road and drove past the watermelon patch. He found a side road to turn around so the truck was headed back toward the main road. He turned the engine off and glanced at his watch in the moonlight. *Ten to eleven.* He thought, *Coach Stan is going to kill me if he pulls monitoring duties tonight. Well, some things are worth dying for.*

"Have you ever made love?" Angelle asked.

Caleb, now in total shock, looked at her in disbelief. He thought briefly before answering, "No."

"Have you ever wanted to make love before?" she pressed.

"If we're being totally truthful, I'd have to say every time I look at you I want to make love to you."

"Did you ever almost make love to anyone?"

"This one girl took me to a movie. I think she wanted to make love. She was beautiful, and her figure was almost as perfect as yours. I was tempted, but I still believe that making love should be reserved for the marriage bed. Will doesn't agree, but he never agrees with anything I say. If we're going to be honest with each other, I'll ask you the same question. Have you ever made love with anyone?"

There was a long pause before Angelle replied, "No, I've never made love."

"Why did it take you so long to answer? If you and Maurice had made love, I would still love you. I know it happens sometimes. I wouldn't like it, but I would still love you."

"Caleb, as God is my witness, I never made love to anyone."

"I want to ask you one other question. Did you panic when Maurice held you and kissed you?"

She looked away as she pondered her response. "I'm not going to answer that. It was a long time ago. Let's not talk about him, or my past." She took his hand, careful to grasp the top of it. She leaned over and began to kiss him on the cheek. Caleb sat there like a stone man, not knowing how to respond, Doc's warning resounding in his head. She reached up and caressed his cheek gently for a moment. Then traced his lips with her finger and eased his face toward hers until their lips met. She reached down and grasped both his wrists with her hands, eased her slender body over until she was sitting on his lap. Their lips began to move over each other's until they were as one. Within moments, the passion became so explosive that she released his hands and wrapped her arms around his neck, pulled him to her as forcefully as her slender arms would allow. They were both nearing a point of complete ecstasy. Caleb was fighting the impulse to put his arms around her and hold her as she was holding him.

"Hold me tightly," she said. "Hold me and pretend we're making love." Caleb, without hesitation or a thought of the consequences, reached around her and drew her soft, warm body to his. For a few seconds, both were feeling pleasure and exhilaration like neither had ever known. Suddenly he felt her tense up and start to tremble in his arms. Her breath quickened even more, and she pushed him away with all her strength, slid over to the door, opened it, jumped out of the truck, and stood there trembling as tears welled up in her eyes.

Caleb panicked at the sight. Guilt overwhelmed him as he sat there a few seconds listening to her frightful gasps. He jumped out of the truck and ran to her. "I'm going to swear to God that I'll never touch you or kiss you again as long as I live. I won't be responsible for you depression and pain again."

"Don't say that, Caleb. I'm going to get control of my emotions. I'm going to get better. I promise you that I'm going to get better."

"Sarah Catherine was right. I'm no more than a common thief trying to steal what will never belong to me. My selfishness is destroying what I love most. I won't do this to you anymore. I'll always love you, but I won't cause you any more pain. As far as I'm concerned, you have no decision to make. You're engaged to someone you must have loved dearly and he's not here. That's why you're here with me, suffering and in tears. Get in the truck. I'll take you back to the campus. I love you enough to give you up if that's what'll make you well."

"Don't say that, please! Swear that you won't give up on me. I know I can love you. Just give me a little more time. I know that's not fair to ask, but..."

"Angelle, get back in the truck. I'm so confused that I don't know right from wrong anymore. My life has been in a whirlwind for weeks now. Sometimes I wish I'd never come to this place. I do know it would've been better for you if I hadn't come."

"That's not true. Never say that again. You belong here. Everybody loves you. Sarah Catherine even said she was sorry for what she said to you. She knows she was wrong now." They drove back to the campus in total silence.

As they neared the dorm, Angelle said, "Drop me off a few blocks from the dormitory. I don't want any of those nosy girls to see me getting out of your truck. They might get the wrong idea and tell the housemother that I was on a date. I could get early sign-in for the rest of the semester."

"That's the last thing I want to happen," Caleb said. He pulled off the road two blocks from her dorm and said, "Good night." Angelle rushed to the dorm. Caleb waited a few minutes then drove slowly to his dorm. *I wish I had a friend to talk to. I don't know what's right anymore. I can't keep hurting her. Why in the world did I have to fall in love with her? Why can't I turn it off, just go to school, and be normal.* He glanced at his new watch and said quietly to himself, "Huh, it's after midnight. I hope I'm not in trouble with the coaches. Now, wouldn't that be a heck of a note if I couldn't get to play tomorrow for breaking curfew. That would be terrible, especially with my folks and Buckie coming to see me play." He parked the truck and eased up the stairs. When he opened the door at the top of the stairs, Coach Stan was coming down the hall.

Caleb wilted and froze in his tracks. Coach Stan looked at his watch, then said, "Caleb, you're about two and a half hours past curfew."

"Uh—yes. Yes, sir. I—I can explain, sir. I worked late and I went to the hospital to see Will and Buckie. Buckie's father was there. He wanted to talk about football and school and a hundred other things. The time just got away from me, and that's why I'm late."

"Oh, really! Is that a fact?" Coach Stan said with a dubious stare.

Caleb paused before answering reluctantly. "No, sir, that ain't right. I've never been a liar, and I don't intend to start now. I was late leaving Buckie's room, but this girl that I'm in love with works nights at the hospital, and she asked me to bring her back to the dorm. Then she asked me if I was hungry. I hadn't eaten all day so we went to get a bite at Mr. Pigg's place."

"Okay, I'll buy that, but I know he closes about ten o'clock. How do you account for the next couple of hours, or should I ask?"

Caleb dropped his head and began his confession. "On the way back from Mr. Pigg's, she wanted to park. But we didn't do nothing wrong. I ain't that kind of person and she surely ain't."

"What you mean, son, is that you did nothing immoral, and she isn't that kind of girl. I know who you were with, and it's inconceivable to me that she'd asked you to park, but I'll take your word for it, however, if you don't clean up your vocabulary, you won't be around long enough to help the team next year."

"I've told you the truth, Coach, and I'm willing to take my punishment. I just don't want Angelle to get in trouble."

"Son, if you brought her back to the dorm at twelve-thirty, I'm afraid it's too late for that. Now you get in the bed and get a good night's sleep. You have a big game tomorrow. I know your folks are coming to see you play. Sleep a little late if you need to because we want you to do well for them."

"That mean I get to play tomorrow, Coach!"

"I think we can overlook your first infraction. The curfew is for your own good. Just don't make a habit of it."

"Why is everyone so good to me?" Caleb murmured as Coach Stan walked away. Stan just laughed and shook his head as he walked out the door.

John David stuck his head out of his door across the hall. "You just dodged a bullet, Caleb. If that had been anyone but Coach Stan, you'd be riding the pine tomorrow night. He's trying to make up for the cruel way he treated you… You actually parked with Angelle?" John David said in amazement. "I can't believe she let you park!"

Caleb put his finger to his lips. "Shhh. Do you want everybody on the hall to hear about it?" He whispered, "It was perfectly innocent. She's a lady. We just talked and—" He grinned and said, "We did some kissing for a brief…hour."

Cliff stuck his head out two doors down and asked, "Does she kiss as good as she looks? Did she give you a frenchie?"

Caleb wilted and dropped his head. "Shhh," John David scolded, "If you don't hush, we might as well post it on the bulletin board."

Tubby Taylor stuck his head out some three doors down. "Did I hear you say Caleb gave Angelle a frenchie?" The doors began to open all the way down the hall. Everyone stepped out and began to cheer and clap for Caleb. Tubby yelled, "I told y'all that Caleb had the hots for Angelle. Now it seems the feeling is mutual!" All up and down the hall guys were asking questions about how it felt to kiss the campus queen and if Caleb had gotten the ring off her finger.

"How do you think it was?" Tubby yelled. "Our hero made the biggest score of his life."

Caleb was turning three shades of pink. Finally he had enough. He threw his hands up and yelled, "Y'all have it all wrong. Angelle and me—"

Everyone yelled, "Angelle and I."

"Whatever," Caleb said. "Anyway, we're just good friends. Even beautiful girls need friends. I don't even know what a frenchie is, but we didn't do anything wrong. I'd appreciate it if you guys wouldn't say anything about this. She needs a friend, and I just happen to be the one she chose."

Travis Carr yelled, "Caleb, you're about the luckiest sucker in the world."

"Luck doesn't have anything to do with it," Cliff said. "Caleb went through hell to get his shot, and he earned it. Let's all go to bed. We have a big game tomorrow."

"Please don't spread any ugly rumors," Caleb pleaded. "Angelle is a very sweet and innocent girl, and she's still engaged. She didn't do anything wrong tonight. I promise all of you that that is the truth."

They all yelled, "Good night!"

The doors began to close. "Get a good night's sleep," John David said, and he closed his door.

After a quick shower, Caleb crawled into bed, but sleep didn't come easy. He recounted every moment and word he and Angelle had shared. Then he thought about Will and his condition and how he might handle him during his convalescence. His mind rolled over to Buckie and Luther and the ballgame. Panic crept in at the thought of playing in front of his parents. His mind continued to roll over and over like a fast moving projector. He tossed and turned until finally, after complete mental exhaustion, he fell asleep. Sometime in the wee dawn hours, the nightmares started. He fielded a punt and it hit his pads and flew up into a Kentucky player's hands. Caleb chased him, but he was always just out of reach as he scored. Later in the dream, he ran the ball around the end. A big safety came up and hit him so hard that he fumbled the ball and almost broke his ribs. He stumbled off the field, and the crowd began to boo. He looked up at his mother in the stands, and she was shaking her head. The dreams came and went for the rest of the night until the bright sun through the window awoke him. He had overslept. He dressed in a flash and rushed to class. He and Dr. DeHaberman came rushing into the auditorium at the same time. She cut her eyes at him over her glasses, but he managed to scoot down the aisle and take his seat before she got to the podium. She began the lecture as Caleb slid into his seat.

Angelle grinned at him. They didn't talk. He returned the grin. After class, they walked out together. Angelle said, "You have a big day today, don't you? I imagine you're pretty excited."

"Scared would be more appropriate. My parents are going to be in the stands, and that scares me to death."

"But Buckie is going to be on the sidelines, and that should make up for it," Angelle said.

"Angelle, I don't really know if I'm good or just—fortunate to have played as well as I have the last few weeks. I'm really nervous about this game. I don't want to disappoint anyone."

"The only person you could ever disappoint is yourself. I know you love to play football, so just go have fun. It's not life or death. There are many things that are more important than being a big football hero, and I know you know that. So just enjoy it."

"You have a good head on your shoulders, as well as a very beautiful one, I might add."

"If I am beautiful, I didn't have anything to do with it. I can thank my parents for that. I look a lot like my mother, and she was beautiful. That's not to say I think I'm beautiful."

"Well, everyone else does."

"Are you coming to the hospital after the game tonight?" Angelle asked.

"I'm sure I will if I'm still in one piece. Oh! I don't know what my folk's plans are yet. If they're going to spend the night, I'll need to spend some time with them."

"I'd like to meet your parents, Caleb. If they are anything like you, they must be very nice people. Do you think that's possible?"

"If I can get to the hospital early enough, and they are going to stay in town, then we might have time for you to meet them."

"Good! I'll look forward to seeing you tonight."

CHAPTER FIFTEEN

After Caleb finished his classes, he went to the club to help Abe as usual. When he arrived, the parking lot was already full. *There must be something special going on in town,* he thought. *I better hurry.* Abe was rushing around trying to take their orders. "Thank heavens you're here," he gasped. "Get your jacket on and give me a hand. We don't have crowds like this except for varsity games on Saturday night."

"What's going on?" Caleb asked.

"They're all here to see you play. There hasn't been this much excitement over a game since … well, I don't think there's been this much excitement over a game in the last ten years."

"Sweet mercy!" Caleb said. "That's all I need, more pressure."

"Then get busy and work off some of that pressure," Abe said. "My gout's acting up." Everyone had to stop Caleb to ask him about the game. They worked steadily until one-thirty, and the crowd began to clear. "Here comes Doc and the Knights," Abe said. "Now, don't be kissin' on that cute little red head. Remember her father's a judge."

"You don't have to remind me," Caleb said smiling. "Who's the older couple with Doc and Mrs. Edith?"

"I've never seen them before," Abe said. "Probably some senator or governor who needs a little campaign money. It happens regularly at election time. Nothing surprises me anymore."

Abe rushed over to greet Doc's party and escort them to Doc's table. He rearranged the tables to accommodate the larger group. Jennifer rolled herself over to the kitchen door to give Caleb a hug. Jennifer tried to give Caleb a kiss, but he gave her a little peck on the cheek. "I had to stop calling you because the judge took the phone out of my room when he got the phone bill this month. He even threatened to take away my allowance if I ever ran up a bill like that again. I've missed talking to you. You know I love you, don't you?"

Caleb ruffled her hair and said, "Princess, I love you, too, but I'm not in love with you. I know you think you love me, but that's not exactly the same as being in love with someone."

"No!" Jennifer snapped. "I do really love you. I have all the clippings of your games in a scrapbook. I'll give it to you as a graduation present."

"That's very sweet of you. I'll cherish it."

"I'd rather you cherished me," she said as she rolled herself back over to the table where everyone was exchanging pleasantries. Abe passed a handful of menus around. Doc kept glancing nervously at Caleb. After taking their orders, Abe returned to the kitchen. Caleb was busy cleaning other tables and he hadn't gone near Doc's party. Abe brought their lunch, and they enjoyed the delicious meal as they talked leisurely. When Abe returned to the table, everyone ordered dessert and continued to socialize for another thirty minutes. Abe's foot was throbbing, so he asked Caleb to see if anyone wanted coffee.

Caleb walked up between Travis and Iris Hodges. Leaning forward, he asked, "Would anyone care for coffee?"

Iris had picked up her glass of ice water and was about to take a sip. She turned and said, "I'd love a cup of coffee, young man." She looked up at Caleb, smiling, gasped, and dropped her glass.

It crashed against the hardwood floor as glass, water and ice went everywhere. A look of horror and disbelief came across her face.

Travis said, "Are you all right, honey?"

Iris continued looking up at Caleb. She stood and said, "I need a breath of air, Travis. Please take me outside for a moment."

Doc, pointing to the patio door, said, "That door leads out to the patio. If you need me for anything, I'll be here."

Iris rushed across the floor to the patio, with Travis in hot pursuit. The judge and Doc sat there looking like the two cats that ate the canary. Edith shook her head and glared at Doc with a look of repugnance.

Caleb rushed to the kitchen for a mop and a bucket to clean the floor.

"What going on?" Jennifer asked, quick to perceive that some sort of duplicity was in progress.

"You two might as well tell her before she blows the whole scheme and makes you two look like a couple of superfluous do-gooders," Edith admonished.

"Tell me what?" Jennifer asked.

"I'll tell her," the judge said. "Young lady, you'd better keep your big mouth shut. I mean I don't even want Lillian to hear about this. Mr. and Mrs. Hodges are Caleb's grandparents, and they don't have a clue as to who he is. I imagine Iris looked up at Caleb and thought she was seeing the ghost of Christmas past—her deceased son-in-law. It gave her a hell of—a heck of a jolt. She'll be all right in a few minutes."

"I don't understand," Jennifer said. "How can you have a grandson and not even know him?"

"It's a long story that's none of your concern, Jennifer," Judge Knight said.

"You'll understand later, Jennifer," Edith said. "It's a little complicated and very personal. Caleb doesn't know they're his grandparents either."

"Oh!" Jennifer said. "I get it, some sort of family squabble, and Doc's trying to promote a reconciliation."

Edith patted Jennifer on the head and commented, "You're very astute, young lady."

Outside on the patio, Travis said, "What's wrong, Iris? I've never seen you act like this before. Are you ill?"

She was still gasping and pale as a sheet. She said, "Did you see … Did you see that young man?"

"What young man?" Travis asked. "Are you all right?"

"Oh Lord! Oh Lord! He nearly startled the wits out of me."

"Calm yourself, and tell me what you're talking about, Iris."

"Travis!" She gasped again. The tears began to run down her cheeks as she murmured, "I looked up and I thought Daniel Morgan had returned from the dead. That he had returned to haunt me."

"Iris, have you completely lost your mind? That's the most preposterous thing I've ever heard you say."

"Oh! Is that so, Travis? Look through that window and tell me what you see." Caleb and Abe were busy on the floor cleaning up the water and broken glass.

"I don't see anything except what I've been seeing for the last hour."

"The boy Travis, look at the boy!" She exclaimed.

Travis stood there looking until Caleb stood up. He was able to get a good look at Caleb's face. "Oh! My heavens, you are right! That young man is the spitting image of Daniel Morgan. I guess the old saying is correct about everyone having a double somewhere in the world. Now, get a grip on yourself. Let's get back to our hosts before we look like a couple of idiots. Please don't repeat what you said to me."

"Travis, I'm no fool!" she snapped. She wiped her eyes and they strolled back to the table.

They took their seats trying to look calm. Travis said in a seemingly casual voice, "Who is that handsome young man that was cleaning the floor, Doc?"

"That's the fabulous freshman, Caleb Morgan, the next all-American football player at Marston. I'm going to marry him someday," Jennifer added.

"She lives in a fantasy world," the judge commented.

"Why is he cleaning tables here if he's financially able to attend Marston and has a football scholarship?" Iris asked.

"He didn't accept a scholarship. His mother has some peculiar notion about charity," Doc said. "She feels that a person should earn his way in life if it's going to have any lasting value. They're very poor farmers from Choctaw County. He has to work to pay for his education."

An apprehensive look flashed across Travis' face. He asked, "What's his mother's name?" Edith and Judge Knight cut their eyes at Doc and watched him pale and squirm for a few seconds.

"Uh, uh, I think it is Mary. Yes, that's right. I'm sure it's Mary."

"And his father's?" Travis asked as his eyes widened and his brows rose.

"I think it was Daniel. Yes, I'm sure Caleb said it was Daniel. He was killed in the war."

Travis and Iris both grew pale and sank low in their chairs. Doc continued his explanation about Caleb. "I was so taken with the boy the first day he came to ask for a job. I later realized that his father and my son, who was also killed in the war, knew each other. My son, June, sent me a picture of Daniel and himself that was taken just days before they were both killed at the invasion of Normandy in forty-four. He's like a son to me now. I've never known a boy like him, with the exception of my son. He has such humility and honesty and strength of character."

"Iris," Travis said, close to tears and in a broken voice, "look at your grandson. Look at that handsome young man." Iris put her hands over her mouth as the tears began to flow.

After an uneasy moment of silence, Iris murmured, "Take me home, Travis. Take me home this minute!" she demanded as the tears streamed down her cheeks.

"Sweetheart, the only way you're getting back to Jackson before the end of the ballgame tonight is by taxi or Greyhound. I came to watch a potential all-American running back, and now, miraculously, I find out that he's my own flesh and blood. I'm about to burst with pride and jubilance. I didn't know we had a grandson! You need to get a grip on yourself."

"Who would ever believe this in a million years?" Doc said, tongue-in-cheek. "This is too bizarre."

"Yes!" Travis said, cutting his eyes at Doc with a dubious grin and nod.

Iris looked up at Doc and said, "Why is he working as a waiter? That's demeaning."

"Like I said, his mother refused to let him accept a scholarship. She has some strange notion that it's charity. She said they don't accept charity. They're hard working farm people with a strict set of values. I tried to give him a Marston Foundation scholarship and he refused it, too. He said a person has to work for what he gets in life for it to have any value."

"It seems I've heard that before," Travis said, smiling at Iris.

"I need to go rest awhile," Iris said fanning her face. "I feel faint. This is too much for me to comprehend."

"Edith, would you mind running Iris home and letting her rest a while?" Doc asked. "I'm sure she'll feel better after a short rest."

"It would be a pleasure," Edith said. They stood and walked out to Edith's car and drove away.

"You could have told me this last week," Travis said. "I've wanted to end this insanity for many years but…"

"I love that boy like a son," Doc said. "I had hoped you'd feel the same when you met him. I didn't know how you'd respond. Every boy needs a grandfather, but I was afraid the wound might be too deep to heal. I'm sorry for meddling in your lives."

"Don't be. I'll be indebted to you the rest of my life.

"I won't take all the credit then. Horace was a party to this duplicity," Doc admitted.

"I suspected as much," Travis said, "and to show him my appreciation, I'm going to give him an all-expense paid vacation on a Caribbean cruise. He's mentioned how much joy the last one brought him," Travis said, giving Doc a quick wink.

"I'll take the money. You take the vacation," the judge quipped.

"I'd like to go with you and mother," Jennifer said, brightly.

"You already did," the judge said.

"I must've been too young to remember," Jennifer said with a shrug.

Travis added, "I've tried to convince Iris to reconcile her differences with Mary for many years. Her response was always, 'Mary knows where we live. It was her decision to abandon her family.' Now, I think it's about time for me to meet my grandson, although I don't deserve to have one. Did you all realize I didn't know I had a grandson?"

"No," Doc said, "but I'm telling you that you have a jewel."

"Yes," Jennifer agreed. "He's wonderful. I'm going to marry him someday. He doesn't know it yet. I fell in love with him out on that patio when he picked me up and danced with me to the beautiful song, *Danny Boy*. There's no one like him in the whole wide world." Her eyes sparkled as she spoke of him.

"She has a full-blown teenage crush on him," the judge said. "It'll be someone else next month."

"There'll never be anyone else," Jennifer said. "You'll see."

Doc motioned for Caleb to come over. Caleb strolled over and said, "May I get y'all something?"

Mr. Hodges stood and faced Caleb. His eyes were teary.

"Is something wrong, sir?" Caleb asked.

"Caleb," Doc said, "get a grip on yourself. This is going to come as a shock." Caleb's heart shot into his throat. All he could think of was that his parents had had an accident on their way to Marston.

"Son, I want you to meet your grandfather, Travis Hodges." Caleb took a deep breath and gave a long sigh of relief. Then, realizing what Doc had said, a feeling of exhilaration ran through his body. They stood facing each other a few seconds. Travis opened his arms and Caleb rushed into them. They stood embracing and tears of joy flowed freely. After a moment they released each other and stood looking into each other's eyes.

"What do I call you, sir?" Caleb asked.

"Just don't call me what I am," Travis said, smiling. "Call me grandfather, son, and I'll call you Caleb Daniel Morgan, my wonderful and handsome grandson. Can you ever forgive me for not being there for you and Mary Margaret all these years?"

"There ain't—I mean there isn't anything to forgive, Grandfather," and they embraced again.

Abe was standing in the kitchen door, watching and listening to the conservation. He wiped his eyes and said, "Now, ain't this a grand ol' day?"

Travis said, "Let me look at how strong and handsome you are." He put his hands on Caleb's shoulders with a firm grip. Then he grabbed him around the shoulder and embraced him again. "I have a grandson," he said in a broken voice. "I never knew you existed until a moment ago, but I swear if I had, I'd have come to see you. I feel so ashamed," he exclaimed, wiping his eyes. "How is Mary Margaret? Is she still as beautiful as she was?"

"I can answer that," Doc said. "She might just be the most beautiful lady I've ever had the pleasure of meeting. Of course, I wouldn't want Edith to hear me say that."

"Did you know she married Uncle Houston last month?" Caleb asked brightly.

"No, I didn't. I never met your Uncle Houston, but he must be a very fine man for her to marry him."

"He is. He's like a real father to me. I don't remember much about my father, but the few memories I do have are wonderful."

"I'd give anything to meet your Uncle Houston and see my daughter again."

Doc caught Caleb's eye and gave a stern look and a quick headshake. Caleb understood his gesture and said, "I'm sure they'd love to see you too, Grandfather."

"Say that again, the grandfather part. I had given up hope of having a grandson."

"Yes sir, Grandfather."

"I plan to hear it for the rest of my life," Travis said. "I'll be attending all your games from now on, even the away games. And you're going to visit us in Jackson. I'm filled with pride and elation, son. This could be the grandest day of my life."

"What about Grandmother?" Caleb asked, somewhat dismayed.

"You don't need to worry about Iris. She'll come around. She's just a very emotional lady. When the initial shock wears off, she'll love you as I do. This silly family squabble is about to come to an end. Doc told me of Mary's silly notion about charity. I do agree that charity is for widows and orphans, but you're family. I certainly can afford to pay for your education. After all, I've done nothing to support you and Mary the last twenty years. I feel extremely guilty about that." Doc's ears perked up to hear Caleb's response to Travis' proposal.

Caleb said, "Grandfather, don't think I'm not grateful for the offer, but I don't need any help. Doc pays me more than I'm worth. I really enjoy working here for him, and Mr. Abe, and Mr. Burt. They're so good to me. They're like my family. I'm not going to stop working here until I graduate." Abe put his hand over his eyes shaking his head and turned and walked into the kitchen and thought, *I love that boy like my son. I don't reckon he needs your money, Mr. Hodges 'cause when Doc's leaves this world, he'll be the richest man in this state.*

Doc's jaw tightened, and he looked at Travis. "That's our boy." Then he laughed and said to Caleb. "Now, if you don't get back there and help Abe clean up, you might have a pink slip with your next check."

Travis reached out to Caleb again and gave him another hug. "I'm so proud to see you, son. This is the grandest day of my life."

Jennifer said, "That's why I'm going to marry him, Mr. Hodges. Isn't he wonderful?"

"Huh!" Caleb said. "Do I have a say in this matter, Carrot Top?" He bent down to hug Jennifer, then returned to work.

"I am going to marry him," Jennifer said firmly. "He may not realize it now. I fell in love with him right out there on that patio the night he picked me up and held me in his arms and danced with me. It was the first time I ever danced. He's the nicest and most handsome and most wonderful boy in the world."

"You'll get no argument from me," Travis said. "Doc, I think I need to go check on Iris. This did come as a shock to her. I imagine she's feeling a little guilty by now."

"We'll all go. You and Horace can get some rest before the game tonight," Doc said.

Will was like a caged tiger in the small hospital room, pacing back and forth and becoming increasingly irritated with his mother's persistent pampering. "Mother!" he said forcefully, "Call Father and tell him to send Clovis back to take you home. I'll be leaving the hospital tomorrow, and I don't think they'll let you move into the dorm with me. I'm fine. I'm well. I need some time to myself."

"Yes, son, I do agree you are doing splendidly. I do need to get back for my Garden Club meeting and my flower gardens. I'll call William tonight when I get back to the hotel. I'll ask him to send Clovis to pick me up tomorrow."

"No, Mother, do it now. You might not be able to reach him if you wait until tonight."

"You're probably right. I'll go now. Are you sure you'll be all right when I'm gone?"

"If I die, Mother, I'll come and get you. I promise"

"Don't be silly, son. You don't seem to realize how serious you injury was."

"Go, Mother!" Will said, shushing her away with his hand.

"All right, if you insist. Just remember, I'll be sitting in our box seats on the sidelines. If you have any complications, just wave for me. I'll come take care of you." She picked up her purse and said, "I'll see you after the game, Will. Please, don't get too excited and run your blood pressure up during the game."

Will dropped his head in disgust and began to shake it.

"I'm leaving now," she said, "but you should be ashamed."

"I know," Will said. "I am," and he grinned at her. He bent low and kissed her on the forehead. "I love you, Mother, but you treat me like I'm still in grade school."

"I just want the best for you, son," she replied and walked out the door.

Will wiped his brow, as if to wipe perspiration from it. He shook his head and said, "Finally, I can have a little peace." He reached for his triple-X white robe hanging on the wall and slipped it on. He waited until he was sure his mother had left the hallway, then cracked his door and peeped out. He waited until all the nurses were out of sight. He shot out of the room and rushed down the hall to Buckie's room. He noticed Gladys coming out of one of the rooms down the hall so he shot into Buckie's room. Luther was sitting near Buckie's bed facing the door, half dozing. Buckie was resting quietly on the bed. Will closed the door quickly behind him, and the noise startled Luther, and he opened his eyes. Luther looked up at Will standing inside the door with his white robe draped around him. He looked like a huge white giant, as big as the door. Luther's jaw dropped, and his eyes widened. He gasped, "Oh my G–O – D!"

Buckie laughed, recognizing Will instantly from Caleb's description and his picture in the program. He said, "Pop, that's Mr. Will James, the all-American football player."

"Lord have mercy," Luther said, "you skeered ten years off my life, Mr. Will. I reckoned Gabriel or one of them other Angels done come to git me. I ain't never seen nobody as big as you."

Will grinned, thrust his huge chest out and said proudly, "They don't come much bigger, Mr. Cummings." He held out his hand. Luther stood up smiling, sporting his new suit and shoes, and they shook hands. "You have quite a boy here, Mr. Cummings. He's a real trooper from what Caleb and the team say about him. I kind of screwed up so I haven't had a chance to come and see him before now. But here I am finally. I'm leaving the hospital tomorrow, and I probably won't get back for awhile."

"You come back when you can and see me," Buckie said. "I ain't going nowhere sept to Heaven." Will glanced at Luther, and Luther looked away.

"I'll certainly do that, Buckie. I'll certainly do that. I see where Buckie gets his good looks, Mr. Cummings. You look quite spiffy in those beautiful duds."

Luther blushed and grinned proudly. "Ain't they purdy? I reckon I ain't nary had no suit likin this 'fore. Hell, I ain't nary had no suit 'fore."

"Well, you should wear it more often, Mr. Luther. You look like a high society, southern gentleman in those beautiful duds. Buckie, I'll be sitting by you and your pop tonight in my wheelchair on the sidelines. You're not going to get too excited when Caleb scores a touchdown, are you?"

Buckie beamed and said, "I sure am gonna get excited. I didn't figure this day would ever come. I'm ready to go right now!"

"It won't be long," Will said. "I'm no doctor, but I'd guess they want you to get a good rest this afternoon. Those games can get strung out sometimes. I know you want to see the end of the game."

"I ain't been doing nothing but resting here for a couple of years," Buckie said. "I'm ready to go now… Are you real sad about not being able to play anymore this year, Will?"

Will thought about the question before he answered. "Yes. Yes, I'm sad about not being able to play. But I brought it on myself, Buckie. I knew those—those thugs were waiting outside for me, but sometimes I'm too hardheaded for my own good. I hurt the team. I hurt the coaches. That's what's killing me. They say you learn from your mistakes. I hope it's true."

Will shook his head as he walked over to the window and gazed out on the street. "My heavens, there must be a thousand cars on the street! You don't think all these people are here for the game tonight, do you?"

"I reckon they ur," Luther said. "That's all they talks 'bout in town and at the mill whur I work. They say if'n Will and Caleb wuz on the team together, there ain't nobody could whup us. And it's true, ain't it Will?"

"You can bet the farm on that, Mr. Cummings."

"Gest call me Luther, please. Ain't nobody calls me Mr. Cummings 'cept…"

"Well, they should, being a gentleman like you are, Mr. Luther. But if you wish, I'll call you Luther. I call all my good friends by their first name." Luther grinned and nodded.

"Now, Buckie, how about I pick you up and toss you up to the ceiling a dozen times or so?"

Buckie laughed at the thought. Luther said, "He could pick me up and do it if'n he wuz a mind to. I done hear'd yo' name called 'bout a million times on that there radjo. But I'd a never believed how big and strong you wuz 'til I seed it wit' my own eyes. How'd you git so strong, Will?"

Will said, "I suppose about half of it was heredity, and the other half was pumping iron five days a week since I was five years old." For the next hour, Luther shot questions at Will and Will enjoyed responding with some pretty tall tales.

Finally, Luther asked, "How'd you know Buckie were in this here hospital?"

"Caleb Morgan is my roommate in the dorm. Caleb made sure all the team knew your son was in the hospital."

"Yeah," Luther said, grinning, "that figure. Ain't he sumpin special?"

"Yes, he is. He's one for the ages. They broke the mold when they made him."

"Pop," Buckie said, "you know all the team came by to see me. Even the coaches came, and I know they ain't got time to be comin' to see me."

"When you're special," Will said, "people take the time. You're a very special young man."

"I still can't believe we're going to the ballgame," Buckie said, getting all excited. "And we're going to be sitting on the sidelines side by side, ain't we Will?" He began to shake.

"If'n you don' calm yo self down, son," Luther warned, "we a gonna be in this here room listening to the game on that there radio again."

Buckie laid back on his pillow. Luther turned on the oxygen, pulled down the mask to hold over Buckie's face for a while. Will leaned over to run his fingers through Buckie's thinning hair. A feeling of deep compassion like he had never experienced before melted his stone heart.

The door opened and Gladys and Angelle walked into the room. Gladys stopped and stood rigid, putting her hands on her hips. Angelle grinned and lowered her head. Gladys said, "You're pressing your luck, Mr. Hot Shot."

"What luck?" Will grumbled. "If I didn't have bad luck, I wouldn't have any luck at all."

"Oh, no, buddy," Gladys said. "There's not going to be a pity party around here today. You're no dummy. You know how fortunate you are to be alive and recovering so quickly. Now get your rump back to your room and get some rest before the game. If you want to know what I think, you and Doc are both nuts. You know you have no business going to the game tonight. What if the ball hits you on the head or someone runs out of bounds and rolls over you?"

Will looked up at Gladys, bobbled his head, and said sarcastically, "What if the sky falls on me, Chicken Little?" He kissed his hand and pressed it to Buckie's forehead. "See you tonight, buddy." He walked to the door, then paused, turned and said, "Angelic Angelle, would you do me this tremendous favor. Call the boy that's madly in love with you, and tell him to bring my game jersey here so I can wear it to the game tonight?"

As Will turned to walk away, Angelle, pink with embarrassment, said "Wait, Will. I don't know who you're talking about."

Will grinned as he said, "Ha!" and closed the door behind him.

Buckie took the mask from his face and said, "He's talking about Caleb, Miss Angelle."

"Like she didn't know that," Gladys retorted, rolling her eyes.

"Go get some rest," Abe said. "I'll clean up. We won't have anyone here tonight, just a handful. It'll be like a night off. I might get home in time to catch the kick-off."

"Why don't you come to the game?" Caleb said excitedly. "You've never seen me play."

"I'd love too," Abe said, "but I don't think that's such a good idea. I've spent a few nights in the can, and I ain't anxious to do it again. Maybe one day it might be possible."

Caleb realized how foolish his suggestion was. He said, "I'm sorry, sir. I wasn't thinking."

"From where I'm standing, I'd say you were thinking real good, son. But that ain't the way life is around here. Just know whether I see you or not, I'll be listening to the game. I'll be just as proud of you as if I was sitting in those box seats by Mrs. Edith and Doc. You've come a long way in a short time, boy. If more people were like you, this old world would be as sweet as Momma's pecan pies."

"Thank you for saying that, Mr. Abe. You know you are like family to me. I reckon there ain't—I mean there isn't anyone that I respect any more than you."

Abe swelled with pride and said, "What's that expression you kids use today? Yeah, I remember. Get out of here and go kick some booty tonight!" Abe put his arm around Caleb and walked him to the door. Abe said, "There'll be fifty friends at my house tonight when I get home. They'll be there with me just to cheer for you. Do yourself proud."

Caleb walked to the truck thinking. *We never realize what deep feelings people hold inside themselves. I don't know why he couldn't come to the game. That doesn't seem right.*

Caleb backed the truck up and started to pull away.

Abe came rushing out of the door yelling for Caleb to stop. Caleb slammed on the brakes and stuck his head out the window. Abe yelled, "Someone named Angelle called and said Will wants you to bring his game jersey to the hospital so he can wear it tonight."

Caleb grinned, waved an acknowledgment, and drove away. He went to the dressing room and picked up the jersey. He continued on to the hospital and walked into Will's room. Will was sitting in a wheelchair, his legs stretched out halfway across the room. Will looked up at Caleb, shaking his head in disgust. "They said that I have to go to the game in a wheelchair. Hospital rules, and this is the biggest one they make. Now, tell me what in the hell I'm supposed to do with my legs? I'll have to prop up my head with my knees if I place them on these foot rests."

Caleb tossed Will's jersey over on the bed. "You'll figure something out. That's what that big brain of yours is for."

"You're right, of course. I just figured it out. I'll get a big jump rope and tie it to my feet and tie the other end to my neck." Will grinned and said, "Man, do I feel good. I feel like I'm making a jail break tonight. Did you ever spend a week in the hospital before? I think I'd rather be in jail. At least they'd let me sleep and not keep poking needles in my ass. If they wouldn't keep waking me up to push a thermometer or pills in my mouth, I might get some rest. Kid, if you're not sick when you get here, you surely will be when you leave."

Caleb responded, "Just be glad that Doc let you go and stop griping."

"That's easy for you to say when you're playing a game tonight. You better play the best game of your life or I'll be on your butt. Oh! I just heard on the radio that the traffic on US 51 is thick as fleas on a dog's back. They think that the game might be a sellout. Corn Shuck, that's unprecedented for a freshman game. It means that they're coming to see you. Not the team, but you."

Caleb held up his hands to show Will that they were shaking. "Don't do that to me, Will. I can't handle any more pressure. I'm more nervous about this game than I was the first time I got to play. You know what a fool I made of myself then. My folks are coming. I never met my grandparents before, but they're here to see me play. I want to make all of them proud. That's why I'm so nervous."

"Come here," Will said, motioning with his index finger. "Come close, I need to show you something." Caleb, somewhat apprehensive about Will's request, slowly eased up beside him. Will thrust both palms into Caleb's sternum knocking him backward across the small room slamming him into the wall. He wilted to the floor, moaning, groaning, and gasping for air. Will also grimaced in pain from his broken ribs.

Caleb regained his breath and staggered to his feet, shouting, "Have you lost your—dang mind, Will? You almost broke my breast bone."

"Sternum," Will said, "and I did it for your own good. That's harder than you'll be hit tonight so now you don't need to have any pre-game jitters. Stop acting stupid. You're the best freshman running back in the nation. It's time you start to realize it."

Caleb rubbed his chest and mumbled, "Don't hit me again, Will. I'm still hurtin'."

"Shake it off, wimp, and get tough! Rub a little dirt on it when you get outside."

"Okay," Caleb said, "just don't hit me again."

"The word's on the street that you're going to make five touchdowns tonight. Do you think that's realistic? Could it possibly be construed as—egotistical?"

"You've been talking to Buckie, ain't you!" Caleb snapped.

"Buckie who? I heard it in the hall and on the radio. They said you've been bragging all over town about how many touchdowns you're going to make for that kid and your family and, of course, the Cajun Queen."

"Now, Will, you stop that foolishness. You know me better than that. Someone's been spreading lies if they say I've been saying that."

Will laughed and said, "Lighten up, Corn Shuck, I'm just joking."

"No you ain't, Will. You ain't joking. You had to hear that somewhere. Buckie's been spreadin' it all over the hospital."

"Let it go," Will said. "Get your mind on the game. Get ready to put on a show for your folks. I'll be there to keep you straight. Don't get caught up in all the hype. Focus on the task at hand, and clear your mind of all distractions. One play at a time. One hundred percent for sixty minutes. Teamwork. Who knows, you might make ten touchdowns. Let the adrenaline work for you. Do you realize what all this means for us next year?"

"Will, I don't think about next year. I don't even think about tomorrow anymore. Today is all I can handle. I have to live for today, and like you said, focus on the game. I have to be the best I can be today. Tomorrow may never come. If it does, it has enough problems of its own."

"Boy!" Will said, shaking his head, "that is the biggest crock I ever heard. You have to live for tomorrow, too. You have to make plans. Prepare for the future, and work your ass off to make things happen."

"I believe that you live for today and shouldn't worry about tomorrow. If you're doing the best you can today, tomorrow will take care of its self. The Bible says that man makes his plans, but God orders his steps. That means you can plan all you want, but in the end, it was God who led you all the way."

"And you really buy that?"

"With all my heart."

Will shook his head saying, "Somebody put a real snow job on you. What about that kid two doors down? Do you believe that it's your God's will for him to lay here and suffer two years while the grim reaper sits salivating outside his door?"

"First of all, He's not just my God, Will, He's everyone's God. Yes, I believe it was God's will for him to lie here two years suffering and eventually to die." That's what sovereignty means. In control of everything. Even life and death."

"Geees!" Will scowled. "That's sadistic."

"No, Will, it's not sadistic. I believe that God has a master plan. He's always working toward its final conclusion. We are not privileged to understand his plans for our life. I love Buckie. His death is going to crush me. But I know that when the Lord takes him, he'll be in a better place. We'll never know how many lives Buckie has touched by his courage and faith in the face of death. He'll receive his crown of glory in Heaven."

Will threw both arms into the air, shaking them violently, and shouted, "Halleluiah, brothers and sisters. I reckon all that's left to do now is to pass the collection plate. That there old Cadillac that I been a sportin' is pert near out of warranty, and I know you fine brothers and sisters don't want yo' good pastor drivin' no old Cadillac. So reach deep into yo' pockets and show me some love."

Caleb lowered his head, shaking it slowly. He didn't respond to Will's cynicism.

"Get out of here," Will said. "You ain't holding no tent revival in my room. Go see your little friend down the hall that's dying. Try to convince him that he's a martyr for a greater cause. I doubt that he'll buy it either."

Caleb walked to the door, looked back at Will over his shoulder, and said, "I know you don't buy it now, Will, but one day it'll hit you like a bolt of lightning. I believe God has a greater purpose for your life than playing football, making love, and getting into bar room brawls... Look after Buckie tonight. If he gets sick, make sure Angelle get him back to the hospital even if he doesn't want to go. He has no business going in his condition."

"Why?" Will snapped. "I thought you believed that our days are numbered."

"I do, but we don't know that number," Caleb replied as he walked out the door.

"Oh yeah," Will mumbled. "You're quick with those cute little comebacks, you cocky snot, but you haven't convinced me of anything. And it's a waste of time trying. I believe in Will James and that's all I believe in."

When Caleb entered Buckie's room, he was sitting up in bed already dressed in his blue trousers and orange jersey. The coaching staff had sent orange Marston coaching caps to both he and Luther. Buckie's was four sizes too large, but he had it on his head resting neatly on his ears. Luther sat in the big chair, dressed in his new gray suit and tie, and looking quite handsome.

"Why aren't you resting?" Buckie admonished.

"Yeah!" Luther chimed in.

"I had to come for a good luck kiss," Caleb said, bending down and giving Buckie a gentle hug and kiss.

"I thought you didn't believe in luck," Luther said.

"I don't," Caleb said. "It just sounded like the right thing to say."

"I've been dreamin' about this night," Buckie said, "and it's almost here. I don't think I can wait no longer."

"Me either," Luther said. "I done hear'd all them games on the radjo and now I'm a gonna git to see one wit' my boy and my own two eyes. Ain't the Lord good, Caleb?" Luther said.

"Mr. Luther, I don't think any of us knows just how good He is to us."

"I sure do," Buckie said. "When I quit wishing on that silly star and started praying, he answered my prayers… Well, most of them anyway." Luther and Caleb glanced at each other.

"Caleb," Buckie said, "if you don't make no touchdowns tonight, I won't be disappointed. I jest want to see you in them bright lights with that beautiful green grass shining under your feet and hear that man on the loud speaker say your name. That'll be good enough for me."

"Me, too," Luther said. "Look a here at them goose-bumps on my arm gest a thinkin' 'bout it."

Caleb held up his arm and said, "Look here, y'all have made them pop up on my arm just talking about it too."

"Please go rest," Buckie said. "I know you ain't been gettin' no rest this week."

"Okay, little brother. I'll go get a little rest so I'll be fresh tonight. Don't get too excited on the sideline tonight. Okay." He kissed Buckie again.

Luther walked to the door with Caleb, gave him a big hug, and whispered, "You ain't never gonna knows how much I 'preciates what you done fer my boy." Caleb nodded and hugged Luther and patted him on the back.

Caleb saw Angelle walk out of the nurse's station and they gave each other a quick wave. Caleb stuck his head in Will's door grinning and said, "I still love you, you reprobate." Will snatched the pillow off the bed and threw it at Caleb. Caleb slammed the door and laughed as he heard Will grimaced in pain.

Caleb walked down the steps and out to the sidewalk. He noticed the old black man he had seen a few days before in Doc's office who suffered with Parkinson disease. The man was shuffling along staggering occasionally and shaking all over. He was holding a brown bag in his hand. Caleb rushed over to him and asked if he could help him get home.

The man responded in a shaky voice, "Thank you son, but I lives jes' down that alley a ways behind Doc Marston's clinic."

"I'll be glad to help you get there," Caleb insisted.

"I be fine," he said and stumbled away.

A few seconds later a police car drove by. Town Marshall was printed on the side of the car. The car came to an abrupt stop, and the marshal jumped out of the car and ran over to the old black man. The marshal grabbed the old man in the collar and yelled, "What the hell you doin' on this Main Street drunk in the middle of the day?" The black man tried to respond but he stumbled into the marshal. The marshal started dragging him toward the car. The old man tried to resist and explain, but the marshal grabbed his night stick and began slamming it against his head repeatedly until the old man collapsed onto the pavement.

Caleb saw red and sprinted to the marshal making a diving tackle, knocking the marshal hard into the pavement. Caleb jumped up and grabbed the old man and tried to pick him up, however, he was unconscious. The marshal staggered to his feet and snatched his pistol from the holster and ran over to Caleb and stuck it into Caleb's back, daring him to move.

Doc was returning to the clinic and witnessed most of the incident from his car. He slammed on the brakes, abandoned the car in the middle of the street, and ran to the scene. "What the hell have you done, Rosco!" Doc screamed.

"I was just doin' my job, Doc, tryin' to arrest this sorry drunk nigger when this crazy fool come running over here and knocked the hell out of me! They both goin' to jail now!"

"You're not taking anyone to jail Rosco! You may've just killed a sick old man who has Parkinson's disease. If he dies, I'll see that you spend the rest of your miserable life in jail."

"He's drunk, Doc! He resisted arrest. Look in that brown bag. I know he's got shine in it. I was just doin' my job. He'll be fine. You know you can't hurt no nigger hittin' 'en in the head," Rosco argued.

Doc picked up the bag, opened it, and pulled out a quart glass jar of milk and a few slices of bologna wrapped in wax paper. He gave Roscoe an incredulous stair for a few second, then yelled, "Pick him up and get him to the emergency room—now!"

"You go get some rest Caleb," Doc said. "I'll handle this."

Caleb reluctantly left the scene and went to the dorm, not believing what he had just witnessed. He tried to rest, however, the sight of the old man crumbling to the ground unconscious and the huge knots that instantly rose on his head sickened him. He couldn't get the picture out of his mind. At five o'clock, he dressed and left the room to join the team and walk to the cafeteria for the pre-game meal. As they walked outside, the players were amazed at the number of cars already in the parking lot. "Great Scott!" someone yelled, "where did all these people come from?"

A few boys answered, "They came to see Caleb, you nut."

"That ain't true!" Caleb blurted. "They came to see the team play."

A dozen voices rang out in concert, "That isn't true."

Coach Shook and the coaches were standing at the window of the coaches' office marveling at the number of cars still rolling into the parking lot. Hundreds of fans were standing in long lines at the ticket booth.

"Everyone loves a winner," Stan said. "Are you up to the challenge, Billy Ray?"

Billy Ray held out his hand. It was shaking. He said, "Coach Shook, why don't you take over tonight? It looks like we're going to have a full house."

"You want me to go out there and blow the game and take all the heat?" Coach Shook said, laughing. "Not on your life, Billy Ray. You get the chance to be the hero or goat. I'm going to hide in the press box. This is unbelievable. To think I told that kid to come back next spring and try out! If that information had leaked to the press, I'd be helping Mavis pull weeds out of her flower bed this evening."

"You remember that I tried to run him off," Stan said, shaking his head.

"I'm not ready for this crowd," Billy Ray commented. "I need your help on the sidelines, Stan. What do you say?" Stan smiled, nodded, and winked.

"Thanks," Billy Ray said, wiping his brow. "I can breathe again."

―〃〜―

"Houston," Mary said, shaking her head, "are you sure you're on the right highway? I'll declare, I believe you've managed to get us lost again. Sometimes I don't think you could find your way out of the cotton field if the mule didn't lead you home."

"Sweetheart, I just missed one turn and it didn't cost us ten minutes. Did you see that sign we just passed? It said US fifty-one. Now I don't think there's more than one US fifty-one in Mississippi."

"Yes, dear, but why is it taking us so long? I told you we should've started earlier."

"We have an hour, sweetheart, and that's plenty of time."

"Oh Houston, I'm so worried. I pray he doesn't get hurt. I don't think my heart would take that."

"Calm yourself, Mary. He won't get hurt. He's so strong you should be praying that he doesn't hurt someone else."

"How fast are you driving, Houston?"

"Fifty miles an hour. Why do you ask?"

"Because, if that truck behind us gets any closer, it's going to come through our rear window. You better pull off the road and let that line of trucks and cars get by us."

Houston shook his head and pulled over and let the traffic clear behind them.

"Satisfied!" he said as he pulled back onto the road.

"No!" she said firmly. "I want you to tickle that carburetor and hightail it down this road. If I have to endure these silly football games, at least I want to see the kickoff."

"Mary!" Houston said, somewhat surprised, "where did you hear an expression like that?"

"Do you think that all women do is cook, sew, and keep house. We do have ears, you know. We hear a lot more than you men think we do."

Houston grinned and tickled the carburetor. He said to Mary, "Now, you pray we don't get a ticket while I'm high-tailing it down the road."

⁓⁓⁓

The team went to the dressing room shortly after five. The trainers and coaches taped ankles and a few knees, and then the players dressed for the game.

⁓⁓⁓

Doc and his guests arrived at the stadium a little after six and strolled to his box seats on the fifty-yard line. The stadium was already half full. Travis was so excited and jubilant about his newfound grandson that he could hardly control his emotions. Iris was still shaken by the revelation at lunch. She was still a little green around the gills. Jennifer didn't help the situation by her persistent chants of 'Go cats go! Win! Win! Win! Go, Caleb!' Mr. Hodges joined Jennifer in her cheer, and soon the entire stadium was rocking to, "Go, Cats go," while Iris sat there wrenching her hands.

The Kentucky team jogged onto the field and were greeted by a few boos. Some cheers were heard from the Kentucky faithful that had traveled hundreds of miles to the game. A few seconds later, a roar went up from the near-capacity crowd as the Marston team appeared in the tunnel. The teams went through their pre-game warm ups. Caleb was so nervous he felt like throwing up as game time drew near.

Doc glanced at his watch. There was still no sign of Mary and Houston. He whispered to Edith, "I can't imagine why they haven't arrived yet. No reason I can think of is good."

"It's going to be all right, James. They may have been delayed by an accident," Edith whispered.

"That's what has me concerned," Doc said, grimly.

Houston pulled into the parking lot at six forty-five. The flagman waved him to the rear of the parking lot, a quarter of a mile from the stadium. "This is a fine how-do-you-do," Mary remarked. "I told you we should have left earlier."

Houston was steamed by now. He said, "We would have been on time if you hadn't have insisted that we break the law. That state trooper kept us on the side of the highway for thirty minutes with his stupid questions. 'Where's the fire?' he said, bobbing his head. I should have told him, up my butt, but I tried to be nice hoping he'd let us go with a warning. The only reason he kept us on the side of the road so long was because he couldn't keep his eyes off you. 'Is that beautiful young lady your daughter, sir,' he said, with a cute little grin. It wasn't any of his business whose wife or daughter you were. I'm going to report him when I get home."

"I'll have to admit he was quite handsome in that smart-looking police uniform," Mary replied, with a snicker.

"That was the first ticket I ever got in my life. Why didn't he stop some of those trucks that kept flying by us?" Houston grumbled.

Mary said in a placating tone, "Please stop complaining. Just park this car and let's hurry." Houston parked their new used car at the back of the parking lot near the place where Caleb had slept when he first arrived at Marston. They rushed across the parking lot to the ticket booth. The line was still fifty yards long. "Now, isn't this a fine how-do-you-do!" Mary complained. "I hope someone has a portable radio. That's the only way we're going to hear the first quarter."

"I didn't drive all the way up here to stand in line," Houston said. "You just wait here and I'll be back in a jiffy."

"Don't do anything foolish, Houston." Houston held his hands up, shook his head, and rushed to the ticket booth. He stepped in front of a very large man in overalls who was about to purchase a ticket. He stuck his head into the window, saying, "I'm Houston Morgan. I have Caleb Morgan's mother back at the end of the line. I'd like to pick up the two tickets that—"

The big man grabbed Houston by the arm, snatched him around, and said, "What you trying to pull mister. I been awaitin' in this here line fer over an hour. Now get your butt to the back of the line and wait like I done."

Houston pulled back and said, "I don't want no trouble, mister, but I have Caleb Morgan's mother back at the end of the line, and she wants to see the kickoff."

"I don't care if you got Mamie Eisenhower back there, Red. Get your butt in line like everyone else done."

Houston stuck his head back in the window and said, "Please, give me the two tickets that—" Before he could finish his sentence, the big man grabbed Houston's shoulder, snatched him around again, and doubled up his fists. Houston backed away and doubled up his fists.

Doc stepped between them and said, "Easy, men. Back off. Easy now."

The big man said, "Doc Marston, what you doin' out here?"

Doc said, "Gus, this is a friend of mine. He drove a long way to get here, and I left tickets for him at the booth. He didn't mean any harm. Get your ticket and let's forget the entire incident."

"Shore, Doc. Any friend of yours is good by me." He reached out and shook Houston's hand. Doc and Houston motioned for Mary to come. They rushed toward the gate at the end of the stadium.

"Do you know everybody, Doc?" Houston asked as they rushed through the crowd.

"I delivered all seven of his kids," Doc said. "He's a hard-working farmer and a pretty good man under normal circumstances. I didn't anticipate this large a crowd," Doc explained. "This is unprecedented. I should have mailed you the tickets. This is all about your son, Mary," Doc said as they hurried along. "These people are here to see your son. I hope that pleases you."

"This is a lot to take in, Doctor Marston," Mary said. "My prayer and hope is that it won't change Caleb. I'm very proud of the young man he's turned out to be."

"You know your son better than anyone, Mary, and I've spent many hours with him the last month or so. From what I've observed, I don't think anything in the world could ever change the person he is now," Doc said.

"It all seems so silly and elementary that everyone could get so excited over a football game," Mary said.

"Mary," Doc explained, "it's not just about the game. It's more about being a part of something special and exciting. Of feeling that you are a part of something bigger than yourself. It brings people together with a common goal. These people work hard all week. The game brings them together. It's almost like we are all part of one big family. We can forget our problems for a few hours and live and die with every snap of the ball. I know it's just a game Mary, but oh! As they say, 'the joy of victory, and the agony of defeat.'"

They walked up to the gate at the end of the stadium where the VIP's entered and all of those who had box seats. Two security guards stood by the gate. "Good evening Doc," they said as they opened the gate.

"My guests are Caleb Morgan's parents," Doc said as they passed. The two guards gazed in awe as Mary and Houston walked by. Houston stuck out his hand and gave them a quick shake.

One guard said, "The chief ain't gonna believe this."

The other guard said, "Did you get a look at that lady. She's gorgeous."

The first guard said, "How you figure that red-headed sucker managed that?"

The other guard remarked, "Beats me. Must be a rich sucker. Let's lock this gate and go watch the kickoff."

A roar went up from the crowd as Will and Buckie were rolled out of the tunnel leading to the field. Angelle and Luther walked by their sides. Two orderlies pushed the wheelchairs to the sidelines. The fans gave Will a standing ovation. Will said, "Do you hear all those people cheering for you, Buckie?"

"They ain't cheering for me," Buckie said. "They a cheering for you."

"I think they are cheering for both of you," Angelle said.

Everyone in the stands began to inquire about the small child in the wheelchair who was sitting by Will. The word spread like a wildfire through the stadium that he was a terminal cancer patient from the hospital who didn't have long to live. The varsity players sitting in the student section began to chant, "Buckie, Buckie, Buckie." In seconds the chant caught on, and the entire stands stood up and chanted, "Buckie, Buckie, Buckie."

Luther's eyes glassed over. He put his arm around Buckie and said, "Do you hear that, son?" Buckie was smiling and tears of joy were running down his cheeks. He was speechless. Will reached over to take Buckie's arm. He held it up and the crowd roared. Seconds later, the two teams came running onto the field. The fans stood and gave another loud roar.

Doc led Houston and Mary down the narrow walk beside the hedges to his box seats. They walked up to the seats. Iris and Travis looked up at Mary. Iris gasped and turned pale. Mary's knees buckled and she almost fainted. Houston grabbed her and eased her down into the seat. Houston, never having met the Hodges, didn't understand what was happening. Travis stood up and walked over to Mary. He reached down and helped her to her feet. They looked into each other's eyes a moment and both wept happy tears. They embraced for a few seconds, and then Travis eased her back down and returned to his seat.

"What? Who?" Houston asked.

"That's my father," Mary said in a broken, almost inaudible voice. Houston put his hands together in a praying position, looked upward, and whispered, "Oh, sweet Lord, thank you." Then he looked at Doc and smiled.

Travis put his hands together and rubbed them briskly, saying, "I don't know about the rest of you good folks, but I'm about to enjoy this game."

"Me, too," Houston said as he stood up to shake Mr. Hodges's hand. "I'm very pleased to meet you, Mr. Hodges."

"Call me Travis. We'll have time to get acquainted later."

Edith took Doc's hand and gave it a gentle squeeze. Smiling, she whispered, "You are wonderful, you old mother hen." The judge glanced at Doc, smiling and nodding his agreement.

CHAPTER SIXTEEN

Caleb and John David were co-captains that night. As they walked out to the center of the field for the coin toss, Jennifer broke the tension with a wild scream that could be heard across the campus. "Caleb," she screamed, "your parents and grandparents are here, and I love you!" The snickers could be heard from across the field. Caleb turned and blew his mother a kiss and everyone clapped. Angelle turned to see who had yelled at Caleb, however, she was unable to determine where the piercing voice came from. She grinned.

John David whispered to Caleb, as they strolled to the center of the field, "You're worse than a sailor, lover boy. You seem to have a girl in every town."

"You better get serious and cut out that foolishness," Caleb scolded. "We have to win this game. I don't want to disappoint Buckie and my folks."

"I'll be with you all the way," John David said. The stands were rocking as the home crowd began to yell and clap in anticipation of the kickoff. They wanted to witness the wonder of the amazing feats of the mysterious number twenty-two who had burst on the scene captivating the hearts of every Marston fan in Mississippi. Yet the question still remained in the minds of some, is he truly great, or were his actions the last few week simply an aberration? If miracles happened again tonight, the question would be settled once and for all.

Iris sat in her seat trembling. She refused to look in Mary's direction. The P.A. announcer asked everyone to stand for a prayer and to remain standing for the National Anthem.

Jennifer asked the judge to help her up. The judge put his hands around her waist, lifted her up from her chair, and stood her close to him with one arm around her. Doc reached around her waist from the other side to help him hold her steady as she braced against the rail.

After the National Anthem was played, the referee tossed the coin. Marston won the toss and elected to receive. The teams lined up for the kickoff. Jennifer was non-stop with her 'Go Cats, Go' cheer. The judge joined in. A few seconds later Houston joined in. Mary put an elbow in his ribs. He stopped and gave her a hard look. "You can sit here with me and listen to me cheer, or you can go and sit in the car. I intend to yell for my boy's team."

"Oh, go ahead and make a fool out of yourself if you want to," she chided.

The Kentucky kicker approached the ball. After a solid kick, it flew deep to the ten yard line on the left hash mark where Cliff was waiting. Caleb was on the opposite hash mark. The kicker had strict orders to kick away from Caleb. Cliff fielded the ball cleanly and started straight up the field. When he reached the twenty, he made a sharp right turn and ran across the field. A wave of seven or eight defenders was converging on him. As they lowered their shoulders to bury him, Caleb shot by him, streaking the other direction. Cliff tossed the ball back to him. Caleb was ten yards down the field before the defenders realized that it was a reverse. Caleb hit the sidelines flying faster than he had ever run before. Only the kicker stood between him and the goal line. The stripes were passing under his feet so fast it was as if he was not touching the ground. The kicker had Caleb pinned against the sidelines and he lowered his head to knock him out of bounds. Caleb put a move on him that defied gravity and should have blown out both his knees. He shot right, leaving the defender flying helplessly out of bounds into his teammates who were standing near the sidelines. Caleb hit his cruise mode and glided the next fifty yards to the end zone and a touchdown. A loud roar exploded from the twenty-five thousand plus fans. It was described in the paper the next day as being as loud as a clap of thunder.

Edith, Houston, and Travis were jumping up and down screaming and hugging each other. Doc and Horace were holding Jennifer between them. She was banging against anyone she could reach, screaming louder than everyone. Mary was fighting the urge to join the insanity. However, she couldn't restrain her smile and the pride she began to feel inside.

Caleb didn't stop as he crossed the goal line. He made a quick circle and continued to run down the sideline toward Buckie. He stopped and walked up to him and presented him the ball. "This is for you, little brother. I love you." Buckie was gasping for air from his yelling for Caleb's run. A photographer from the Memphis paper snapped a picture as Caleb handed Buckie the ball.

The photographer tapped Angelle on the shoulder and whispered, "What's the deal here with the kid?"

"I'll tell you in a minute," Angelle said. She turned on the oxygen and put the mask over Buckie's face.

"Now don't get too excited, Sugar Boy," Caleb said, "Because I'm not through. This is your night." Luther put his hand to his face and fought the tears.

One official had thrown a flag, and it floated down. The referee saw what Caleb had done. He rushed over to grab the flag and handed it back to the other official. "No flag!" he yelled. "No flag!" Then he looked at the official who had thrown the flag and commented, "There's no penalty for a little humanity." A fresh ball was tossed to the official and Marston kicked the extra point.

After Buckie's respiration eased somewhat, Angelle turned off the oxygen and motioned to the photographer to come to her. She stepped back a few steps and whispered into the photographer's ear. He continued to nod as Angelle briefly told him the story of Buckie and Caleb.

"Thanks, Miss. That's a heck of a story," the photographer commented.

The Wildcats took the kickoff and ran out to the twenty-two yard line. They began to pound the middle of the Marston line. Each Marston lineman was outweighed by at least twenty pounds a man.

Will rolled his wheelchair back a few feet from the others and cleared his throat loudly. Angelle looked back at him, and he motioned for her to come. She stepped away from Buckie and walked up next to Will. "I need to know one thing, Angelle. What are your intentions where Caleb is concerned?"

"I don't know what you mean," Angelle said, totally caught off guard and somewhat surprised by his question.

"I think you do," Will said. "You know he's crazy in love with you."

"I don't know that," she said somewhat uneasily.

"Cut the act, Queenie. Caleb is the only real friend that I have, and he's not like anyone I've ever known. He's genuine, sincere, honorable, and gullible as hell. You could destroy him, you know. If you love him, you should take off that ring and throw it in a river somewhere and tell him so."

"I should get angry with you," Angelle said, "because this is none of your concern. But I'm not going to do that. I know you are his friend. I don't want to hurt him. There are things in life that you have no control over." She held up the ring. "Life is not as simple as you make it out to be. I didn't ask him to fall in love with me, and the last thing I need in my life at this time is to fall in love with him."

"The hell you say," Will argued. "Life is as simple as you make it. You just make up your mind and do what has to be done, and damn the consequences."

"No, Will." she said gravely, shaking her head. "Sometimes the consequences are more painful than we can bear. You don't understand. Some things take time to work themselves out. They may never work out. That's where Caleb and I are now. We're going to have to wait and see if things work themselves out."

"Well, I suggest you don't wait too long to make up your mind, Angelle, because you don't find a Caleb Morgan in every Christmas stocking. He's becoming a high-demand commodity very fast. Right now you have the inside track. You can't dangle him forever."

A roar went up from the crowd when the Wildcats fumbled the ball on their own thirty yard line and Marston recovered. "We'll talk again one day," Will said and rolled the wheelchair over near Buckie.

Two plays later, Caleb shot through the middle of the Kentucky defense on a quick trap. He flew by the linebackers and safety so fast that no one touched him and he sprinted into the end zone.

For the next two hours, Caleb put on a show that could only be described as super-human. He rushed for almost three hundred yards, averaging over twenty yards a carry, and scoring six touchdowns. When the final horn sounded, Marston had chalked up a 41 to 14 victory.

After Caleb's second touchdown, Mary had joined Doc's joyous group and was yelling as loud as Jennifer.

Buckie became nauseated and his fever began to rise near the end of the game. Angelle had to rush him back to the hospital as the game was ending.

After the horn sounded to end the game, Caleb sprinted over to the sidelines in front of Doc's seats, leaned over the hedgers, and received hugs or kisses from everyone except his grandmother. She sat there with her lips pursed, fighting the tears.

Mary took Caleb's face in her hands and kissed him. She said, "Son, I was wrong. I was wrong not to let you play football. Please forgive me."

Travis grabbed Caleb, almost pulling him into the stands and kissed him on the forehead. "My grandson, I love you. I am so proud of you." Travis turned and looked at Iris. She turned away, as tears ran down her cheek.

"I have to go now," Caleb said. He looked at Iris and said, "I love you, Grandmother," and he jogged away. Iris broke out in tears and began to weep uncontrollably.

Houston nudged Mary. Mary laid her pride aside, stood up, rushed to her mother, and reached out to her. Iris stood up to put her arms around Mary and they embraced and wept.

After the long embrace, Iris said, "Now, I want to meet my wonderful grandson. Can we go see him, Travis?"

"We'll have to fight the crowd," Doc said, "but I'd fight a dragon to get you there."

Travis grabbed Doc's hand with both his and shook it briskly. "You are a saint, Doctor James Marston. This truly is the best day of my life."

"I'll agree he's a saint," Edith said, "but sometimes he's a devilish saint."

"I've been called a lot of things," Doc said, "but devilish saint isn't one of them. Y'all get behind me, and I'll bulldoze through the crowd and get you to the dressing room."

"I had every intention of going to see him, Mrs. Hodges," Jennifer said. "Did I tell you that I plan to marry him someday when I can walk?"

"I think you've told everyone in the state that," the judge said.

"All of you are going to be my in-laws one day," Jennifer said confidently.

Mary smiled. Houston said, "I'd like to have some red-headed grandchildren someday." They muscled their way through thousands of jubilant fans who didn't want to leave the stadium. After circling the stadium, they managed to get within fifty yards of the dressing room. Hundreds of adoring fans waited outside just to get a close look at their real-life hero.

Coach Shook had allowed the press into the dressing room. They all wanted an interview with Caleb, and they wanted the details about the young child on the sidelines. "He's the sweetest boy in the world," Caleb said. "It was his dream to see a Marston game, and his dream came true tonight."

"Is he actually dying?" one writer asked.

"He can still read the paper!" Caleb snapped. "He's very ill. I won't say any more about how serious his condition is. I'd appreciate y'all not writing anything about his condition."

"How much longer does he have to live?" another writer asked.

"Only the Lord knows that," Caleb said, "but Doc said he's on borrowed time." The instant those words came out of his mouth, Caleb realized his mistake.

"This would make a terrific human interest story," another writer said. "Dying child's last wish comes true. If only we had a picture to go with the story."

"Please, don't write that story," Caleb pleaded. "He's not a story, he's a wonderful child and it's about to kill his father." Caleb tried to change the subject so he added, "My mother and stepfather and grandparents were at the game tonight. They had never been to a Marston game before." He continued, "Did you know that my grandfather is president of the largest bank in Jackson?"

"That's nice," one of the reporters said, "but we have to run to get the story in the morning paper. Thanks for the interview." They rushed toward the door.

Caleb lowered his head and said, "I'm still a stupid fool. Why did I even talk to them? I'm going to have to hide the paper from Buckie tomorrow morning. Why did I even talk to them?"

The orderly was pushing Will through the tunnel to the dressing room when Coach Shook and the staff caught up with him. "Will," Coach Shook said, "we're pulling out for Kentucky at eight in the morning. We're going to miss you."

"Let me think," Will said, "how would Corn Shuck put it? Oh yes, stupidity begets stupidity. You reap what you sow. I can't blame anyone but myself for my stupidity. I knew those rednecks were probably waiting outside the bar for me. I let you and the coaches down, not to mention the team and fans. Now, I'm reaping the whirlwind of my pride. If you want to take my scholarship away, that'll be justice."

The coaches couldn't believe what they were hearing. Coach Shook said, "Will, you're the heart and soul of this team. As hard as it is to stomach now, if you learned anything from this, it might be your salvation." Will sat there tight-jawed, nodding. "We want you to rest and get well and get ready for spring training in March. We'll be like an army without a general the rest of this season. But our hope is that the team will rally around each other and work harder than ever. We're not giving up on this season. We got a taste of victory last week, and it was very, very sweet. Oh! By the way, the sheriff called this afternoon. He said he'd rounded up all the thugs that almost killed you. He has them behind bars waiting for you to come and identify them. I told him it might be a few weeks before you're able to drive up there."

"I know. Doc told me. Call him back, Coach, and tell him to let them go. Tell him that they attacked me from the rear and I didn't get a look at any of them."

"Will, I know that's not true," Coach Shook said. "You don't intend to settle things yourself, do you? If that's the case, you haven't learned a thing. You might get killed next time, or you might wind up in jail for a long time. This is a matter for the law."

"That's all I thought about while I was in the hospital, looking up at the gray ceiling the last few days. They cost me a lot, but you can't be around Corn Shuck Morgan from Choctaw County with his providence and hard work philosophy and not have a little of it rub off on you. It's a hard pill to swallow, but the truth is that I probably deserved a good ass-kicking for the way I treated one of the boys. I think he took it a little too far, but I've done things almost as cruel. I could have done time in slammer, but my father always pulled strings and managed to get me out of trouble. Those rednecks don't have anyone on their side." Will shook his head and said, "I'm going to try to forget it, and that ain't frickin' easy for me. Pardon my French."

The coaches walked up to Will and patted him on the back. Coach Shook said, "I like the way you're thinking, Will. Come by in the morning before we pull out and give the team a little pep talk. Just watch your language." The coaches laughed and hurried down the tunnel to the dressing room.

Coach Shook whispered, "I told you men that it was a good idea to move Caleb into Will's room."

"I think that was my idea," Billy Ray said.

"If I remember correctly," Coach Parrish said, "it was Will's idea."

"You got that right," Ollie said.

"Huh!" Coach Shook grunted, "You dumb line coaches can't remember anything. I know it was my idea."

"Yeah," Ollie said, "I may be a dumb line coach, but I remember who wanted Caleb Morgan to come back in the spring and try out." He began laughing boisterously.

Coach Shook doubled up his fist and gave Ollie a fake punch in the belly. They all laughed as they walked into the dressing room.

⸙

Angelle and Luther had rushed Buckie out of the stadium and into the ambulance. Buckie was pale and nauseated. His fever was still rising as the ambulance pulled away from the stadium. Buckie's gray face was still beaming with joy and excitement. He couldn't stop talking about the most wonderful night of his life, as he fought for life.

⸙

Caleb walked outside the dressing room. A giant roar went up from the thousands of adoring fans. They all rushed toward him to get an autograph or just get a closer look. Caleb was embarrassed at all the attention. Then he heard Jennifer's unmistakable, piercing voice. "Caleb, we're over here." He spotted the judge's six-foot-four frame over the sea of heads. He started working his way through the fans, shaking hands and thanking people for their compliments. He signed a few programs as he plowed closer and closer to his family.

Mary pushed her way through the last group of fans and Caleb held out his arms to her. They embraced. She whispered, "I was wrong not to want you to play football, son. Forgive me. You have a gift from the Lord, and I was wrong not to encourage you to use it." Houston was slapping Caleb's back and patting his head. Mary backed away, taking Caleb's hands. She said, "I want you to meet someone very special." She led him to Iris.

Iris wiped the tears from her face as they approached. She held out her arms and they embraced. "Please forgive me," Iris whispered. "I've been a fool for too long. I'm going to make it up to you and Mary Margret somehow, if it takes the rest of my life."

Caleb whispered, "There's nothing to make up. You're here now, and we're a family again. That's all that matters." Everyone took turns hugging Caleb and expressing their love and admiration for him.

Jennifer was sitting in her wheelchair, feeling left out. She was starting to pout when Caleb turned, reached down, scooped her up, and swung her around. The mass of fans had crowded around to watch Caleb as he was greeted by his family. When he took Jennifer in his arms and began to swing her around, they let out a tremendous cheer.

"Carrot top, my sweet princess," Caleb said, as he whirled her. Then he began to kiss her, going from cheek to cheek. Jennifer managed to steal a few kisses from his lips. "Did you think I would forget my number one fan, sweetheart?" Caleb said, looking into her gorgeous kaleidoscope eyes.

"I want to tell you a secret," she whispered in his ear. "I'm going to therapy on Monday, Wednesday, and Friday now. The therapist said I'm showing tremendous progress, and with determination, I may be walking before next year."

Caleb was surprised and responded, "Did he really tell you that?"

"Not in so many words, but I know he doesn't want me to get my hopes up too soon."

Caleb caught the judge's stare, and he shook his head ever so slightly. Caleb whispered, "Don't get discouraged and give up. It may not happen that fast, but don't give up."

"You know I won't," Jennifer said. "I'm going to dance with you at my graduation. You promised, and I'm holding you to it."

"I keep my promises," Caleb said.

"I love you," Jennifer said in a whisper.

"I love you, too," Caleb said, smiling.

"I hate to throw cold water on this blissful occasion," the judge said, "but I have to be on the bench bright and early." He glanced at his watch.

"I can't wait to get to the bank tomorrow morning," Travis said. "I called all my board members and employees and close friends this afternoon and told them to listen to the game tonight because my grandson was going to shine. And how you did shine!" Travis said, patting Caleb on the back.

"Mary, you and Houston are going to spend the night with us," Edith said.

"Oh no! Edith, we can't impose," Mary said.

"What imposition?" Edith remarked. "We have four bedrooms and three baths and a very large house. James and I use only one bedroom." She laughed and said, "Now we're not going to take no for an answer." Mary looked at Houston.

"That sounds fine to me," Houston said. "I wasn't looking forward to a four-hour drive tonight. But we'll have to leave early because I have a job interview at two o'clock tomorrow in Kosciusko."

"What!" Caleb blurted, still holding Jennifer as she snuggled her head against his cheek, stealing an occasional kiss.

"I didn't want to say anything to you in case it didn't work out," Houston said. "I filled out a job application at the school bus plant last week. They wrote me a letter and told me to come in for an interview. I'm not getting my hopes up."

"I don't know why not!" Caleb said excitedly. "You can fix anything. You're the best mechanic in Choctaw County. Oh! Uncle Houston, that would be a godsend. But what about the cotton crop? You haven't finished picking it, have you?"

"If I get the job, I'll let the boll weevils have the rest of it. I'm tired of eating poison. I don't have much more than a bale left in the creek bottom, and I can pick it on the weekends."

Mary chimed in, "These good people aren't interested in all this Choctaw County talk. You two can talk later."

"On the contrary, Mary," Travis said. "I'm interested in anything that will make your life a little easier. Houston, I know the plant manager. I can call him and pull a few strings for you."

"That's very kind of you to offer, Mr. Hodges, but I'd rather get the job on my own merit. If they don't think I can do the job, then I feel that I shouldn't have it. Mary and I have prayed about it. We're still making it on the farm, although the cotton crop seems to get smaller each year. The land is just worn out."

Doc began to think. *I know Joe Smiley, the plant manager pretty well myself. If Houston's that talented, he should get the job. Everybody needs a little help occasionally. I'll make the call tomorrow. It certainly wouldn't do any harm to mention that Houston is Caleb Morgan's stepfather.* Edith glanced up at Doc. She knew his mind was already spinning and contriving a plan.

Jennifer whispered in Caleb's ear, "I didn't want to tell you this, but Emma made me promise. She said to tell you that she's flying into Memphis Saturday morning. She'll be staying with Doc and Mrs. Edith. She and Chris are coming to the homecoming game and ball. She said she wants to dance with you and talk to you. Promise me you won't dance with her. She can't be content with Chris. She wants all the good-looking boys, but I told her she wasn't going to have you."

Caleb smiled as he said, "You're right, she can't have me." He laughed again and said, "I'm all yours."

"Don't tease and make fun of me," Jennifer whispered. "You didn't mean that, did you?"

"I didn't ask you to marry me," Caleb whispered, "but I'll always love you."

You will one day, Jennifer thought. *I'll never love anyone but you, and you'll never marry anyone but me.*

"Unload that arm-full, Caleb," the judge said. "We have to hit the road." Caleb kissed Jennifer on the nose and sat her in the wheelchair.

His grandparents gave him a final hug, said goodbye, and left for Jackson.

"I'm going to the hospital and check on Buckie," Caleb said. "If he's all right, I'll run over to Doc's house for a minute to say goodbye. I want to hear more about the new job, Uncle Houston."

"I don't have it yet," Houston said, "and I refuse to get my hopes up."

"Son," Mary said, "you have to be exhausted. Don't feel that you have to come and say good bye. I'm sure you need some rest."

"I feel wonderful," Caleb said. "If it weren't for Buckie's condition, I'd say I feel better than I've ever felt before. I have grandparents that love me. You have your parents again. How can life get any sweeter for us?" He kissed Mary and Edith and slapped Houston on the back. He broke through the crowd that was still milling around and ran for his truck.

CHAPTER SEVENTEEN

Caleb jogged up the stairs at the hospital and down the hall to Buckie's room. Buckie was still smiling and gasping for breath as Angelle sat by him with the mask over his face.

Luther grabbed Caleb, hugged him, and said, "You done made Buckie and me proud o' you tonight."

Caleb patted Luther on the back and said, "Thank you, Mr. Luther. It was a good night for everyone." Buckie was motioning for Caleb to come to him. Caleb walked up beside him, leaned over and said, "Did you have fun tonight, little brother?"

Buckie nodded and said, "It was more beautiful than I ever dreamed it would be," Caleb. "I believe you could fly if you really tried. It looked like your feet weren't even touching the ground when you was running down that field."

"Only the angels can fly," Caleb said.

"You think when the Lord takes me to heaven, He'll let me fly? Or just let me run fast like you?"

Caleb glanced at Luther, never sure how to respond to Buckie's heart-rendeing questions. He pondered the question for a few seconds, then responded, "Buckie, I believe the Lord loves you so much he's going to let you do almost anything you want to do, even fly, and run faster than me." Buckie's smile brightened and he squeezed Caleb's hand. Caleb bent over and kissed his forehead and noticed a lump under the sheet at Buckie's side. He gently lifted the cover and the game ball was snuggled against Buckie's side.

"He insisted," Angelle said, shrugging and smiling.

"Buckie," Caleb said beaming, "I met my grandparents today for the first time in my life and my parents were at the game, too. This was one of the best days of my life."

"I'm happy for you," Buckie said in a whisper. "If I could meet my mother it would be the best day of my life too."

"I'll keep praying that she'll come to see you, Buckie," Caleb said, ashamed for giving Buckie false hope.

"She better come soon," Buckie murmured, "'cause I ain't feeling so good no more."

Gladys came marching in and said, "Sweet peace and rest I hold in my hand young prince. We're going to get you a good night's sleep now that the game is over. You go get some rest, too, Luther." She glanced at her watch and said, "It's almost eleven. You go, too, Angelle. You've had a long hard day. I'll take care of our prince now."

"I thought you were off tonight." Angelle said.

"I swapped shifts with Ann Marie. I just came on duty. Y'all go get some rest because this prince is in good hands tonight."

"I think I'll go over to the hotel and rest for a couple of hours," Luther said.

"Good," Gladys nodded. "You need it as much as Prince Valiant does tonight. If you don't start getting more rest, you'll be laid up in a bed of your own. Oh, by the way, Caleb, you were unbelievable on that field tonight. No one could have imagined a crowd like that on a Thursday night. The traffic was so horrible I had to get out of the car and walk over here. I left my Harvey Dan stranded in the traffic jam griping and using some unsavory words I don't care to repent. Everyone said your talent was phenomenal but seeing is believing, and I couldn't believe what I was seeing. Take my advice and marry some young beautiful girl," and she glanced at Angelle and winked, "and have a dozen boys. Coach Shook might never retire if he had that to look forward to."

"Yeah," Luther said. "You two fits like a hand in a glove. You both real purdy and ain't nobody in this here world any gooder you two, and you both got smarts too. I bet yo' chillen would be more pretty than any chillen in this here world."

"Somebody call a preacher," Buckie managed to joke, trying to laugh. "We gonna get them hitched 'fore the night's over. I been knowin' they was perfect for each other longer'n any of y'all."

Gladys leaned over Buckie and raised the sheet, popping the needle in his hip. She kissed him and said, "Good night sweetie." Buckie's eyes closed before she could straighten up. "He was totally exhausted," she said. "Now everyone scoot. I'll sit here awhile. We're not too busy tonight, thankfully. I'll keep a close eye on him, Luther. You know I'll call if there are any complications."

They all walked out and Caleb waited for Angelle to sign out. They walked downstairs.

Angelle gave a big sigh, commenting, "I thought we were going to lose him before we returned to the hospital. He can't hold on much longer."

"He's fighting death hoping to see his mother," Caleb said. "She's the reason he's living tonight."

"Why do you think God would want to take him at ten years old?" Angelle asked. "I do have faith, Caleb, but I don't understand."

"I don't think there is any way to understand the ways of the Lord. All we have to hold on to at a time like this is what the scriptures say. 'All things work for good for those that love the Lord.' I know that he loves the Lord, and I know that the Lord loves him. I want him to grow up and enjoy life, but that obviously isn't God's will. After all, how can this life with all its pain and sorrows and sin compare to spending an eternity in glory with our Lord and Creator? I'm certainly no saint, but I do know my scripture. Mother saw to that. 'Eyes have not seen, nor ears heard or the mind conceived all the wonderful things that God has in store for those who love him.' When Buckie closes his eyes the last time, the Lord's going to reach down and take his hand and he's going to be with Him for all eternity. And this I know, he'll be in a better place."

"That's a beautiful answer, Caleb. I may rest a little easier after hearing that."

"I can't take credit for it. It came from the eternal One. My concern is for Luther now. That boy is his life, and I don't know how strong his faith is…I'll run you back to the dorm now. Hop into my beautiful carriage, Cinderella. I have to hurry because I promised Mother and Uncle Houston that I'd run by Doc's house and visit with them a few minutes if Buckie was all right." He opened the door and let Angelle get in and rushed around the truck. "Angelle, I feel so strange tonight. I've felt joy like never before when my mother and grandparents finally reconciled their differences tonight. Then I see Buckie and Luther and I tumble to the depths of despair. I feel like I'm on an emotions roller coaster. I feel like I'd like to sleep for a month and not have to face the inevitable."

Angelle listened and thought, *Oh Caleb, if I could only tell you about the emotional roller coaster I've experienced for half of my life, and I do understand how you feel. I feel the same way.* He cranked the truck and pulled away and began to pour out his heart. "I thought playing football would be the most wonderful thing in life when I first arrived. So much so, I was willing to lie and deceive the one person that loved me more than anyone in the world. Now I realize that, as much as I love to play, it's just a game. I'd give it up in a heartbeat if it would change Buckie's condition, or if it meant that you and I could spend our life together and have a family and love each other for the rest of our lives. Those are the things that really matter in life. Something wonderful happens, and then something tragic happens. There doesn't seem to be much peace anymore."

Angelle listened and felt Caleb's pain in her heart, although she had endured more pain and torment in her life than anyone should have to endure. She realized that she loved him more than anyone in the world now, and her concern was not for herself, but for the kind and compassionate country boy that had stolen her heart forever and given her a reason for hope and peace in her life. She took Caleb's hand in hers and squeezed it gently and snuggled against him and said, "Life is going to be wonderful someday. I know it will. It has to be. You didn't forget that you said I could meet your parents if we had time. I'd love to meet your parents if you don't mind. The housemother knows that I took Buckie to the game. I'm sure I won't get in trouble if I come in a little late."

Doc's warning rang out like a clap of thunder in Caleb's mind. *If I bring Angelle to his house to meet my parents, he'll surely realize that I didn't heed his warning and that she must have some feelings for me.* His heart began to race again. "Uh, it's kinda late. Are you sure you won't get in trouble? You know you can't afford to get in trouble. You won't be able to work. I'd never forgive myself if I was responsible for that. What if someone sees us out after curfew?"

"Don't be silly. Who's going to see us at Doc's house? Oh, please, Caleb," she pleaded as she snuggled against him again. "I know it'll be all right."

"You know I could never refuse you anything," Caleb said, as he turned toward US 51.

"Tell me about your grandparents. You've never mentioned them before."

Caleb told Angelle the story of his mother and father's marriage and why he had never met his grandparents. He finished just as he pulled into Doc's driveway.

"That's a tragic story with a beautiful ending," Angelle said. "I understand why you were so excited tonight."

Caleb opened the door for Angelle. "Look!" he said excitedly, "That's our new car over there. Uncle Houston said it was in good condition. It looks practically new. He bought it just so he and Mother could come to see me play football." He paused and said hesitantly, "Angelle, ah…" and there was a long pause.

"What's wrong?" She asked, perceiving that Caleb was very uneasy about something.

"Uh, uh," Caleb continued to stammer, finally able to say, "Can we pretend to be friends when we go in?"

"Why? Are you ashamed of me?" Angelle asked, revealing a look of complete disappointment.

"Oh, Heavens no!" Caleb responded. Now he was backed into a corner and he had to make a choice whether to tell her the truth about Doc's warning or tell her that his mother had warned him not to get involved with a girl until he had secured his diploma. Either answer would hurt Angelle—and that was the last thing he wanted to do. He had to think quickly. He despised lying, but to spare Angelle's feeling he would even consider that. He was so panicked that he couldn't think of a lie. He made a decision and said, "Angelle, I know you are going to think this is silly, but my mother is kinda old fashioned about marriage and dating and all that. She warned me about coming to school and getting involved too quickly with a girl. She said I might stop studying and not make my grades. I've only been here a few weeks, and you know, I'm head over heels in love with you. If she knew how I felt about you, I don't know what she'd say or do. Can you understand that?"

Angelle gave a sigh of relief and said, "I hope to be a mother someday, and that's the same advice I'd give my son or daughter. Let's go in and meet them. Don't worry."

Caleb smiled and thought *I guess the truth is always better, even if it's only a half truth.*

"So this is where Doc lives?" Angelle said, "I imagined it would be a three story antebellum mansion. This house looks just like the other houses on this street."

"It's larger than it appears," Caleb said, "and quite beautiful inside. Look at that gorgeous rose garden. It's Mrs. Edith's pride and joy."

"Everything's beautiful," Angelle said, "even the yard and shrubbery."

Edith had noticed the lights in her driveway and she came to the door, somewhat surprised by Angelle's presence. "Y'all come right in. Everyone's in the den having coffee and cake. Come join us." They followed her down the hall to the den and walked in.

"Angelle!" Doc said, seeming more surprised than Edith. "What a pleasant surprise. I think this is the first time we've had the pleasure of your company in our home, even though I've invited you to come for dinner numerous times. But I know how busy you are with your studies and work." He glanced at Caleb with a curious look and said, "Let me introduce you to Mary and Houston Morgan up from Choctaw County. I'm sure Caleb has already told you that they were here."

Mary walked over and reached for Angelle's hand. Angelle quickly put them behind her back and gave a polite curtsy. "You are a lovely young lady, and a nurse, too." Then she cut her eyes at Caleb and gave him an accusing look.

Houston commented, "Mary's description was an understatement, young lady. You are absolutely gorgeous. Are you a nurse or a student?"

"Both," Doc said. "She's my favorite Marston Foundation scholarship recipient. You have to be brilliant and dedicated to receive the scholarship. She's both."

"Mrs. Morgan," Angelle said, "you are more beautiful than Caleb described, and Mr. Morgan, your hair is redder than he said."

Everyone had a good laugh except Doc and Mary. They both seemed uneasy, and Caleb knew why.

Angelle smiled at Doc and Mary and said, "I want to apologize for intruding on this family gathering, but Caleb came by the hospital to check on Buckie after the game. When he mentioned that he was coming over to your house for a few minutes, I knew how much concern you have for Buckie's condition. I thought you might want an update after the stressful game he attended. Caleb and I have a mutual interest in Buckie's condition, so I asked him if I could tag along to give you the report."

"Oh," Mary and Doc said in concert, smiling again. Houston said, "Oh," seeming disappointed.

Angelle continued, "We almost lost him on the way back to the hospital. I could barely detect his respiration. His heartbeat was so slow I could barely pick it up with the stethoscope, and he lost consciousness. It scared me, Doc. We kept the oxygen on and when we put him in the bed, the respiration increased. He eventually opened his eyes as he re-gained consciousness and seemed to be doing much better when we left. Gladys made Luther go get some rest. She said she'd watch Buckie closely tonight. She traded shifts so she could go to the game. She'll be there all night."

"Gladys is a jewel," Doc said. "I don't know what we'll do when she retires. I fear we'll lose you too when that fiancé of yours returns from the service."

Angelle's eyes shot toward Caleb. Doc's comment seemed to pierce Caleb's heart, and a sick look came over his face. Angelle was quick to respond, "Who knows, Doc, he may fall in love with one of those beautiful German girls and never come back, then I can work for you as long as you'll have me."

Houston and Mary both glanced at her hand and saw the ring. Houston realized that this gorgeous creature that had so impressed him was not going to be his future daughter-in-law. He stood there and boldly proclaimed, "The young man would have to be a complete fool, blind, or an idiot to marry someone else with this gorgeous young lady waiting for him over here."

"Houston!" Mary scolded, "that kind of talk was crude and inappropriate."

"I said it, and I'll stand by what I said, Mary. I'm sorry if it offended anyone."

Doc, always quick to quell a riff, said, "I'm inclined to agree with Houston, Mary. If I was forty years younger and free like a bird and hadn't already met the most wonderful and beautiful lady in the world, Angelle would be at the top of my list." Angelle's cheeks became rosy with embarrassment.

Mary put her finger to Houston's lips and said, "Not another word, you red-headed plow boy." Everyone had a big laugh as the tension eased and they all sat down. Caleb sat on the sofa by Houston and began to fire questions at him about the job prospect, the crop that was not yet harvested, and how the new house was coming.

Edith and Angelle cornered Mary on the other sofa and bombarded her with questions about country life in rural Choctaw County. They were fascinated with her stories of gardening, canning, smoking meat, picking cotton, plucking chickens, skinning wild game, and all the chores a country lady had to perform just to survive. A far cry from what city life was for Edith and the privileged class. She described what life was like before the electric lines had been stretched only a few years earlier. Mary was not ashamed of her country heritage and spoke proudly of her life on the farm. She was a proud woman and dedicated to her family and her church. She offered no apologies for her lifestyle. It took only a few seconds to realize she was a woman of high breeding and extraordinary character and intelligence.

"I don't know how you do all that and maintain your beauty and health," Edith said.

"It's truly a labor of love," Mary said, smiling brightly.

Edith smiled and said, "I think it might be easy to love a life of a little more luxury."

Houston commented, "If I get the job, I'll let Gus Clemmons pick the rest of the cotton and corn on halves. He lives just a ways down the road, and I know he can use the extra money with nine head of kids. He'll finish in a few days, but I ain't counting my chickens too soon."

Doc sat there silently, smiling inside his heart, with his usual grace and dignity, enjoying all that he heard. After all, this was the family of the young man who would someday be his only heir.

This was the girl that he loved as a second daughter. He knew she would never replace his birth-daughter, lost in childbirth, but she was certainly a good substitute. He looked lovingly at Caleb, then Angelle, and thought. *What a wonderful couple they would make if circumstances were different. But that certainly may never happen. I have every confidence that Wellington will get her on the road to recovery soon. I have to believe that he will, if anyone can.*

Doc broke his silence and said, "We haven't had two lovelier young ladies in this house since—since Lillian and Annie Laurie Black were here over twenty years ago. Annie Laurie was Miss Tennessee and runner-up in the Miss America contest some twenty year ago. Of course, Edith will always be the most beautiful lady in the world to me."

"He knew he better add that," Edith said. They all laughed together again.

Caleb looked at his watch. "Oh my goodness, it's late. We have curfew and we're already late. I don't want Angelle to get in trouble by keeping her here so late with all this home talk." He hugged Houston, then turned and kissed Mary. They embraced tenderly.

"I love you so much, son, and I'm very proud of you. But remember why you're here. Keep up with your studies. You're still finding time to do your daily scripture readings, aren't you?"

Caleb backed away slightly. "I won't lie to you, Mother. With school, football, study, and work, I don't have much time to sleep. No, ma'am, I don't think I've read them more than a couple of times." As Caleb thought about it, he wasn't sure he'd read any.

"Let me remind you, son, I don't think your education will do you any good in Hell. Don't abandon your priorities. Order your life accordingly, and everything will work out."

"Yes, ma'am," Caleb said and kissed his mother again, and turned to walk away.

"Don't speed," Doc said. "I'll cover the situation if need be. After all, Angelle was here in consultation about a patient's medical condition. I think that precludes any concerns you have about curfew."

"Thank you, Doc," Angelle said. She put her hands behind her and bowed politely, as was her practice instead of shaking hands. She said to Caleb's family, "I'm glad to have met all of you. It's evident where Caleb gets his good looks and manners." Turning slightly, she continued, "Doc and Mrs. Edith, I had a wonderful time. I love your home. I'm going to take you up on that standing invitation to come for dinner someday."

"When that young soldier boy of yours gets back, I want both of you to come. I'm dying to meet him," Doc said.

"Likewise," Edith said.

Doc and Edith walked them to the door. Doc said, "Don't be a stranger, Angelle. It's been wonderful seeing you away from the stress and hurry of the hospital. We should do this more often. Maybe Caleb will bring you back for dinner some night soon. Edith is quite the chef. If we ever lose Chef Paul at the club, I'm going to put her to work full-time."

"Our door is always open to you two," Edith said and kissed Angelle, then Caleb. "You two would make a beautiful couple... if it weren't for that big rock on your finger, but that could be remedied easily."

Doc gave Edith a hard look, then said, "No speeding, young people."

"No, sir," Caleb said. "I never go too fast."

Angelle snickered as they walked to the car and said, "I don't imagine you could speed if you wanted to."

Caleb opened the door for her and said, "Are you laughing at my honeymoon truck?"

"Nope, but I'm probably the only person on campus who doesn't."

"When I graduate and start making a living, the first thing I'm going to do is buy a nice second hand car."

Caleb pulled away as Edith and Doc stood waving at them. "They would make the perfect couple," Edith said. "Why did you look at me as if I tooted in an elevator?"

Doc laughed as he put his arms around Edith and kissed her. He commented, "You didn't see the real Angelle tonight. You saw a facade. She's a fragile young woman. I've told you about her past. She's having problems again, and Wellington has agreed to take her as a patient. What she doesn't need at this time in her life is conflict. I think Caleb is in love with her. I've cautioned him about encouraging her in any way because of her love for that soldier. Any involvement with Caleb would only increase the guilt and conflict that she's already feeling. It's just best that they stay friends."

"Best for whom, Doctor Freud!" Edith snapped. "I think you may be meddling in something that doesn't concern you. Who are you to tell Caleb not to pursue the girl that he obviously loves? I saw it the moment they walked in together. Furthermore, she's in love with him. I'm no physician or psychiatrist, but as a woman, I can recognize when two people are in love. Did you see how quick she was to offer an excuse for coming over here? She knew the hospital would call you if Buckie's condition was critical. She came here to meet the parents of the boy she loves. She wanted to make a good impression on them. I don't suppose you noticed that she couldn't keep her eyes off Caleb."

"We have company, Edith. They may hear us and think we're quarreling out here."

"Isn't that what we're doing?" Edith asked. "I've never meddled in your business, James, but I think you're meddling in their business. I don't suppose you heard her say the young soldier might find someone over in Germany and get married. That wasn't a joke, it was a wish."

"We can talk about this later," Doc said. "Let's get back to our guests."

"I've stated my position," Edith said. "There's nothing to discuss. You are wrong this time, James!"

They turned and walked in. Doc whispered, "It won't be the first time I was wrong, but I think I'm right this time."

"Wrong," Edith whispered.

"Right," Doc whispered.

They walked into the den and sat down. Houston said, "I had hoped that those two were more than friends. She's precious."

"Yes, she is," Doc said, "but I wouldn't get my hopes up. She's engaged to a nice, young soldier and seems to be very much in love with him."

"That's right, Houston," Mary said. "Caleb is not yet eighteen. The last thing he needs right now is to get involved with a girl. It'll be hard enough for him to keep up with his studies and play football. A girlfriend at this time would only complicate his situation."

"My feelings exactly," Doc said, giving Mary a nod and supportive smile.

"Well, I don't agree with either of you," Houston said. "Getting involved with a girl like Angelle might be worth getting a little behind in your studies. College is temporary, but a girl like her may not come along but once in a lifetime."

"My feelings exactly," Edith said with an even more agreeable smile. "I think they were meant for each other."

"Well, it's not going to happen," Doc said, "so you two cupids don't need to get your hopes up."

Edith looked at Houston, smiled, and winked. "More coffee and cake?" She asked.

"Sounds like a winner to me," Houston said. "I don't think I ever tasted cake quite this delicious. Mary is a marvelous cook, but I don't think she ever made a cake like this."

"It's some kind of cream cheese cake with fruit filling. It's James's favorite. I'd like to take credit for it," Edith said, "but Clotile, the wife of our chef at the club, is a master pastry chef. She bakes an assortment of cakes and pies. They're all delicious. She makes James a different one every Thursday. James eats the entire cake before the weekend is over."

"With a little help," he said in self-defense.

Mary sat there with a look of concern on her face that was obvious to Doc. He had spent a lifetime studying faces. He knew when a patient was not telling all the truth about their medical condition. "What's bothering you Mary," he asked. "That beautiful glow has left your face."

"You're very perceptive," Mary said. "I'm concerned about my son."

"Mary!" Houston blurted, "I was just kidding about the girl. Caleb's a very responsible young man. Sometimes I think he's too responsible. He's not going to do anything foolish again."

"I wish that was it, Houston, however, that's not my concern. You heard what he said about working and football and studying and not having time to read his Bible."

"Yes," Houston responded. "We all heard and we knew it was going to be a problem, but he's strong, intelligent, and determined. He'll be all right. His responsibilities will lighten up when football is over."

"I've been thinking about that scholarship, Doctor Marston. It goes against my fabric for him to accept it; however, these are extraordinary circumstances… Do you think the offer is still open?"

Doc began to laugh. "That offer would be good at any college or university in this nation, Mary. Do you want me to tell Coach Shook?"

"Let me think and pray about it for a few days, and I'll let you know. My son's health and emotional well being comes before my pride."

Houston looked toward heaven and mouthed, "Thank you, Lord."

CHAPTER EIGHTEEN

As Caleb drove along Angelle eased over next to him, put her fingers around his arm and tightly squeezed it. She said, "I see what you were talking about. Your mother's very protective of you. But remember this, Mr. Super Star, some day I may take you away from her."

"You already have," Caleb said. "You can have me tonight. We can drive to Memphis, get married, and be back tomorrow before noon. To soften Will's favorite expression, 'To heck with everyone else.' Now what do you say to that proposal?"

"It's a beautiful proposal, but I still need a little more time. There are things in my life that are still unresolved, and I have to work them out first. If everything works out right, I'll accept your proposal, hopefully soon."

Caleb leaned over, kissed her cheek, and said, "You know you're driving me crazy. When are you going to take off that ring and let me take you out to movies and start dating like other people do. I'm sick of hiding like a thief and stealing kisses where no one can see us. If you let him hold you, why won't you let me hold you when we kiss? That tells me you trusted him, but you don't trust me. You don't know how that hurts me."

"I want you to hold me as much as you want to hold me but … I need more time. If you truly love me, just be patient with me."

Caleb shrugged and said, "What choice do I have? You're the only girl I'll ever love. I'll wait forever for you."

"I've been thinking about the ball. I'll let Will escort me to the ball if you're going to be with me all the time. I saw another side of him today. Behind that stony façade, there's another person. I saw compassion in his eyes when he visited with Buckie today."

"Oh great! Will actually came to see him today? That's answered prayer."

"I'll go with him, but I don't think I can dance with him. If he takes my hand and puts his arm around me, I know what will happen. I might be so afraid that I'll panic. Then we'd all be embarrassed. I'd be so ashamed. The entire school will think I'm insane."

"Stop worrying about that. I have a plan. You aren't going to have to dance with him. Only me."

Angelle squeezed his arm tighter and laid her head against his shoulder. "You make me feel so secure." Caleb turned at the red brick entrance to the college and drove slowly toward the dorm. "Pull off to the side of the road for a second and kiss me, Caleb. I need to feel your warm lips against mine before we say good night."

Caleb eased over to the side of the road. Before he could stop the truck, Angelle's arms were around his neck, and her warm lips were moving over his. She cradled his face in her hands and moved as close as she could against his body. She began to smother him with passionate kisses. He felt her warm body against his and the warmth of her firm breasts against his chest. Her breath was hot and rapid. Her lips moved quickly over his. Her mouth widened and he felt her warm soft tongue begin to caress his lips. The sensation was blissful, more so than any feelings either had ever experienced. Caleb became so aroused, he began to tremble. He grasped the steering wheel tightly, fighting the urge to put his arms around her and hold her as tightly as she was holding him. The passion continued to build as their lips opened wider and wider and their tongues began to probe deeper and deeper. Angelle was panting and gasping. After a few minutes, she eased her hand down his chest and then slowly to his firm muscular thigh. Her respiration quickened even more. Suddenly she stopped kissing him, took both hands and reached down quickly easing her skirt up to her panties. She placed her leg over his lap and managed to squeeze her body between his and the steering wheel. Slowly she eased down until her body rested on Caleb's lap, and they could feel their forbidden parts almost touch, separated only by a layer of thin clothing. She gave a huge sigh and their lips met again as her kisses became wild and more passionately than ever. She began to move her body slowly against his.

Caleb was trembling uncontrollably. He gasped the steering wheel so tightly that his arms began to shake. Breathing rapidly, he felt faint, in total ecstasy like he had never imagined. His head was spinning, and his heart was pounding. He knew these sensations were forbidden. At that moment, he totally lost control. Nothing mattered now but unbridled pleasure. He was under her spell. Caleb felt the warmth of her body move against his. His trembling became more pronounced. He managed to stammer, "What, what, what are we doing?"

Angelle, hardly able to speak, murmured. "I, I'm showing you how much—I love you and why—I want you to wait for me."

Caleb was battling eighteen years of virtue and fidelity, yet desire of the flesh was winning this battle. Knowing this was not the time or place for what they were almost doing, he gasped, "You have to move. This is wrong and very dangerous, and it is not the right time."

"I never knew I could feel this way after…If this is wrong, I don't want to do right. I want you to make love to me."

"Don't you realize what you are saying and where we are?"

"I know," she gasped, "just kiss me a little longer and we'll stop. Just pretend we're making love. I didn't know this kind of feeling existed. I don't want you to stop."

"Angelle, my love," Caleb whispered, breathing harder than ever, "we have to stop this now before it—it goes too far. Then we won't be able to stop." Angelle's kisses began to smother him. "We have to stop now!" Caleb pleaded, "I'm losing control."

"We're not doing anything wrong, are we?" Angelle said. "We're not actually making love, are we?"

"Oh goodness!" Caleb gasped, "if this isn't making love, I don't think my heart could take the real thing. If you don't stop, I'm afraid those threads won't stop us. We have to stop, or you'll feel shame and guilt tomorrow. You may never want to see me again."

"All right," Angelle said, but she didn't stop.

Caleb couldn't fight her and the sensation he was feeling. His blood was almost boiling. His entire body was about to erupt with complete ecstasy. He knew Angelle was experiencing the same uncontrollable sensation. He was so consumed with pleasure that he had not notice the lights that were nearing from behind them.

A red light began to flash alongside his truck. His head jerked around in time to see a Campus Security car stop next to his truck. Panic, fear, and dread surged through both their minds as Angelle bounded off his lap, frantically pulling her skirt down. "Oh, my heavens!" Caleb gasped. "What have I done? Doc can't get us out of this mess. This is the Lord chastising me and I deserve it. I've ruined your life." He thought, *She's going to lose her job and I can't imagine what everyone is going to say when they hear why she's confined to the campus. What have I done to her?*

Angelle had eased down in the seat, nervously trying to straighten her wrinkled skirt. She wiped the moisture from her mouth and face and tried to fit her nurse's cap on her sweaty rumpled hair.

Two uniformed security officers stepped out of the car with flashlights in hand and ambled over to the truck. Caleb recognized them as the two officers who almost arrested him for trespass and vagrancy when he was sleeping under the oak tree before school began.

"Are you two love birds students at Marston?" one officer asked, with the light still shining in Caleb's face.

"Yes, sir," Caleb said, trembling.

"Let me see your student I.D."

"I don't carry mine with me," Caleb said.

"Neither do I," Angelle said, her face as red as a spring beet.

"You two look like you just ran a marathon. Your faces are flushed," he said with a chuckle. He glanced at his watch. Caleb's stomach sank.

"You look familiar, kid," the other officer said.

"Yes, sir," Caleb quickly responded. "We met under the oak before school started. You two were going to take me to jail for vagrancy."

"I remember you, kid. What's your name?"

"Caleb Morgan, sir."

The other officer said, "Hell of a game, kid. We met your parents tonight. Doc was bringing them through the gate at the end of the stadium. Your mother's a beautiful lady. Your old man is— very lucky. You played a heck of a game tonight, Caleb. But I still have to take you two love birds to the dorm and report your curfew violation. Sorry kids."

"I don't care if you report me, but Angelle really isn't late. She's the nurse who brought that sick boy to the game tonight. He was very ill after the game, and she took him back to the hospital. She had to talk to Doc Marston about his condition, and that's why she's late. She works late every night and they know it at the dorm."

"Then there shouldn't be a problem. What has me confused is what kind of work you two were doing on the side of this road almost three hours after curfew."

"Well, uh, we were, uh, uh." Caleb couldn't think of a single lie.

Angelle leaned forward and looked at the officer. "I asked him to kiss me before we got to the dorm. The dorm mother doesn't let girls kiss in front of the building after a date. Caleb's parents came to the game tonight. This is the first time they've ever seen him play. He went to Doc's house to tell them goodbye before they left for Choctaw County. I went with him because I've never met his parents. We talked a little too long. Doc said he would talk to the dorm mother if necessary. That's the whole truth."

The officer stuck his head in and shined the light on Angelle's face. He asked, "Are y'all like uh, dating." Angelle flashed the sparkling diamond ring in his face. "Oh! You two are engaged. What you think, Willis?" he asked the other officer.

Willis leaned over to take a good look at Angelle. "Shucks Grover, if I had a gal that looked that good, I don't think I'd have made it this far before I pulled over. Let um go."

Grover said, "Y'all get goin' and in the future, find a better place to do your spoonin'."

Caleb was soaked with perspiration for a couple of reasons as he watched the officers pull away. He quickly started the truck and pulled away. He wiped his face and said, "That was too close. We're playing with fire and almost got burned in more ways than one."

"I'm so ashamed, Caleb. I don't know what came over me. I promise you that I've never done anything like that before in my life."

"Not even with—?

"With no one," she said in near tears.

"I won't put you in this situation again. This has to end tonight. No more slipping around and stealing kisses in dark places. No more pretending that we're just friends. It's not fair to him, you, or me. I don't care if Doc knows that I love you. I'll take that scholarship and find another job to take care of my extra expenses. You have to make up your mind about whom you love and whom you want to spend the rest of your life with. If it's not me, it'll almost kill me, but somehow, I'll live. I'll never truly love anyone but you. All that matters to me is your happiness and your health. I love you enough to give you up if that's what's best for you."

"I do love you, Caleb. There, I said it. But …"

"There's that word again. I know it'll break my heart some day. I just know it will."

Angelle eased over by Caleb again and put her arm around his shoulder. "You're so kind and considerate, and always say the most wonderful things. All I can do is ask you to wait for me. Please be patient with me."

As they neared the dorm, Angelle said, "What did you mean when you said, 'I don't care if Doc knows that I love you?' And why would you want another job? Why would he care if we were in love?"

"I'm sure you realize it, but in case you don't, I'll tell you. Doc is very protective of you. He lost a daughter at birth and he feels like you were sent to replace her. He knows all about your past. He's afraid if you get involved with someone at school, it might cause a conflict in your mind that makes you feel guilty. The conflict might worsen your depression."

"He meant you, didn't he?"

Caleb nodded.

"Why didn't you tell me that he felt this way?"

"I felt like some things are better unspoken."

Fear came over Angelle's face. She became panicky. Her hands began to tremble. She said, "He's talked to Dr. Wellington. I'll never get well. That's the only reason he would say that."

"Calm yourself. That's not rational thinking. I agree with Doc, even though I couldn't stop loving you if it killed me. His only concern is your well-being. If you were thinking clearly, you'd understand his rationale. Your problem is fear and guilt. Doc is only trying to protect you. He thinks that putting you in a situation that might add to your guilt might worsen your condition."

Angelle put her hand on Caleb's face and said, "Do you really believe that, Caleb? Do you really believe that?"

"I don't just believe it, I know it. Those are the exact words Doc used."

"Are you sure?" Angelle questioned again.

Caleb tried to explain his feelings. "That's the reason I didn't tell you about it. I knew you'd twist it around and find something to get worried about. Angelle, you're going to get well. You're going to put all those fears behind you, and you are going to have a wonderful life. Is it because you think you can never let me hold you and make love to you that you continually ask me to wait for an answer? Or is that wishful thinking on my part? If that's your reason, I'll marry you just the way you are, even if it means I can never hold you or even make love. I'll still marry you and take care of you and love you the rest of our lives. Are you waiting to get well before you tell me that you love me and will marry me? Or is it because you're still confused about who you truly love and want to spend the rest of your life with?"

Angelle calmed somewhat and said, "I can't give you the answer you want now. I'll just ask you to wait a little longer." Caleb pulled up in front of the dorm. She leaned over, kissed him on the cheek, and hopped out of the truck. The door was locked so she rang the bell. Caleb pulled a short distance down the street and stopped. The housemother opened the door, and Angelle explained why she was so late. The dorm mother nodded, smiled, and closed the door behind Angelle.

Angelle bounded up the stairs and ran into her room with a brightness on her face that had been absent for half her life. The lights were still on, and Sarah Catherine was sitting on her bed, twisting her hands in near panic. "Where have you been?" She snapped. "I've been in a near panic waiting for you. I almost asked Miss Mills to call the hospital and ask if you were there. The only reason I didn't call was because I didn't want to get you in trouble in case you were doing something stupid. Do you realize what time it is? Did you get in trouble with Miss Mills?"

Her face still beaming, Angelle shook her head and sat down on the bed. "Sarah Catherine," she said, "tonight I experienced emotions, sensations, and feelings that I didn't know existed. I didn't think I would ever be able to feel like I did tonight."

"Oh my heavens!" Sarah Catherine gasped. "You had an orgasm! Oh! Sweetheart, please tell me you didn't make love with him tonight? You're not ready for that in your condition."

"Why should I tell you anything?" Angelle said, still smiling. "What happens between two people in love is personal."

Sarah Catherine put her hand to her face, looked away, and whispered, "You did. You actually made love to him." She turned and looked at Angelle's smiling face, reached out, and grasped her hand lightly. Angelle's jerked it away from her grasp and panic returned to her face. "How could you possibly make love when you can't allow anyone to touch you?"

"Did I say we made love?" Angelle retorted.

"I just assumed—You didn't? You didn't?" Angelle began to smile again and shook her head.

"Thank heavens. What were you talking about?" Before Angelle could respond, Sarah Catherine began to laugh. "If it wasn't sex and it made you feel that wonderful, maybe we can bottle it and sell it and make a million bucks."

Angelle explained. "We kissed, and I held him closely. We didn't actually make love, but I wanted to. It was the strongest and most pleasurable sensation I've ever felt. That's all I'm going to say about it. He makes me feel alive again. I love him more than life itself. I'm going to get well, if for no other reason than to love him for the rest of my life and make him happy. I have a reason to live now. I'm going to crawl out of this black hole and start to live again. I have something to live for now. I actually remembered how I felt before—when life was beautiful. I loved my mother and father so much, and how much love and happiness we had as a family. I felt that sensation again as I held him and kissed him."

"Does that mean the engagement is over and you plan to marry Caleb? Did you tell him you would?"

"No. I still don't think the time is right. When I can let him put his arms around me and hold me closely without any fear and with nothing but love in my heart, that will be the right time."

"Are you sure that he'll wait for you no matter how long it takes?"

"He said he'll wait forever, and I believe him. He even said he would marry me if I never get well. I believe he loves me that much."

"How are you going to break the news to Maurice? That's going to be heartbreaking."

"I haven't thought that out yet."

"Now, don't get angry with me for asking this, but suppose Maurice gets a leave and shows up here. You go out to meet him and that old feeling that put that engagement ring on your finger comes back, what then? Will you be able to tell him that it's over face to face?"

"I'm not going to think about that now. I'll have time to think about it later. I'm as close to heaven now as I've ever been."

"How did you get back in the dorm without a hassle?"

"I just told Miss Mills the truth."

"The whole truth?" Sarah Catherine asked with raised brows.

"Nothing but the truth," Angelle said, grinning sheepishly. "Well, the truth, less about ten minutes."

Sarah Catherine laughed and said, "That must've been a steamy ten minutes. I could use a few minutes like that myself." They both laughed. "We better get to bed, sweetie. We have class in less than six hours."

"I'll never get to sleep," Angelle said. "I'm too excited."

"I'm excited for you, but try to get some sleep. You have a long day tomorrow, and there's the homecoming ball Saturday night. If you don't get some sleep, you'll look like the wicked witch of the west tomorrow. I know you don't want that hunk of burning love to see you like that."

"Oh, goodness!" Angelle gasped. "I had almost forgotten about the ball. I wish I could forget about it. I think it's going to be a catastrophe."

"Sweetie, get off that roller coaster. Everything is going to be all right. Think what a wonderful life you're going to have very soon."

"I don't know how you put up with me, Sarah Catherine. Everything about me is gloom and doom. I love you because you're so understanding and kind to me."

"Sweetie, no one deserves a little kindness anymore than you. Now, get undressed and let's hit the sheets."

CHAPTER NINETEEN

After Caleb arrived at the dorm, he quickly showered and crawled into bed. Unfortunately, he battled his pillow all night, as was his practice the last few weeks. He was finally sleeping deeply when Emil's alarm clock exploded at ten until eight. It rang for five minutes before John David came rushing in to turn it off. He shook Caleb. Caleb opened his bloodshot eyes. John David commented, "The dorm cleared when your fire alarm went off. You have five minutes 'til class. Of course, after last night's incredible performance, you might think you don't have to go to class anymore, stud. By the way, Coach Simpson came by about midnight for bed check. I told him you were visiting with your folks. I hope I wasn't lying."

"Most of it was true," Caleb said, grinning as he grabbed his pants and shirt and put them on. He snatched his shoes off the floor and slid his feet into them without socks or tying them.

"Maybe you'll let me in on the part that wasn't true sometime later," John David joked.

"I don't think so," Caleb said, grinning with bloodshot eyes as he ran out the door. He rushed back into the room a few seconds later, snatched his notebook and pen from the small table, and shot out the door again.

John David shook his head with a foreboding look and said, "He's faster than a speeding bullet and can leap tall buildings in a single bound, but even Super Caleb is no match for the broken heart. When you fall for an engaged girl, you're setting yourself up for a gigantic fall. With his tender heart, I don't know if he could survive it."

Caleb sprinted up the steep hill and across the campus and ran through the door into the classroom just as the bell sounded. The entire class stood and applauded him. When they stopped clapping, he blushed as he stood there. In an exaggerated country boy voice, he said, "Aw, shucks, folks, it weren't nuttin'"

"Not for a super Corn Shuck," one of the boys yelled.

Good grief, Caleb thought. *Will's been spreading that nickname all over this campus. That kind of name catches on.*

Will had dressed in his street clothes long before daylight. He'd been pacing the floor ever since, waiting for Doc to release him. Elizabeth had returned at eight a.m. to say goodbye as she waited for the chauffer to drive her to Birmingham. The chauffer arrived at shortly after eight, but Elizabeth insisted on waiting until her baby was released before leaving. Doc arrived at eight-thirty. Will had almost worn a hole in his boots pacing by the time Doc arrived. Doc gave him a thorough examination and a dozen cautions about his activities and conduct for the next three months. Then he said, "I'm going to release you now. You're free to go."

"Son," Elizabeth said, "I know how hard-headed you are. You are your father's child, but I expect you to follow Doctor Marston's instructions explicitly. Do you understand?"

"Sure, Mother," Will said flippantly as he threw his arms up in a victorious celebration and yelled, "Free at last, free at last. Praise God, I'm free at last." He began to paraphrase parts of the poem, *Invictus*. "Under the bludgeonings of chance – and Tex and friends – my head is bloody, but unbowed, just cracked. I thank whatever gods may be for my unconquerable soul – and my hard head. Because I am the master of my fate. I am the captain of my soul." Then he placed his long muscular arm around Doc's shoulders, almost enveloping him and patted Doc on the head, saying, "Thanks, Doc, for pulling me through."

"If you believe that poem, son, I doubt that you believe I had any part of your recovery. I know that poem very well and in its proper sequence. I think the author must have been a confused and a misguided soul if he thought he was the master of his fate or the captain of his soul. I think it should have read this way. Out of the night that covers me, black as the pit from pole to pole, I thank the one true God for my unconquerable soul. And concluded it with, God is the master of my fate and the captain of my soul."

"Ah Doc, all that deep religious philosophy is a little too heavy for me. I just live and let live. You know, laissez les bon temps rouler. That means— "

"I know what it means, Will," Doc said with a look of repugnance. Doc put his arm around Elizabeth and said, "Take a good look at this lady, Will. She loves you a hell of a lot more than you love yourself. Do you realize that you came about this close to dying?" He put his fingers together, leaving about an eighth of an inch between them. "If you only knew how many fools about your age that I've pronounced dead because they thought they were invincible. If you want to kill this sweet lady, just continue with your reckless lifestyle. The next time you may not have a guardian angel looking after you. I think you need to slow down and do a little soul searching. Try to decide what's really important in life and what your goals are. I think a good place to start might be at church next Sunday."

"Oh, no!" Will snapped, shaking his head. "I took that trip when I was a youngster. That's not for me. I don't need it. I get preached at every day from Mr. Providence."

"Then you should consider paying a little attention to his advice. He may be pure country and appear a little slow to one with your intellect, but he has his priorities and values in order."

"I'll give it some thought, Doc," Will said, patronizingly. He leaned over and hugged Elizabeth, and kissed her goodbye. "Be careful on the way home, Mother. Now, I'm out of here, folks," and he shot out of the room.

Once outside, Will stopped by his car and glanced at the glistening sun. "Sunshine, oh marvelous sunshine at last. Man do I feel wonderful!" His car was in the rear parking lot near Doc's office. Will jumped in, started it, and squealed out toward the street. He slammed on his breaks, squealing the tires again.

Doc had walked out the back of the hospital. He stood and watched Will's antics and shook his head. He yelled toward Will's car, "There are sick people in here, Will!"

Will looked back at Doc, grinning, and yelled, "Like I don't know that, Doc. I know something else. If you don't get them out of that antiseptic morgue, they're all going to die!" He gave his deep machine gun laugh and drove quickly out into the street and peeled away.

Doc gave a deep sigh and murmured, "That boy has a death wish, and it may very well come true."

~)|(~

I could eat the hind end of a Billy goat, Will thought. *Let me see.* He glanced at his watch. *Caleb is still in class, and the cafeteria doesn't open for another two hours. It's a little early, but I think Mr. Pigg might let me in. I know he's been barbecuing since daylight. That food sounds wonderful.* He flew down the street and headed north on 51. Mr. Pigg's place wasn't open, but he let Will inside. He had just pulled the first Boston butt from the smoker grill. Will stuck his nose into the air and breathed deeply, commenting, "That smells divine." Mr. Pigg loved compliments so he heaped the freshly cooked pork on two po-boy buns. Will devoured both, plus a quart of soda, in record time.

"Didn't they feed you in the hospital?" Mr. Pigg asked.

"The food was atrocious. No salt, no pepper, no seasoning, only children's portions. If Mother hadn't been there to get me a burger and a shake occasionally, I'd have starved. I swear it wasn't fit for a pig…" Will considered his comment and said, "No offense intended."

Mr. Pigg laughed and responded, "None taken."

"Those po-boys were a culinary masterpiece," Will said as he paid Mr. Pigg. He then started back toward the campus. As he drove, he remembered he had left so hastily that he hadn't said goodbye to Buckie. The small boy had aroused deep feelings of compassion and love that he had never experienced before. He drove back to the hospital and parked.

Will dared not let Doc see him return so soon after his earlier bold and childish antics. Actually, he didn't want anyone to see him. He had observed from his father that any show of emotion, such as compassion or sympathy, was viewed as weakness in a man; however, he felt compelled to ease up the stairs and say goodbye. He looked around like a thief before entering Buckie's room. He was stopped at the door by a young and quite attractive nurse that he didn't recognize. She was coming out of Buckie's room. She was obviously a new employee.

"Are you family?" she asked curtly.

"Nope!" Will responded with a slight head bobble.

"Then I think it best that you not go in at this time. His father is with him. The child had a rough night. The staff thought they were going to lose him a few times. He's sleeping comfortably now and quite heavily sedated."

"Then he won't mind if I come in and speak to his father if he's sleeping, will he?" Will retorted with an I-got-you grin. "Now get out of my way." He used his elbow to ease her aside and started through the door.

"Well! I never," she gasped in disbelief.

"Well, you have now," Will said, "and you should do it more often. After all, it brings out your inner beauty and a beautiful sparkle in your eyes." Her mouth gaped open. She covered it with her hand, and stood there speechless and confounded by

Will's remarks. Then she began to smile. Will winked at her and walked inside.

Luther was nodding in the big chair, half asleep. Buckie was asleep, an ashen pallor to his face. Luther continued to doze. Will lightly touched him on the back as he passed. He knelt down by Buckie's bed, leaned over, and kissed him on the forehead. Buckie's eyes opened slightly, and he tried to focus. He reached out slowly for Will's hand. Will took his tiny hand in his and held it gently. Buckie managed to say in a drugged voice, "You ain't so tough, are you, big boy?"

"Tough enough to hammer you," Will whispered, holding up his other arm in a fist, shaking it with a smile on his face.

"You don't scare me none," Buckie said, managing a grin.

"I don't imagine anything scares you, kid," Will said. "You just might be the bravest boy in the world."

"I ain't so brave, Will. I'm kinda scared to die, but I don't want Poppa and Caleb to know it. But my preacher, Brother Branch from back home, came by yesterday. I told him I was a little scared 'cause I ain't been baptized. He said, 'What hinders you from being baptized now, my child?' He took some water, said a prayer, and put a few drops on my head. Then he told me, 'In the eyes of the Lord, this is just as good as being baptized in Mr. Cyrus Blackard's pond back home.' And I trust what he says."

"I'm sure of it, too," Will whispered.

"He told me to remember this. 'To be absent from the body is to be with the Lord.' I reckon the Lord will take care of me until my poppa and momma get to heaven," Buckie said.

Will's usually cold and indifferent heart was breaking as the dying child poured out his heart and soul to him. He was fighting the tears. He leaned over and hugged Buckie tenderly and whispered, "You are going to be fine, Buckie. I swear to you that you are going to be fine." Will turned and looked out the window to keep from crying. *Men don't cry in my family,* he told himself, *and I'm not real good at lying. He's not going to be fine. They're going to lay him into the cold, dark earth, and his life will be over and soon forgotten. Why was he born to suffer like this? If there is a God, why would he take this child's life? What has he done to deserve such torment? If there is a God, I want no part of him, if this is his kind of love. I feel sick,* he thought. *I feel sick of lying, and I feel sick of dying. I'm even sick of living right now. I'm sick of loving people. All that happens is that you get hurt if you love someone. I can't believe I let Caleb talk me into this. This is not who I am. This is not the real me. What am I doing here? I don't get involved with other people and their problems. Hell, I have enough troubles of my own without taking on the troubles of the world. I'm getting out of here. I feel like I'm smothering. I feel sick.*

Buckie squeezed Will's hand and said, "I love you, Will. Thank you for being my friend." Will grabbed his face with both hands, leaned over, putting his face between his knees, and began to wail. Luther jumped up from his shallow sleep, rushed over, and put his arm around Will. Buckie leaned over the side of the bed to put his hand on Will's head. He stroked it tenderly. "Don't cry for me, Will. Please don't cry anymore. It's going to be all right. I ain't scared no more. If you don't stop crying, Will, I'm going to cry, too. I don't want to be sad no more."

Angelle had opened the door quietly and observed the last few seconds. She had heard some of what Will had said to Buckie. She continued to stand in the doorway, fighting the tears. She dared not enter with tears in her eyes. She closed the door quietly, but left a small opening. She listened in amazement.

Will raised up slowly. Buckie reached out and wiped Will's tears away. "You're a tough guy, Will," Buckie said. "Tough guys don't cry."

"I guess I'm not… I guess I ain't so tough, kid," Will said, sniffling and wiping his face.

"Yes, you are, Will. You're the toughest guy in the world." Buckie said.

I always thought I was, Will thought. "Kid," he said, "if you want me to be the toughest guy in the world, that's just what I'll be." He raised his fist again and said, "I'll start by hammering you," and he faked a punch at Buckie.

"Now—you're my Will again," Buckie said.

Luther bent over touching Buckie's cheek and said, "Cryin' ain't no sign o' weakness, son. It be a sign o' love."

"I suppose I'd better leave and let both of you finish your naps before that cute little crabby nurse comes back and has me arrested," Will said.

"Fore you go, I got to tell you something," Buckie said, "'cause I may never see you again."

"Oh, yeah, kid. You might just be tougher than me."

"Will, I been worrying about you," Buckie said.

"About me? The tough guy? Why would you worry about me? Doc gave me a clean bill of health this morning. I'm free to go."

"No, Will, that ain't it. I'm worried about not seein' you in heaven."

Will turned and looked at Luther. Luther returned a blank look. Will looked at Buckie, hesitated a second, then said, "I don't think you need to be worrying about that. I know you and Caleb will be there. I ain't got many friends, and I sure can't afford to lose them."

"But you ain't been baptized," Buckie said, shaking his head.

"Now, who gave you that bogus information?" Will said. "My mother is Episcopalian. I suppose I am, too. I was baptized as an inf—as a child. She even took me to church when I was younger. Now, put your mind at ease, 'cause Ol' Will is going to be just fine."

After a few hours of rest, Gladys had returned early to relieve a nurse who had an emergency at home. She knew that Buckie had had a bad night, so she came rushing in. She walked over to Buckie, embraced him, and kissed him on the cheek. She commented, "I heard you had a rough night, sweetie. Are you feeling better?"

"I am now that Will come to see me again." His voice was a whisper. "I reckon I got the most famous friends in the world."

"It's more like infamous," Gladys said grinning, as she nudged Will. "Has Doc released you yet?" Gladys asked with a hard look.

"No," Will said. "I escaped. I'm going to the dorm now, Buckie. You can believe this," and he held up his muscular right arm as he said, "I'd give this right arm if you were able to go with me. I'll be back soon. I need to hurry over to the dressing room before the team leaves for Lexington."

Luther tried to stand, but Will put his hand on his shoulder and said, "Keep your seat, Mr. Luther." Will patted him on the back and looked at his weary, bloodshot eyes. "You need some real rest, sir." But no words of comfort came to his mind. He patted Luther again on the shoulder and left for the campus.

Will drove to the stadium and walked into the dressing room where the team was preparing to depart for Kentucky. The varsity players rushed over to greet him. Will put his hands out and said, "No hugging and kissin', boys. The ribs are still a little tender." The coaches came out of their offices and walked over to greet him. "I wish you could make the trip," Coach Shook said. "Just your presence on the sidelines would be a boost to the team's morale."

"You know how I feel about that, Coach. I screwed up and let everyone down, and it's killing me."

"Don't get too discouraged," Coach Shook said, "'cause it ain't over, boy. You have two more glorious years. People are waitin' to see you and Caleb out there together. Two potential all-Americans."

"You can scratch that potential," Will said.

"You want to talk to the team, Will? They're tired of my same old crap." Will nodded, a little apprehensive. "Take a seat, men, Will has something to say."

The room quieted as everyone took a seat on the benches in front of their lockers. Will ambled up between them and started his talk. "Men, I'm not a very good speaker. I've always let my actions speak for me. I guess I learned the hard way that sometimes talking can be a little less hazardous to your health.

Caleb begged me to go with him last weekend and not to go to Memphis. I'd give anything if I had heeded his advice. I didn't, and I'm paying for it now, and so are you, as well as the coaches. We had something very special started. It felt wonderful, but I blew it. I'd give anything short of my life to have my health back and lead you onto that field tomorrow, but I can't. I still remember that little demonstration of teamwork that Coach Shook used when he told us to put our hands together. He made Caleb crawl up on top of our hands then we, as a team, threw him up so high he pissed in his pants." Everyone laughed. "Oh," Will said, "he didn't volunteer that information."

After the laughter ceased, he continued. "Listen to what I'm going to say. I'll tell you why I'm so damn good. I don't want to sound egotistical—the hell I don't. That's who I am. I'm a good football player. No—I'm a great football player. In case you didn't know, I made all-American last year. It's what I live for. If President Eisenhower walked in here and asked me if I played football, I'd tell him I play great football. If he disagreed, I might kick his ass. My passion is football. My love is football. My life is football."

The coaches cut their eyes at each other, wondering if they had made a mistake asking Will to address the team.

Will continued. "But I didn't win that game last week. No one person wins a game. We, as a team, won the game last week. It took all eighty plus of us to win. I don't know if we'll win another game. I hope we win all of them. But I promise you this, and it's my secret to being a good football player. If you'll walk on that field tomorrow and say to yourself, and believe it, 'We are winners,' and then reach down inside yourself and give everything that you have – leaving nothing in the tank, one-hundred percent for sixty minutes, you can walk off the field winners, regardless of the score. Am I right, coaches?"

"Yeah! Yeah!" the coaches yelled and clapped, as did the team.

Coach Shook said, "It's hard to argue with success, but I'd give a little more thought to kicking the president's butt." They all laughed and rushed to Will. They called out, the slogan, 'One hundred percent for sixty minutes!'

"That's it!" Coach Shook yelled. "Grab your gear and let's go win another game." He took Will's hand and shook it, as he said, "You are a hell of a football player, Will, but that speech was more impressive than any game you ever played. What are you doing this weekend?"

"I'm going to the library and try to find a dozen books that I haven't read. Then I'll go to my room and wart the hell out of my best friend."

CHAPTER TWENTY

Caleb finished his morning classes and rushed out of the building to get to work. He heard Rachel yell at him. He stopped and waited as she jogged over.

"Hey, hot shot! What's up?" she said.

"Your head is, and I think it's on fire."

Rachel smirked and said, "If we can dispense with the insults for a second, I'd like to know if we are still on for the homecoming ball?"

"A promise made is a debt unpaid," Caleb quipped.

"That's not very original, but true. I'm glad you didn't back out, or I wouldn't have gone. I've drawn you a map. It's in my purse." She opened it, fumbled around a few seconds and said, "Here's the map. It's only four miles from the campus. Just go North on fifty-one for three miles and turn left on 'Possum Corner Road. Continue for one and a quarter miles. You can't miss it. It's only fifty yards on the other side of the white, wood-frame church on the left. The road is spelled like it sounds, 'Possum." She spelled it for him, and Caleb grinned at her.

"What's so funny, the name? I imagine you ate 'possums and coons before you came up here to civilization."

"Back in those sticks, we ate everything," Caleb said. "We ate snails, grub worms, earth worms, roaches, rats, and grasshoppers.

You ain't et 'til you've had a plate of grub worms served over rice and sawmill gravy."

"Stop!" Rachel yelled, throwing her hands up. "Enough already! You're making me sick. I'm sorry I criticized your community."

"You can keep that paper with the map on it. I'm not that dumb," Caleb said.

"I don't know, after all you're a jock, aren't you?" she quipped, smiling and wrinkling her freckled nose.

"There you go again. You're never going to get a boy with those snide remarks."

"Who said I want a boy. I'm holding out for a real man. By the way, do you think that old relic you drive will make it all the way to my house and back?"

"Oh, we're not going in my old truck. Angelle Noel was selected to be in the court. Will is taking her. We're all going in his new red convertible."

"Hold on a minute, shorty," Rachel retorted, "I don't like being on the same planet with that—I won't call him what he is. It's not Christian. I'm sorry if I insulted your truck. I don't mind riding in it. It's become quite the talk on campus. Anyway, my father volunteered to let us use his car if we need transportation."

Caleb shifted his feet and rocked from side to side as his mind raced thinking of how to convince her that they must go with Will. "The truth is always better than a lie," he commented. "I know it's an old—"

"Cliché," Rachel interjected.

"Thank you, Will. I mean Rachel," Caleb said facetiously. "Be that as it may, we have to go with Will and Angelle."

Rachel put her finger to Caleb's nose and pushed. "No, we don't have to go with Will and Angelle," she said flatly. "You may have to go with them, but I'll be staying home before I get in a car with that—that lecherous…"

"Please hear me out, Rachel, before you interrupt again. I'm going to be late for work anyway." Rachel cocked her head sideways with a smirk, and waited. "It's like this. Angelle is engaged."

Rachel threw her head back looking skyward and blurted, "Like I didn't know that. Furthermore, she's gorgeous and drives all the boys around here crazy and, I might add, professors, too."

"Let me finish—please. I sit by her in class, and we're very good friends. When she found out that she'd been selected to be on the Homecoming Court, she asked me to escort her. But I had promised you that I'd escort you. She said she wasn't going if I couldn't escort her. I finally convinced her to go with Will. But she said she would agree only if we all went together. She has some strange ways, and she doesn't trust Will any more than you."

"Are you telling me that the Angelle I know, actually talks to you? I've heard she doesn't talk to any boys. She just speaks French when they come on to her."

"We're really good friends. I wish we were more than friends, but you know."

"Yeah, that ring. It's a killer, isn't it?" She laughed. "Just remember, she's not the only fish in the sea."

"You can do better than that," Caleb said, grinning.

"I suppose if I get a pin for my nose, plugs for my ears, and patches for my eyes, I might force myself to do this—for you. But be forewarned, you'll be indebted to me for life. The first time I hear honey, sweetie, chick, darling, broad, or any other demeaning word come from his mouth, I'll put my fist in it. He's ruined the reputation of dozens of girls already. I don't intend to be another one. I truly don't like him, Caleb."

"I kinda sensed that," Caleb said.

"Now, don't misunderstand me. I have to love him because the Bible tells me I must love everyone, but I don't have to like him or egotists like him. There's a difference in loving and liking. He makes my skin crawl when I look at him."

"Oh! You know him?" Caleb asked, somewhat surprised.

"Heck no, I don't know him. We must have the same free hour because he comes strutting into the library two or three times a week acting like he's the world's gift to women. That's where I see him."

"Has he seen you?"

"I should hope not. I hold my book up to my face and peep over it."

Why would you peep—Caleb thought better of voicing his thought. *Just let sleeping dogs lie.* He was quick to say, "I appreciate what you are doing for Angelle. I'll sing at your wedding, or dance at your funeral, however the saying goes."

Rachel looked at him cockeyed and said, "Are you sure you graduated, hay seed?"

"I have my sixth grade diploma on my wall in the dorm," Caleb said smugly.

Rachel doubled up her fist and put a shot directly into his sternum, knocking him backward almost to the ground. "Touché," she said. "I'll see you at six-thirty sharp. Don't you dare be late, or I'll show you my upper cut."

"Uh—uh—uh," Caleb stammered.

"What! Out with it," Rachel snapped, cocking her head.

"Uh, there's one other little problem…" After a long pause, he continued, "Angelle won't dance with Will. She said she wouldn't go if she had to dance the first dance with him."

"And—" Rachel snapped as she put her hands on her hips, giving Caleb an incredulous stare.

"Uh—uh," Caleb continued to stammer.

"Did you hear a word that I said," Rachel blurted.

Caleb dropped his head. A sick, disappointed look came over his face. "I guess she won't be going then…"

"Are you trying to put a guilt trip on me?" Rachel said sharply. "It won't work!"

"I'm really in love with Angelle. It breaks my heart that she won't get to go," Caleb said. "I'm sorry that I asked you to…"

"Well—you should be, knowing the way I feel about Will," Rachel retorted.

As Caleb turned to walk away with a sinking look on his face, he said, "I'll pick you up at six-thirty sharp."

Rachel watched him walk away. His shoulders were drooped, and his head was hanging. She watched for several seconds, then yelled, "I'll do it for you. What do I care about my reputation? Why should I care if they think I'm one of Will's bimbos. I'm not dating anyone anyway."

Caleb turned, a smile broke across his handsome face, and he started to run toward her. Rachel threw her hands out and barked, "Stay away from me, shorty. I'm subject to knocking your head off if you come any closer." Caleb stopped, his face beaming, and he began blowing her kisses as he jogged backward down the hill. Rachel wanted to be angry, but the look on his face made her smile. She stood there smiling and shaking her head as he jogged away.

―※―

At noon, Angelle walked slowly down the canopied walkway behind the hospital and stopped in front of the door with a sign that read, 'Dr. Wallace Wellington, Psychiatrist.' She stood in front of the door a few seconds, then reached for the handle. Her hand was trembling. She pulled it back. After a few seconds, she visualized Caleb's face. She reached out, grasped the handle, made herself open the door, and walked inside. A middle-aged lady with graying hair sat at a small desk in front of a window. A beautiful little girl about five or six years old sat on a pallet next to the desk with a coloring book and two dolls in front of her. The lady looked up and smiled very pleasantly at Angelle. She asked, "May I help you? I'm Janice Wellington, Dr. Wellington's wife. He's semi-retired but still works a few days a week. I fill in for a real receptionist, since he doesn't handle many cases anymore." She had a calming voice and a pleasant smile, and Angelle's fears eased somewhat.

"I'm Angelle Noel. I think Dr. Wellington is expecting me."

"Have you met Dr. Wellington before?"

"No, ma'am," Angelle responded nervously.

"I thought you might have because he and Doc are such good friends. Wallace said Doc thinks of you as a daughter. You seemed a little nervous when you walked in. Don't be. Wellington is a kind person. You're going to be very comfortable when you meet him."

The door opened and a tall, distinguished looking gentleman walked out. He said, "Miss. Noel, I presume. I'm Dr. Wellington. It seems we have a mutual friend by the name of Dr. James Marston." His voice was deep, warm, and rich, with a calming tone, almost as if he were smiling with his voice. He walked up to Angelle and put his arm on her shoulder. She flinched and jerked away. "Sorry if I startled you," he said and reached for her hands.

Angelle quickly put them behind her, bowed politely, and in a nervous voice said, "Thank you for seeing me, Dr. Wellington."

"You know, I haven't taken a new patient in over a year. As a favor to my best friend, I agreed to see you. Let's go back to my office and get acquainted." He led her into his office. Angelle had never been inside a psychiatrist's office. She didn't know what to expect. The room was very homey with beautiful pictures on the wall. A magnificent mahogany desk was located near the back of the spacious room. A half-dozen framed degrees were hanging on the wall behind it. The desk was well organized with only a lamp, pen set, writing pad, a box of tissues, and a phone on its polished surface. A gorgeous, shiny leather sofa with pillows was situated across from two comfortable looking chairs with a coffee table in front of them. The lighting was recessed, soft and soothing. Angelle thought, *This would make a beautiful living room for someone.*

"Let's get comfortable, Angelle. You sit in that chair and I'll sit near you." Angelle sat on the edge of the chair and clasped her hands tightly together, leaning forward.

"I should tell you that anything we discuss in this room is privileged and is in strictest confidence." Angelle nodded and forced a smile. "There are obviously things in your life that are causing you pain and discomfort. We are going to try to find out what they are. Then, we'll be able to resolve them. Why are you are here, Angelle? What do you hope to gain through these sessions?"

"I, I want to be like everyone else, Doctor Wellington. I've been too ashamed to get help before, and I didn't have the money. But things are different now. I've fallen in love with someone, and … and I can never marry him because of the way I am."

"Tell me how you are, Angelle. I want total honesty."

"I have horrible nightmares almost every night. I have these feelings of panic that come over me. They frighten me badly, and sometimes I want to die. I—I can't let anyone touch me or even hold my hand."

"What other feelings are you experiencing?"

"Sometimes I feel like everything around me is getting black and closing in on me. I have a sinking feeling that frightens me so horribly that I feel faint. My heart almost comes out of my chest. I have a terrible pain in my stomach and then my legs hurt. Slowly the feeling eases and the light returns. I'm left with the fear of it returning soon. I couldn't live if that feeling stayed with me very long. I hate those feelings. They're too horrible to actually describe. Sometimes I have this hopeless and helpless feeling that lingers. I want to cry. No one knows how it feels unless they have experienced it. It's actually a hundred times worse than I have described when I'm experiencing it." She lowered her head and said, "I feel ashamed even telling you this."

"There is no shame in this room, Angelle, only truth. The most wonderful healer that ever lived said, 'You shall know the truth, and the truth shall set you free.' You need to know that I am a psychiatrist and also a Christian. I'm not the healer. The Lord heals, and He has given doctors the tools that allow them to accomplish that. You are suffering from depression and anxiety brought on by insecurity, fear, and possibly guilt. Now, let me ask you a few more questions. I see you have a beautiful ring on your finger. Did you let that young man hold you and kiss you? Were you at ease with him?"

"No. I've never let anyone hold me or kiss me, except my parents. I did kiss someone, but I wouldn't let him hold me."

"Someone loves you enough to give you that ring. Does he know your condition?"

Angelle hesitated, and then said, "He said he loves me and wants to marry me. Yes, even under these conditions, he still wants to marry me."

"He must love you dearly. Why did you hesitate before you answered?"

Angelle shrugged and shook her head.

"I want you to tell me about your home life. What was it like before you came to Marston?"

"My mother and father were the most wonderful parents in the world. They loved me and took care of me. There was so much love and happiness in our family."

"Why did you say they were and they loved me? That's past tense."

"Because they're both deceased," Angelle answered.

"How long have you had these feelings?"

"Since I was about eleven, after my mother died. My father was killed by a thief while he was on patrol when I was ten. He was a policeman in New Orleans. A few years later, my mother was …" Angelle put her hands over her face and began to weep. There was a long pause. Finally, Angelle said, "I wasn't sick before they died. I loved my life. I was really happy as a child."

Wellington rocked back in his chair a few seconds, then said, "Would you like a soda? I have some in the refrigerator in the other room."

"No, sir," Angelle said.

"What happened to your mother, Angelle?" She lowered her head and began weeping.

"No more tears, sweetheart." Dr. Wellington handed her a tissue from his desk to wipe her tears away. "It's quite obvious that their deaths are related to your fears. Unless you are willing to talk about those times, we have no place to begin the healing process."

"Dr. Wellington, it's so hard to talk about my mother's death. I've tried to forget it every day of my life. That night still haunts me. I dream about it. It's always in my mind." She lowered her head and said, "I killed my mother. She would be alive if I had just …"

Wellington rocked back in his chair. He remembered an article in the newspaper some six or seven years earlier about a double murder in New Orleans. A mother had walked in on her husband raping his stepdaughter. She shot him, but he grabbed the gun away from her and killed her before he died. The child, a young girl, was found by the police, running naked down a street in New Orleans. For personal reasons, Wellington prayed that Angelle was not that child. His face turned gray, and a fear welled up inside him causing him to feel faint. He took a deep breath and pushed away his fears.

"Angelle," Wellington said calmly, "why would you think you killed your mother? I know you didn't kill your mother."

Angelle's head was still bent low as she whispered, "I killed her when I didn't tell her. I should have told her what he was doing to me. Or I should have run away. She would still be alive if I had not been a coward… Can you help me to forget this, Dr. Wellington. Will I have to live with shame and guilt the rest of my life?"

"Now we have a starting place, Angelle. It won't be easy for you because you have to be willing to face the pain that comes before the healing."

"Doctor, I think I would walk into hell to be well again and to be able to really be close to the boy that I love so dearly. The only happiness that I have felt since … is when I'm with him. But I can't even let him hold me. I can't make him wait forever. I won't do that to him. I love him too much, so if you don't think I'm going to get better, please tell me so I can stop seeing—"

"If you have determined that you're going to get better, that's the first step. I don't lie to my patients. It may take a long time for you to heal because the wounds are obviously very deep. I see a few patients on Mondays and Fridays, but I'm going to make an exception in your case. We are going to meet on Wednesday as well, if you can work that into your schedule."

Angelle nodded, somewhat disappointed by the Doctor's answer. She said, "Doctor Wellington, that's not the answer I wanted to hear."

"Angelle, I don't usually say what I'm going to say to you, but you're very special to a lot of people that I love. I'm going to be brutally honest with you because I want you to get well almost as much as you do. My fear is that you came here hoping, as they say, for a quick fix. Sweetheart, there are no quick fixes for your condition. There's medication that seems to help some people. In your case, that would only be a band-aid over a gigantic wound. I'm here to guide you through the pain and recovery. But you'll never recover until you're able to stand up and face the world, unashamedly, and say, I was raped by a monster. It cost me my sanity and almost cost me my life. It did cost my mother her life, but I did nothing wrong. I acted as a child would in fear and dread. I will no longer live in fear and dread of the past. It cannot harm me any longer. I was a victim, and now I am the victor."

Angelle put her hands to her face and began to sob. After a good cry, she stood up, wiped her eyes, and, with a look of despair, said, "Dr. Wellington, you don't think I'm going to get well do you?"

Dr. Wellington quickly responded, "Angelle, it doesn't matter what I think. It's what you think that will ultimately determine whether you recover or not. Yes, I think you are willing to do whatever it takes to get well. Now, sit down and take a few deep breaths, because we have a lot to talk about."

Angelle sat down and said, "Dr. Wellington, he may not want to wait for me if it takes too long. I won't ask him to wait for me. I love him too much to ask him to waste his life on me."

"If he truly loves you, he'll wait forever. Angelle, what you don't understand is that you have to do this for you. This is not about him or anyone else. This is your life and your happiness that we are concerned with. You have to believe that. No one wants to live in fear and dread when there is hope and help. You may decide that this isn't the boy that you want to spend the rest of your life with. He may change his mind about you. There can still be a wonderful life ahead of you with or without this young man…I want to hear more about your dreams next session. You might not realize it, but we've made significant progress today," Dr. Wellington reassured. They talked a while longer as Wellington tried to gain her confidence. "I'll see you in two days. If you need me before then, pick up the phone and call me, day or night." Angelle stood, forced a smile, and left for the hospital to begin work.

———

As soon as the door closed behind her, Wellington grabbed the phone and rang Doc's office. Vivian, Doc's receptionist answered, and he asked for Dr. Marston. He had to wait for a minute or two before Doc picked up the phone. "Doc Marston here."

"You can be damn glad that you're there instead of here," Wellington said, "because the next time I see you, I'm going to kill you."

"What in the Sam Hill are you raving about, Wellington?"

"As if you didn't know!"

"I'm busy, Wellington, and in no mood to play games. Unfortunately, I'm not semi-retired, whatever that means. Some of us still have to put in a day's work. We can talk about what has you in such a huff on the golf course Friday."

"Not so fast, slick," Wellington snapped, "I'm talking about the beautiful little princess that you pawned off on me."

"Explain yourself, Wellington, and be brief."

"Did you know about her condition and past history?"

"I certainly did. I screen all the Marston Foundation applicants thoroughly before I award a scholarship."

"You knew everything?"

"Everything," Doc answered confidently.

"You knew about the baby?"

"What baby!" Doc snapped.

"You didn't know she had a child in the mental institution while she was in a catatonic state?"

"No!" Doc gasped. "That wasn't in any report that I received. What happened to the child?" There was a very long pause before Doc said, "No! That's impossible. We can't be talking about the same person... That's impossible!"

"Yes, it's possible and true. It's my Grace. My adopted Grace is Angelle's child. Now, you've asked me to try to help Grace's mother recover. Her recovery may cost Janice and me our daughter. That would destroy Janice."

"Wellington, I am so sorry. I didn't know. I swear I didn't know. I would have tried to get her to go to Memphis for treatment if I'd known. I'll still do it. I'm so sorry."

"No. No. I won't let you do that. I feel an obligation to this sick, pathetic young lady. After all, she is Grace's mother, and she's so sick. I'm going to do all I can for her, even if it costs us our daughter. I have to believe the Lord sent her to me."

"How did you get the child?" Doc asked. "I thought you went through an adoption agency."

Dr. Wellington told the story. "You remember, I worked at the East Louisiana State Hospital in Jackson, Louisiana after I finished my medical degree from Tulane. Dr. Cleveland and I became good friends. Dr. Cleveland knew Janice and I lost our daughter in a car wreck when she was a senior in high school. A few years ago he called to tell me of Angelle's situation. She had been in a catatonic state for over a year. Imagine a thirteen-year-old child who didn't even know she was alive. Angelle had had a baby six months after she was admitted. They doubted that she would ever recover. He said it was a gamble to adopt the baby, but the odds were that no court would ever allow an institutionalized child to keep a baby, even if she recovered. Dr. Cleveland said her recovery was very doubtful at best. When I told Janice about the situation, she became so excited that we took the chance. Grace is legally adopted, but you know how courts are about situations like this. I never even asked for the mother's name. I didn't want to know."

"I don't know what to say," Doc murmured. "That explains a lot of things that Caleb told me about her. He said she wakes up at night screaming, 'Don't take my baby.'"

"Oh, my Lord," Wellington exclaimed, "she didn't tell me that. She did tell me she had horrible nightmares. Her nightmares are obviously based on her suppressed memories of childbirth and someone taking the baby away."

"I work with the girl every day of the week, and I had no idea her condition was this critical," Doc confessed. "She seems very stable at work. I might add that she's one of the best and brightest nursing students I have ever worked with. I love her like a daughter. I did know that she had suffered from depression and anxiety in the past. I knew she was suicidal when she was younger. After hearing about what she went through, I can understand her state of mind. After being raped and sodomized for almost a year, she lay there and watched her mother and the stepfather kill each other. But it seemed that she was recovering."

"Well, thank heavens you specialized in internal medicine and surgery and not psychiatry. But seriously, James, this child should actually be in a mental institution so she could receive full-time treatment. She's in no condition to be attending school and holding down a job with so much pressure and responsibility."

"We can't be talking about the same person, Wellington."

"Unfortunately we are," Wellington said. "I'm going to do my best, but if there isn't significant progress after a time, I'm going to recommend commitment. I know you're busy. I'll keep you abreast of her progress or lack of."

"Please, do, Wellington. I had no idea she was that troubled. I should have been more cognizant because of her past. It would have been a miracle if she hadn't had problems somewhere down the road. She's in good hands. She's top of my prayer list. I have every confidence in you."

CHAPTER TWENTY-ONE

After his encounter with Rachel, Caleb drove to the club and worked the rest of the day and evening. He and Abe cleaned up, and he rushed to the hospital.

Buckie was weaker than the night before. The lines in his face were more pronounced, and his eyes were bloodshot and sunken back. Buckie barely recognized Caleb. He was in and out of consciousness. Even Luther knew that the end was at hand.

Luther said, "Let's go git some more coffee, Caleb. I won't be able to sit and watch if I don't git a big cup." They walked into the waiting room, and Luther filled his cup with black coffee that smelled and looked like used motor oil. They walked back down the hall as Gladys was entering the room with the sedative. They followed her into the room. Caleb felt the gray shroud of death hanging over the room. Buckie never felt the needle. He was near the sleep of death and everyone felt it.

Gladys bent over and kissed Buckie, then turned to Luther, hugged him, and whispered in a broken voice, "You have to be strong, Luther."

"You want me to stay with you tonight, Mr. Luther?" Caleb asked.

"Ain't no need o' both us sittin' up all night, Caleb. You go git a good night sleep."

They sat silently for a while. There was nothing left to say. The end was near. Angelle eased in and said, "You try to rest tonight, Mr. Luther. We don't want you getting sick." Luther wiped the sleep from his eyes, and patted her on the arm. Angelle asked, "Are you leaving soon, Caleb?"

"I reckon," he said as he stood. "Mr. Luther might get a little rest if I'm not here to talk to him." Caleb bent over and gave Buckie a long kiss on the cheek. He ran his hand over his soft brown hair and fought the tears. He hugged Luther and said, "I'll see you tomorrow." Luther just nodded.

Caleb and Angelle rode back to her dorm. Caleb never looked at Angelle or spoke a word to her. Angelle eased over close to him, continually looking at him. He stopped in front of the dorm. Angelle said, "Why are you angry with me?"

"I'm not angry with you, Angelle. I'm just wondering why the Lord needs to take Buckie away from Luther. He doesn't have anyone but Buckie. He's been a wonderful father. I'm doing what should never be done. I'm questioning the sovereignty of God. It's tearing up my guts."

"You're thinking what I've been thinking for a long time," Angelle said, "and I know it's wrong. But how do you stop your mind from wondering. I'm fearful about what's going to happen to Mr. Luther when… I need to go," Angelle said. "I'm about to get behind in my studies. I'll be up most of the night. Kiss me goodnight, then I'll run."

Caleb hesitated a few seconds, then answered slowly, shaking his head. "No I won't. Not tonight. I feel like I'm stealing someone else's kisses. I may never kiss you again. Not until the ring on your finger is the one that I place there."

"I know I'm hurting you when I encourage you. It hurts me too. I need a little more time to settle things in my mind. I know you don't understand. My feelings for you are strong and deep. All I can do is ask you to wait for me."

"That's not an option. I have no choice. You have my heart through all eternity."

"Then kiss me, and show me that you'll wait for me."

"No. It's better that we don't kiss anymore. It's too painful, not knowing if you'll change your mind tomorrow or next week. If Maurice surprised you and drove up here now, what would you do? Don't answer that. I don't want to know."

"Are you saying that you'll never kiss me again?"

"Angelle, I don't know what I'm saying anymore. My mind is in a fog, and everything is clouded. I've never had this feeling. If depression is worse than this, it must be horrible."

Angelle thought, *Pray you never find out.* As she leaned over to kiss him on the cheek, he turned and their lips met for a few seconds. She opened the door, stepped out, and said, "You'll feel better when the sun rises tomorrow. It has some healing power. Believe me, I know about depression."

"Your kisses have healing power, too," Caleb responded, then murmured, "even to a liar and thief."

Angelle blew him a kiss and said, "You're not a liar or a thief. You're just in love. Isn't it a wonderful feeling?" She walked toward the door, turned, and walked backward, blowing kisses with each step.

When she finally entered the building, Caleb drove away mumbling. "I am a thief. I'm trying to steal someone's girl. I'm just a dirty rotten thief, Lord, and I can't do a thing about it." He drove slowly down the hill. The thought of Buckie dying sickened him. He parked and trudged up the stairs to his room.

Will was sprawled out on his cot with a couple of dozen books scattered on the bed and floor where he'd thrown them. If he didn't like the first few chapters, the book went sailing against the wall then to the floor. He read novels as fast as most people read comic books. Occasionally, he'd slow up if he found a steamy part in the book. He read the pages faster than most could turn them. Caleb walked up beside him and said, "Are you fanning yourself with the pages?"

Will held the book up and let Caleb look at the title. 'Great Expectations' by Charles Dickens. "This is the biggest crock of crap I ever tried to read. This is the sixth time I've tried to read it, and it gets more disgusting each time. If that little bitch, Estella, slapped me like she did Pip—Pip. Who names a kid Pip? Or Miss Havisham. How many Havishams have you ever known?"

"Strangely enough," Caleb quipped, "that's my mother's maiden name."

Will turned his head sideways giving him a dubious stare. Caleb had to laugh.

Will continued his criticism. "How does a cake last a hundred years? The maggots, rats, and roaches would've eaten it in a few days."

"How are you, Will?"

"I'm going to be fine now that Mother's gone back to Birmingham."

"She loves you, Will. You're very fortunate to have a mother like her."

"You love me too, but you don't treat me like a ten-year old, do you?"

"I reckon I don't," Caleb admitted.

"What's with that reckon, crap?" Will chided. "Get that hillbilly jargon out of your vocabulary. You're a college man now. Learn to speak like one."

"I reckon I'll try," Caleb said, grinning. "I'm glad you are back to normal."

"They're going to get their asses kicked tomorrow without me," Will said.

"Yep! You are positively back to normal."

"Well, you know it's true. If you and I were playing tomorrow, it wouldn't even be a contest. Now, let me get back to the moldy cake and all the cobwebs. Maybe I read it too fast last time. You know it's a classic."

Caleb collected his bath supplies and started out the door to go to the shower. He heard a bang against the wall, then came the sound of the book hitting the floor.

You Shall Know the Truth

Saturday morning came. Football fever broke out like a smallpox epidemic in the hill country and small towns of north Mississippi. The losing streak was finally over. There was cautious optimism of another victory. Everyone who knew football understood that the odds were against Marston's team winning again without Will; however, hope springs eternal, and without hope the spirit dies—even football spirit. So there was great hope for a second straight victory. Even though the faithful had suffered through three horrendous years of losing, they never lost faith, and the single win was enough to re-kindle the flames that burned in the heart of every Marston faithful.

Caleb and Will rose early and went to breakfast together. The dining hall was empty with the varsity away. Most of the freshmen were catching a little extra shut-eye. Will ate like a starved horse. "What do you have planned for today?" Caleb asked.

"I'm going to walk and jog about ten miles. Then I'll see if I can pump some iron."

"Don't be stupid," Caleb snapped. "Do some light walking. Wait until the ribs heal before you hit the weights."

"My legs feel like jelly from lying in bed a week. I hardly have enough strength to lift my fork."

"You look like you're doing a pretty good job to me," Caleb snickered.

"I need food to regain my strength. You never ate hospital food, or you'd understand. I imagine I lost twenty pounds last week."

"That won't hurt you," Caleb said, patting Will on the tummy. "You were getting a little pudgy around the midsection anyway."

"The hell you say," he growled, snatching his T-shirt up. The muscles in his stomach looked like an over-sized washboard.

Caleb eased his chair away from Will's reach because he knew Will's big fist was about to pound him. "Just kiddin'," he added. "I have to go to work now. I won't be able to listen to the game with you tonight. We'll have a huge crowd at the club with the game far away, but I'll see you when I get in about eleven of so."

"Don't wake me when you come in," Will said.

"You won't be asleep because if we win, you'll be too excited to sleep…"

"If we lose, I'll have the red ass so bad I won't be able to sleep. On second thought, I don't think I'll hang around this monastery. It's too quiet with the varsity away and all the freshmen out doing … whatever the hell freshmen do. I think I'll ride out to the Briar Patch this afternoon and have a few beers and listen to the game with my redneck buddies. I haven't seen Slim or Queenie or any of my redneck buddies since before the season started. I should be back by midnight, unless I get lucky," and he grinned.

"Gee whiz, Will! Promise me you won't go out there," Caleb pleaded. "I know all about that place. That's where you were coming from the first night I met you. I pulled you to a room and you tried to kill me. The kids in class call it the Devil's Den. Haven't you learned your lesson about places like that?"

"Get off my case, Corn Shuck. I'm as safe as a baby in its mother's arms out there. Those rednecks love me. I'm not going to do anything stupid. I know what condition I'm in. What do you take me for, a moron? Those locals put in a hard week's work. They're looking for a place to blow off a little steam after a week of the same old mundane grind Monday through Friday. You need to loosen up – live and let live, and give me a little credit."

Caleb stood up, disgusted with Will. He began to chastise. "There is no hope for you, Will. You look for trouble, and yes, I think you're brilliant, a brilliant fool." He backed away from the table hurriedly, placed his tray on the counter, and stomped out the door.

The Briar Patch was a honky-tonk north of Marston on 'Possum Corner Road, a short distance past Rachel's home. The joint probably straddled the two unmarked state lines. No one actually knew whether it was in Tennessee or Mississippi. No one seemed to care. It was on private property down a narrow private road about a half-mile from the main road. The building itself was a dilapidated, old frame structure with a rusty tin roof that sagged in the middle. It should have been condemned years before now.

A tall, rawboned character that went by the name Slim owned the joint. The locals hung out at the place on weekends to drink Slim's moonshine liquor, cheap keg beer, and wine. There was always hope that some local skirts might show up. However, they seldom did. Whenever they did, there was sure to be trouble. Slim kept a shotgun under the bar and made sure everyone knew it. Slim's regular clientele entertained themselves by playing cards, shootin' pool, swapping lies, and an occasionally dice game might break out on the pool table. Most weekends, some local rednecks who aspired to be famous country stars like Hank Williams or Grand Pa Jones would bring their guitars and fiddles and entertained the crowd with the hope of receiving enough tips to pay for their libations. The place reeked with the foul odor of rotgut moonshine and beer that had spilled into the large cracks of the rough hardwood floor.

Slim was a shrewd businessman who didn't want trouble with the feds, the sheriff, or the local religious denominations. A few regular drive-by customers were churchgoers who always seemed to come after dark. A killing or bad beating could cause trouble for Slim's very lucrative business. His joint was there, and everyone knew it. Since there had never been a serious incident and its location still in question, the locals let bygones be bygones and ignored its existence. Of course, the local sheriffs from Mississippi and Tennessee came by at election time for a campaign donation. The joint was open seven days a week, but it didn't start buzzing until about five on Friday. Then it didn't slow down until late Sunday night.

Will was a regular during the off-season. He was quite the hero of the local boys. The usual crowd loved their football, and they loved their hero even more. Will seldom had to buy a drink. He had never been involved in a rumble at the place. On occasions, as he put it, he had gotten lucky because Slim had a bar maid who was divorced. She was quite attractive and had a terrific body. She was in her late twenties, and she had taken a fancy to Will the first time he walked into the joint. Will usually got lucky when she was at work, if he was willing to wait until near dawn when she got off. She went by the nickname Queenie. No one knew her real name. She was a queen to the local clientele. She ran the local boys crazy. She was not easy to get and extremely selective. Will never had to grovel. She was his anytime he wished. During the previous year after football, he wished quite often. Queenie never made any demands of him. She knew they were from different worlds, and she was satisfied with their relationship just as it was.

Will arrived at the Briar Patch early and began drinking immediately. That night everyone listened to the game on the radio. Will screamed and beat the bar with his fists after almost every play. He chugged another beer often, and with every bad play Marston made, he would shout, "That would never have happened if I was there."

Queenie pleaded with Will to ease off the booze. She hadn't seen him for weeks, and she had better things planned for him that night. By the time the game was over, another loss, Will wasn't in any condition to drive or walk anywhere. Shortly after midnight, Queenie asked for the rest of the night off to take Will to her place to sleep it off. The crowd had dwindled to a few hard liners, so Slim agreed.

Caleb had put in a hard day at the club. The evening crowd was unusually large. Doc and Edith came in around seven, and Doc turned on the radio. The next two and a half hours were misery for everyone. Marston played their hearts out, but they were no match for the Wildcats. Marston managed to drive for one touchdown and one field goal, but they couldn't stop the Kentucky offense without their all-American. The game ended with a 27 to 10 loss for Marston, pretty much as the experts had predicted.

Doc turned off the radio. He and Edith walked over where Caleb was cleaning tables. Caleb wore a long, dejected face. "I suppose you know that Buckie probably won't make the night," Doc said. "It's a miracle that he's still with us." Caleb nodded. "I feel helpless," Doc admitted. "Sometimes, especially at times like this, I feel like I should have been a farmer or banker like my forefathers were. It's not so hard to let an elderly person who has had a full life, slip away to be with the Lord, but I'll never get used to losing a child, although I'll never question the Lord's will again. I'll come get you if we lose him tonight. I know Luther will need your comfort."

Mrs. Edith said to Caleb, "We haven't told Luther yet, but James has spoken with Mr. Pride at the funeral home about the arrangements. We don't want Luther to have to go through that ordeal."

"Mrs. Edith, you're the sweetest lady I've ever known, and you are married to the most wonderful man that ever lived."

"Oh, if that was only true," Doc said, patting Caleb on the back. "But it's the kindest thing anyone ever said to us. What does Jennifer call you? Danny Boy? That fits you. Good night, Danny Boy."

Edith put her arms around Caleb, hugged and kissed him on each cheek. "God took our son, and I know he's in a better place, but he didn't forget about us. He sent you to us." They left the club to go home.

Caleb and Abe didn't finish cleaning until almost eleven. Caleb rushed to the hospital and went to Buckie's room. Luther was sitting in the chair, a tormented look on his face. His eyes told a story of grief, misery, and fear. Gladys had already given Buckie a shot, and he was asleep. Luther stood up and tried to stretch when Caleb walked in. He had sat for so many days that every bone and joint ached. "Let's go to that there waitin' room out there 'cause I need a smoke," he said. They walked to the waiting room. He rolled a cigarette and took a huge pull off it, let the smoke out slowly, then gave a big sigh. "You knowed he wanted to see his momma 'fore his time come, didn't ye?"

"Yes sir. He's been praying about it for a long time," Caleb answered.

"I knowed she weren't a comin'. I reckon she be laid up summers wit' some no 'count trash likin' she done 'fore I marr'd her." His head lowered slowly. "I hear'd what them boys at the mill was a sayin' 'bout her. They was a sayin' if'n you had a candy bar or a dime she'd take a ride wit' you and give it to you. If it weren't fer Buckie, I wish to God I'd a never knowed her."

"We can't be worrying about her now, Mr. Luther. That's over and done. We have no control over what people do. Some are self-destructive. We just have to keep on praying and hoping God answers our prayers."

"I quit a prayin' fer her a long time ago," Luther said. "I knowed it weren't a doin' no good. She were no good when I marr'd her, and I reckon she's still ain't no good."

"You want me to stay tonight and let you go get some rest?" Caleb asked. "I don't mind. You look so tired and worn out."

"Boy, you done worked all day and night. You need yo' sleep more'n me. I can sleep in that there cher gest fine. I ain't a wantin' to leave wit' the end so near. But I 'preciate the offer." Luther finished the cigarette and they walked back into the room. There was an eerie feeling of death hovering over the room. Buckie labored for breath while Luther fought the tears.

Gladys came in and kissed Buckie goodnight as usual before she left the hospital. She spoke some consoling words to Luther, and she went home.

Caleb stood by Buckie and ran his fingers through his hair and leaned over and kissed him. Angelle walked in and hugged Luther and walked over by Caleb. She looked down at Buckie fighting for life, and a tear ran down her cheek. She hugged and kissed him gently. "I have to get back to the dorm now. Are you coming Caleb?"

"I suppose," Caleb said, as he put his arms around Luther. "If things go bad, Doc promised to call me. I'll be here for you. I'm going to be with you as long as you need me."

Luther's face wrinkled and he began to cry and said, "I knows you will, boy. I knows you will." He lowered his head, continuing to cry, and said, "Buckie say to me tonight, 'When I go to be with Jesus, Poppa, would you ask Caleb to say a few words at my funeral, if'n he ain't too busy.' He said, 'ain't nobody loves me more'n him, and he's my brother.'"

Every muscle tightened in Caleb's body. His face hardened. He grasped his hands tightly and thought, *Lord, why would You take this precious child that loves you so much, and leave Luther with nothing? I know you are a God of love and mercy. You healed the sick and cured the leper and even raised the dead. Why wouldn't you show this precious child a little compassion? Why didn't you answer our prayers? This child doesn't deserve to die this way. I know I ain't got no right to say these things to you, but you know my heart, and I can't hide my feeling from you. I do have faith Lord, but I don't understand. I'll never understand why. Why not me Lord? I've had a good life. He's had nothing but misery and pain. I would have gladly taken his place.*

"If it be too hard fer you to do, I know he'll understand," Luther said.

"You know I'm going to do whatever he wants. He is my brother in spirit and so are you."

Luther sat down in the chair as Caleb and Angelle walked to the door. Luther asked, "Did Marston win? Buckie were too sick to listen, so we didn't even turn on the radjo."

"No," Caleb said. "It was the same old thing without Will."

Luther nodded and said, "I 'spected it."

Driving back to the campus, Caleb appeared to be in a daze, never taking his eyes off the road or glancing at Angelle. She knew he was deeply troubled, but she had never seen him in this distraught condition before, and her heart was breaking for him. Caleb stopped in front of the dorm and Angelle whispered, "You want to talk about it, my love?"

Caleb shrugged, saying, "I don't know what to say other then I'm heartbroken about Buckie and Luther. I feel like my mind's in a fog. I can't even think straight. It's hard to imagine what Luther's going through."

"I understand your pain," Angelle said. "I love them, too. I'm also worried about Mr. Luther." They sat for a moment. She put her arm around his and said, "Please don't stop loving me, or give up on me. You know I have deep feelings for you. You make me feel like I've never felt before, but I need just a little more time. I know that's hard for you to understand but ..."

"Would you like to talk about it?" Caleb asked.

Angelle shook her head, leaned over, and kissed his cheek. She opened the door and walked to the dorm. Caleb drove to his dorm, still in a fog of confusion and heartache. When he arrived at his room, Will wasn't there. It was near midnight. He became deeply concerned about Will. The silence was deafening, and his ears seemed to roar. He turned off the lights and tried to rest. Sometime between three and four in the morning, he finally went to sleep.

He sat up at six a.m. and looked at Will's bed. "What has he done this time," Caleb mumbled. He was deeply concerned, but he quickly slipped on some clean clothes and drove to the hospital, anticipating the worse. Luther was asleep, and Buckie was alive. *Thank God,* Caleb thought. Luther woke up and walked to the bed. Buckie's eyes opened as he raised his head slightly and said, "Pop, I'm hungry."

Luther kissed him and hugged him as Caleb stood by, smiling. "What does you wants to eats?" Luther asked.

"I want pancakes with lots of syrup," he said, breathing easier than he had in days. Some color had returned to his face.

"I don't know if they got 'um today," Luther said.

"I'll get him some," Caleb said. "I'll be back in a flash." He hurried out of the room, sprinted down the steps to the Marston Café and ordered pancakes. In ten minutes, he was running up the stairs to Buckie's room.

Doc was just coming out of the room when Caleb returned with the pancakes. "Buckie's doing better today," Doc said, smiling. Then he whispered, "He's cheating death, you know, and it can't last. There's no way he should be alive today. In all my years, I've never seen anyone cling to life like he has. It's as if he's waiting for something to happen. I think he wants to end his misery, but he won't give up hope."

Caleb whispered, "Buckie wants to see his mother before he dies, Doc, and we know it's a hopeless wish. No one knows where she is. He prays for it constantly. If that doesn't break your heart, then you don't have one."

Doc shook his head. "God have mercy on her soul. If she only knew what he was going through." Doc looked at the paper plate covered with a napkin.

"Pancakes," Caleb said. "He woke up this morning asking for pancakes."

Doc patted Caleb on the back, shook his head again, and continued his rounds.

Luther took the plate of pancakes, cut them into small pieces, and began to feed Buckie. "I put lots of butter and syrup on them," Caleb said.

"Gest the way he likes 'um," Luther said.

Buckie ate almost a third of one. "I don't think I can eat no more, Poppa, but it shore was good. Thank you, Caleb." Then Buckie looked at his father and said, "Poppa, you don't look so good. You ain't been sleepin' none, have you?"

"You don't worry 'bout me, son, cause I'm gonna be fine."

"We lost the game, didn't we?" Buckie asked. "I wanted to listen, but I just couldn't stay awake."

Caleb nodded. "If Will had played, we might have had a chance, but we lost the game."

"You reckon the Lord will let me see you and Will play next year when I'm in heaven."

Caleb looked at Luther. Luther shook his head and shrugged. Neither Luther nor Caleb knew how to respond to the child's sincere question. "I can't answer that," Caleb said. "All I know is that you are going to be the happiest boy in the world when the Lord reaches out and takes you in his arms. Who knows, he might let you play on a football team in heaven and you might be the best football player ever."

"Tell me more about heaven, Caleb. I ain't really ready to go, but I thought I was going to the Lord last night. I ain't never hurt so bad or felt so sick." Luther sat down and hung his head low.

Caleb took Buckie's hand and tried to explain all that he knew about heaven. "When you get to heaven, the first thing the Lord is going to do is give you a new body like Jesus, perfect and beautiful in every way. You'll never have pain or nausea again. There won't be any sadness or sickness there. Then he is going to give you a mind like His, where everyone loves each other. There'll never be any hatred or jealousy, only love. The beauty of everything around you will be more glorious than anything you can ever start to imagine. There will be eternal happiness in the presence of God. I'm sure He has a million more things in store for us that He has not revealed to anyone."

"You think I'll be able to fly in heaven?" Buckie asked, showing a little excitement.

"The angels fly, don't they? Why not you?"

Buckie was pleased with Caleb's answer, and he tried to smile. Then a troubled look came over his face and he said, "I think I'm still gonna worry a little about my momma. Do you think I'll see Momma in heaven?"

"If she loves the Lord, you'll see her in heaven, Buckie. We're going to pray for your mother. Aren't we, Mr. Luther?"

"Shore we are," Luther said. "Buckie knows I pray fer her ever day."

"Poppa said she was a wild rose, and the mostest beautiful girl he ever saw. She just weren't cut out to be no momma. That's why she left us. Ain't that right Poppa?"

Luther nodded and forced smile.

"Oh." Buckie remembered, all excited. "Look what my Sunday school class sent me in the mail I got yesterday." He reached under his pillow and pulled a beautiful get well card out and opened it. A five-dollar bill fell out. "They all signed it and even sent me this money. They said they all love me and can't wait 'til I get well and come back to church. They are good boys, and I love them, too. I wish they hadn't sent no money. I know most of 'um ain't got no more money than me and Poppa have."

"They sent it to you because they love you," Caleb said. "They want you to buy something special with it. That's what people do when they truly love you. It's called a sacrifice."

"Is that why you come to see me all the time? I know you don't have time to come here every day with all you do."

"No, Buckie, it's no sacrifice. It's more a labor of love. I have truly learned to love you and Mr. Luther these last few weeks as much as I love anyone in this world, and that includes my mother and Uncle Houston and Doc and Mrs. Edith. I love them as much as my real parents."

"I been worrying about you missing study time," Buckie said. "I reckon I won't worry no more about that. Are you going to marry Miss Angelle?"

Caleb couldn't help but laugh. "You're an astute little cupid," Caleb said. "There's nothing in this world I'd like any more than marrying Angelle Noel. I truly love her. I love her as much as I love you. But as we all know, she wears a ring. Someone may have stolen her heart before I met her. Only time will tell."

Buckie smiled and said, "You are going to marry her, I know. I see the way she looks at you. Us men know them kind of things, don't we, Pop?"

Luther raised his head slowly, hiding his face so Buckie wouldn't see his tears. "I reckon us men knows them kinda things, son. Yeah, he's gonna marry her. I gest knows it."

Then Buckie's face turned grim. He said, "Momma ain't comin', is she, Caleb?"

"I don't know, Buckie. I honestly don't know."

Buckie began to tire from all the exertion. He said, "I'm gonna take a little nap now, Pop. I'm feeling a little tired and sleepy." Luther pulled the chair up close to Buckie and cradled his small head in his hand as he often did. He said, "We'll quiet down and let you get a little nap."

"I have to run anyway," Caleb said. "Abe and I'll have a large lunch crowd today, I'm pretty sure." He kissed Buckie and said, "I'll be back after lunch to check on you. You sleep as long as you need to. I love you, little brother," and he rushed off to the club.

―)⟨⟨―

Caleb was right. The crowd was huge. Actually it was the largest Sunday crowd that Caleb had served. As he and Abe rushed around trying to accommodate the crowd, their tongues were almost hanging out. Caleb whispered to Abe as they passed, "I don't think any of these rich women up here know how to cook." Abe burst out laughing and quickly hustled into the kitchen trying not to bring attention to himself.

The next time they met in the kitchen, Abe said, "These ladies don't have to cook. They all have cooks and maids at home, and they give them Sundays off."

"How long have you been doing this?" Caleb asked.

"I don't know. Over thirty years I imagine."

"Oh, Mr. Abe, if I thought I had to work like this for thirty years, I might want to die young."

Abe smiled and said, "I don't have to do this, son. I don't have to work anymore. I do it because everyone needs a reason to get up in the morning. I'm not bragging, but I think I do a pretty good job."

"Oh, yes, sir. You do a great job, but how would you make a living if you didn't work?"

Abe put his arm around Caleb and walked him out of the kitchen where Clotile and Chef Paul were having words. Two of the helpers were working frantically to keep up with the orders. As they left the kitchen, they heard a skillet clang against the wall. Clotile yelled, "I'm doing it as fast as I can. If you think you can do it any faster, get your coon ass over here and do it yourself!"

"Caleb, I'm going to tell you something that only my wife, my son, and possibly Mrs. Edith knows. When Doc hired me and saw that I could do the job, he explained something to me. He said, 'Abe, most people don't make plans for their retirement. They think they are going to work and be healthy until they die. In most cases that doesn't happen. If you'll stay with me and run the dining hall like I want it run so I can retain a good medical staff, I'll buy you five shares of stock every month as long as you're employed here. When you retire, you will have so much money you can buy a home in Beverly Hills or on the beach in Miami.' He began to buy Standard Oil stock for me. He said, 'We'll always need gas and oil. I think that'll be a safe investment.' Doc kept his word. I don't know exactly how much it's worth now, but let me put it this way. I could give my wife the checkbook, and I don't think she could spend all the money in our lifetime. Now, do you know why I say I would die for that man?" Caleb stood there in disbelief, with his mouth gaped open.

Caleb asked, "What does having a good dining hall have to do with retaining a good medical staff?"

Abe explained, "I wondered the same thing, so one day I got the courage to ask. He said it had nothing to do with his doctors, it was the wives that he had to keep happy. If they had a classy place with excellent food where they could bring the family to eat and swim and socialize, they were more likely to be contented to stay in this small college town. Doc doesn't miss a trick. He wanted to give up when his boy was killed, and his dreams died, but he didn't. He made himself go on, and since you've been here, he's the same ole Doc that he was before.

"Son," Abe continued, "if my revelation surprised you, then you are really going to be shocked at what else I'm going to tell you." Caleb eyes widened with anticipation. "Guess who'll be the richest man in Mississippi when Doc moves on to glory?"

"I can't imagine," Caleb said with a headshake.

"Well, I'm standing right by him," Abe said. "Now get your butt back to work and look like you're enjoying it."

"You can't be talking about me, Mr. Abe, 'cause I've heard they don't pay teachers and coaches that well, and I don't think there's any oil on our small farm either. So that doesn't make any sense."

"Are you pulling my leg?" Abe asked.

Caleb didn't look down, as he had before. He said, "No, sir."

"I reckon I'm speaking out of turn, and Doc might kill me if he knew I told you this. You are not going to be a teacher, you're going to be a doctor, and you'll inherit the entire Marston enterprises."

"No, sir, Mr. Abe. I don't take things that I don't earn. Anyway, I'm not smart enough to be a doctor." He laughed and said, "Those stocks wouldn't be a bad thing, but I won't wait on tables for these rich folk for thirty years to get rich from them."

"Time will tell," Abe nodded confidently, and they went back to work. Caleb wanted to get off a little early to check on Buckie and also to see if Will had made it back; however, the members and their guests continued to roll in. It was after three p.m. before the last family cleared out. "Let's hit it hard," Caleb said, "because I need to get away as soon as possible." Abe was beat, but they worked frantically until the floor and tables were spotless.

"This was harder than any football game I've played in," Caleb said. "I'm exhausted."

"Son," Abe cautioned, "if you don't work a little more sleep into your schedule, you aren't going to make the year." They sat down for a minute to catch their breath before they walked out to the parking lot.

"The boy's about to die, and his mother never came," Caleb said.

"The Lord's in charge of that too," Abe replied. "You did all that you could do to make the child's last days happy ones. Be satisfied with yourself. I know the Lord is. I'm going to church now. I hope my pastor keeps it under three hours, or I'll be snoring out loud. We did a good job today, son. I don't reckon anybody realized it, but I did. I suppose that's all that really matters."

Caleb jumped into his truck and rushed to the dormitory. He flew up the stairs and into his room. "Where's Will!" Caleb yelled down the hall. "Has anyone seen Will today?" He heard a dozen "No's" echoing back from the other rooms.

CHAPTER TWENTY-TWO

Caleb was sweaty so he shucked off his sweaty clothes, bathed, and put on clean ones. He shot out the door and down to his truck to go to the hospital. He found a parking place across the street from the hospital and parked. As he started across the street, he saw a very unusual sight. A neatly dressed, attractive lady, who appeared to be in her mid-twenties, was sitting on the bottom step to the hospital holding a young black child. She had her head down as she held the the child close to her breasts. The child was asleep. The sight was strange to say the least, and Caleb couldn't take his eyes off her. As he neared her she raised her head, and a look of surprise came over her face.

Caleb slowed his pace slightly and looked at the child closely. It was obvious that the child was of mixed blood. He had long black fine wavy hair, and his complexion seemed only a few shades darker than Angelle's. The child was beautiful. Caleb's attention then focused on the woman. She grabbed her purse, snatched out a newspaper clipping, quickly glancing at it. She then looked up at Caleb. Caleb's heart stopped, and he felt a choking sensation in his throat. His blood pressure shot up, and he felt as if the top of his head was about to explode. *Oh my God*, he thought. *Oh my precious and merciful God, please don't let this be Ruby...* Ashamed of his prayer, he was quick to think, *Oh, forgive me Lord for my hypocrisy. Please, let this be Ruby for Buckie's sake, and please have mercy on Luther if it is.*

The attractive young lady said, "You're Caleb Morgan, aren't you, sir?"

Caleb stopped cold in his tracks, turned slowly facing her, and was barely able to say, "Yes, ma'am."

"I don't want to impose, but could you spare me a minute?" Caleb's heart raced faster. He wanted to know who this lady was, yet fearful of the truth.

"Certainly," he said.

She opened the paper clipping again, glanced at it, and said, "I thought it was you from this picture."

Caleb eased up beside her and knelt down. Deep in his heart he wanted to hear her say, 'That was kind of you to grant that dying boy his last wish.' There was a short pause that seemed to last forever. Then she said, "My name's Ruby Cummings, and that's my boy in that picture." A tear ran slowly down her cheek. Caleb tried to swallow and felt ill. His knees became weak, and he sat down on the steps beside her. There was another silence that never seemed to end. Ruby wiped her tears with her hand and said, "I know they don't want to see me but—but I just had to come. I wanted to look on my little boy's face one more time. I done wrong. I know I done wrong. I ain't never done nothing right in my life. Sometimes I wish my father would of killed me when he was a beatin' me. I wanted to come back a million times after I left, but I knew Luther wouldn't have taken me back after what I done."

Fear and panic gripped Caleb, and Ruby sensed it. "I know what you thinkin'," she said. "You thinkin' Luther might kill me when he sees what I done," and she looked at the child. "I ain't gonna let Luther see me. I just want to slip up there when everyone's a sleepin' and look on my sweet boy's face one last time. I was a hopin' you'd come back tonight after everyone's sleepin', and hold my baby for me so as I could slip up to Buckie's room and take one last look at my sweet baby. Would you do that for me, please? I beg you?"

"I need to tell you something, Mrs. Ruby. Buckie prays every day that he'll see you before he dies. Doc Marston said he should've been dead months ago, but he's been fighting death and praying that he'll see his mother before he dies. He said to me just this morning, 'I reckon I ain't gonna see my momma.' Mrs. Ruby, I think the Lord sent you here to answer a dying boy's prayer."

She leaned away from Caleb, with fear in her eyes, shaking her head, and said, "Oh no! I can't do that. I could never face him or Luther again after what I done. No! No! No! I ain't gonna do that. I ain't no good, and I don't want them to think no worse of me than they already do." She looked at the child again.

"There must be some good in you, Mrs. Ruby. You're taking care of that child, and you came back to see Buckie."

"I ain't no good, Caleb, that's why I got this child. Can't you understand that?"

"I understand your fears, but you need to understand that Buckie may not be here tomorrow… Now I've had time to think about it. I think we need to get up and walk up those stairs and into Buckie's room while there's still time. You need to say to him, I'm your mother, Buckie, and I love you, and I'm sorry I left you. You can't imagine what that would do for a wonderful little boy who loves you, even though he doesn't remember you. Luther doesn't have a cruel bone in his body. He'll be sick about what he sees, but he won't do or say anything in front of Buckie that would hurt you or your child."

"You don't understand, Caleb. I'm weak, and I'm lower than trash. I can't do that. Buckie's better off with a memory, even though it's a bad one. You don't know what I've done. You're a decent person, and you can't imagine the things I've done in my life."

"Have you ever killed anyone?"

"Only my soul," she murmured.

"Everybody makes mistakes in life," Caleb explained. "It's not how we begin, but how we end, and it's never too late to change."

"I can't do it, Caleb. I ain't strong like you. I just can't."

"Oh yes, you can, and you will! You have to!"

"I know you love Buckie very much because of what you done for him, and you're taking time with me. Most folk spit on me and my baby and say nasty things to me when they pass us, so I have to tell you why I won't do it, then you'll understand."

"I don't need to know why, Mrs. Ruby," Caleb insisted. "All that matters is that you're here, and you are a dying boy's answered prayer."

"I won't walk into that room and pretend to be something I ain't. My shame is too great." Ruby said.

"Then tell if you must, but it won't change a thing. You know what you have to do. I think Buckie's happiness is of greater concern than any shame you might feel."

"You're not going to like what you hear, but I'm going to tell you everything. Then you'll understand why no one is as low as me, and I won't bring no more shame on them. My pa weren't nothing but white trash like me. If he weren't beatin' me, he was a doin' it to me. I married Luther to get away from him. I learned early what boys wanted from me and how I could get what I wanted, and I used it." She paused and the tears ran down her cheeks.

"You don't need to tell me anymore, Mrs. Ruby. I knew all this because Luther's my friend, and he told me everything."

"He didn't know the half of it," she said and continued. "When I was living with Luther, I was slipping out every day doin' it with half the boys in town. Then this boy come along who had a nice truck, and he treated me nice. I thought he had money. He told me he loved me, and he gave me things. One day he asked me to run away with him. It was the biggest mistake of my life and I've regretted it every day since then. Buckie was a sickly baby, and I was young and stupid. I didn't think of what I was doin' to him or Luther. Luther was the only man who ever treated me with respect and love, and I abandoned him and my child.

That boy took me to a motel just outside of Memphis and we shacked up for a few days. I woke up one mornin', and he was gone. Two days later the man who owned the motel came in and said he wanted his money." She wiped the tears again. "I told him I didn't have no money. He told me he was callin' the law and having me arrested. That scared me bad. He asked me where my man was. I told him I didn't know. I reckoned he wouldn't be comin' back. I pleaded with him not to call the law. I said I'd work or do anything if he wouldn't have me arrested. He grinned and said that he supposed we could work out something for a few days. He shoved me back on the bed and crawled on top of me and done it. Later that night he come back and done it again. The next morning I got up and put on my clothes to try to slip away. He met me in the door, pushed me back to the bed, and pulled up my dress. The door opened behind him, and a big mean lookin' woman was standing there. She come a running in, stomping, cussing, and swinging a big butcher knife in her hand. She lunged at me, and I rolled off the bed and ran around it. She made a swipe at me but missed. My shoes came off, but I managed to get out of the door and run to the road. I run until my feet were bloody, then I walked until I saw this truck stop. I straightened my clothes, and tried to fix my hair. I walked into the café and asked the man behind the counter if he had any work. He shook his head and gave me a dirty look. I asked him if I could sit a while. He told me not to hang around too long. 'We don't need your kind around here,' he said. When I started to sit down, this big ol' truck driver motioned for me to come over. I sat down by him and he asked me where my shoes were. I shrugged and didn't answer. He was eatin' a big hamburger and fries. I hadn't eaten in three days, and I was starving. He asked me if I was hungry and I nodded. He yelled at the man and ordered me a burger and fries. They brought the food over and he asked me where I was headin'. I told him I didn't know, but I needed a job, and I stuffed the food down. He told me that he'd buy me a pair of shoes. I left with him, and we drove toward Memphis. He pulled over at a small store, went in, and bought me a cheap pair of shoes. They were too big, but I was glad to get them. He drove a while longer, almost to Memphis, and then he found a place to pull over. I knew what was comin'. He said, 'It's time to pay for the shoes, sweetie.' Then he drove into Memphis and pulled over and told me to get out. I walked the streets of Memphis for two days looking for work. I slept in back alleys on cardboard boxes at night. I was about ready to go to the river and end my misery." She continued to weep as she poured out her heart.

Caleb put his hand on her shoulder and said, "Please, don't tell me anymore. I think I understand what happened next."

"You don't know all of it, Caleb. You don't know how many times I wanted to come back to Luther. I didn't know how good I had it with Luther until it was too late." She continued her story. "I was starving by then and desperate. I walked into this cheap hotel and bar on one of those back streets and asked the bartender if he had any work. I told him I was starving and desperate and willing to do anything. He grinned and looked me up and down. Then he glanced around the bar. There were two girls sitting at a table painted up like dolls, with low cut tops, and dresses pulled up above their knees. He said he might have some work for me if I cleaned up good.

I knew what he meant. I should have gone to the river and jumped in, but I was cold, hungry, sick, and scared to die. I sold my soul that night and became a whore. I had almost got the courage to go back to Grenada somehow and ask Luther if he'd take me back. But after that night, I knew I had burned my bridges.

The other girls took pills to get up and pills to go to sleep. It didn't take me long to see why, so I joined them and lived in a drunken dope fog world for years.

We had this Negro man who worked there cleaning and fixing whatever was broken. Some of the girls would let him have it every now and then. They laughed and called it freebies. One morning after I'd been working all day and night, I went to my room to go to bed. I was drunk and I had taken two dope pills, but somehow I managed to get my clothes off and fell on my bed. The last thing I remember is the Negro man walking in my room and closing the door behind him and saying to me, 'Ruby, will you give me a little?' I passed out and I swear I don't remember a thing after that. The next month I didn't get no period. The next month, it didn't come either. The boss made arrangements for me to take care of the problem, as he put it. I didn't take no pills or drinks for a few days until my brain kinda cleared up. I thought, 'I'm already going to Hell for what I done, but I ain't goin' to Hell for killin' my baby.' When I went to the mirror to fix my face, I didn't recognize myself. I felt shame for the first time in my life. I didn't hate my momma and poppa no more. I pitied them. I didn't hate Luther for marrying me and getting me pregnant no more. I blamed myself for what I'd become. I got what little money I'd saved up, slipped out the back door, and went to buy me some decent clothes. I got a room in a cheap hotel, and every day I walked the streets of Memphis lookin' for work. My money finally played out, but I swore I wouldn't go back to that place, even if I froze or starved. I was walking north out of the city when I saw this little café. I had one dollar left, so I figured I'd eat my last meal. I walked in and sat down. This elderly lady walked over and said, 'What can I get you, young lady?' I smiled. I hadn't smiled in years. I don't reckon anyone ever called me no lady before. I said, 'I have one dollar. Get me whatever that'll buy.' She looked at me kinda strange, then she said, 'Your man leave you, honey?' I told her that I left him years ago. 'You fallen on hard times?' she asked. I told her I'd been looking for work for over a week, and I ain't got no place to go. 'You're a pretty girl, clean, and nicely dressed, and you speak reasonably well. I don't know why you can't find work.' I shrugged, 'cause I couldn't tell her the truth. 'I'm sure cooking is beneath your dignity,' she said, 'but I just lost a cook. I haven't had time to hang a sign out front.'

"I answered her, Oh! nothing is beneath my, whatever you said. If she only knew what I meant, she would probably have kicked me out, but she didn't. Then she asked me if I could cook. I told her I haven't done much cooking lately, but I could learn. Oh, please, give me a chance. I don't have nowhere to stay and I don't have any money, I pleaded. 'I don't know,' she said. She thought about it a few seconds. Then she said, 'What the hell, these rednecks wouldn't know a hash from a rash anyway. Alice can teach you what you need to know."

Caleb didn't interrupt Ruby again. Her story was almost unbelievable, and Caleb wanted to hear it all.

Ruby continued her story. "Her name was Mrs. Ray. She was the kindest lady I've ever known. She had a little room over her garage that she usually rented, but she never charged me. I worked from five in the morning 'til nine at night, and I learned to cook good. When the day come and my baby was born, I named him Lucky. Mrs. Ray called a midwife for me. When the baby come out, Mrs. Ray took a long look at him and said, 'Ruby, we got a problem. I don't care what you did before you came here, because you are the best employee I ever had. But I can't have that baby crawling around the café behind you calling you momma. We'll both be out of business, or they'll burn this place down with us in it. He's going to have to stay in the kitchen for awhile.'

"So that's what we done. She was better'n any grandma could have been." Ruby stroked Lucky's soft wavy hair and said, "He's a good boy, and he's real smart, too. I love him. I swore to myself that I wouldn't do to him what I done to Buckie. Mrs. Ray loved him as much as I do. She died last month." Ruby put her hand over her eyes to hide the tears.

"Her lawyer come to see me a few days after she died. He said that Mrs. Ray had left the business and house and property and a sizeable sum of money to me. She didn't have no family of her own.

A few days later some men in expensive lookin' suits come to see me and offered to buy me out. Seems they want the property to build a shopping center. If I sell, I ain't ever goin' to have to worry about money no more. I know I don't deserve any of it. I'd give it all away if my boy up there was well. I got money, now. Maybe if I had had money before, I might coulda helped Buckie."

"No, Mrs. Ruby. All the money in the world would not have helped Buckie. Doctor Marston did everything humanly possible to help him. Only the Lord could have helped him, and in his wisdom, for His reason, He chose not to."

"Now, you can understand why I won't bring no more shame on Luther and Buckie. No one would want to let their dying child know that his mother was a whore."

"We all make mistakes, Mrs. Ruby. Buckie don't care what you've done. He still loves you. You need the courage to walk in and tell him that you've made mistakes, but you never stopped loving him. Ask him to please forgive you. Actually, he already has. He said to me, 'I don't want Momma feeling bad about leaving us. She just weren't cut out to be no momma.'"

"No. I can't do that. I just want to see my boy before he's gone. I'm going to pay his hospital bills, and everything else and—"

"No, ma'am. It's already been taken care of. Dr. Marston paid all the bills. He's very rich, and he loves Luther and Buckie just like I do. You save your money and take care of that child. You'll need it."

An elderly couple dressed in their Sunday finest walked by. They stared in disbelief. The woman said, "Did you see that, Homer. Does that trashy woman have no shame?"

"I don't know what the world is coming to," Her husband replied. Caleb was shocked speechless.

"That weren't nothing," Ruby said. "At least they didn't spit on us or use those filthy words. They just said what everyone thinks. My baby doesn't deserve to be treated this way, even if I do."

"I'll come back at nine tonight. Do you have somewhere to stay until then?" Caleb asked.

"I have a car," and she gestured at the car across the street near Caleb's truck. "It was Mrs. Ray's. I'll get Lucky a bite to eat and drive down south to Grenada. I might ride out by Mrs. Mattie's house and Luther's old house. She was a nice lady, and she loved Buckie. I wonder if she's still living? I hope so. Then I'll take Lucky to the lake and let him play by the water. You won't forget, will you?"

Caleb told her, "No. I'll be here at nine sharp. There's a nice big waiting room just inside those doors to the left. There shouldn't be anyone in there at that time of the night. I'll meet you there." She nodded and thanked him.

CHAPTER TWENTY-THREE

Caleb didn't go to see Buckie. Rather, he drove nervously to Doc's house. His hands were trembling on the steering wheel. Edith greeted him at the door with a kiss and commented, "If you're here to see Doc, he went to the club for a quick nine holes before he makes evening rounds. Is something troubling you? You look pale and uneasy, son."

"It's Ruby. She came to the hospital. She saw the article in the newspaper about the dying child. She knows it's Buckie, and she wants to see him. But she won't go up and face Luther. She wants to slip up tonight and see Buckie while he's sleeping. She's too ashamed to face them. I have to ask Doc what to do."

"He'll know," she said confidently. "You run tell him. He'll know what to do. You try to relax. Everything usually works out for the best."

Caleb rushed to the club and jumped on Doc's Cushman cart. He drove off to find Doc. Doc saw him coming from a distance. He and Wellington halted their game and watched as Caleb, driving fast as the old three-wheeler would travel, came up to them. Doc was sure Buckie had died. Caleb pulled up beside him and said, "I'm sorry for interrupting your game Doc, but I had to talk to you about an urgent matter."

Thank heavens, Doc thought, relaxing a bit, realizing that his thoughts were unfounded. "Then tell me, son."

"It's about Ruby," Caleb said nervously. "She's here."

"Praise God!" Doc said.

"I don't know about that," Caleb said. He told Doc everything that Ruby had confided in him. Doc listened intently, almost in disbelief to the heartrending story. When Caleb finished, he asked, "What should I do, Doc?"

"You know what you have to do, Caleb. She has to face Buckie and Luther. The child has to come first. She has the rest of her life to deal with her situation. Right now, the child must come first. She actually appeared to be repentant?" Doc questioned.

"She sounded as sincere as anyone I've ever known."

"Are you saying there is hope that she and Luther might be reconciled?"

"I'd say it's up to Luther. I think she loves him. Doc, how do I get mixed up in these situations?"

"I imagine the Lord put you smack dab in the middle of this one, son, otherwise you wouldn't be there. I'll meet you at nine sharp to help with the situation."

"Oh Lord, thank you. I was hoping you'd say that, Doc."

"At least something good occasionally comes out of a newspaper," Doc chuckled.

Caleb rushed back to the hospital and into Buckie's room. Buckie lay there gray and laboring for breath. Buckie was nauseated and in pain, but he managed a smile when Caleb walked over and kissed him. Luther was also glad to see him.

"He ain't eat nuttin' since yesterday," Luther said.

"Well, Buckie, how about a nice cup of vanilla ice cream," Caleb said.

"I reckon I might try a few bites of ice cream," Buckie said.

"I'll be back before a cat can blink its eyes." Caleb scooting out the door.

"Why you reckon he loves me so much, Pop?" Buckie asked.

"I reckon some folk gest full of love," Luther said, "and he be one of um."

"I jest know I'm gonna see him in heaven, Poppa, and Miss Angelle and Mrs. Gladys and Doc and you. I hope I see my momma. I ain't feelin' so good no more. I don't want to leave you Poppa, but I jest—I jest don't know how I can hold on no more. Tell me one more time about my momma. Tell me what she looked like and how she talked, so I'll know her when I see her in heaven."

"Son," Luther said, laboring for the right words, "I reckon she'll be 'bout the prettiest gal in heaven. Pretty long hair, colored likes sands on the banks of that lil ol' winding creek 'hind our house. Green eyes that's sparkles likes the stars on a dark winter night. Skin so soft and white, it feels like a baby kitten's fur. When she calls yo' name, her voice is gonna sound sweeter'n the music that ol' hound dog made when he were treein' a coon down on the creek bank 'fore you got sick. You'll know yo' momma, 'cause she'll find you."

Tears formed in Buckie's eyes and he said, "Oh, Poppa, why didn't she come see me? I know she left 'cause of me. Sometimes I wish I weren't even born. If I hadn't been born, she might a stayed with you. I know you miss her."

"Son—oh son, don't ever talk like that. She left 'cause I shouldn't aught a marr'd her. She were too beautiful fer me. I were ten year older'n her. She weren't nuttin' but a chap herself when I taken her into my house. It were my mistake for bein' a fool. But sometime even good things come from fools likin' me, 'cause I got you to proves it. I wouldn't change that fer a million dollar. You has made my life worth a livin'."

Caleb burst through the door with a cup of ice cream and a spoon. Gladys had seen him hurrying out of the room and asked if there was a problem. Caleb explained about the ice cream. Gladys went to the nurse's station and gave him a cup of ice cream from their freezer.

"You musta sprouted wings," Luther said. "How'd you get back so quick."

"Gladys gave it to me from the freezer in the nurses' station."

"She be a sweet lady," Luther said.

Caleb took the top off the cup and began to feed Buckie. He managed a few bites, then said, "I can't eat no more, Caleb, but it sure is good."

"You want the rest, Mr. Luther. I'm sure you haven't eaten either," Caleb asked.

Luther nodded. "I ain't one fer wastin' no food." He finished off the cup. They sat down and talked for a long time until Buckie went to sleep.

Caleb said, "I need to go to the dorm and check on Will. He didn't come back last night, and I'm worried sick about him. I'll be back in a couple of hours."

"You don't need to do that," Luther said. "You need to study and rest. I don't want you a makin' no bad marks cause of us."

Caleb smiled and kissed Buckie gently on the forehead. He said to Luther, "If I fail, it won't be because of you two. This sweet child has taught me more than any of those professors ever will. You two have taught me about courage and faith and love and forgiveness."

Luther blushed and said, "You gest an angel, Caleb. You gest an angel come to get us through this hell." He began to cry.

Caleb put his arm around Luther. "I'm no angel, Mr. Luther. The truth is that you and that child have taught all of us more than you will ever know. I don't think any of our lives will ever be the same after knowing you and Buckie. That's why I'll remember you and Buckie every day for the rest of my life."

Luther wiped his tears and said, "I love you, my friend."

"I'll be back in a little while," Caleb said as he left. When he arrived at the dorm, he saw Will's car in the parking lot. *Thank you, Lord,* he thought as he bounded up the stairs and into the room. Will was sprawled out on his bed snoring. "Will," Caleb said, shaking him. Will slapped at him.

"Go away and let me get some sleep," Will growled, pulling the sheet over his head.

Caleb got a whiff of his breath. The fumes nauseated him. He backed away and said, "Get up and get a shower, you sot. You smell like a pig pen in rainy season. I have some good news. Ruby came back. Did you hear me? Ruby came back. I hope it's good news. Doc thinks it is, and Doc always knows best."

"Ruby, Ruby," Will slurred, in a drunken stupor. "I heard about Ruby. She was hot as a six-shooter. All the rednecks wanted some of Ruby. They got some, if they paid. I didn't get none of Ruby. Everybody wanted to know where Ruby went." He started to dry heave. Caleb grabbed the wastebasket and held it under Will's mouth. He continued to dry heave, but nothing came out.

Duck, the team clown, heard the commotion as he walked by and looked in the door. No one ever just walked into Will's room. He saw Will's condition and snickered.

Caleb, irritated by his callous demeanor, snapped, "I don't think this is funny at all, Duck."

"Look at mister all-American," Duck scoffed, "lying there like a skid-row bum, puking his guts out. You'd think he'd have learned a lesson after almost getting his brains knocked out."

"Just go away," Caleb said. "He has problems that no one knows about."

"Yeah. He has real problems. I wish I had some of his problems. You know, trying to figure out what to do with those millions he's going to inherit."

"Either come help me get him to the shower or get John David to help."

"I ain't lost my mind," Duck said. "I'll get John David." He snickered again and said, "When he comes to, tell him if he feels something fuzzy in his throat, swallow it quick, because it might be his asshole."

"I heard that, Duck," Will slurred. Duck grew pale, turned, ran out the door and down the hall into his room, and locked his door.

Will rolled over and looked up at Caleb. His eyes looked like a florescent road map. "Go get my pistol, Corn Shuck, and shoot me," Will slurred. "I have to get some relief."

Caleb tried to pull Will to his feet. "Don't hit me, Will! I'm taking you to the shower. You ought to be ashamed to be so filthy drunk."

"I'll go anywhere with you if you'll help me get over this nausea. Take me to the hospital. Take me to the morgue. Hell, just knock me in the head." Will sat up and almost knocked Caleb down.

Caleb yelled for John David to come over. John David walked across the hall and stuck his head in the door. "Give me a hand," Caleb said. "We're going to sit him in the shower under some cold water."

John David widened his eyes, looked at Caleb, and asked, "Are you sure about this?"

"He's agreeable," Caleb said. They pulled Will to the shower and let him soak for an hour. Then they helped him back to his bed. John David took a handful of alka-seltzers, put them in a glass of water, and Caleb forced the foaming drink into Will's mouth.

"I'm getting back to my room before he sobers up enough to kill us," John David said. "You'd do well to take a hike yourself."

"I'm all right now," Will said. John David gave a quick finger wave and scooted back to his room.

"Just how much did you drink, counting last night and this morning?" Caleb asked.

Will held up two fingers and said, "Three."

"I know better'n that Will. Three beers wouldn't faze you."

"No," Will mumbled. "Three cases."

"That could have killed you, Will. You don't deserve any sympathy. I hope you puke all day and night. Maybe you'll learn a lesson."

Will held up a finger, his head bobbling, trying to hold his eyes open, and said, "I think I learned my lesson."

"I certainly hope so," Caleb responded.

"Yeah," Will said. He held up the finger again, his head still bobbling, and said, "two's my limit from now on."

"Are you thinking straight, Will? Can you talk to me now? You said something an hour ago that has me concerned."

"I'm fine. My head's not spinning so fast now, Corn Shuck. What's your problem?"

"I told you Ruby was back. You said some things about a Ruby. Do you know Ruby?"

"I don't know any Ruby. What did I say?" Will asked.

"You said she was a prostitute,"

"Oh, I don't know that Ruby personally, but I do frequent this sleazy bar and cat house in Memphis sometimes, just to see how the low-lifes live. I heard some of the local riff-raft talking about a Ruby that worked there a few years back. They still come in looking for her. She must have been a real queen."

Caleb sat down and gazed out the window at the beauty of nature and the tree leaves that were beginning to turn bronze. *What a mixed up world we live in,* he thought. *There is so much beauty and splendor around us, yet there is so much pain and ugliness out there. Why is life so difficult and uncertain?*

"What's troubling you, Corn Shuck?" Will said.

"Ruby is Buckie's mother," Caleb said, "and she's here."

Will struggled to sit up. He looked at Caleb's dejected face. "Kid. Friend," he said earnestly, "you can't carry the problems of the world on your shoulders. Your knees are going to buckle, and you'll become a raving lunatic. You need to lie down and take a nap sometimes. The world will look brighter when you get some rest. I have to get something in my stomach, just in case I have to throw up again." He grinned as he remembered Duck's joke and said, "I think I'll yell down the hall and ask if anyone knows where Duck's hiding."

Caleb managed a grin and said, "Don't do that because he might go home. He's a clown, but he's a pretty good lineman."

"I have to remember that one," Will said, still grinning. He stood up, grabbed his head, and let out a painful moan.

"How did you get home, Will? Please tell me you didn't drive."

Will twitched his mouth, wrinkled his face, and finally concluded, "I don't remember."

John David yelled from across the hall, "Some cute little blonde drove him back. She blew the horn, and about six of us went out. We had to pack him up the stairs. A tall, rough looking character followed her here in his car. He picked her up and they left."

"Slim and Queenie," Will said, nodding. "They're the best."

"Yeah. We all need friends like them. They let you get so drunk that you passed out, and then were nice enough to bring you home. Everybody needs friends like that."

"It was a little more involved than that," Will said smugly. He started stomping around the room and getting irritated. "Where's my damn trousers?" he growled.

"I imagine the girl still has them!" John David yelled. "You weren't wearing any when you came back."

"Oh, that makes sense. I'll get another pair," he said and proceeded to get dressed. He began to rub his stomach. "Do you hear my stomach growling?" he asked. Caleb shook his head. "Oh!" He yelled, "now it's hurting. It feels like a train's rumbling through it. I have to get something to eat now. I don't think I've eaten in—two days. Wanna come?"

"I have to study a while. Then I'm going back to the hospital at nine tonight. You go ahead. Please, don't do anything stupid—again."

Will started out the door and mumbled, "I wish Mr. Pigg's place was open on Sunday."

Caleb read a few chapters in his books and worked on some algebra problems. He tried to compose a theme that was due the next week. After studying for a few hours, he realized that he was accomplishing nothing. He could see only Ruby's face and the beautiful child in her arms, and he felt deep empathy for both. He shuddered at the thought of the conflict that was imminent if Doc insisted that Ruby face Luther and Buckie. Knowing Doc as he did, he knew it would happen.

Will hadn't returned when it was time for him to leave, so he drove back to the hospital. When he arrived, he felt as if he was breaking out with hives.

Doc pulled up in front of the hospital and walked across the street where Caleb was waiting. "Doc," Caleb said as he neared him, "I feel faint. I'm so nervous that I'm stinging all over."

"It won't kill you," Doc said. "I'm a little uneasy about this myself. But we'll do what has to be done." They walked up the front steps and into the hospital. They eased slowly into the main waiting room. Ruby was sitting there, pale and frightened, with the child snuggled in her arms.

"Who, who," she stammered, "who's with you, Caleb?"

"This is Doctor Marston, Buckie's doctor, and a good friend of Luther and Buckie. He's come to help."

"I, I—I didn't want you to tell anyone," Ruby said, trembling. She cut her eyes slowly at Doc with a look of guilt and panic in them.

"I'm not here to judge you, Ruby, only as a friend. I want the best for everyone," Doc said in his calming and compassionate way.

"You want me to leave, don't you?" her fear turning to despair.

"On the contrary," Doc said. "You're the answer to a precious dying child's prayer. I want you to stand up, go upstairs, and answer his prayer. You owe him that much. He still loves you very much."

Ruby began to tremble, and her breath quickened, as she grew pale and even more nervous. She managed to stand, appearing ready to bound out the door. Doc stood in front of her. "Oh no," Ruby said. "I could never do that. I'm too ashamed. I reckon I better go, Caleb."

"Ruby," Doc began, "if you run now, you'll regret it for the rest of your life. There is no shame here, only compassion. No one is judging you. We're asking you only for love and compassion. The simple truth is more important than your personal feelings. It's time to face the truth, and the truth is that that child loves you. Buckie doesn't know or care about your past. He just wants to see his mother before he dies. He may not be with us tomorrow. He should have left us last night. You'll have to live with a new shame if you don't see him. You've straightened your life out, and you are a wonderful mother to that precious child in your arms. We've all done things in the past that we're not proud of. If we realize we were wrong and change our behavior, the Lord will forgive us, even if men won't. Then we can forgive ourselves. We all know that love covers a multitude of sins."

Ruby sat back down, shaking her head and trembling.

"Mrs. Ruby," Caleb pleaded, "Mr. Luther still loves you, and Buckie loves you, too. Mr. Luther isn't going to hurt you. He would never hurt you. He's one of the kindest persons I've ever known."

"I don't care if he hurts me," Ruby said. "I deserve it. It's my baby that I'm fearing for. I know how Luther feels about black people."

"You don't have to worry about Luther," Caleb said. "I know he wouldn't do anything that would hurt Lucky or upset Buckie. Please—get up and do this for Buckie… Also, do it for yourself. You know it's the right thing to do."

She sat there rocking back and forth, trembling and in near tears. She stopped rocking, took a deep breath, and let it out slowly. She stood up with Lucky in her arms and reached for Caleb's hand. They began to walk up what seemed to be the longest flight of stairs in the world. When they reached the top and walked onto the floor, Gladys and Angelle were standing at the nurse's station. Angelle saw them and nudged Gladys's arm. They didn't breathe because they realized instantly that it was Ruby. They stood frozen as they watched Ruby, Lucky, Doc, and Caleb move slowly across the floor toward Buckie's room.

As they neared the door, Gladys let out a long sigh and murmured, "Luther, poor Luther. He'll never survive this. That's the final straw."

"Do you want to go in with them?" Gladys asked.

"Not on your life," Angelle said. "I want to run. I feel sick."

"She might have been raped," Gladys whispered. "We don't need to be too quick to judge."

"I'm not judging," Angelle said in a whisper. "I'm afraid."

"I'll go in first," Doc said, "and prepare them for the shock." He opened the door and eased in. Buckie had not been given his sedative so he was still awake, lying there, laboring for breath. The football that Caleb had given him was in his hands, and Curley was snuggled next to his face on the pillow. A bright smile broke across his face as Doc walked toward him. Luther, exhausted and half out of his mind with worry, was in the chair next to the wall, fighting fatigue and depression. He sat up and tried to smile.

"How is my best buddy tonight?" Doc asked.

"I ain't feeling so good," Buckie said, "but I'm a making it all right."

"Well, you'll be feeling a lot better in a few minutes," Doc said. "I have some really good medicine for you tonight."

"Don't give me no shot now, Doc, 'cause Caleb ain't been to see me yet," Buckie pleaded. "I'm kinda afraid to go to sleep tonight."

"I want you to prepare yourself for a very special surprise," Doc said, smiling. "You too, Luther. I want both of you to promise me that you won't get too excited when it happens. Promise me, Luther, that you'll act like a Christian gentleman."

"Whatever you wants, Doc, if'n it'll makes my boy happy, it'll shore make me happy."

"All right, everyone stay calm. Caleb, bring them in." Caleb opened the door and walked in, followed slowly by Ruby who held the child close to her breast. Caleb reached out for the child, and Ruby handed him to Caleb. Luther looked back over his shoulder, let out a gasp, and the blood drained from his face.

Doc took Ruby's hand and led her over to the bedside. "Here's the answer to your last prayers, Buckie. God is merciful. This beautiful lady is your mother."

Ruby looked down at the frail, gaunt, and pale child that she had abandoned, and the tears began to stream down her cheeks. A glow that sparked like the sun on early morning dew broke across Buckie's face. He reached up to her and said in a whisper, "Momma, oh, Momma, is it really you? I ain't dreamin', am I? You do love me. You came to see me." He began to cry. Ruby put her arms around him. They embraced as their tears of joy and love mingled as they cried together.

Ruby began to kiss his sweet face, saying, "Please, forgive me. Oh, please forgive me, son. Only God knows how much I wanted to come and see you … and I didn't even know you were sick."

Luther stood up, trembling. Shock turned to disbelief, then anger. He eased over to Caleb and whispered in Caleb's ear, "That nigger baby hers?" and looked down at Lucky. Caleb gave a sick nod. Luther began to back toward the door, turned, and walked out of the room. Doc walked over to Caleb and took the child. He gestured for Caleb to follow Luther.

Buckie's tears quickly turned to joy as he and Ruby looked at each other, happiness and joy beaming from their eyes. "I wanted to come see you many times," Ruby said. "But I was too ashamed, Buckie. I know I done wrong, and I don't expect that you'll ever forgive me."

"That don't matter no more, Momma, 'cause you did come to see me. I ain't gonna be here much longer, Momma. I'm going to heaven, and I want you and Poppa to come to heaven to be with me someday."

"I love you," Ruby said. "I swear by all that's holy that I do love you, my child. I thought of you every day since I left. I can't make up for all those lost years I wasn't there for you, but I had to come and tell you that I always loved you."

"You ain't leaving now, are you, Momma?" Buckie said with a frightful look.

"I'll stay as long as you want me to," Ruby said. "And when you get well—"

"Momma," Buckie interrupted, "I ain't gonna get well. I'm fixin' to be with the Lord. But I'm gonna wait for you and Poppa in heaven. We'll be a family again. We gonna be a family again 'cause I know Poppa still loves you. You done come home."

Lucky opened his eyes and realized he was in the arms of a stranger. He began to whimper and look around. When he saw his mother, he reached out, calling, "Momma, Momma." Ruby took him in her arms.

Buckie's eyes widened. He hadn't noticed the child. His eyes brightened and he said, "Momma, do I have a real brother?"

"I suppose you do, Buckie."

"You ain't got married again, have you?"

Ruby stammered as she answered, "Uh, no, son. It was just—"

Doc interrupted, saying, "A blessing Buckie. Your brother is a blessing."

"What's his name?" Buckie asked, beaming with excitement.

The small child said, "Lucky. Me Lucky."

Buckie's eyes became wider as his mouth flew open. He blurted, "He can talk good as me, Momma. How old are you, Lucky?" The child held up one fingers, and said, "Two."

Ruby said, "He just made two, but he's a smart two."

"Can I have a hug from my brother?" Buckie said, smiling and reaching for Lucky.

"That's your brother, Lucky," Ruby said. "He wants a hug. Is that all right?" Lucky smiled and nodded. Ruby put him by Buckie and they hugged each other.

"You're beautiful," Buckie said, "just like our momma. Can I touch your hair?" Lucky smiled and nodded. Buckie ran his fingers through the coal black, wavy hair and said, "Your hair is softer than cotton, Lucky, and it is shiner than silk and black as midnight."

Lucky ran his fingers through Buckie's thinning hair and said, "Soft too."

"Oh, Momma, thank you for coming to see me and bringing my brother. I reckon this is about the best day of my life."

You Shall Know the Truth

Doc put his hand on Ruby's shoulder and said, "I'm going to ease out for awhile and let ya'll get reacquainted. Buckie's waited for this night most of his life. You don't need to be concerned about where you're going to stay. I keep two rooms open at the Marston Hotel down the street a couple of blocks. When I have friends visiting, they'll have a place to stay. After you have a good visit, I'll take you and Lucky down to the hotel and get you settled in. There'll be no charge. The rooms are already paid for. I can't tell you how happy I am that you came."

"But Doctor Marston, I can't stay at that hotel," and she gestured at Lucky.

"You don't worry about that," Doc said. "There'll be no problem."

Luther had walked downstairs and sat on the concrete steps. He rolled a cigarette and sat there staring into space, taking deep pulls from the cigarette, shaking his head.

Caleb sat down by Luther and put his arm around his shoulders.

"How could she do that, Caleb," Luther said, lips quivering and teary-eyed. "How could she bring her black bastard baby to see Buckie? Don't she have no shame?"

"Oh Luther, you should have seen the happiness and joy in Buckie's eyes when he saw Ruby and the child. You should be so happy for him."

"He ain't gonna feel no joy when he knows he got a brother. I knowed she were trash when I marr'd her, but I never knowed how low she were."

"No one but you can change the way you feel about black people. I can promise you this, Buckie doesn't care what color his brother is. He's just gotten a little taste of heaven tonight."

"You know I'm happy fer him. I'm happy his momma come to see him, but why did she have to bring that, that, that baby with her?"

"I talked with her for a long time today. I know the pain and shame she's carrying in her heart over her mistakes. She wanted to come back to you, but she was too ashamed."

"I'd a slammed the door in her face if'n she'd a brung that baby to my house."

"No you wouldn't have, Mr. Luther. You love her too much to have done that. Love means forgiving. Love means forgiving a million times if necessary."

"I ain't nary gonna forgive her fer what she done!" Luther said, jumping up and pounding his fist into his palm. Doc had walked up behind them. He stood at a distance and listened to them talk.

"She ain't like that anymore," Caleb said. "She gave up her sinful life when she found out she was having a child. She took a job as a cook and raised the baby like a decent woman should. You can't understand how hard her life's been as a white woman with a black child. Ruby could have given him away or had an abortion, but she didn't. Her very words were, 'I might spend eternity in hell for what I done to Luther and Buckie and the way I lived, but I ain't doin' to him what I done to Luther and my baby.' She's been a wonderful mother to Lucky."

"That don't change nuttin', Caleb. Any white woman what'll lay with a black man ain't fit to live."

"You don't mean that, Mr. Luther. That's just pain, exhaustion, heartache, depression, and years of stress gripping at you. You're a better man than that. Let me ask you this. If he was a white child, would you forgive her?"

Luther sat back down, put his hands over his face for a minute before responding. "I don't know what I'd do if things was different. I can't say. I just feel sick."

Caleb said to him, "I'm not going to judge you, Mr. Luther. I ain't walked in your shoes. I suppose most folks around here feel the same way you do. I just never learned to hate people because of the color of their skin. The best friend I ever had was a colored boy named Little Willie. We grew up together. We ate together and played together. We worked and picked cotton and hoed the crops together. I'll love him and his family 'til my dying day. His father didn't have but four or five acres, and he planted cotton like us. He and his wife helped us get our crop in every year. If we hadn't had them to help us, we would probably have killed ourselves trying to get the crops in before winter and the rain set in."

Doc walked over to Caleb and Luther. He eased up beside Luther, kneeled down, and put his arm around him. "Luther, I know how much pain and sorrow you've endured for such a long time. My heart is breaking for you. I know what just happened didn't help your emotional condition, however," Doc emphasized the however, "it took a lot of courage for Ruby to walk into that room and face you and Buckie. She's going to stay with him until the end. I expect you to conduct yourself in a manner befitting a gentleman until she's departed. I'll not leave until I have your word on that."

Luther put his hands over his head and thought awhile. He said, "I ain't gonna treat her no way, Doc. It's gest like she don't 'xist to me no more. I won't be mean or ugly to her. I'll gest be there fer my boy 'til the end comes." He began to weep. "Then I'll take my boy home." He began to wail, and then said, "I'll bury him and it'll be over."

"Won't you at least—" Caleb began. Doc quickly put his hand on Caleb's shoulder and shook his head.

"I'll accept that," Doc said, "knowing the condition you're in. I would suggest that you allow Ruby a little extra time with Buckie. My concern is that Buckie will sense your hostility toward the child. That wouldn't be good for him. No one should have to endure conflict on their death bed. Later you can go up and stay with him."

"I done thought 'bout that, Doc. I'll do right by my boy. You ain't got to worry 'bout that no more. But I ain't a leavin' that room no more 'cept to git a bath and shave," Luther said.

"Buckie will be asleep soon," Doc said. "You can go up in a few minutes. I'll take Ruby to the hotel. She looks almost as tired as you. Let's get a coke and sit here a while and enjoy this cool breeze and try to get our priorities in order and emotions under control. After all, this is about Buckie's happiness. We'll have a lifetime for tears and regrets later."

Lucky had snuggled up next to his newly discovered brother. Buckie looked up lovingly at Ruby and said, "Momma, why did you leave us? Was it my fault? Poppa said I was a sickly baby. Was it 'cause I cried all the time and was always sick?"

"Son, I was just sixteen when you were born and too foolish to realize what I was doing. There is no real excuse for what I done. I reckon I thought about you a million times over the years. I knew Luther wouldn't take me back after what I became. I tried to forget that you existed, but it weren't no good trying. I jest felt guilty and ashamed. I finally convinced myself that you and Luther would be better off if I didn't come back. I didn't know you was sick, or I'd a been back long ago. You do believe that, don't you, son?"

"I believe whatever you say, Momma, 'cause you did come to see me."

"Baby, I done some bad things in my life, and I feel some real shame for them. I can't take back what I done, but I learned some things the last few years. There are some real good people in this world who love you even though you done bad things. And I ain't that foolish girl I was back then. I had changed my life, and I was trying to get the courage to come and see you when I saw your pitcher in the paper. It was like time stood still when I looked at your beautiful face on the front page of that paper. They said you were sick. I knew I had to come back to see you and get the courage to face Luther. I had to tell you how much I love you and to ask you and Luther to forgive me. I reckon too much water's done run under the bridge for that to happen, so I'm jest gonna stay with you as long as you want me to."

"You didn't marry nobody while you were gone, huh, Momma?" He looked at Lucky.

Ruby gave a painful smile and caressed his cheek gently and said, "No, Buckie... That's the result of one of the bad things I done. God can even take bad things and turn them into something beautiful." She reached out and ran her fingers through Lucky's soft wavy hair. "Luther's still my husband, I reckon, unless he divorced me for abandonment."

"He ain't divorced you, Momma," Buckie was quick to say. "He prayed you'd come home like I done."

Doc eased through the door followed by Gladys and Caleb. "Gladys is going to give Buckie his pain shot now so he can get some rest tonight," Doc said. "He'll be asleep in a couple of minutes. I'll take you to the hotel and you can get some rest."

"Oh, Doc, do I have to go to sleep now?" Buckie pleaded. "I ain't felt so good in a long time."

"I can promise you your mother will be here in the morning," Doc said. "You can talk and visit all day long."

"Okay," Buckie said, smiling. "Ain't my brother beautiful, Doc? I done got my Christmas present and my birthday present all at one time. Momma's my Christmas present and Lucky's my birthday present—and it ain't even Christmas, or my birthday."

Ruby turned away quickly and wiped the tears from her eyes. Then she knelt down and kissed Buckie. She took Lucky in her arms and said, "I'll see you early in the morning, my sweet child. I love you son. I've always loved you."

"I love you, too, Momma, and I love my little brother. Thank you for comin', Momma." Ruby leaned over so Buckie could kiss Lucky. Gladys gave him the shot and his eyes closed while he was smiling.

"Ruby," Doc said, "I imagine you perceived some hostility in Luther's face when you came in." Ruby nodded. "I've had a good talk with him, and he promised not to say or do anything that would upset Buckie, your child, or you while you are here."

"I knew he'd be angry," Ruby said, "and I don't blame him. I jest want to be here for my boy. I know I can't make up for the lost years, but I want him to know that I do love him and I did want to come back."

Doc nodded and said, "I think he realizes that." They walked downstairs and out to the steps. Luther was still sitting there, smoking one cigarette after another. Ruby paused for a second and looked at him. Luther cut his eyes at her, and then quickly looked away.

"I'll see y'all tomorrow," Caleb said and started across the street to his truck. Angelle ran down the steps and yelled, "Hey! Did you forget me, Caleb?"

Caleb put his hand to his forehead and glanced at Doc as he said, "I can't believe I forgot that you asked for a ride back to the dorm." Doc continued to walk with Ruby toward the hotel. Caleb and Angelle hopped into the truck and started back to the college.

"Forgive me," Caleb said. "I've thought of nothing but you ever since that first day I saw you. But now my head's in such a whirlwind I don't know what I'm doing."

"I understand," she said. "I feel the same way." Caleb drove back somberly to the dorm. There was no mention of a goodnight kiss when they arrived. Their hearts were broken over Luther's pain and bitterness, and the inevitable end to the life of the child who had stolen their hearts. Angelle took Caleb's hand and gave it a gentle squeeze. They managed smiles, then she walked to her dorm and Caleb drove slowly back to his dorm.

—⫸⫷—

Doc took Ruby's arm and escorted her into the hotel. He walked boldly into the lobby and up to the registration desk. Some of the guests were sitting in the lobby chatting and sipping coffee and other drink. Their whispers could be heard across the lobby as Doc escorted Ruby and the child to the desk clerk. Doc turned and gave them a hard look. "Clovis," Doc said, "this is Ruby Cummings, a close friend of mine. She'll be staying in room one-zero-one until further notice."

Clovis's eyes widened and his mouth gaped open. His breath quickened, and he began to stutter, "Uh, uh, uh."

"Did I not speak clearly?" Doc said, his voice rising.

"Oh! Oh! Yes, sir, Doc. I heard what you said but…" He reached behind him and opened the office door.

The owner, Jasper Clemens, was sitting at his desk reading the evening paper. He never looked up. "A problem, Clovis?" he asked.

"I'm waiting for my key!" Doc said boldly.

Jasper, recognizing Doc's voice, laid the paper down, leaned back, and looked out the door. He saw Doc, Ruby, and the child in her arms. Jasper looked away quickly as if the situation might resolve itself without his involvement. Doc's temper raged, and he slammed his fist down on the counter, yelling, "Hand me the damn key now, Clovis—or I'm coming across this counter to get it!"

Clovis was so frightened that his face turned white and he began to shake. "He'll fire me if I give you the key, Doc," he whispered.

"Now listen to me, Clovis, and you, too, Jasper, you hypocrite. I own the bank, in case you've forgotten, which holds the mortgage on this place, which incidentally happens to be about two years delinquent. If I don't get the key this instant, I'll foreclose and own this place by eight a.m. The first thing I'll do is fire the whole lot of you bigots. And by the way, Jasper, do you actually think there is an intelligent person in this town that doesn't know you creep into the quarters every Saturday night about eleven to visit a certain lady of color—and sneak out before dawn?"

"Give him the key," Jasper snapped, "and be quick about it."

"One other thing, Jasper," Doc said, "I'm holding you personally responsible for the safety of this lady and her child while she's a guest in this hotel."

"There'll be no problems, Doc. I'll guarantee it," Jasper said nervously.

Clovis snatched the key off the board and handed it to Doc. He whispered, "I'm sorry, Doc." Doc nodded and gave him a wink.

Ruby looked at Doc in total amazement and thought, *What kind of man is this to have so much power and still have so much compassion?* They walked down the hall to the first room. Doc opened the door and walked in with her. "I think you'll be comfortable here. If you have any trouble, just call. I'm in the book."

Ruby stood there with an awe-inspired look on her face and said, "Why would you do this for me, Doctor Marston, knowing what kind of woman I am?"

Doc gave her a warm smile and said, "What did our Lord say to the woman accused of adultery? 'Neither do I accuse you. Go and sin no more.' If the Lord forgives us of our sins, who am I to do any less?"

"But Doctor, I ain't nothing but white trash, and you know it."

"Ruby, I despise the word trash when it applies to one of God's children. When I was coming into town this morning, I saw a drunk staggering down the highway. He was clutching a fifth of whiskey in a paper bag. He stumbled and fell to the ground. Even as he fell, he turned and landed on his back to protect the bottle. The contents of the bottle were more important than the pain of the rocks on his flesh. Would you call him trash?" He smiled and said, "Most people would. But he's someone's sick child, an individual with a serious illness who needs a friend. But he's not trash."

"Did someone stop and help him?"

"I picked him up and took him home to his mother. I know the family well. His mother is a precious lady who's cried herself to sleep many a night over his condition. We put him to bed."

"God bless you, Doctor Marston," she said with quivering lips. "God bless you."

Lucky stuck out his hand to Doc.

Ruby sniffed and said, "That's his latest thing. He wants to shake hands with everyone."

Doc smiled and took his small hand. He shook it, then kissed it gently. "You are truly a lucky young man, Lucky, to have this lady as your mother. A more appropriate word would be blessed. I'll see you two tomorrow. Get some rest," and Doc left for home.

CHAPTER TWENTY-FOUR

Caleb trudged up the stairs. Will's car was not in the parking lot but Caleb didn't notice. He had more pressing concerns. The dorm was quiet. Caleb took a shower and returned to his room. As he lay in bed, eyes wide opened but unfocused, a quagmire of questions with no good answers rolled through his mind. He thought, *I wish Will would return. I know he could distract my thoughts with his warped philosophy of life.* His mind was so tormented over Luther and Ruby's situation that he never even thought of Angelle. Caleb forced his mind to think about meeting his grandparents and how wonderful it was to have met them. He almost smiled when he recalled his mother's embrace and her confession. Caleb stood up and walked to the door. He could see the light radiating from under John David's door, so he eased across the hall and tapped on his door.

"Come in," John David called out. Caleb eased in and sat down on the cot by him. John David put his Bible down, and speaking softly, said, "You look troubled, pal." His roommate was sleeping deeply on the other cot.

Caleb nodded as he asked. "Why is life so painful sometimes? I thought college would be light and joyful, but there's so much pain and sadness all around me that I just want to run and hide somewhere and pray it goes away. Everyone pats me on the back and tells me how terrific I am, but if they could see the heartache inside, they'd pity me instead."

John David put his arm around Caleb and said, "You have a gift from God, and it's not football, it's love and compassion. With that gift comes sorrow and pain. You can't fix all the problems of life. Doctor Marston has the same gift, and you need to learn a lesson from him. He does everything humanly possible for his patients, but when he's done all he can, he moves on to the next patient. Doc accepts the will of God for each patient. I also believe totally in the sovereignty of God. I don't think he created the world, gave it a spin, and then retired to some distant place, just leaving us to spin aimlessly through life until our time comes. I do believe He knows how many hairs are in our head, and He does know when the sparrow falls to the ground. I believe that God determined that Buckie will meet him in paradise at a specific time, predetermined by His will and knowledge. You can find that in Psalms 139, if you don't believe me. Now it's time to accept God's providence. Turn your troubles over to the Lord. Say, 'Thy will be done,' and truly mean it. You can't orchestrate the concerns and problems of this world. You are not that great and wonderful. Accept what you can't change and change what you can. Then accept the will of God."

"John David, you always know how to lift up my spirits. You are going to be a wonderful preacher and counselor."

"I pray you're right. If you think I don't have problems and sorrows in my life, listen to this. I have a sister who has been through two marriages already. She's only twenty seven. She's an alcoholic, and I suspect worse. She has two children by different husbands. My parents are raising them. I hope to get them when I marry and graduate. The doctors have told her if she doesn't quit drinking, she won't live to see her thirtieth birthday. She's destroyed her liver. I have bruises on my knees from praying, but you can't help a person who refuses to be helped. I'll never quit praying for her. I've asked myself a million times why she chose that path in life. You know my father's a preacher?" Caleb nodded. "She had sound Biblical guidance and teaching for seventeen years. When she graduated, she left home and joined the wild side of life. Her name is Hanna. Add her to your prayer list, please."

"I will," Caleb said. "I promise you I'll pray for her every day."

"Where is everybody?" Will yelled as he entered the hall. "This place is like a morgue. Caleb, where are you? Does anyone know where I can find Duck?" And he burst out laughing.

"He just had to do that," Caleb said.

John David looked at Caleb and began to laugh. Then he commented, "Only Will could survive that experience."

"He has more pain than either of us. Anyone who could hate his father—Well, I can't imagine it. Thanks for being here for me, John David."

"It's my pleasure. You've brought a little sunshine and hope into all our lives. Even Will's a different person since you arrived."

Caleb walked across the hall and said, "What's all the commotion about?"

"I missed you, mommy," Will said in a childish voice.

"I missed you too like I miss the mumps," Caleb said, snickering. Will grabbed him with a big bear hug. They tussled a few seconds until Will's ribs began to ache, then they went to bed.

Caleb rose at dawn and rushed to the hospital to check on Buckie. Luther was sitting in the chair by the bed. He looked up with bloodshot eyes and said, "He had a bad night, Caleb. They had that ox'gen on his face all the night. He's a strugglin' to stay alive."

"He's going to keep struggling, Mr. Luther. He's trying to catch up on ten lost years."

Doc came in and took a look at Luther and said, "You look sick, Luther."

Luther nodded and stretched out his stork-like limbs. "I ain't a feelin' too spry this here mornin'."

Buckie's eyes opened, and he looked around. A frightened look came across his face. "Where's Momma and my brother?" he gasped.

"She'll be here any minute," Doc said.

"You didn't send Momma away, did you, Poppa?"

"Buckie!" Luther snapped, "you knowed I wouldn't do that to you."

"Don't you remember, son?" Doc said, "I took her to the hotel last night so she and Lucky could get some rest. Now, you stop worrying. She'll be here in a few minutes."

A tear ran down Buckie's cheek, and he said, "I don't want my momma to leave again."

"Don't you believe us?" Caleb said, bending over and giving him a gentle hug.

"I reckon I do if ya'll say so. What time is it, Caleb?"

"It's barely daylight, little brother. Give her a little time to dress the baby and get him a bite to eat. Then she'll come. Okay?"

"I reckon I was actin' a little like a baby, huh, Caleb."

"Under the circumstances, little brother, I don't think so."

"Doc," Luther said, "come and drink a cup o' coffee wit' me, if'n you got time."

"I'll be glad to have a cup with you, Luther, but what you need more than coffee is eight hours of sleep."

"Sit wit' my boy a minute, Caleb." Doc and Luther walked outside the door. Luther said, "I don't wants no coffee, Doc. I been thinkin' all night. You been so good to us, I gest want you to know I ain't gonna be mean to Ruby no more. I ain't gonna be ugly to that—that baby either. He can't help if he were born to a whore."

"You've made a good decision, Luther. The child didn't ask to be born, and he's in for a difficult life. But If you think the child has problems, it won't compare to what Ruby's facing. She's already been cursed, spit on, and called every filthy name imaginable. Ruby's not that foolish young girl that abandoned you ten years ago. She's lived through hell just to survive since she left you. Now she's turned her life around. We need to give her our respect for what she's done the last few years. There's something else you don't know. Ruby's wealthy now. Oh, not a millionaire, but she'll never have to work again. She admits her mistakes. She wanted to come back to you before now, but she thought you wouldn't have her after her sinful life. Obviously, she was right."

"Doc, I ain't ever gonna forgive her, if'n that's what you a'thinkin. She brung all this on herself. I don't care 'bout no money. Me and Buckie done good wit' what I made. She knowed she coulda come home to her boy, but now it be too late."

"I'm sorry you feel that way, Luther. I've always felt that a repentant person deserves a second chance. I've seen pride destroy people's lives." Luther nodded, and they walked back into the room.

Doc checked Buckie's vital signs carefully and commented, "You seem to be doing very well today, son." He turned and gave Caleb a grave look. "I'll be back later," he said, giving Luther a pat on the shoulder as he passed. When he opened the door, Ruby was standing there with Lucky in her arms. "Did you have a good night?" Doc inquired.

"Yes, Doctor Marston. We both got a good night's rest."

"Come right in. Buckie's on pins and needles waiting for you."

Ruby eased across the room, glancing at Luther. Luther was sitting against the wall, a stoic look on his face.

Buckie reached out to his mother and brother. Ruby bent over to kiss him and sat Lucky on the bed. Lucky leaned over to hug Buckie and said, "My brudder."

Buckie hugged Lucky saying, "You're my beautiful brother, and I love you."

"I wuv you, too," Lucky said.

Luther stood up, hardly able to hide the jealousy and resentment in his heart. He said, "I'm a goin' and have a smoke and some coffee, son. I won't be gone long."

"It's all right, Poppa. Why don't you go sleep a while? You look so tired. Momma and Lucky are gonna stay here with me."

"I ain't goin' nowhere!" Luther snapped. "I'm yo' Poppa, and I need to be here wit' you."

"Don't be mad at me, Poppa. I was just thinkin' about you."

Luther, realizing his anger and jealousy had reared its ugly head, became ashamed and quickly responded. "Son, I ain't narry been mad at you in my whole life. If'n it sounded like I wuz, it's gest 'cause I don't know half what I'm sayin' no more."

"I have to get to class, Buckie," Caleb said, "but I'll be back after work." Caleb walked over to Luther who had started out the door and he said, "Please, Mr. Luther, go get a few hours rest. It won't change one thing, you not being here. Buckie'll still be here when you get back, and you might be a little better company when you've rested."

Luther realized what he meant, nodded, and said, "I gest might do that, Caleb. You ain't nary steered me wrong."

"Good." Caleb said. "That makes me feel better."

Luther turned back to Buckie. "Son, I thinks you be right. I'm a gonna get a little rest at the hotel. I be back when I git rested a little. I know you be in good hands." Ruby's eyes shot up at Luther, but he was walking out the door.

⊸⫟⊷

Caleb returned to the campus for class. He took his seat by Angelle, and his dejection was written on his face.

"Caleb, you need to get a hold on yourself. You look depressed. If anyone can recognize the signs of depression, it's me." Angelle continued, "You've let yourself get too involved."

"If you love someone, I don't know how you can keep from getting involved."

"I know," Angelle said. "He's the sweetest and kindest little boy I've ever known. I'm heartbroken for him. He's in such pain and agony all the time. It might be a sin, but sometimes I catch myself wishing that the Lord would take him and give him some relief."

You Shall Know the Truth

Caleb looked into her beautiful, pain-filled eyes and said, "I hate to admit it, but I've had the same thoughts. God forgive us. He's letting Buckie live for a reason." Dr. DeHaberman stormed across the stage. Caleb said, "We better zip it up. I don't know how forgiving she might be this time."

At noon, Caleb jumped into his truck and started to the club. Angelle was walking down the sidewalk. Caleb pulled over beside her and said, "I thought you had a one o'clock class."

"I dropped it today." Angelle responded. "It was an elective, and I don't need it to graduate. I want to spend more time at the hospital. I really love working there with Gladys and Doc. You go on to work. I'll make you late."

"I don't care if I'm late."

Angelle opened the door and crawled in. "You're depressed. You'd never say something like that if you weren't."

Caleb admitted that he might be. "I've accepted the inevitable where Buckie is concerned, but my fears are now about Luther. He won't survive this. He has nothing to hold on to. I don't know if he has much faith."

"He will survive,' Angelle said. "You can live with pain. You have to get up each day and make yourself go on. It's painful, but you can live with it."

"I pray that you're right. I suppose no one knows that any better than you." Caleb said.

A look of surprise, then shock, flashed across Angelle's face. "Why did you say that, Caleb?"

Caleb realized what he had said. He thought for a second and said, "I don't know why I said that. Forget it."

"No. I won't forget it. What do you know about my past? Tell me," she pleaded.

Caleb drove up in front of the hospital, stopped, and looked at the fear and sadness in her eyes. "Do you really want me to tell you what I know about you and your past?"

"I certainly do," Angelle responded.

"I know everything."

"You couldn't know everything. How could you?" Angelle exclaimed.

"I know you were sexually abused as a young girl by your stepfather, and your mother was killed by the monster that abused you." Horror spread across Angelle's face, and she put her hands over her mouth and gasped. "I know that you spent over a year in a mental institution. When you were better, you were sent to an orphanage in Monroe, Louisiana. You attempted suicide when you were there. You graduated from Ouachita High school as the valedictorian, and Doc gave you a Marston Foundation scholarship. You make straight A's, and you're a brilliant and beautiful girl. You fight with depression and anxiety and have ever since the night your mother was killed. Did I leave anything out?"

"How could you know that?" she gasped. "Who else knows that?" She began to tremble, and weep.

"Stop crying. No one else knows the truth but Doc. It might be better if they did. The shame and guilt is not yours. Put it where it belongs, and get on with your life. Doc screens all the applicants before he gives them a scholarship. When I told him that I was in love with you, he was concerned that I might be putting too much pressure on you. The only reason he told me any of this was because he thought my loving you might cause you too much conflict, because of your engagement. Doc told me because he loves you very much and doesn't want any unnecessary stress in your life. He actually threatened me, and he was serious. I lied to him and told him I wouldn't see you anymore. I really tried, but I couldn't stop seeing you. You're the most wonderful thing in my life."

Caleb sighed deeply and continued. "I understand now why you won't let me hold you. But all of that happened a long time ago. You have to put the past behind you, and learn to trust people. The thing that worries me most is that you said you let Maurice hold you. That tells me that you love him more than me. You trusted him, and you don't trust me. You know the last thing that I want is to cause you more pain. I've wished a million times that I didn't feel the way I do about you. But really, you don't just choose the person you fall in love with. It just happens, even if that person doesn't love you."

Her rapid breath eased somewhat. She said, "Do you think I haven't tried to trust you? I'd give anything to have you put your arms around me and hold me close. I get up every morning and pray that I won't be sick anymore or have a panic attack. Most days I feel pretty good, especially when I'm busy at work or with you. Then out of the clear blue that feeling starts to come over me. It's so horrible I can't describe it. It's a helpless and hopeless feeling. I just want to run and run. But that doesn't help even if I do. After awhile, the feeling eases up. I live in constant fear of its return. I think I'd die if it lasted too long. Sometimes I've been walking down the street and that panicky feeling comes over me so bad that everything turns black, and the hopeless feelings return. It's like I'm in a black pit and it's closing in on me."

"But you're not going to die. You are going to beat this illness. You know why you feel this way. When you tell Dr. Wellington what you just told me, and all of the story, he'll be able to help you. That's what he does. Don't you think you can trust me?"

"I know I can trust you."

"Then hold out you hand and let me hold it."

She turned away for a second and then began to slowly extend her arm. Caleb reached out and very, very gently put his hand in hers. He began a gentle squeeze. He felt her hand start to tremble, and she snatched it from his grip, breathing heavily again. "You still have no confidence in me," he murmured.

"That's not true. I do have confidence in you. But I have no courage, only fear."

"You're going to beat this illness. I know you are because Doc said Dr. Wellington is the best in this country."

"You knew about him, too," she said, still shocked that her secret had been revealed.

"Yes, Angelle. I'm the one who told Doc that you needed to be in treatment because you were having emotional problems. He thought you were doing fine because you hide your feelings so well."

"How could you have known I was having problems? Because I won't let you hold me?"

"That was part of it… Your snooty roommate let me have an earful outside the dorm a few weeks ago. She told me you suffered from depression and had panic attacks. She said you were sick and I was the reason for it worsening. I got so angry with her that I wanted to kick her rump when she stormed off. But deep down, I knew she was right."

"She's a busy-body and should mind her own business," Angelle said angrily. "I'm going to tell her that tonight."

"Please don't do that. She loves you and was only concerned about your well being. If it were not for her, you wouldn't be in treatment. I'm glad that you're finally going to get some help, even if it costs me your love."

"I'll always love you, Caleb, even if we never marry."

Caleb looked at her and said, "I'll never marry anyone but you." He glanced at his watch and said, "Now, I really am late for work. You take courage because you are going to get well."

Angelle kissed her hand and placed it on his lips and said, "You better scoot now, my love." He smiled and pulled away in his truck.

Angelle stood and watched until he was out of sight. Then she walked sheepishly over to Dr. Wellington's office and quietly slipped in. Janice Wellington was sitting behind the desk typing. The beautiful child was taking her afternoon nap on the pallet.

"Good afternoon, Angelle," Janice said. "Dr. Wellington is expecting you. Go right in." Angelle eased by the desk. She looked down at the child, stopped, and knelt down by her. Angelle reached out and brushed a lock of hair from the child's face and commented, "This is the most beautiful child I've ever seen. What's her name?"

"Grace," Janice said hesitantly.

"Is she your granddaughter?" Angelle asked.

"No," Janice said, the blood leaving her face. "She's my daughter."

"Oh, I'm sorry," Angelle said quickly, embarrassed because she surely had offended Janice.

"She's adopted," Janice explained.

"Oh," Angelle said again, somewhat ashamed of her prying.

Wellington had heard Angelle come in. He was standing in the door waiting for her. He heard the conversation, and he gazed at Janice with a doleful look.

"Come right in, Angelle," he said calmly. She felt more at ease than before. She walked in and took a seat on the couch with her hands on her knees.

"You seem to be more at ease today. Have you had a good day thus far, Angelle?"

"Well, I'm not scared to death today, if that's what you are asking."

"I can sense that. Have you had any problems since our last session?"

"I slept well last night. Thus far today, I feel better than usual."

"You said you have awful nightmares occasionally. Tell me about them. Can you remember any of them?"

"I don't want to remember them, but—yes, I remember all of them. They are almost the same each time. Must I do this?"

"Only if you want to get well. I've done extensive studies on nightmares and published numerous articles in the medical journal about my findings. They might just hold the key to unlocking those deep feelings of insecurity that are hiding in the recesses of your psyche. It's a starting point."

"They're all horrible. I don't know if I can talk about them."

"You came for help, Angelle. I told you it would be painful at first, but with the pain comes healing. We have to retrain our psyche by facing our fears. Then we can understand why we feel the way we do. Only then will the torment of these feelings begin to subside."

Angelle nodded, and her eyes went dead.

"Okay, let's start walking through this hell."

"I'm in this white room. It's so bright it's almost blinding. It feels like I'm being ripped apart. I'm in so much pain that I think I'm dying. Then I hear this baby crying and I see a man dressed in all white holding up a baby. He lays the baby by my side, then the baby begins to nurse from my nipple. A woman comes in and takes the baby from my arms. I try to fight her to keep the baby, but she's stronger than me. She pulls the baby from my grasp and takes it away. I began to wail and scream, don't take my baby from me! I scream and cry until I wake up. Then I feel sick... I can't imagine why I would dream that."

Wellington sat there rocking back and forth with his hands behind his neck looking aimlessly at the ceiling.

After a long silence, Angelle looked up at Dr. Wellington and asked, "Are you all right, Doctor?"

Wellington lowered his hands from his neck and looked at Angelle. "How long have you been having this dream?"

"It was the first nightmare I had when I was well enough to leave the institution. It wasn't much later that the others started."

"Tell me about another recurring one, and that's all we'll get into today. I need some time to try to consider their meaning."

"This man takes me by the arm and pulls me down this long hall. He forces me into the bed. Then he holds me down and does unspeakable things to me, and then the pain is unbearable. I can't even talk about it."

"You don't have to tell me what happened. I understand." Dr. Wellington said. "That dreams is the way it actually happened, isn't it, Angelle?

Angelle nodded, put her hands over her face, and began to cry. Wellington grabbed some tissues and started wiping her face. "It's all right to cry, Angelle. You cry all you want, but be confident of this. That demon is coming out of you before we finish. We know where he lives now, and we are going to destroy him."

Angelle wiped her eyes and said, "Do you really think there's hope for me?"

"Let me put it this way. I think there are three things that must happen before you can be healed. First, you must want to be healed. Second, you must believe that you will be healed. Third, you have to be willing to pour out your heart and soul, no matter how painful that might be, and face your individual demons.

"Do you remember how many demons Christ cast out while he walked the streets of Jerusalem? Now a demon doesn't attack a strong person, only the weak. I believe that a demon is attacking your mind because of sin. I don't mean your sin, but your weakness because of the sin that was done to you. We're going to attack your demon by putting everything on the table. I'll help you learn to face your demon. With God's help, Angelle, you'll tell your demon that he is no longer going to control your mind with feelings of guilt and remorse over the tragedy that happened to you when you were a child. Yes, Angelle, I think you are going to get well. Let me give you a little exercise that has worked with many of my patients. Have you ever been hurt by an anxiety attack?"

"I don't understand what you mean. It's the worse pain imaginable," Angelle said.

"Yes, it's mental anguish, but has it ever physically hurt your body?"

"I suppose not—physically," she admitted.

"The next time that feeling starts to come over you, say this to yourself. 'You can't hurt me. I'm not going to fear you anymore. Come on give me your best shot because I know you can't hurt me. I'm not going to live in fear and dread of my next attack. You can't hurt me, and I'm not going to worry about you,' and you have to believe it."

"Dr. Wellington, I know you are a brilliant psychiatrist, but that seems too easy. I can't believe anything could be that easy." Angelle said skeptically.

Dr. Wellington continued. "I didn't say it was easy. I said it's worked for some patients. It'll only work if you believe it'll work. Your depression is deep-seated, and we're going to work hard to get to the root of it. The anxiety is a result of fear, stress, and depression. Remove the stress and the fears, and the panic will resolve itself… I think we've covered enough today. I'll see you Wednesday."

"Dr. Wellington, I can't tell you how much better I feel after talking with you."

"Don't get too high, and don't get too low. Just stay under control, and don't forget our little exercise if needed."

Angelle walked out feeling better than she had in years. As she rushed to the hospital, she was thinking, *You can't hurt me anymore. I'm not going to worry about you anymore. Come on give me your best shot.* She said aloud to herself, "I didn't really mean that. I don't want any shot at all. But you can't hurt me anymore because I'm not going to worry about you."

―✦―

Wellington looked at his watch, grabbed the phone and called Doc. Vivian walked into Doc's office and said, "Your golfing buddy's on the phone."

Doc took the phone and said, "I can't play today, Wellington. Some of us still have to work for a living."

"Friend," Wellington said, "and I use that term loosely. I just met with your young beauty queen. She knows that she had a child, but she's repressed it. She has nightmares about the delivery, and the nurse that took her child away."

"I was afraid of that," Doc said. "Does that change anything?"

"You know it doesn't, however, Janice is about to go nuts. Angelle touched Grace's hair today and said she was the most beautiful child she had ever seen… On a lighter note, we'll need to move the tee time an hour later," Wellington said. "A certain ex-friend of mine has me tied up until one p.m."

"I can live with that," Doc said. "Oh, I almost forgot. Burt said tell you the next time I saw you that you need to stop spending money on hopeless lessons and just play the slice."

"You tell that smart-ass that if he'd cut the trees on the left side of the fairways and widen the fairways on the right, I could play my slice. Good bye!" Doc could hear him grumbling. "You wait until I see that smart aleck pathetic excuse of a pro. I'll—" Doc hung up the phone and burst out laughing.

"Something you want to share?" Vivian asked.

"Not in a million years," Doc said, still laughing as he went to his next patient.

CHAPTER TWENTY-FIVE

After work, Caleb hurried to the dressing room. The team was dressing, and the atmosphere was gloom. The coaches came out of their office where they had been locked up for two days. Coach Shook said, "Team, let's get ready to win a homecoming game for our students, parents, and alumni. Virginia's pretty good this year, but I still believe in you. If we set our minds to the task at hand, and we're prepared, we can win. Do you believe it?" The team gave a half-hearted, "Yeah," and a few claps. They stood up and started to the practice field. When they were all out of the dressing room, Coach Shook looked at the coaches and said, "We have problems, and I don't mean with Virginia."

They went over the game plan and tried to run a few new plays. The practice was a disaster. After an hour of stumbles, fumbles, dropped passes, and missed blocking assignments, Coach Shook called the team together and said, "Sit down." He shook his head and said, "I've been around here thirty years, and I can truly say that this was the worse practice I have ever endured. If you've given up, we need to forfeit the remaining games and just go fishing. If you've lost confidence in me, I'll go over to the administration building and resign. I'll have no part of a team that has lost its heart and desire to succeed. Most of you were here last year. We didn't win a game then, but you never gave up. You never stopped believing that victory was coming. This practice is over. If it's like this tomorrow, I won't be here on Wednesday."

Will was standing behind the coaching staff, and he stepped around them and said, "May I speak, Coach?" Coach Shook nodded.

"I'm a real asshole," Will said. "I suppose I'll die an asshole. It runs in my family. I've heard you can't change a leopard's spots, but I'm trying. I'm captain of this team. I should be leading you to victory. But, as you know, I did something very stupid. My football is over for this season, but your season's not over. I'd gladly lose a few fingers if I could lead you onto that field Saturday afternoon. I'm ashamed of what I did, and I'm ashamed of what I just witnessed. These coaches have spent every weekend and most nights in that office trying to come up with a plan that'll make you winners. How did you repay them? By moping and dragging around like you just lost your girlfriend to your best buddy. I heard some of you mumbling that you wish it was next year. We don't live our lives in the future. This is nineteen-fifty-five. How do we know we'll be living next year? This is our time. We don't worry about next year. We won a ball game two weeks ago. I never thought I'd see this team quit."

Every head was down, and the shame could be seen on their faces. Some of the seniors motioned for the team to huddle around them. After a few seconds, they circled the coaches and in one voice yelled, "We're ready to practice now, Coach Shook!"

For the next hour, the team worked like a well-oiled machine. Coach Shook called them together and said, "Men, if you play like you practiced today, we may have a surprise for the Cavaliers Saturday."

The team shouted and ran for the dressing room. As the coaches walked slowly to the dressing room, Coach Shook said, "At times I'd like to kick Will's ass, then at other times I'd like to hug his neck."

Stan added, "Men, we better be a little more tolerant of Will James. He might just be President someday, if he sets his mind to it."

Billy Ray commented, "As much as we regret what happened to him, it might be his salvation."

"I whole-heartedly agree," Coach Shook said. "If we think he was good this year, just wait until next year. He's going to make up for this year."

For the next four days the excitement rose to a fever pitch on campus in anticipation of homecoming and all the activities that encompassed it. Many students had invited their girlfriends or boyfriends to the dance and parade on Saturday. The students were involved in everything except class work that week, busying themselves making huge signs to be displayed all over the campus, and building and decorating dozens of elaborate floats for the parade. Will had taken up permanent residence in the library, occasionally attending a class when he became bored with the reading. He seemed to enjoy undermining his professors when he caught them in a blunder. They knew they dared not make a mistake when he was present. Most were pleased when they saw his chair vacant.

Caleb, as usual, found himself in a whirlwind of distress, going in a circle to class, to the club, to practice, to the hospital, and then trying to study late at night. Nothing had changed at the hospital. Luther had tried not to show his true feelings concerning Ruby and the child; however, he was a very transparent person. It was a deathwatch, and Luther didn't sleep anymore. He looked closer to death than his son. The love that Buckie had shown for his mother and brother seemed to smolder inside Luther like a fire that was sure to explode soon.

Every night after Buckie received his shot, Caleb and Angelle drove somberly back to the campus. No longer did they talk about their love for each other. Their private lives were put on hold while they waited and dreaded the inevitable. Angelle simply leaned over and gave Caleb a tender kiss on the cheek when they arrived at the dormitory.

Buckie had refused to give up after his mother's return. Every day was like Christmas to him, savoring the love and affection of the mother he had longed for all his life.

On Thursday after a short practice, the coaches and team walked to the hospital to make their last visit to see Buckie. Will didn't come. Buckie became so excited over the team's visit that he almost hyperventilated and went into an uncontrollable tremor. The team and coaches were quick to give him a pat on the head and words of encouragement. They were also quick to ruffle Lucky's hair or give him a pat on the head. Not a single player looked at Ruby with contempt. Then they returned to the campus.

Gladys had watched the long procession of athletes file by the nurse's station. This time she stood there with an approving smile. She glanced at Angelle and said, "Those are some good kids, and Coach Shook is one fine man."

Angelle smiled and said, "They all love him, especially Caleb, because he gave him a chance."

"I'd probably kiss his feet if he had saved my job," Gladys said jokingly.

Buckie settled down after the team left. Ruby sat down by him and held his hand while he and Lucky resumed their picture game. Ruby had brought pictures, and Buckie would hold up a picture and Lucky would try to identify and say the name of the picture. If he couldn't pronounce the name, Buckie would tell him and Lucky would repeat it.

A few minutes later, Will peeped in the door looking around like a thief. He eased in, and Buckie saw him. "Look, Momma, that tough guy's comin' to beat me up. But, he ain't really that tough." Ruby whirled around with a frightful look, not knowing who to expect.

Will sat a package on the floor and walked over to Buckie's bed. "I'm just kiddin', Momma. That's the all-American, Will James, and he's my friend."

Will took Ruby's hand as he said graciously, "It's my pleasure to meet you, ma'am. You have a mighty tough kid here."

"And this is my little brother, Lucky," Buckie said proudly. "Ain't he beautiful, Will?"

"I reckon he's about the prettiest little fella I ever seen," Will said.

"You ain't sposed to talk like that, Will," Buckie chided. "Everybody knows you a, uh, uh ..."

"What he's trying to say, Mrs. Ruby, is that I'm a genius," and he winked at her.

"Yeah," Buckie said. "That's the word. Caleb says that Will can read a book 'fore he can get to the bathroom and take a cra— Oops. Sorry, Momma." Ruby smiled and nodded. "And he said, if Will didn't like a book, he would throw it into the trash can."

"Is that all you and Caleb do, talk about my bad habits? I would have thought you two might've talked about some of your girlfriends or something interesting."

Buckie blushed and said, "Aw, Will, I ain't got no girlfriend."

"What's in that bag over yonder?" Buckie asked, grinning with wide eyes.

"What bag?" Will said, shrugging his shoulders.

"You know what bag. I saw you put it down," Buckie said excitedly.

"Oh, that bag. It's the most prized possession that Marston has ever had."

"What! What! What!" Buckie said more excited.

Will walked over, picked up the bag, and eased back close to the bed. He said, "This bag contains the actual ball that I used to score the winning touchdown that broke the longest losing streak in the nation. I was going to keep it for a souvenir, but there is someone very special to me that I think would like it even more than me."

Buckie's lips began to quiver, and his eyes became teary. He said, "You mean me?"

Will eased the ball out of the sack and handed it to Buckie. Buckie began to weep.

Will wiped Buckie's eyes with his handkerchief and said, "I had a few tears in my eyes too when I trotted off the field and put the ball in a special bag." Will had written his name in bold letters on the football. Under his name, he had written "The winning ball that broke a thirty-five game losing streak." Will bent over and kissed Buckie on the forehead and said, "I'm out of here, kid. I don't want to monopolize your time with your mom and brother."

"I don't know what that big word means, but please come back and see me when you can," Buckie said. Will shook Ruby's hand again and said, "It was a real pleasure meeting you, Mrs. Ruby." Lucky threw out his hand. Will reached down and shook it and said, "You might just be the prettiest kid I've ever seen, with the exception of my best buddy here," and he patted Buckie on the head, kissed his cheek, and walked out the door. He met Luther coming toward the room. Will waited for him and put his arm around him and said, "Mr. Luther, you have to be strong like your boy in there. I wish I had his courage and strength of character."

"Will, I'm a fearin' that I'm a thinkn' more 'bout me than my boy, now. I'm scared, Will. I don't know if I can live wit'out my boy."

"You are going to be all right," Will encouraged. "He got that heart and courage of a lion from you. You'll be all right."

"What I got to live fer when he gone?"

"You have yourself to live for. You have your memories of the good times. People survive. They make themselves go on after these horrible things happen. The sun will rise again, and with every sunrise, the days will get brighter for you."

Luther grabbed Will, hugged him, and began to cry on his shoulder. He thanked him for his encouragement. Luther walked back into the room and sat in the chair against the wall.

"You want to sit here by your son?" Ruby asked softly.

"I be fine here. I sit by him all night long. He knows I be here fer him if'n' he needs me. I would'st ever leave him." Luther couldn't resist the opportunity to hurt Ruby for her past sins. He saw the pain on her face at his words, and deep in his wounded heart, he felt shame.

"Momma," Lucky said, "Buckie come home wit' us?"

Buckie gave a pitiful look at Luther and said, "I wish you and Momma could go home with Poppa." Using all of his strength, he held the football up and said, "Poppa, look what Will give me. I shouldn't ought took it 'cause—"

"Yes you should, son 'cause he wouldn't a give it to you if'n' he didn't want you to have it. Them folk been a lying 'bout Will James. He ain't no bad boy. No mean boy would a done what he done fer us."

Later, after work, Caleb rushed to the hospital. He spent an hour with Buckie and his family. Buckie's condition was critical, and his time was near. He was fighting death with every labored breath, yet he held on to the ball that Will had given him. He couldn't wait to show his prized possession to Caleb.

Gladys and Angelle were constantly in and out of the room making sure Buckie was comfortable and fearful that the end would come before dawn. The pain and nausea was so severe that Gladys had to double the morphine. She came in with the syringe and said, "Good night, sweetie. You've had enough excitement for the day. It's time to rest."

Caleb and Angelle drove slowly back toward the dorm and Angelle said firmly, "I'm not going to the ball Saturday."

"My heart's not in it either, but it's your responsibility to go. You were selected by the students and faculty, and it's too late to back out."

"But my heart's not in it either and …"

"And what?"

"I can't dance. I've never danced in my life. I'd look like a fool stumbling all over the floor."

Caleb looked at his watch, and his eyes lit up. "We can fix that now." He drove by the entrance to the college and drove as fast as the old relic would carry them to the parking lot at the club. The concrete parking lot was well lit. He hopped out of the truck, walked around, and opened the door for Angelle. "Come on and get out," he insisted. "It's time you learned to dance."

"But there's no music."

"I'll sing if you can tolerate it." Caleb reached out his hand, palm down, and Angelle nervously came near him. "Now you hold my hand. I won't close mine. I'll ease my arm around your side so I can guide you. All I know how to do is the box step. Then he thought, *That ain't exactly true. Darlene taught me to waltz, but I don't think Angelle is ready for that.* "Mother taught this to me. I promise I won't put my hand on your back or hold you. Now relax. That's the most important thing."

Angelle managed a snicker and said, "Easy for you to say."

"Ready?" Caleb asked.

Angelle nodded halfheartedly. Caleb began to sing *Danny Boy*. Angelle placed her hand on his shoulder and took his hand very, very gingerly. Caleb began to dance the box step with her. She was stiff as a poker, and he had to muscle her around with his arm against her side. "Would you please relax!" He barked. "I haven't bitten anyone in weeks."

Angelle giggled and said, "This is hopeless. I feel foolish. I'll never learn to dance."

"If you don't relax, we are going to look foolish. Close your eyes and think of the most pleasant thing you've ever done."

Angelle paused, and then after a few seconds said, "I can't think of anything pleasant I've done, except—kiss you."

"There won't be any kissing here tonight," Caleb said. "We have business to tend to, plus we're both late. As much as it pains me to say this, think of some pleasant moment with Maurice before you came here."

Angelle seemed to wilt at Caleb's suggestion.

"I'm sorry I said that. It was a stupid thing to say. I only said it out of jealousy."

After a brief silence Angelle said, "I remember something very pleasant that happened recently. I'm ready to start again."

"I probably don't want to hear what it was."

She laughed and said, "You might. It was the first time I ever saw you when you were in those overalls, and you thought I was a maid. I won't say what I thought you were. I laughed all the way to the hospital. But I didn't forget your eyes and handsome face."

"All right, now let's get serious. Close your eyes and think of something pleasant," and he began to sing again. She relaxed somewhat and they began to dance. The longer they danced, the more her fears subsided. Before Caleb could say, 'You have it,' she snuggled close to him and laid her head against his chest, and they felt as if they were in a fancy ballroom or at the Governor's Ball.

"I never knew dancing could be so enjoyable," she whispered.

"You're very good," Caleb encouraged. "You're light as a feather. We're not going to embarrass anyone." Before Caleb could finish speaking, Angelle wrapped her arms around his neck, planted her soft lips on his, and held him as tightly as she could. He provided no resistance. He was under her spell again and very close to heaven.

Burt lived in a modest home provided by the club only a block from the clubhouse. He had walked out to the number one tee to start the watering system, as was his practice every other night. He saw Caleb and Angelle dancing in the moonlight and chuckled at Caleb's singing. He continued to watch until the dancing stopped and the passionate kissing began. He waited, but it seemed to have no end. He glanced at his watch and thought, *They are both late for curfew. I better break this up before it gets out of hand, and they get kicked out of school.* He began his slow stroll toward them.

They were oblivious of his presence until he taped Caleb on the shoulder. Caleb jumped and almost screamed. Angelle did let out a scream.

"It's all right!" Caleb shouted. "It's just Mr. Burt. He's the pro here."

Burt looked at Angelle, thinking. *This has to be Angelle. She is one gorgeous young lady.* "I hate to do this to you kids, but it's time for you two to be in bed, and I don't mean the same bed."

"I can explain everything, Mr. Burt. You see—"

"Of course I see, son. What you two were doing is as old as Adam and Eve. It's perfectly natural. However, there's a time," he glanced at his watch again, "and a place, and I don't think this is either. Do you two want to get booted out of school?" Angelle stood silently, almost shivering with fear and embarrassment.

"Let me try to explain, Mr. Burt," Caleb pleaded.

"You have two seconds to get in that truck. I want to see your tail light disappear in ten seconds." They both ran to the truck and sped away, or at best, tried to speed away.

"Oh, to be young again," Burt sighed. "If I'd had a girl that beautiful in college… Well, it might have been worth getting kicked out for." Burt walked back to the green, shaking his head, and saying, "I've never seen anyone so beautiful. It's no wonder she's driving him nuts."

"Don't you ever kiss me like that again unless you mean it," Caleb chided.

"But I did mean it," Angelle said sliding over close to him, laying her head against his shoulder. "I'm hoping very soon I'll be able to tell you that I love you, and I'll marry you when we graduate, but I need just a little more time."

―✦―

The team didn't practice on Friday so Caleb was able to put in a full day's work at the club, avoiding Burt as much as possible. He thought the evening crowd would be an overflow because of homecoming, and he was correct. The place was a madhouse as expected. The crowd piled in early and stayed late. He and Abe rushed around until it seemed they were meeting themselves coming and going. Doc and Edith, as they often did, donned the white waiter's jacket. They pitched in and served the members and guests until the overflow eased. At ten p.m. the last guest exited the dining hall. Abe and Caleb dropped their shoulders and collapsed into seats. "That was the worse yet," Caleb commented.

"I've seen it this bad, but never worse," Abe agreed, wiping the perspiration from his face. "This kind of night makes me think of retirement. But I'll be here as long as Doc needs me. Look at this mess," Abe said. "You'd think these rich folk grew up in a pig sty."

"You look really tired," Caleb said. "Go on home and I'll clean up."

Abe forced himself to his feet. "Let's get to it, boy. It ain't gonna clean itself." They locked the door at midnight and walked out into the crisp clear night. The moon was full and bright. The stars looked like those hanging on a Christmas tree. "It doesn't get any prettier than this, son," Abe mused. "I got to make a few 'coon hunts when I was a boy. This kind of night brings back some sweet memories. The old black man that took me was a very kind gentleman. He was the closest thing I ever had to a poppa. He died suddenly, a stroke they said. It took me a while to get over it. Ten years later, Momma died. I still think about her every day. If you think we worked hard tonight, son, she put in a day like this every day of her life. I never heard her complain. She was a sweet lady… A sweet, sweet lady." He shook Caleb's hand and murmured, "See you tomorrow," as he crawled into the old Ford.

Caleb glanced at his watch and shook his head. "Too late to go to the hospital," so he crawled into the truck and went to the dorm. The dorm was quiet. He showered and went to bed.

At daybreak he sprang up and dressed quickly. He shook Will. Will took a swing at him, but missed. Will snatched the sheet up over his head. Caleb backed away and said, "I know you're awake. We need to pick up the girls at six thirty sharp. You'll be ready, won't you?"

"I changed my mind," Will mumbled. "I'm going to Memphis. Got a call last night from a hot chick up there. Couldn't resist her offer."

"Don't say that, Will!" Caleb pleaded. "Please don't do this to me. You'll ruin my life if you don't go."

"What life!" Will barked, sitting up. "Get your ass out of here, and let me get some sleep. Of course I'll be ready."

"Don't ever do that to me again, Will," Caleb snapped. "My heart stopped beating. Do you have a tuxedo? This is a formal dance, whatever that means."

"Doesn't everyone," Will quipped, motioning for him to go. He rolled over, putting his pillow over his head.

"I'm leaving, Will, and I promise you that you'll have a great time. I owe you for this."

Will snatched the pillow off his head and barked, "If she turns out to be a dog, you're dead. I have a reputation to live up to."

Caleb went out the door murmuring, "More like live down. It's not your reputation I'm concerned about." *Oh well, he and Rachel can only kill me once.*

—⁂—

As usual, Caleb went to the hospital. Angelle had arrived earlier, and she met him at Buckie's door. "Thankfully, there's been no change since yesterday," she said. "He's still holding on, but now he sleeps most of the time. Doc just left. He said this boy is one for the ages. Before I forget, Rachel said to inform you that she's going to dress at the dorm with me. 'You will pick us up at the dorm, and don't dare be late.' Those were her exact words."

Caleb smiled and said, "That sounds like her. She always has to be in control. And does she have a sharp tongue. I'm dreading the confrontation between her and Will. You're going to see a battle of wit and insults tonight. Will's probably going to kill me before the night's over, if Rachel doesn't beat him to it."

Caleb went into the room and gave Luther a hug. He was slouched over in the chair holding Buckie's hand. "He ain't doin' so good, Caleb. I'm a fearin' it's 'bout…"

"God's in control, Luther. He's promised that He'll never put a burden on us too big for us handle. Ask Him for strength to get you through this, and He will. When I look at my little brother lying there, waiting to be touched by the hand of God, I see a beautiful child who lived with hope and faith and epitomized love. That means he was love. Emil taught me that word. He was my roommate before I went to the athletic dorm. He and Buckie have a lot of the same wonderful qualities."

"I kinda figured that's what it meant," Luther said. "I can't read nor write, but you knowed that. Ruby said she wuz gonna teach me, but she left 'fore … I ain't never loved nobody likn' I love my boy, but you ain't fer behind."

Caleb bent over to kiss Buckie and whispered, "I love you, little brother." He sat down by Luther and asked, "Are you and Ruby making it all right here together?"

"She ain't no bother ifn that's what you a askin', gest long as Buckie's happy."

"Do you still love her, Mr. Luther?"

Luther wobbled his head a few times, paused, then said, "You don' quit lovin' somebody 'cause they no good."

"Then what's the problem? I know she loves you."

"I mighst still love her, but I can'st forgive her. She done made her bed, and I ain't a crawlin' in bed wit' no whore."

"So you don't believe a person can change?"

"If'n' I was weak 'nuff to taken her back, she'd gest leave again. I ain't strong 'nuff to raise no chap by myself no more. I ain't raisin' no chap wit' no momma no more. I seed what it done to Buckie, and I knowd what it done to me… Caleb, all my life I hear'd what them town folk was a sayin' 'bout me 'hind my back. They was a sayin', 'There goes that dumb redneck, Luther Cummins.' I swore they'd nary say that 'bout my boy. I made shore he got schoolin' ever' day of his life so he wouldn't turn out likin' me."

You Shall Know the Truth

"Mr. Luther, you did better than right by your boy. No child ever had a more loving and caring parent than you. Now, I know I'm meddling, but I have to say this. I think you are wrong about Ruby. I do think people can change. No. I know they can change if they have a reason. Ruby has changed, and I don't think she'd ever leave you again. But I know life would be hell with two whites trying to raise a half-black child. I don't know if I would be willing to take on that responsibility either, knowing how most people in the south feel about blacks."

"That ain't the problem!" Luther snapped. "That boy ain't the problem. I don't hate no black people. I don't hate nobody. I don't hates them peoples what made fun o' me all my life. What Ruby done be my problem."

CHAPTER TWENTY-SIX

Caleb realized that he had made Luther face the truth about Lucky. He had put the seed in Luther's mind and prayed it would grow. Hopefully, Luther would admit that the child was all that stood between his and Ruby's happiness.

Ruby and Lucky eased into the room. Luther took a seat against the wall. Buckie opened his eyes slowly and looked up at Caleb. "I knew you'd be here when I woke up," he said. "I dreamed about you and Angelle last night. You two got married right here where you standing. Brother Branch and Poppa and Momma and everyone was here in the room."

Caleb forced a smile and said, "Did I kiss her?"

"You didn't quit kissin' her. My dream went away, and you was still kissin' her."

"I like your dreams, and I wish I had a few like that," Caleb chuckled.

"It ain't gonna be no dream when you kiss her. One day she's gonna marry you. I jest know it. I wish I could be here to see it."

"I'm here to make you feel better," Caleb said, "and you're making me feel like a king, but you always did make me feel better."

"You know that ain't true. It's like the sun shines on my face ever time you come to see me. I jest lay here and think about you running down that field, and them boys trying to catch you. I can almost see your face grinning as you run to the end of that field. I wish I coulda seen Will make that touchdown that won the game. I got so excited, I almost wet the bed."

"You didn't almost wet the bed," Luther said grinning. "You did wet the bed!"

"Aw, Poppa, you didn't have to tell um that," Buckie said blushing. "But it's true."

"I don't want you to waste all those sweet words on me," Caleb said. "Save some for these three people who love you dearly. I have to go to work now, and I need to go to the game this afternoon. I have to take Angelle to the homecoming ball tonight. I don't know if I'll see you before tomorrow morning, but I'll be here at sunrise. That's a promise."

Buckie reached his shaky hand up and took Caleb's. The strangest look came across his face, as if to say, 'This is goodbye, Caleb. I won't be here tomorrow.' Caleb bent over and hugged him tenderly for a long time. Then he kissed his cheeks and forehead.

"This is not goodbye, little brother. I'm going to be with you through all eternity. That's another promise I'm going to keep." Buckie's eyes softened. A bright smile came across his face and he said, "I'll be a waitin', number twenty-two."

—≻ʒ|ฅ↼—

Caleb made short work of his duties on the golf course and rushed over at ten-thirty to help Abe in the dining hall. The members and guests began to flood the dining hall at eleven, just after the morning parade. At eleven-thirty, Doc and Edith came in, followed by Judge Knight and Jennifer. Jennifer stopped at the entrance and said, "Go ahead, Father. Caleb will come to get me. I want to talk to him." Caleb spotted them and rushed over to Jennifer. Her kaleidoscope eyes sparkled even brighter as she waited for Caleb to get to her. She threw up her arms and gave Caleb a big hug. "Kiss me, Danny Boy." Caleb gave a boyish grin and kissed her tenderly.

"I've missed you, sweetheart," he said. "You don't call anymore."

"My ole tight-wad father took the phone out of my room. He said he wasn't made of money. But I've been thinking about you every day. My physical therapist said I'm the most determined patient he'd ever worked with. If heart and desire was all a person needed to get better, I was definitely going to make it. I told Mother what he said, but she said they tell everyone that. She still discourages me. But I'm going to make it, Danny Boy. We're going to dance all night at my graduation. I asked Father to take me to the ball tonight, but he said he had to get back and work on some cases tomorrow. Are you going to the ball?"

"Yes. I'm not very excited about it, but someone asked me to take them, and I couldn't say no," Caleb said.

"I wish you had. I'm jealous of her, whoever she is," Jennifer confessed.

"She's a nice girl," Caleb responded. "You'd like her."

"Pretty?"

"You don't think I'd go with a homely girl, do you?" Caleb joked.

Abe grunted loud enough to be heard from across the room and gave Caleb a hard look.

"Duty calls, sweet princess. I'll roll you over to the table."

"I wish we could go out on the patio and talk for a while," Jennifer said. "There's so much I'd like to say to you. Why don't you sit with us in our box seats?"

"I'd love to, but the freshmen team always sits together in the student section. I wouldn't want them to think that I thought I was better than them. They've been good to me."

"I love you, Danny Boy. I'll always love you."

"I love you too, sweetheart. I'll always love you."

"Someday you'll really mean that," she said with conviction as Caleb rolled her up to the table.

"It's good to see you, Judge Knight," Caleb said.

Judge Knight stood, extending his hand, saying. "We're already looking forward to next year, my boy. Doc was just telling me that the entire stadium is going to be sold out by May. According to Jennifer, you have one more game this fall."

"Yes, sir. We play Ole Miss next Thursday. We've heard they have the toughest team in their conference. They're undefeated."

Abe grunted again, so Caleb said, "Y'all have to excuse me now. Abe's getting behind, and I don't want to get him upset." Edith motioned to Caleb with her index finger to come.

Caleb walked around the table to her. Edith said, "You better never be too busy to give me a kiss." Caleb blushed, bent down, and kissed her sweet cheek.

"I read in the paper today that Angelle was selected to be in the homecoming court. I have this beautiful gown that I bought for the Governor's Inauguration Ball a few years ago. The bust line was a little too low for—for someone my age, and I didn't wear it. It's a really lovely gown. It's a petite. I noticed the other night that Angelle is a petite. She has the figure to fill it out nicely. Tell her it's hers to keep. I won't need it. I'd have given it to her sooner, but I just found out that she was on the court. I put it on the seat of your truck. Will you see that she gets it?"

"I'll take it to her as soon as lunch's over. Oh, Mrs. Edith, she'll be thrilled. Thank you so much." He rushed over to help Abe.

"If you are through socializing and making time with all the ladies, you might give me a hand." Abe said in a somewhat irritated voice.

"Yezza, Mr. Boss man," Caleb quipped. Abe gave him a hard look and slapped at his butt. Caleb was too quick and scooted away.

The dining hall began to clear at one o'clock, giving the guests time to get to the stadium before the afternoon kickoff. Abe was in a foul mood because Doc had made arrangements for professional help for that night. He was expecting another overflow crowd. Abe mumbled and grumbled through the entire lunchtime about having to work with a bunch of amateurs. "I told Doc I could handle the job myself," he grumbled. "I'll spend all night cleaning up their mess and tellin' them what to do."

"I don't think so," Caleb said. "He said he employed two professional waiters from Memphis that were off on weekends."

"You know what that means," he barked. "It means they ain't worth their salt if they don't work on weekends. The big tips come on the weekend."

"You're just afraid they'll show you up," Caleb said laughing as he ran out of the kitchen.

Abe yelled, "You better run, you smart butt, 'cause you ain't that good a friend." Abe whispered, "But he might be right."

"I'll bet you never admit that to him," Clotile said.

"Mind your own business woman, and keep the food coming," Abe snapped.

"What food, fool? I don't have an order," Clotile answered sharply. Abe stomped out of the kitchen mumbling.

By one-thirty, the hall was almost spotless, and Abe said, "Get out of here or you'll miss the kickoff."

"Are you sure?" Caleb asked, wide-eyed.

"I said it, didn't I?" Abe snapped, still huffed about the unwanted help.

"Then I'm out of here. I do hope the night goes well, and I'm sorry I—"

"Scoot," Abe gestured. "Out!" Caleb ran for the door, and Abe yelled, "Are you going to wear that waiter's jacket to the game?" Caleb snatched it off and ran for the kitchen. Abe reached out and grabbed it as Caleb passed. He said, "I'll take care of it. Have a good time, boy. I wish I could go with you."

―⁀╲▎╱⁀―

Caleb flew to the hospital and ran up the stairs with the gorgeous gown in his arm. Angelle was behind the desk. He rushed over and handed it to her. "Mrs. Edith sent it to you. She bought it for the Governor's Ball, but said it was a little too revealing for her age. She said keep it. She didn't want it back."

Angelle held it up in front of her, and the tears began to stream down her cheeks.

Gladys walked out of the office and saw Angelle with the beautiful gown in her hands. "Where did you get that magnificent gown?" she asked.

"Mrs. Edith sent it to me for the ball. She said I could keep it."

Gladys held it up, inspected the label, and gasped. "This is a Christian Dior from Paris, France. Do you have any idea what it must have cost? I'd be afraid to wear this if it was mine. I'd build a glass case and display it."

"Do you like it, Angelle?" Caleb asked.

"I would think the tears should answer that," Gladys said. "You realize Angelle is supposed to be at the game sitting on the sidelines with the other maids during the game, don't you Caleb."

"No. I've never been to a homecoming game before."

"She conned me into writing a bogus excuse saying it was critical that she work today because of a critical shortage of nurses. That part is true, but what I didn't say was that the reason for the shortage was because they were all going to the game. She said she was too embarrassed to make a public spectacle of herself in front of all the fans. I shouldn't have done it, but Angelle can be very persuasive."

"I'm late for the game," Caleb said. "See you tonight in the most beautiful gown at the ball."

Caleb bounded up the steps of the stadium looking for a seat. He heard Will's bugle voice bellow out. He looked up and spotted him near the top row. Caleb took a seat by Will. "I can't believe you're sitting up here with the freshmen team and peasants," Caleb quipped.

"Well, it's not by choice, I'll assure you. Coach Shook banished me from the sidelines. He said we couldn't afford any more penalties. I'm thinking about slipping down on the visitor's side, and flashing their signals to our team."

"You wouldn't!" Caleb gasped.

"Nah. I'd get kicked out of the game. I'll probably be ready to get out of here anyway if they don't get their fingers out of their—"

"Will! There are girls everywhere. Be a little more discrete."

"Corn Shuck," Will said, somewhat amazed, "your vocabulary has increased a thousand-fold since I've been rooming with you."

"Glad you noticed, Will? And those PhD's didn't help at all."

"I missed the crowning of the queen before the game. I was in the dressing room trying to build a fire up their—"

"Hush Will!" Caleb chided. "Don't talk like that with all these girls sitting around us."

"Show me Rachel!" Will demanded.

"I can't tell one from another from this distance, especially with those large hats on. They all look alike from here." Caleb lied. Rachel was a head taller than the other maids sitting on the bottom row on the fifty-yard line. Her long hair was ablaze in the bright sunlight."

"That one with the flaming red hair must be a beanpole. She towers over the others," Will said, laughing.

"It's time for the kickoff, Will. Stop worrying about that. She's beautiful, and you won't be disappointed. Let's watch the Game."

"I better not be disappointed. I don't get nervous about much, but this is giving me the he-bee-gee-bees. You know I have a reputation to uphold."

Marston kicked off. The crowd let out a roar, and all jumped to their feet. The Cavaliers ran the ball to the forty-yard line and quickly marched down the field. Will went berserk after every play, screaming loud enough to be heard in down town Marston.

Caleb was embarrassed, but he dared not show it. Will's passion for the game consumed him. He was dying as he watched his team get mauled on the field, knowing what a difference he could have made. Caleb spent one of the most miserable two and a half hours of his life listening to Will rant and rave after every play. Mercifully, the game finally ended. Unfortunately, the score was 28 to 7 in favor of Virginia.

Providence and Hard Work Series
You Shall Know the Truth

Will stood up and said, "Kick my ass, Corn Shuck. Kick it in front of all these people. That loss was entirely my fault. I am one damn fool!"

"Try to forget about it, Will. There's always next year. Let's get cleaned up, and go have a wonderful time."

"I was feeling bad enough, and you have to go and remind me of that."

"I have to go pick up my rented tux from the cleaners downtown. I'll be back as soon as I can."

"You better run," Will said. "With this traffic, you'll be an hour getting out of here."

"Good idea, Will." He bounded down the steps, jogged across the campus and down Main Street to the cleaners. He was back at the dorm in thirty minutes.

Will had already showered and was dressed when Caleb rushed in. Will looked very handsome and dignified in his tux. He had class and breeding, and there was no concealing it. Caleb stood and admired him a few seconds.

"What!" Will asked. "Do I have a spot? Is my tie crooked?"

Caleb shook his head and said, "You look terrific, Will. You're going to knock Rachel off her feet when she sees you."

Will gave a prideful smile and said, "When you got it, kid, you got it. Now you get to it, kid. You don't want to keep the Cajun Queen waiting." Caleb showered and shaved. Will helped him get dressed. Caleb knew as much about donning a tux as he did putting on a football uniform the first time. After he was dressed, Will backed away and gave him a long hard look.

"What's wrong?" Caleb asked. "Do I look that bad?"

"Nah. You look like a country gentleman."

"Will, I have to ask you something. I don't want you to fly off the handle when I do. But I need to know. I've heard rumors that you got a girl pregnant last year, and they say she had an abortion. Is that true?"

"It's really none of your damn business, but to ease your virgin mind, I don't know if I got her pregnant or if it was someone else.

She was sleeping with half the boys on campus, but she fingered me. I don't know how I could have gotten her pregnant. I always practice safe sex. I don't know a damn thing about an abortion."

"Did your father know about her pregnancy?"

"Yeah. Her father called him and told him it was my kid."

Caleb continued his persistent questioning. "Did she have an abortion?"

"I don't know. I didn't hear from them again. She didn't come back to school this year."

"Thank you for telling me that, Will. I feel a little better now. Let's go to the ball."

Will and Caleb started down the steps. Will became nervous again. He said, "I can't believe you talked me into this. Tell me the truth. Is she a dog? I can handle it. I don't want to freak out when I see her."

"Calm down, Will," Caleb said in a placid voice. "I think she's beautiful. All you have to do is dance the first dance with her, and please be nice to her. She's a preacher's kid."

"What!" Will gasped. "A preacher's kid! You didn't bother to volunteer that information before."

"It didn't seem important at the time. After all, you're not going to marry her, just dance with her."

"In one night, you've managed to tally destroy my reputation, Corn Shuck."

They hopped into Will's car and Caleb said, "Put the top up, Will."

"No way, pal. Women love to ride with the top down."

"Not with hats and formal gowns on."

Will let the top up and said, "Satisfied?"

Caleb answered, "I'm sure they will be."

As Will pulled away, he asked again, "Tell me one more time what she looks like. What do her legs look like? Shapely, no big ankles, I hope."

Caleb shook his head and cut his eyes at Will, saying, "I don't believe this. Okay, for the last time. She has flaming red hair and gorgeous green eyes. She's beautiful. Her figure'll knock your eye balls out."

Will slammed on the brakes, throwing Caleb into the dashboard, bumping his head.

"Have you gone crazy!" Caleb yelled, holding his head.

"Red hair!" Will yelled. "Freckles, too, I imagine. I guess she milks the cow and slops the hogs and wears rubber boots to class."

"Nope. No rubber boots," Caleb said laughing and gave Will a little punch in the ribs.

Will let out a yelp and barked, "What are you trying to do, maim me for life!"

"Sorry. I forgot."

"I hope you appreciate this, Corn Shuck. There's nobody in the world I'd do this for but you."

"You might be surprised, Will. You might actually enjoy the ball."

"Oh, I'm quite sure of that now. You've really whetted my appetite after that info."

They pulled up in front of the girls' dormitory and Caleb hopped out. Will sat there. Caleb motioned for Will to come. "The dance starts in fifteen minutes."

"That's what has me concerned," Will mumbled, easing out of the car. They walked to the door and stepped inside.

Angelle and Rachel were sitting nervously on the edge of the sofa in the parlor. They stood up. Angelle gave Caleb a nervous smile and timid wave. Rachel gave them a smirk. They started to stroll toward the boys. Will whispered, "Is that her?"

"That's her, Will. Didn't I tell you she was beautiful?"

"What's wrong with her?" Will whispered. "I've never seen her on campus. Why couldn't she get a date? Something smells fishy here."

"She didn't want a date. She's very selective about who she dates. She said she was taller than most of these boys."

"If she asked you, Corn Shuck, she couldn't be too selective."

"Shut up, Will! They'll hear you."

The four nervous young people met in the center of the parlor. Caleb said, "You ladies look absolutely gorgeous in those beautiful gowns. Rachel, I'd like you to meet Will James, my roommate. Angelle, I believe you've already met Will."

Will reached out to shake Rachel's hand. To his amazement—and the fact that she was wearing heels—he was looking her squarely in the eyes. "Damn, Will gasped. "Just how tall are you, woman?"

"Tall enough to spit in your eyes," Rachel snapped. Will took her hand. Rachel clamped down on his with a vice-like grip. For a few seconds it was a battle of strength and will until Rachel's hand turned blue. She tried to pull it back. Will slowly released it.

"What do you do in your spare time, Red, run a dairy?" Will quipped.

"Not that it's any of your concern, Will James, but I do milk a cow in the morning and in the evening most days. I bathe and wash my hands and feet at least once a week. Any more sarcasm? Everyone isn't born with a silver spoon in their mouth like you."

"Touché," Will said, wide-eyed. "With your spunk and size, you should've been a boy. We could use a few like you on the team."

"We better get going," Caleb was quick to say. "We'll be late." He frowned at Angelle and shook his head. Angelle grinned.

They walked out by Will's car and Rachel said, "I knew I should have bought us corsages."

Will looked at Rachel and gave her a smirk, then reached into the back seat of the car and took out two small boxes containing beautiful orchids. "Caleb and I bought these for you two lovely ladies. Let me pin it on you Rachel, and he took the corsage and reached for the top of her low cut gown.

"I don't think so!" Rachel snapped. "Angelle, pin mine on and I'll pin yours."

Will reached in the back seat and took out another small box containing boutonniere for him and Caleb.

After the pinning was over, Caleb said, "I can't take credit for that, ladies. Will bought them. I never went to a dance before, much less a formal dance. I didn't know we were supposed to buy them."

"I didn't know it either, Caleb," Angelle admitted, a little embarrassed.

"Let's walk," Angelle said. "It's only a few blocks, and it's such a beautiful night." They strolled toward the Student Union. Rachel kept her distance from Will. Angelle took Caleb's arm in hers. There was no talk as they strolled, and Caleb felt the tension mounting between Will and Rachel. *If we don't get there soon,* Caleb thought, *they are not going to make it,* so Caleb picked up the pace. They arrived a few minutes before the ball was to begin and walked across the spacious ballroom toward the bandstand.

The ballroom was a picture of architectural magnificence. Doc had spared no expense in its construction. Dozens of brilliantly lighted chandeliers hung from the cathedral ceiling. The floor was constructed of flawless, shiny red oak. Dozens of mahogany tables surrounded the spacious dance floor. They weaved their way through the mass of students to the tables next to the bandstand that was reserved for the queen and her court. They took their seats and waited nervously for the first dance. The band continued to warm up their lips and their instruments, making a fractured sound.

Dr. Timothy Walker, the Dean of Students, walked onto the bandstand and held his hands up for quiet. He was a very popular Dean, being groomed as the next president. The students all gave him a hardy round of applause. "Thank you, students," he began. "We all wish the game had turned out a little differently, but all is not doom and gloom. The future has never looked brighter. Good times are coming," and he glanced at Will and Caleb and gave a little wink. "Just a reminder, not that I think I need to remind you, because everyone knows that alcohol is not permitted on the campus—at anytime.

"Now it's my pleasure to introduce to you the nineteen-fifty-five homecoming court and queen." He asked the court to stand, and he introduced them and their escorts. Everyone clapped and whistled as they were being introduced. Angelle received the loudest applause and most cat-calls. "We always reserve the first dance for the court and their escorts," Dr. Walker informed. He held his hands high and said, "Let the music begin." Then he and the other faculty members retired to an adjacent meeting room.

The court and their escorts stood and walked to the center of the dance floor. Rachel was more hesitant to get up than Angelle. Will held out his hand to her.

"Are you sure you can dance, rich boy?" Rachel needled. "You look pretty clumsy on the football field."

"Just take my hand, and hold on for the ride of your life—honey," Will countered.

"If you call me honey again, you're going to be minus two front teeth."

"All right, sugar," Will retorted as he took her hand and pulled her to her feet. They walked to the center of the floor. Rachel said, with a scowl, "We might as well get something straight right now. I'm not your woman, your honey, your gal, your chick, or any other demeaning word. My name is Rachel. Some call me Red, and I'm not offended. Do we have an understanding?"

"Feisty," Will said. "I like that in my women."

Caleb held out his hand. Angelle was reluctant to take it. "It's all right," Caleb whispered. "Just like last night with a little better music. Think of something pleasant." She took his hand, and they walked out on the floor. The lights began to dim. A huge silver ball with beautiful multicolored lights was hanging from the ceiling. It began to turn, creating a magical effect. The band began to play the beautiful Glen Miller melody, *Moonlight Serenade*.

Will took Rachel's hand, reached around her, pulling her tightly to him, and began to dance.

"You're holding me a little tight, aren't you?" Rachel protested.

"You'll be holding on to me in a few seconds, Red." He began to spin her around and around as they glided across the dance floor. Will was as light on his feet as Fred Astaire. Five years of ballroom dancing as a teenager had paid dividends.

Surprisingly, Rachel was equally as adept. "You're pretty damn good," Will commented.

"Don't you know how to pay a girl a compliment without using crude language?" Rachel chided.

Caleb took Angelle's hand, palm open, and reached around her waist snuggling his elbow against her side to guide her. They began to dance slowly. Angelle was so nervous and stiff that they almost stumbled when Caleb tried to turn with her. "Close your eyes, and remember the kiss last night," he whispered.

Angelle closed her eyes, and Caleb could hear her murmuring, "You can't hurt me. You can't hurt me."

"Heaven knows I could never hurt you," he whispered. "Why would you think that?"

"I know you wouldn't," she whispered. "I wasn't thinking about you." She closed her eyes again and began to relax. Caleb felt as if he was truly dancing with his shadow, with only the soft touch of her hand grasping his, and his arm nestled against her side. Angelle was light as a feather on her feet, and very, very smooth after she relaxed. They appeared to be a normal couple enjoying each other's company. Hundreds of envious young male eyes watched Caleb dance with the most beautiful and mysterious girl on campus, imagining it was them instead of their 'Golden Boy.'

Everyone became fascinated watching Rachel and Will as they began to put on a show, whirling around and around as they glided from one end of the floor to the other. They were so smooth, they could have been a scene from a Fred Astaire and Ginger Rogers musical. Rachel was fighting the urge to enjoy herself, although she was losing the battle. *What can't he do?* She thought. *What a waste of humanity.*

The dance ended and they walked back to their seats. "You two were amazing," Angelle said excitedly. "Where did you two learn to dance like that?"

"If you got it, you got it," Will said smugly. "Of course, five years of ballroom dance instruction and three years of barroom dancing didn't hurt."

"I learned to move like that trying to stay out of the way of Bessie's hooves when I milk every day," Rachel joked.

"I don't care how ya'll learned, because you two were poetry in motion," Angelle said.

The band struck up a fast jitterbug tune. Will said, "If you were impressed with that, kid, hold on to your drawers 'cause you ain't seen nothing yet." He reached down and grasped Rachel's hand. She began to protest, saying, "You'll never get me on the floor for that fast music." She protested all the way to the center of the floor. Will began to twirl her around, catch her, and spin her around and around again. When he realized that Rachel could keep up with the more difficult moves, he picked up the pace. Will spun her around, hoisted her to his hip, then twirled her around again. He held her around the waist and tossed her into the air, catching her on the way down, then sliding her between his legs, reaching around and pulling her to her feet.

Then Will led Rachel into a different style. Their acrobatic antics caught the attention of the other kids. Many stopped dancing and gave Will and Rachel the center of the floor while they watched and clapped in amazement. Will began to feel the flesh pull from his broken ribs, but his pride and super ego wouldn't allow him to stop. As the music came to an end, he grabbed Rachel's waist while holding her hands to her side and tossed her into the air flipping her over his head. Her gown slipped down to her head exposing her long shapely legs and stockings all the way to her shiny white-laced panties. She tried to push her dress up as Will lowered her toward the floor. Will held her hands firmly and eased her to a soft landing. "You big dummy!" Rachel scowled, snatching her gown back over her legs. "Don't ever do that again." Will's side was aflame with a burning pain after that move. He slowed the pace as the dance came to an end. "I've never been so embarrassed in my entire life," she said, continuing to blast him as they walked to their seats. "Everybody in the building knows what color my panties are now."

"I don't," Will quipped, then whispered, "but the night's still young."

"And you never will," Rachel snapped.

After they sat down, Will said, "Red, never say never. You may have to eat those words someday."

"When hell freezes over!" She shot back.

"You two were good enough to be on Broadway with moves like that," Angelle commented. "How did you keep up with him, not having practiced those moves?"

"I was just trying to stay alive," Rachel admitted. "Anyone who would get on the dance floor with that maniac has to be insane."

"You two looked like you were having so much fun," Caleb added.

"If you thought it looked like fun, you can dance with him next time because he won't drag me out there again. Everyone on campus is going to be laughing at me next week."

"I don't think anyone saw your—your under-clothes," Angelle said, trying to sooth her anger. "It all happened so fast."

"I was looking up at the ceiling, and I saw them," Rachel said. "I felt like I was exposed for ten seconds."

"Calm down, Rachel," Caleb said softly. "Angelle's right. It happened so fast that it was hardly noticeably."

Before Caleb could finish consoling her, one of the boys yelled from across the room, "I like your white drawers, Rachel, especially the ruffles."

Rachel slid down in her chair, putting her hand over face.

Will let out a cough, winced, and doubled up in pain.

Rachel looked at him, knowing his physical condition, and her anger quelled somewhat and she asked, "Are you all right?" showing genuine concern.

Will sat up, holding his side, grimacing in pain, and said, "I won't be jitter-bugging with you or anyone again tonight. I think I tore my ribs apart again."

"Well, you deser—" She looked away and felt a little guilty about what she intended to say.

"I'd like to dance again," Angelle said, "when they play another slow tune."

"That's why we came," Caleb said. "I'm ready." Caleb looked across the hall and his eyes widened as he saw Chris and Emma enter the ballroom. His heart quickened. *I don't know why I should worry about them*, he thought. *They came to have a good time, too. He wouldn't start any trouble here.* The band began to play Caleb's favorite song, *Danny Boy*. He and Angelle looked at each other and smiled warmly. He stood and extended his hand. They stepped onto the floor and began to dance. After a few seconds, Caleb felt her soft, warm cheek touch his. They moved around slowly, lost in each other's arms.

Will stood up, extended his hand, and said, "Dance?"

"Why not," Rachel retorted. "My reputation is in the toilet anyway." She smiled and they began to glide slowly around the floor. Rachel fought the urge to place her cheek against his for a few seconds, but finally her inhibitions were conquered by his seductive charisma. She gave in to her desire and laid her head softly against his cheek. Will smiled, held her closer, and laid his head against her cheek, and they glided as one around the room. Rachel caught a glimpse of Caleb dancing with Angelle. She could see the open palm and his hand close to her back, yet not touching. *What a terrible way to live your life,* she thought. *What horrible experience could have done this to her? Such beauty and kindness, yet she may never be able to experience love. God have mercy on her and Caleb.*

Caleb looked up as Chris and Emma glided by. Emma looked at him and mouthed, "Dance with me." Caleb smiled and shrugged as if he didn't understand her. He turned Angelle away quickly and tried to dance away from them. In seconds, Chris and Emma danced by him again. Emma looked at him and whispered, "Dance with me."

Chris heard her and stopped abruptly, holding her at arm's length, and said, "Who were you talking to?" He turned and saw Caleb and Angelle dancing nearby. His face hardened and his nostrils flared. He said, "Were you whispering to that SOB?" Caleb heard him and quickly danced away from them.

Emma became angry and said, "What if I was? You don't own me. I'll dance with anyone I wish to."

Chris snatched her arm and led her off the dance floor, saying, "I don't care to dance with you anymore." He led her to their table. "I'm going to get some air," and he motioned to a couple of his cronies and they walked outside. Chris went to his car and pulled a fifth of Jack Daniels from under the seat and broke the seal. He turned it up and drank until the fumes came out of his nostrils almost choked him. Then he handed the bottle to his pals.

The song ended and a dozen young freshmen boys rushed over to Angelle's table and asked if they might have a dance.

Angelle held up the ring, smiled, and said, "I don't usually dance. You all can see I'm engaged. Caleb's my friend. I asked him to escort me tonight because I'm on the court and had to come. Thank you all for asking, but, no, I don't normally dance with anyone but my fiancé."

"Ah, heck," they said and walked away disappointed.

"You handled that quite well," Will said. "You could be a diplomat with a tale like that. Don't you realize that it's obvious to everyone that you're in love with Caleb?"

Angelle blushed and lowered her head.

"You're meddling, Will James," Rachel chided. "Can't you see you're embarrassing her?"

The band began to play another slow tune, and Rupert Barnes, a six-six center on the basketball team eased up timidly to their table and asked, "May I have this dance, Rachel?"

"Hell, no!" Will barked. "Can't you see she's with me?"

Rupert whirled around and started to rush away. "Wait, Rupert," Rachel said. "Will doesn't speak for me. I'd love to dance with you." She stood and gave Will a smirk and walked out to Rupert who was trembling by then. He looked sheepishly at Will, hoping to get his approval. Will gave him a reluctant nod, and he and Rachel began to dance.

"What was that all about?" Caleb commented, smiling. "Could it be that you actually like Rachel, huh, huh?"

"She's okay, except for the smart mouth," Will admitted. "She's a hell of a dancer. Not many gals can keep up with me. Why do you think she wanted to dance with Ichabod? I'd have danced with her if she wanted to dance."

"Because she's a polite, well-mannered young lady. Something you could work on," Caleb retorted.

Will watched them dancing and felt a little twinge of jealousy for the first time in his life. When the dance ended and Rachel returned to her seat, she gave Will a stern look and came unglued. "Don't ever do that to me again! This is not a real date anyway! I'm doing this for Caleb and Angelle." Will shrugged and seemed a little wounded.

"I need to go see a man about a dog," Will said. "Be back in a few second. He put his finger in Rachel's face and said, the next dance is mine, Red, and you are my date tonight."

Will went to the restroom. Caleb asked, "Are you angry with me, Rachel?"

"The jury's still out; however, I have to admit, he's as confident and smooth on the dance floor as he is on the football field."

"That means you kinda like him?" Caleb asked, grinning with raised brows.

"No!" Rachel snapped. "Although I did enjoy dancing with him. Who wouldn't? I felt like a ballerina on the floor with him. I loathe people like him. They think they're better than everyone else. They have no compassion or regard for anyone but themselves. They're egotistical and selfish. After what he did last year, I think he's lower than a snake's belly."

"Please, don't tell him that," Caleb pleaded. "I have to live with him."

"I don't intend to tell him anything after tonight, shorty. I did this for you and Angelle." Rachel's demeanor changed, and she smiled, saying, "I'm glad I did, for your sakes. You two are a beautiful couple on the dance floor."

Providence and Hard Work Series
You Shall Know the Truth

Now I need to—how did he put it? Go see a man about a dog. Tell him I went home when he returns," and she laughed and went to the ladies room.

"What did she mean about last year? What did he do to make her dislike him so vehemently?"

"Everybody thinks he got a girl pregnant here at school and that he helped her get an abortion."

"Did he?" Angelle gasped.

"He possibly could have, but he swears that he knew nothing about an abortion, and I believe him. Will doesn't lie. His father might have gotten involved, but I don't know that for a fact. It's only gossip, and I don't like gossip."

"It's obvious Rachel thinks he did. Who was the girl?"

"I don't know. She didn't return to school this year."

"I need to go powder my nose, too," Angelle said smiling. "You better not dance with anyone while I'm gone either. I can be a tiger when I get jealous." She gave Caleb a smile that warmed his heart.

The band began to play the beautiful tune, *Unchained Melody*. Caleb loved the song, and he turned to watch the band and the man singing. He wished that Angelle was there to dance with him. He was enjoying the music, patting his foot keeping time with the music. Suddenly, he felt a tap on the shoulder, and he jerked around quickly. He was shocked to see Emma standing there smiling at him. She was wearing her most beautiful and exquisite gown. "I knew you were too bashful to come over and ask me to dance," she said with her teasingly seductive smile, "so here I am, asking you. When I heard that song and the words, 'I hungered for your touch,' I couldn't sit there any longer because that's the way I've felt about you these last few weeks."

"I didn't want to start any trouble tonight," Caleb said. "You know how Chris hates me. You look very beautiful in that gorgeous gown. Not that you're not always beautiful."

Emma sat down in Angelle's chair and said, "If Chris said things like that maybe I might think more of him. I've thought of nothing except that wonderful night with you. I asked father to let me come to the ball. He said it cost too much to fly me home, and it was a ridiculous idea anyway. I wanted to come and go to the ball with you. So—I called Chris and he bought a ticket for me, and here I am…wishing I was with you. Now let's dance. I want to hold you again like before."

Caleb began to stutter, "Ah, uh, uh, where's Chris?"

"Outside," Emma said, "drinking with his buddies, I'm sure. Now get up and let's dance." She reached out, took his hand, and led him onto the floor. She wrapped her long slender arms around him pulling him close to her and whispered, "I think I've fallen in love with you… No. I am in love with you." She put her lips to his neck and began to kiss him. Caleb began to panic, praying the dance would end before Angelle returned from the restroom or Chris returned.

Will and the ladies returned to their seats and spotted them dancing.

Chris and his gang finished most of the fifth, and Chris stuffed the bottle down between a row of thick hedges. He said, "Let's get back inside. I have a few things to get straight with Emma."

Angelle's face paled with a look of dismay, and she whispered, "Who's that beautiful girl dancing with Caleb?"

"I don't know if you can call that dancing," Rachel retorted. "I don't know if she had any dinner, but I know what she'd like for desert. I've never seen her before, but I'll assure you that she's high society. I bet that gown cost almost as much as yours, Angelle… And look at that expensive jewelry."

"Her ol' man can afford it," Will said. "He's a federal judge from Jackson. Her name's Emma Jean Knight, and she's here with Chris Black. They are kinda semi-engaged, Will said. You know, an expected arranged marriage to keep the blood pure and the filthy lucre in the family."

"You should know about that," Rachel said. After a few seconds, she realized how harsh and judgmental her comment had sounded. She said, "I'm sorry Will. That was crude and totally uncalled for."

"I kind of left the gate open for it," Will said. "Uh oh!" Will whispered. "This might get interesting ladies. Here comes Goldilocks."

"What?" Angelle said. "What do you mean? What's wrong?"

"Just look at Chris Black storming between those tables. This fight's been brewing for a long time."

Chris rushed onto the dance floor, pushing everyone aside, and ran up behind Caleb. He jerked Caleb around by his shoulder and shot a hard right to Caleb's temple. Caleb knees buckled, and he crumbled to the floor. Chris pounced on him and began pounding Caleb's face.

"Oh, hell no!" Will barked. "He ain't playin' that game!" He shot across the floor, grabbed Chris by the back of his collar and snatched him halfway across dance floor. Will let out a painful groan and grimaced in excruciating pain. He lifted Caleb to his feet. Caleb was dazed, seeing stars and still half out of his senses. Will put his arm around him and started leading him toward the door. He yelled to Chris, "Come on, Goldilocks. Let's see how you do in a fair fight!"

Chris stood up, dusted himself off, and retorted, "I'm right behind you, big boy."

Angelle put her hand to her mouth, crying and pleading for Caleb not to go with Will. The students boiled out the door behind them, excited to see a fight, especially this fight. Caleb kept shaking his head, trying to regain his faculties. The students formed a big circle around Will, Caleb, and Chris. Caleb's mind began to clear somewhat. He looked around and realized what was happening. He put his hands out and blurted, "I ain't goinna fight you, Chris. This ain't right." Emma wormed her way through the students with an excited and pleased smile on her face.

Rachel put a hand on Angelle's shoulder and said, "You wait here, and I'll try to stop them," and she ran out the door.

"What's the problem, cow patty?" Chris taunted.

"Are you chicken?"

Caleb, still trying to shake off the grogginess, managed to say, "I ain't chicken. I just don't believe in fightin'. It's a childish and ignorant way to settle a dispute. There're no winners."

"Oh yeah!" Chris yelled. "There's going to be a winner," and he ran at Caleb.

Will backed away, saying, "Kick his sorry ass, pal."

Chris shot a quick right at Caleb's chin. Caleb ducked. Caleb continued to hold his hands out backing away and saying, "I'm not going to fight you, Chris! Now stop it!" Chris shot another right at his chin, barely grazing it. Caleb continued to back away, protesting as Chris ran at him with a barrage of rights and lefts. Caleb ran backward, avoiding the hits.

"Come on, Caleb!" the boys began to yell. "Fight him." Chris's arrogance and insolence slightly exceeded Will's if that was possible, and his fellow students despised him. They wanted Caleb to deck him. Caleb kept backing away from Chris's wild swings. The students began to crowd in closer and closer, and their screams became louder and louder.

Caleb stumbled back into a group of students, and Chris finally had him corralled. He fired a quick right, catching Caleb squarely on the nose. The blood spewed down his mouth and chin. Instinctively, the first law of nature was evoked, and Caleb fired a hard right uppercut to Chris' jaw, and he crumbled like a piece of cheap pottery. Caleb backed away. He felt and tasted salty warm blood gushing down his mouth and chin onto the expensive rented tuxedo jacket. A roar went up from the students so loud that it sounded as if the football game was still in progress. The students rushed around Caleb and patted him on the back, then returned quickly to the ball. Caleb's heart fluttered as he looked at Chris lying there motionless.

"He's all right," Will assured Caleb. He grabbed a cup of punch from one of the boys as they passed and dashed it in Chris's face.

Chris regained consciousness, began to cough and spit out punch. Angelle came running out of the building and over to Caleb. "Are you hurt?" She asked, reaching up and touching his bloody face and swollen eye.

"Ouch!" Caleb said, backing away. "I'm all right. I didn't want to fight."

"Like hell you didn't!" Will barked. "That punch would have decked Joe Lewis. I wish we'd sold tickets. We could've made a fortune."

Emma knelt down by Chris giving a scowling look and yelled, "Get up. You're all right. I'm ready to go. Take me to Doc's house—now."

Chris took her hand and staggered to his feet, screaming, "This ain't over, you son-of-a-bitch! This ain't over by a mile. One lucky punch, that's all it was!"

"It's over!" Caleb responded flatly. "It's over!"

Chris staggered away holding on to Emma and continued to shout, "You stay away from Emma or I swear I'll kill you next time. It won't be a butt shot either. It'll be between your fricken eyes."

"You won't live to talk about it!" Will blurted. "You better leave well enough alone, and get your sorry ass out of here."

"Shut up, Chris!" Emma snapped. "Haven't you made a big enough fool out of yourself already."

"We better get away from here quickly," Will said. "The dean'll be coming out that door any second to see what that roar was all about. With blood all over your face and clothes, you'll have a lot of explaining to do." They rushed toward the sidewalk and hurried down the street. At a safe distance, they slowed their pace. Will patted Caleb on his back and said, "I was proud of you, Corn Shuck. I think you've seen the last of that sorry rotten—"

"What are the kids going to think of me now?" Caleb said. "I'm not proud of me."

"I don't approve of fighting either, Caleb," Rachel said, "but he didn't give you a choice. I think he was angry enough to kill you."

"There's always a choice," Caleb said. "I could have walked away."

"Don't be stupid," Will said. "He had no intentions of letting you walk away. You did what you had to do, and I'm proud of you."

"Look at this tux," Caleb said, feeling sick. "It's ruined. I don't know where I'll get the money to pay for it."

"Cold water," Angelle commented. "Cold water removes blood. But we need to soak it quickly before it sets."

"Forget the coat," Will said. "I'll pay for the damn thing. Take it off and throw it in the trashcan. The night's still young. Where do you ladies want to go now? I know a little place about ten miles up fifty-one just over the line that'll be rocking by now. What do you say, ladies?"

"I say, have you lost your mind? My next stop is home!" Rachel retorted.

"It's not even eight o'clock," Will barked. "What's with you, Red? Don't you like to have a good time? Talk some sense into her, Angelle."

"Caleb needs some medical attention," Angelle responded. "His nose is still bleeding, and he needs ice for it and his swollen eye."

Will was still pleading and mumbling as they walked up to the dorm door. Angelle said, "Come in, and I'll get some ice. We can stop that nose bleed." They went inside, and Angelle tended to Caleb's injuries. "Take off the jacket, and I'll take it up to my room and soak it in cold water. They'll never know the blood was on it when you return it." Caleb eased the jacket off, and Angelle took it up stairs and put it in the sink to soak.

When she returned, Rachel said, "You can take me home now... All of you."

Will gave Caleb a disgusted look, and Caleb shrugged apologetically. They walked to the red convertible and crawled in. As they drove, Will said, "I have another idea."

"Nope!" Rachel responded.

"Here me out, woman! Mr. Pigg's is on the way to your house. I'm famished. How about it, gang? I know you ladies didn't eat before the ball."

"And how would you know that? Are you psychic?" Rachel retorted.

"Girls don't eat when they're nervous. You two were so nervous when we arrived, your faces were paler than a cadaver. What about it?"

"I could eat a bite," Angelle said, "now that the excitement's over. I know the food is excellent."

"I could eat a goat," Rachel said. "And yes, you're right, I didn't have any dinner, Mr. Smarty Pants."

"Good," Will said, "we finally agree on something."

They headed north on US 51. Angelle eased over close to Caleb and whispered, "Tell me more about Emma, and why Chris obviously feels threatened by you. Why did he threaten to kill you if you didn't stay away from Emma? I can understand why he's so jealous. I know she's gorgeous and rich and high class. I could understand why you might like her more than me, but—"

"Slow down," Caleb whispered, amused by her description and concern. "She means absolutely nothing to me, even though she is gorgeous and wealthy and very, very high class. But, I love you. Nobody but you…will never love anyone but you. Emma is a flirt and a tease. It runs Chris crazy. She's flirted with me a few times at the club. That's all."

Angelle snuggled up to him and put her head over on his shoulder, looking up into his smiling eyes, and said, "That's what I wanted to hear you say."

"Here's the turn," Will announced. "It's not too late for you gals to change your mind."

"Nope," Rachel said.

"Aw, come on, Red, where's your sense of adventure! I'd like to take you two queens into that place and let those rednecks see what two good-looking gals look like."

"Nope!" She pointed down the road and said, "Home." Then pointed at the road leading to Mr. Pigg's place and said, "One or the other."

"I can see it's going to take a while to train you," Will said.

"Huh!" Rachel responded, wrinkling her face. "You should live so long."

Will reluctantly turned at the intersection and grumbled all the way to Mr. Pigg's place. Most of the ballgame crowd had eaten earlier, and the place wasn't crowded. Will pulled in and parked. They unloaded and walked in.

Mr. Pigg looked at Caleb, shook his head, and asked, "Where was the train wreck? Did anyone else get killed?"

"Nope," Caleb said. "Only my reputation."

"Your reputation!" Rachel snapped. "Mr. Pigg, I'd like to ask you a personal question. Do you know what color my panties are?"

Mr. Pigg winced, giving her a wary look. "Of course not," he responded.

"Then you're probably the only person in Marston County who doesn't know," Rachel said.

Mr. Pigg continued backing away, holding his hands out saying, I ain't touching that. He turned to Will and said, "Sorry you weren't out there to help our boys today."

"Not as sorry as I am," Will responded, remorsefully.

"We'll get 'em next year," Mr. Pigg encouraged.

"If Will doesn't pull one of his idiotic stunts again, we might," Rachel said.

Will leaned back giving Rachel a hard look, becoming irritated and hurt by her persistent badgering, and commented, "Do you have a personal vendetta against me?"

"I was simply stating a fact," Rachel said, grinning and realizing she had struck a nerve.

"You don't worry about me, Red. I'll be there. There'll be hell to pay for my—mistake. I'm paying for it now, but they'll pay later."

"Let's order," Caleb said, trying to quell a smoldering volcano.

"Good idea," Will responded.
"Great idea," Rachel added.
"Stupendous idea," Will enhanced the comment.
"Colossal idea," Rachel topped his adjective.
"Enough!" Caleb yelled. "We'll all have indigestion."

Mr. Pigg had stood near them, his head moving from side to side as they verbally jousted. "What do we have here, a lover's spat?"

Rachel put her hands on her hips and looked up at Mr. Pigg as if he had called her a dirty name.

Caleb's hand shot up quickly, and he said, "I want your famous pork po-boy and a Coke. Angelle, what would you like? He has barbecue plates with beans, slaw, potato salad, and even ribs."

"I'm not that hungry," Angelle said.

"That's understandable," Caleb said, giving Will and Rachel a hard look.

"Could I get half of a po-boy? I like beef better."

"Sweetheart," Mr. Pigg said, "you can get anything you want, even me when you get tired of that washed-up prize fighter." He gave her a little wink.

Will's steam had cooled somewhat. He said, "What do you want to eat, Red?"

"What are you having?" Rachel queried.

"I'm going to eat three pork po-boys," Will said, nodding.

"Then I'll have three myself," she mimicked.

"What?" Will gasped, his mouth gaped open. "Do you have a hollow leg?"

"Don't worry, I'll pay for mine," she said.

"Don't be foolish," he said. "Make that four po-boys for me," Will said to Mr. Pigg, giving Rachel a fake smile.

"Make it four for me, also," Rachel smirked.

Mr. Pigg threw up his hands and rushed back behind the counter. In record time, he brought out a large platter of po-boys piled so high they could have fed half the population of Rhode

Island. "Do you two mind if I sit and watch?" he asked. "I've never seen any two people eat that much before...Not in a week."

Will looked at Rachel and grinned. She returned the grin. The contest was on. Will began to stuff the po-boys down. He finished two before Rachel had her napkin tucked in. He had eaten three before. *Four might be stretching it,* he thought, *but no woman will ever beat me at anything, especially not this redheaded chili pepper.* He was halfway through his third one as he watched Rachel nibble on hers like a mouse. *I got her now,* he thought as he finished the third one.

Mr. Pigg walked over and cautioned, "You better not eat a fourth one, Will. It's going to make you sick."

Caleb and Angelle leisurely ate their meal, enjoying each other's company, and watching Will make a fool out of himself. Will chewed and chewed and chewed as it became more and more difficult to swallow. Rachel continued to nibble on her po-boy, smiling at him. Will managed to get half of the fourth one down, but he was starting to feel strange. He laid the last half down and said, "I think I'll wait on you, Red. It looks like we'll be here until dawn before you finish your other three."

"I have no intentions of eating the other three. I'm taking them home so Mother won't have to cook dinner tomorrow."

Will's jaw dropped. He gave her a strange look, realizing he'd been had. He didn't know whether to get angry, laugh, or get sick. He didn't have to decide. Suddenly, he jumped up and ran for the restroom. They could hear him heaving and heaving. Rachel burst out laughing.

Caleb wanted to laugh, but he didn't want Will to hear him. He snickered quietly and said, "You're a wicked woman, Rachel. You realize he actually likes you, and you know, he doesn't like many people."

Rachel retorted, "That's his problem. He needed a lesson in humility..." She continued, "Caleb, I've often wondered just how you two became so close. Your personalities are so opposite."

"You don't pick your friends, they pick you, and he picked me. I have no idea why. But I love him like a brother. There isn't anything in this world he wouldn't do for me, or me him."

"How can you tolerate his—?"

"Because there's another Will inside him that wants to get out. He hasn't yet learned how to let him out, but I'm going to help him."

"Good luck, miracle boy. I hope I live to see that day," Rachel said skeptically.

Caleb told her, "When he comes back, go easy on him because he's a volcano ready to erupt at anytime. Nobody's ever got the best of him before."

"I'll get off his case. I've had my fun for tonight," she said earnestly. "May I get a bag for these po-boys Mr. Pigg?"

Mr. Pigg handed her a paper sack and said, "Put them in the refrigerator tonight. Just warm them tomorrow and they'll be fine."

Will sneaked out of the restroom, red-faced with embarrassment and said, "Are we all through?" He waited for Rachel's cutting remark. It didn't come.

They all said, "Yes."

Then Will reached for his wallet. He frantically slapped every pocket, but there was no wallet. "Oh shit!" he mumbled. He gestured for Caleb to come to him.

"You got to be kidding," Rachel whispered. "This is priceless. Mr. Cool, the richest boy at Marston, doesn't have a penny on him."

"Don't say anything," Angelle pleaded. Rachel laughed under her breath and nodded.

"You have any money?" Will whispered with a fearful look. "I'll pay you back as soon as we get to the dorm."

Caleb slapped his pants and said, "All I have is some change on me. I didn't bring any money. I didn't think we were going anywhere except to the ball."

"Now, ain't this a revolting development," Will muttered. "This ain't happening to me."

Rachel stood up, opened her small purse, and took out a twenty-dollar bill. She walked over and put it on the counter, turned, walked back, and sat down with a smug look on her face. Mr. Pigg had watched the boy's embarrassment and had no intention of making them pay for the food. But he couldn't resist the opportunity to watch Will eat a little humble pie, knowing him as he did. He fought the urge to burst out laughing. He picked up the bill, then looked at Will and Caleb and shook his head. He grabbed Rachel's change from the cash register, put it on the counter, and walked back to the kitchen, shaking his head, hardly able to restrain his laughter.

"You give her the change," Will said. "I'm too humiliated to face her wrath and that venomous tongue."

"I'll pay her back Monday," Caleb said. "This could happen to anyone."

"I'm not anyone," Will snapped. "I never did anything so stupid in my life."

"Well, you have now," Caleb said, "so get over it." They walked back to the table. Caleb handed Rachel the change and said, "Rachel, I'll bring the rest of the money to you Monday if that's all right. We both messed up."

"I'll pay for my four po-boys," Rachel said. "But I really need the rest of the money. That was my lunch money for this month."

Will felt guilt for the first time in his life and said, "We'll run back to the campus and get my wallet. You'll need some money before Monday."

"Tomorrow's Sunday. I'll be at church all day. I won't need it until Monday. Don't worry about it. It's no big deal. It could happen to anyone. Even you." She couldn't restrain her laughter. They all began to laugh. They laughed so loud even Will began to chuckle. Mr. Pigg walked out of the kitchen, laughing so hard his eyes became teary.

"See, Will, you can laugh at yourself without getting angry," Caleb said. "Laughter is the music of the heart. It's the best medicine in the world. At least that's what Uncle Houston always says."

They walked out, loaded up, and started to Rachel's house. Rachel directed them. They turned on 'Possum Corner Road. "You should recognize this road, Will. I think you drove down it a few dozen times last year."

"And just how would you know that?" Will questioned.

"Nobody in this county drives a new red convertible except you, plus you drive like a bat out of hell and dust our house every time you pass. Everybody knows that you hang out at the Briar Patch on the weekend. There are no secrets in this community. And I know who you go to see. She lives about a half mile down this road. Jacob and I ride our bicycles down the road all the time, and we've seen your car parked in her yard at dawn a dozen times or more. Anything else you want to know about yourself?" Rachel said smugly. "There's the church on the left. The parsonage is just a few yards past it."

The parsonage was a small white frame house with a weathering tin roof. The yard was clean and well groomed. A few shrubs grew close to the steps of the front porch landing. The porch light was on. Will hopped out and ran around to open Rachel's door. She hopped out before he was able to get around the car. She hurriedly walked to the small porch. Will hustled to keep up with her long stride. At the porch, she turned and said, "The night was … entertaining, to say the least."

"I had a nice time, too," Will said. "When will you be available to do it again?"

"Are you asking me out on a date?" Rachel said with an appalled look on her face.

"Uh, I think that's what I did," Will said. "Did I not make myself clear?"

"You, you, you must be kidding. If we were the last two people on this earth, I wouldn't date you."

"Stop kidding," Will said. "How about next Saturday?"

"Are you—did you hear me? This was not a date. I did this for Caleb, so good night."

"Wooh! Wooh! Wooh!" Will said, walking around in front of her, blocking the door. "What about the good night kiss? I'm not letting you off that easy. It's traditional to give your date a good night kiss. I'm a very traditional guy."

"I'd sooner kiss a goat than you, Will James. I have a little brother that thinks you walk on water. I'd hate for him to know the real you."

"Why do you say things that you don't mean?" Will said. "I know you're dying to kiss me."

"You are unbelievable… My dad'll be coming to the door any minute. I'll let him tell you why I won't kiss you good night."

"He won't be doing that, Red. He trusts you. That's what preachers do. They trust people. That's why you live in this shack. I'll bet there's not a member of his congregation that doesn't live in a better house than this one."

Rachel's face became as red as her hair and she said, "This isn't a shack to ordinary people. There are dozens of these people that live in worse houses than this one. We're warm in the winter and comfortable in the summer. That's all anyone needs in life. Now, get out of my way before I scream."

"Is that your final word, Red?"

"It was my final word the first time you asked."

"Okay. What time do services start tomorrow?"

"Ten o'clock in the morning. Why would you care?"

"If I don't get a kiss, I'll be here sitting by you tomorrow morning, telling everyone that you're my gal. I'll tell them what we did tonight."

"You wouldn't! Not that we did anything that I'm ashamed of except…"

"I would, and I will," Will said firmly.

"No one needs to be in church anymore than you, but not sitting by me."

"One little kiss, and I'll let you off the hook." Rachel looked at Caleb with fiery eyes. Caleb had heard everything, and he slid down in the seat.

"One little kiss, and positively no tongue," she said. "I'll knock you crazy if you do."

"Well, one kinda little kiss. However, I would want you to know that I'm kissing you if you accept my terms."

"Do you swear that you'll never tell anyone that I let you kiss me?"

"Red, do I look like a kiss and tell guy?"

She stood there for awhile rocking back and forth and finally stopped, put her hands behind her back, and said, "Go ahead and get it over with."

"This is not a lynching," Will said. "It's supposed to be enjoyable."

"You better get it over with before I start screaming."

"Just one other thing," Will said, "and I will."

She gave Will a disgusted look, put her hands on her hips, and waited.

"It's not much," he said. "You have to promise to close your eyes. I can't kiss a girl with her eyes open. It's meaningless if the eyes are open."

"It's meaningless anyway, but if it'll get you off my porch, I'll close my eyes." She resumed her position of disgust and, with a slight smirk, said, "Look my eyes are closing. Now, get it over with quickly."

"Tighter," Will said. "I can still see those fiery green emeralds" Rachel closed them tightly, causing her face to wrinkle even more. When Will was sure they were securely closed, he tiptoed around her, took a giant step onto the dew kissed grass, making no noise, and crept quickly to the car. The door was still open, so he eased the door shut, and reached for the key.

"What are you waiting on," Rachel said. "My eyes are closed. I'm waiting in painful anticipation."

Will started the car. Her eyes popped open. Her jaw dropped, and she couldn't believe what had happened. Will stuck his head out the window and said, "Gotcha. 'He who laughs last, laughs best.' See you at ten a.m." He turned around, still grinning at her.

"You didn't get anyone but yourself," Rachel yelled. "That kiss you didn't take is going to drive you crazy. It was your first and last chance, and you blew it, big boy. Sleep well." She opened the door, went inside, and turned out the porch light.

Will pulled away and said, "You know she's right. I was looking forward to that goodnight kiss. She's the only girl that I never kissed good night. You were right, Corn Shuck. I like the kid. It may take awhile to get her under control, but she has potential."

"Will, I'm going to give you the same advice you gave me. Give it up. She's absolutely forbidden fruit."

Will looked back over the seat at Angelle snuggled up next to Caleb. He said, "I gave you some bogus advice, didn't I?"

"Like Rachel said earlier, the jury is still out on that. She still has that ring on... You two have nothing in common except football. She does love football," Caleb said.

"I'll give her two weeks before she's groping at my feet," Will said, trying to convince himself that there might be a chance for him. "Did you two notice what a great dancer she is? And those eyes, beautiful green eyes. I didn't even have to bend down and get a cramp in my back when we danced." Will rambled on about Rachel's good qualities, ignoring Caleb and Angelle.

Angelle put her hands to Caleb's cheeks and began a kiss that lasted until Will pulled up in front of the dorm. He looked back over the seat and said, "You two need a room."

Angelle looked up at Will somewhat embarrassed by his remark and said, "Let's go see if the blood came out of the jacket." They went into the dorm lobby, and Caleb waited while she ran up to get the jacket. She lifted the jacket from the red water, rinsed it a few times, and thought, *They'll never know it was bloodsoaked.* She wrapped a towel around it and ran downstairs. She handed it to Caleb. "It looks clean," she said, brightly.

"Thank you. Did you have a good time? You know this was our first date."

"When I'm with you, I always have a good time."

"Will you marry me?"

"Possibly…possibly I'll do that—someday."

"I certainly hope you wouldn't kiss anyone else the way you kissed me unless you intend to marry them."

Angelle looked around the parlor making sure the dorm mother was not there. She put her arms around Caleb and kissed him passionately. After the kiss, she stepped back and said, "Do you mean like that?"

"You know exactly what I mean, you beautiful, heavenly creature. Good night, my love."

"See you tomorrow morning at the hospital," Angelle said, the words sending chills down her spine. For a brief few hours she and Caleb had been able to escape the impending heartbreak.

Caleb hopped into the car and Will pulled away. "I just met the girl I'm going to marry," Will announced, "and I owe it all to you."

Caleb almost swallowed his tongue, hearing Will's words. "I don't want to discourage you, Will, because I don't think you could ever do better than Rachel. But there's a little problem you haven't considered."

"What might that be?"

"One word. Loathe. I think that's the word she used to describe her feelings about you. Yep. That's it," Caleb said

"You continue to underestimate me, Corn Shuck. She's crazy about me. I'll have her begging me for a date in a few weeks. I can turn on the charm when necessary."

Caleb took time to digest Will's proclamation. They parked at the stadium and Will said, "I'll never sleep tonight. Let's go to The Briar Patch and sit and talk awhile. I have to make some plans. I need Rachel's class schedule and a little more information about her hobbies, likes and dislikes, and what she does in her spare time."

"That's easy, Will. She goes to class, the library, then home, milks the cow, and studies. You heard her. That's why you never saw her before. She's not a party girl, Will. She's a home-girl."

"Did you see those legs?" Will asked, totally oblivious to Caleb discouragement. "Long and shapely. She meets every requirement that I set for the woman I want to marry. Beautiful, great personality, intelligent, sense of humor, great legs, and all the other equipment in the right places. You know what I mean. Large enough to give me big offspring. No runts. The most important quality is that she's a virgin. Let me qualify that, a virgin now."

"You left out the most important quality, Will. I didn't hear the word love."

"You know my feelings about love. It's an old-fashioned, out-dated, over-rated concept fostered by women to trap a man. Marriage is about sex, plain and simple. When you've sown your wild oats and it's time to settle down and raise a family, you find a woman that meets your qualifications and can satisfy your sexual desires, and you marry her. I do believe in commitment, faithfulness, respect, and responsibility. Things my father never learned. Those qualities make a winning football team as well as a successful marriage. You say you love Angelle. Describe love to me."

"I want to be with her. I want to take care of her. I want to hold her and make love to her. There is nothing I wouldn't do to make her happy. I want to grow old with her, and I want her to have my children."

"Huh!" Will said. "That's a little extreme, isn't it?"

"Which part?" Caleb asked. Will thought a second, then shrugged. Caleb continued, "I think you need to slow down and think about this. Tomorrow you might feel this way about someone else. You don't fall in love and start thinking about marriage after the first date. That's not your style."

"Corn Shuck, you have a lame memory. What did you tell me about Angelle the first time you saw her. You hadn't even talked to her."

Caleb grinned and said, "You got me there, but I knew she was the one."

They stepped out of the car. Will leaned against the hood and said, "Did you see the way she danced with me. She didn't dance like a preacher's kid. She was silky smooth and limber as a switch. Those firm breasts were pressed against my chest. I can still feel them."

"Don't talk like that, Will. You make it sound dirty," Caleb chided.

"Sure," Will said, "and I suppose you didn't notice Angelle's breasts or that blonde siren's breasts against your chest? Do you think they don't know how it affects a man? They love it! Why do you think they wear those low cut dresses revealing as much as they can without being arrested."

"I'm not going to talk about that any more, Will. I'll tell you this and I'm through. When you fall in love, you'll see that it's not at all about sex, and what I said is not that extreme. I don't want to burst your bubble. I'm happy that you liked Rachel. But you and I both know rich boys don't marry poor girls. They play with them and have their fun, but when the time comes to marry, they marry from their own class. I don't think you should get your hopes too high. Rachel's different from any girl you've ever dated. She's heard things about you that she'll never accept or forgive. You'll never get a date with her."

"Why are you trying to discourage me?" Will said. "I thought you'd be overjoyed that I've found someone like Rachel that I could really get involved with."

"It's hard to talk to you, Will. I know how you blow up when someone doesn't agree with you. I just don't want you to get hurt. Rachel isn't going to date you. She has a preconceived notion about wealthy people like you. She'll never change her mind. She'll find a nice quiet, intelligent, reserved young man who shares her beliefs and values, and that's who she'll marry. That's what girls like her do."

Will became angry and his face turned red. Caleb backed away and said, "That's why I can't really talk to you."

"You go to hell!" Will yelled, snatching the car door open. He jumped back in the car and peeled rubber half way across the parking lot.

Caleb put his hand to his forehead and said, "When will I learn to keep my stupid mouth shut? What have I done now?" Caleb stood there a few minutes looking into space. Finally he said, "Not tonight, pal. I'm not going after him this time. He'll be drunk before I could get to the Briar Patch. He'd whip my butt if I did. Anyway, there are people around here tonight that are not spoiled, over-indulgent, child-like, egotists that have some real problems."

CHAPTER TWENTY-SEVEN

As Caleb stood there disgusted with himself and Will, Doc's Plymouth came flying across the parking lot. The car skidded to a stop near Caleb. *Oh my Lord,* Caleb thought. *Have mercy on Mr. Luther.* Caleb ran to the car, snatched the door open, and jumped in expecting to see Doc. He was shocked speechless to see Emma behind the wheel. She pulled away quickly before Caleb could speak or protest. Emma said nothing, but drove swiftly through the campus with a big smile and continued to US 51.

"Would you like to tell me where we're going, and why you kidnapped me?" Caleb finally asked.

She cut her eyes at him giving him an impish grin. "You'll see," she said.

Caleb became concerned and extremely nervous, knowing Emma as he did. "Does Doc know you're out in his car?"

"Of course. I told him I wanted to go for a ride and get something at the drive-in."

"Oh," Caleb said, somewhat relieved. "We're going to the drive-in?" He received the same impish grin.

Caleb looked out the window as they flew by the 51 drive-in. "You just passed the drive-in," he said as his heart began to race. Emma laughed and continued to drive swiftly. "Tell me where we're going?" he insisted. "Do you know what time it is?"

Emma turned down James Marston Lane. In seconds they flew by Doc's house. Caleb slid down in the seat as they passed. She continued down the street passing Burt's house. Caleb looked and the lights were off. *He doesn't water the greens tonight,* he thought. He was sure what Emma had in mind, and his heart rate continued to rise. "Uh—do you think this is a good idea?" he asked.

Emma pulled into the driveway that went by the pro-shop and continued to the maintenance shed and parked in the darkest spot behind the pro-shop.

She was wearing a short skirt and a tight white sweater. She was a gorgeous sight in the moonlight. Caleb's heart raced as he pondered how he was going to get out of this predicament without embarrassing or hurting Emma. No sooner than she had turned off the lights she slid over close to him and said, "I want to apologize for Chris's behavior. He's a fool and spoiled rotten. I hated to go to the dance with him, but it was the only way I could get to see you again. I wanted so desperately to be with you tonight. I'm in love with you, Caleb, and I think you have feelings for me, too. No one ever kissed me the way you did before or made me feel that way. I've dreamed of nothing but this moment for weeks, and here we are together at last. I have to confess that I was very jealous when I saw you with that attractive girl with the beautiful brown eyes and olive complexion. Then I saw that large diamond on her finger, sparkling. I knew you couldn't afford one that large, so I asked the girl sitting by me about her. She said you two were just friends and her fiancé' was in the service… Put your arms around me and hold me and kiss me like before." Caleb didn't have time to respond before her warm moist lips were on his and she had eased over in his lap.

"Put your arms around me and hold me close like before," she whispered. She began to smother him with her passionate kisses. They were wild and hungry in a near savage way. He had never been kissed like this before, even by Angelle. He fought the urge to yield to her seductive magnetism; however, after a few minutes in each others' arms he began to feel powerless. The longer they kissed the deeper he fell under her spell. When their passion heightened to an almost uncontrolled state, she snatched her sweater off, unhooked her bra, and gently eased Caleb's face to her full, large breasts and continued to hold him tightly, stroking his head. Caleb had lost all control and Emma knew it. She had him where she had dreamed of. Caleb was so deeply under her seductive spell that he lost all will power. His mind was in a fog of ecstasy and unbridled passion. She stopped abruptly, crawled over the back seat, unbuttoned her skirt, snatched it off, and slid her panties down. She began to plead, "Come to me quickly, my love."

Caleb looked back over the seat at her beautiful naked body gleaming in the moonlight. Never having looked on a woman's naked body before, he felt faint and breathless. He'd never seen anything so perfect and so beautiful. His heart jumped into his throat racing out of control. He desperately tried to fight the temptation to ease over the seat and make love to her, although he knew he would regret for the rest of his life. He couldn't take his eyes off her as she reached for him still pleading for him to come.

He regained some senses and managed to stammer, "I, I—I can't rob you of your virtue in the back seat of a car. I can't do that to you."

"I'm not a virgin," she confessed. "Chris and I—come to me," she pleaded desperately. "I want you, and I know you want me."

Caleb's resistance was melting away as he continued to gaze on her beautiful and perfect body. He put his hands on the top of the seat and started to swing his leg over the seat as a battle raged inside him, and the temptation began to overpower him as it seemed to pulled him toward her, while his conscience kept saying, "Don't give into temptation. You'll never forgive yourself."

He never had to make the decision because a bright light hit his face like a bolt of lightning.

A familiar voice broke the spell as Burt yelled, "Doc, is that you?" Burt stuck the light to the window revealing Caleb's horror. Then the light flashed on the back seat. The light stayed on the back seat a few seconds. Emma grabbed her skirt and balled herself up trying desperately to cover her body.

"Roll the window down, son," Burt said. Caleb's ecstasy turned quickly to panic and shame. A pain like a searing poker hit Caleb's stomach, and he felt sick.

Caleb rolled the window down slowly and stared into the light. Burt turned off his flashlight. "What were you two thinking? Do either of you have a brain in your head? Do you want to ruin your lives? I'll guarantee you that neither of you had any protection for what you were about to do. Take Emma home. We'll talk about this tomorrow. I can't believe what I'm seeing. You are the last person in the world I would ever have thought—I can't imagine what Doc and the judge would do," Burt said, shaking his head.

"You're not going to tell Father, are you, Mr. Burt?" Emma pleaded. "Father would kill me—and Doc..."

"No. I'm not going to tell anyone. I couldn't hurt them. I think too much of them. Get dressed and get off this property immediately. Don't ever pull this stunt again, either of you."

Burt trudged across the grass, shaking his head. Emma dressed quickly without a word and they drove by Burt as he stood in his doorway.

"That was the most embarrassing thing I've ever experienced," Emma said. "You don't think he'll tell Doc, do you?" Emma asked nervously.

"No. He'll do what he said."

"I wish he hadn't come," Emma said angrily. "It wasn't any of his business what we were doing. We're adults now. Is there some place safe where we can go? I'm so in love with you. I don't think it's wrong to make love to the person you're going to marry. I can't wait four more years." They passed Doc's house as he was getting into Edith's Cadillac. Emma stomped the gas pedal to the floorboard. "Did he see us!" Caleb gasped.

"He never looked up. He seemed to be in a hurry. Must have an emergency at the hospital."

Caleb's heart sank as he considered what the emergency could be. "Take me to the dorm quickly. I think I know what the emergency is."

"Oh, no!" Emma protested. "I won't be back until Thanksgiving. Let's go somewhere else."

"Take me to the dorm, now!" Caleb demanded. "I think my friend just died. There are other doctors on call tonight. That's the only reason Doc would go out at this time—unless he's looking for you."

"He's not looking for me. I use his car every time I stay with him."

"Hurry!" Caleb said.

"All right!" Emma responded, somewhat irritated at his tone. "I'm going to tell Chris that it's over between us. He's selfish and despicable sometimes. I'll tell him that I'm in love with you. You better watch out for him, Caleb. He's mean enough to do something really bad to you. He cursed you all the way to Doc's house."

A voice in Caleb's head kept saying, *Tell her that you don't love her. You'll have to tell her someday. Do it. Do it now.* "Ah—ah—ah." That was all he could manage.

"Did you want to say something?" She said, looking curiously at him.

"Just hurry. I think a boy that I love just died."

"You were serious back there, weren't you? I thought you were making excuses not to park with me because you're kinda old-fashioned and timid. I should have known better because you weren't timid before I crawled into the back seat."

Thank the Lord you did, Caleb thought. *Thank the Lord twice that Burt came along. I almost made the biggest mistake of my life. Now, I have to face Mr. Burt, not to mention the Lord.*

"Why are you so silent?" Emma said, sensing coldness in his demeanor. "Hold my hand while I drive," she said, giving him a teasing smile.

"You just drive with both hands, and put the pedal to the metal."

They wheeled into the parking lot and stopped in front of the dorm. John David was returning from the Ball. He noticed Doc's car skidded to a halt. Emma draped her long arms around Caleb before he could escape and said, "Kiss me like you love me, or I'll hold you here until you do. Give me a kiss that'll last until Thanksgiving." Caleb put his arms around her and kissed her passionately, but Emma didn't want to release him. "You can do better than that," she said still holding on to him.

"Please, Emma, I really have to get to the hospital. Now let me go!"

"All right, party pooper, but when I return, we're going out of town to some secluded place where we won't be interrupted. I'll be dreaming about it. I know you will too."

She released him and he said, "Good night, Emma," and ran to the stairs. Emma pulled away.

John David had stood and watched the lip-lock for a good two minutes and waited for Caleb. "It looks like you won the fight and the prize," he said with an edge to his voice.

They started up the stairs and Caleb said, "You wouldn't believe me if I told you what happened."

"All I have to say is that seeing is believing,"

"I don't have time to explain," Caleb said, rushing into his room stripping off the rest of the tux. "I'll explain later what you think you saw because sometimes seeing can be deceiving."

"I'm not judging you. You don't have to explain anything to me. Emma is the kind of girl who could make a monk scale the wall. If you say it was an innocent kiss, who am I to dispute you? I believe you. I'm not sure Angelle would, but what I don't understand is when did the switch occur?"

"That's a long story, and I don't have time to defend myself. I think Buckie just died. I saw Doc rushing toward the hospital. We'll talk later."

"Do you want me to go with you?" John David asked.

"I think it would be better if you didn't go right now. Luther won't be in any condition to talk to anyone. He and I got pretty close these last few weeks. I might be able to comfort him."

"Go!" John David said. "I don't need an explanation about the kiss. Heck, I'd probably kiss her too, if I got the chance ... and I'm engaged."

Caleb dressed in record time and ran out the door. John David's door was open. As Caleb passed the room, he yelled, "I was kidnapped!"

John David yelled back. "If I weren't engaged, she could kidnap me any time she wanted."

Caleb glanced at his watch as he ran down the stairs. "Midnight," he said. "What a terrible time for Buckie to meet the Lord. Luther won't rest for days."

He flew up the stairs at the hospital and saw Doc as he was coming out of Buckie's room.

"Is it over?" he gasped, rushing up to Doc.

"Gladys called me and said she thought he'd died. She couldn't find a pulse. By the time I arrived here, she was able to find a slight, irregular pulse. He's in a coma but he'll never come out of it."

"Does Mr. Luther know?"

"He knows. He just sits by the bed holding Buckie's hand. His head is down, and he just stares at him. God forgive me, but I hope the end comes quickly. I don't know how much more he can endure."

"Is Ruby here?" Doc nodded.

"Should I go in?"

"No. Not now. He doesn't need company, he needs closure. I hope he doesn't have a gun at his house. Go get some rest, Caleb. Tomorrow's going to be a bad day. He'll need you then."

Caleb went back to the dorm and tried to sleep. His mind wouldn't stop rolling. The events of the week and particularly this night kept flashing through his mind like a fast motion picture.

Will crept in around four a.m. He didn't seem to be drunk. Caleb pretended to be asleep. Will quietly undressed and crawled in bed. Caleb felt a little better now that Will was back. He managed to get a few hours of sleep. At dawn, Caleb crawled out of his sweat-soaked bed and dressed quietly, being careful not to wake Will.

Caleb and Angelle arrived at the hospital about the same time as the sun was rising. They spent the morning standing by Luther and Buckie. They tried to comfort Luther and Ruby. Lucky couldn't understand why his brother wouldn't wake to play with him. At ten-thirty, Caleb said "I have to go to work, but I'll be back as soon as the lunch crowd leaves, Mr. Luther."

"Please comes back," Luther whispered in a broken voice that was almost inaudible. Caleb nodded, gave him a hug, and went to the club. The dinner crowd was large as usual. Abe and Caleb rushed around serving them. After everyone left, they cleaned the place in record time. Caleb went out to get in his truck. Burt came walking up and stood by the truck.

"We didn't actually make love, Mr. Burt. I wanted to but thankfully you came up and saved me. There's nothing you can say that'll make me any more ashamed of what I almost did, so let me have it."

"Was it your idea to come back here?" he asked.

"Does it matter?"

"It matters to me."

"Doc's car came flying into the parking lot at school. I thought Buckie had died so I ran and jumped in the car. I didn't know Emma was driving. She pulled away before I could get out. She didn't tell me where she was headed. I didn't know her intentions until she parked where you saw us. The rest was absolute sin on my part. I'm not faulting her for what happened. I could have gotten out of the car and walked away, but I didn't. I am truly in love with Angelle, and I can't believe what I almost did. I'm very ashamed."

Burt scratched his head and looked at Caleb's repentant eyes. He said, "Who was it that said, 'The best of men are men at best?'" Caleb shrugged. "Son, I'm not condoning what you did. But there's always a lesson to be learned from our mistakes. Listen, and learn it well. There's many a good man who fell into that trap and ruined their lives. The most notable was King David. His life was never the same after his sin. The lesson to be learned is never to allow yourself to get caught in a situation like that. There's absolutely no human power in this universe stronger than a woman's seductive charm. They've always known it. Delilah, Ruth, Cleopatra, Helen of Troy, Marilyn Monroe, Elizabeth Taylor, and millions of other beautiful women have it. They were all so desirable they could make a man climb a black locust tree just to catch a glimpse of their beauty. Emma's right up there with the best of them. There's not a man living who wouldn't turn his head to catch a second glimpse of Emma's beauty. Guard yourself against getting into that situation, and you won't have to fight the temptation. Now—it's over as far as I'm concerned. I'll never mention it again."

Abe came to the door and said, "Doc just called and said tell you—it's over. I'm sorry to have to give you the bad news, son."

Caleb's heart sank. Remorse quickly turned to sorrow. A tear ran down his cheek. "Oh Lord," he murmured, "please give Mr. Luther courage to make it through these next few days."

"I'm sorry, Caleb," Burt said. "I know how much you loved that little boy. Can I do anything?"

Caleb answered, "You already have." Caleb jumped into his truck and rushed to the hospital and up the stairs. Doc, Angelle, and Gladys were standing by Buckie's door. Caleb ran over to them and asked, "How's Luther?"

Doc shook his head with a grim look and replied, "He wailed for a long time, and now he's draped over the body. I've already called Mr. Pride at the funeral home. I told him to give Luther a couple of hours before he comes for the body. I'll make all the arrangements with Luther when he's calmer. I'm going to suggest a service at ten a.m. tomorrow. He doesn't need all this stress hanging over him too long. It'll give him time to go home and rest. He's in no condition to make a decision now."

"What about Ruby and Lucky?" Caleb asked.

"Thankfully, the child is sleeping in her arms. She just sits in the chair next to the wall and weeps silently," Doc said.

"Can I go in, Doc?" Caleb asked. Doc nodded.

"I'll go with you," Angelle said. They eased in and walked up by Luther and put their arms around him.

Luther sat up and leaned back against them. He put his arms around them and said, "Look at my sweet boy. He's a sleepin' so peaceable now. He ain't a hurtin' no more, is he, Caleb?" He began to weep again.

"He looked into the face of God this morning," Caleb said, "and he's not hurtin' any more. The Angels took his hand and led him to glory, Mr. Luther. Buckie has a new body and the mind of Christ. He wants you to mourn for him for a while, then he wants you to get up, wipe the tears from your eyes, and thank God for taking him to heaven."

"I'm a gonna try to do what you say, Caleb, "But I'm a feelin' so empty inside, liken I ges lost everythin' what was import' to me."

"We're here for you," Angelle said, "and we love you so much."

Luther leaned his head on their shoulders and said, "I couldn't o' made it if it weren't fer you two. Ain't nobody Buckie loved more'n you." Then he leaned forward and put his head on Buckie's breast and sobbed. Angelle never realized that Luther had held her tightly in his arms.

Angelle and Caleb walked over to Ruby. Caleb leaned down and kissed her cheek. "My heart breaks for you, Mrs. Ruby. I feel your pain."

She took Caleb's hand and squeezed gently. "I didn't know people like you existed until I come here. I'm never going to forget your kindness to me and my boys and …"

The door opened and Brother Branch eased in. Luther stood as Brother Branch hugged him and whispered words of comfort and encouragement in his ear. Luther nodded and said, "My boy shore love' to go to church and hear you a preachin'. He loved them boys in his Sunday School, too. Look at all them letters they writ to him. Ever Sunday they writ him a new one. Before Caleb come, he was a'readin' them ever time I got back to the room. My boy was so happy 'fore he got sick." He broke down crying again.

Luther turned to Angelle and Caleb and said, "You git back to work, Miss Angelle, and you go git some rest, Caleb. You canst do no more good here. I'm gonna be fine. I gest want to spend a little more time wit' my boy 'fore they come to git him."

"I've come to take Luther home," Brother Branch said. "I'm going to stay with him tonight if he needs me. Will I see y'all at the church?"

"I'll be there," Caleb said. "Buckie asked me to say a few words, but I'd be there even if he hadn't."

"Y'all stop worrying about Luther," Brother Branch said. "I'm going to look after him until he's feeling better."

"I'll be outside, Mr. Luther, if you need anything," Angelle said.

Caleb walked over and gave Luther a tender embrace. There was sadness in Luther's eyes, but Caleb could also see relief. "I'll be praying for you, and I'll see you at the church, Caleb said. He walked over to the nurse's station and said somberly to Angelle, "He's doing better than I thought he'd do. I suppose when the end comes, it's actually a relief after all the years of suffering and pain."

Caleb turned to walk away and Angelle asked, "Where are you going?"

"I don't know. Just out into the light."

"I wish I could go with you."

"Do you?" he asked with coldness in his voice that Angelle had never heard before. "Then take off that ring and walk out of here with me. We'll never look back."

"That's not you talking, Caleb," she said. "It's exhaustion and heartache. Go get some rest. You've been our rock too long." He walked away and murmured, "If you only knew."

Caleb went to the golf course. It was crowded as usual. Everyone was having a great time, laughing at each other's bad shots, and telling dirty jokes. A few had beer in their golf bags, and they were all having a merry old time on the course. It seemed to anger Caleb. He walked the rough and watched the merriment and felt contempt for everyone he saw enjoying themselves. "These rich clowns don't have a care in the world," he mumbled, "or do they just not give a ...?" He stopped under a large oak tree away from the fairway and sat down. He put his head between his knees and began to cry. When he could cry no more, he sat up, and leaned back on the trunk of the tree and began to watch again. Then, to his surprise, he saw Doc and Wellington trudging down the fairway pulling their carts behind them. *I can't believe Doc could come and play golf after what just happened?* he thought. *Doesn't he have a heart?*

Doc hooked his ball into the rough near where Caleb was sitting. He walked up and noticed Caleb sitting somberly under the tree. "What are you doing out here?" Doc asked. "I would've thought you had enough of this place without coming here as tired as you must be."

Caleb shrugged and responded, "I don't know. It seemed to be as good a place as any to have a good cry. Why are you here?" Caleb asked sharply.

Doc leaned the club against the cart and walked over to Caleb. He took a long look into his eyes. Then he began to speak softly. "Son, be careful how you judge. If you judge, make a right judgment. You know I seldom play golf on Sunday. That's family day at my home. Do you have any idea how many times I've walked into a room and pronounced a person dead? A person that I dearly loved who is now deceased? No, you don't, and you can't imagine. The first rule in my profession is to separate yourself from personal involvement or you'll go insane. I've never been able to keep that rule. I've never loved a patient any more than I loved that boy. I want to cry out to God, why? Why didn't you give me the skills and knowledge to help him? Why did you leave Luther so alone? There are more questions than answers. Sometimes the burden gets so heavy, I have to walk away. This is how I get away from it. I'm walking off the stress and frustration now. I imagine that's what you are doing out here. Am I right?"

"You're always right, Doc. Forgive me."

"I wish that was so. Now, get up and walk with us. You can pull my cart. The exercise will be good for you. It's the greatest stress reliever in the world."

"Hit the ball, Wellington. You've been standing over it five minutes."

"I'm trying to remember which trick I used yesterday on the practice range."

"I think I heard you say it was #37," Doc said with a chuckle. Caleb laughed deeply for the first time in weeks. Caleb walked the remainder of the nine holes. When they finished, Doc said, "I spoke with Brother Branch and Luther after they removed Buckie's body. They agreed to have the services at ten a.m. tomorrow. I'll come by the dorm at six to pick you up to ride with us. Edith may be going, too. Gladys and Angelle said they wanted to come in Gladys' car so they could get back for their shifts. You know, in case we needed to spend more time there with Luther and Ruby. I'll see you in the morning."

"I do feel better Doc," Caleb said. "I appreciate you coming by and getting me out of the dumps, and I'm sorry for ..."

"Go have a good dinner and get some rest. Tomorrow will be equally as stressful."

The gorgeous sunset with exquisitely brilliant colors of the rainbow spread across the western sky. Caleb looked in awe and murmured, "How can anyone look at that glorious sight and not believe in God? No one except God can paint a canvas like that."

As he continued to drive toward the college, he thought, *I need to go see Buckie.* Then, realizing he would never see Buckie alive again, his sadness returned. He drove slowly to the dorm and went to the cafeteria. Will was there, eating silently and alone, as was his custom. Caleb walked over and sat down by him. "Buckie is dead," he said. Will pushed the half-eaten food away and lowered his head.

After he considered Caleb's words for awhile, he looked up at Caleb, glassy-eyed, and said, "I loved that boy, too, and I'm going to miss him... I'm sorry for blowing up at you last night. I finally realized what you were trying to tell me after I drove half way to Nashville. I almost didn't get back. I was running out of gas. I found a service station near Memphis on the way back. I was running on fumes by then... I know you don't think I have a serious thought in my head except for football, but I was serious when I said Rachel got to me last night. I've thought of nothing but her ever since I left her on the porch wanting to kill me. They weren't sexual fantasies either. I want to date her and prove to her that I can be a gentleman. I believe I could fall in love with her. It hurt me when you said she would marry some reserved young man with the same values and interests that she has or something on that line. Will you help me, please?"

Caleb realized that Will was serious. "I'll do all I can for you. You know that. But, it won't be easy. You'll have to prove to her that you've changed your lifestyle and that you're interested in her as a person instead of what you might want from her."

"I can do that. It won't be easy, but I think I can do that."

"You're serious about her, aren't you?" Caleb said, smiling.

"As serious as I have ever been in my life." Then Will asked, "How did Luther take it? Is he all right?"

"Better than I thought he would. Just the relief of it being over had to help. Doc's picking me up early tomorrow morning to go to the funeral. You want to go with us?"

"Hey, you know me. I can't handle situations like that. Tell Luther—well, you'll know what to say to him. Will you do that?"

Providence and Hard Work Series
You Shall Know the Truth

They went to the dorm. Will tried to read while Caleb tried to study. Neither got much accomplished. There was a somber mood in the dorm after everyone received the word that Buckie had died. Caleb finally gave up on the books. After Will had crashed a dozen books against the wall, he turned out the lights. Caleb spent the next few hours in darkness thinking about his beloved friend. He planned what he would say at the services to honor him and give solace to Luther and Ruby and those that loved Buckie so dearly.

Caleb rose at dawn, showered, shaved, and put on the beautiful suit that Doc had given him. Will watched him dress as he lay in bed. Caleb glanced at his watch and said, "Time to go. Are you sure…?"

"I'm sure," Will said. "Y'all be careful and give Ruby and Luther a hug for me. Tell them—" Will paused, shook his head, and slumped his shoulders.

It was a gray dreary day as Doc and Caleb drove south on US 51. Caleb gazed out the window, oblivious of the sights and sounds outside. The heartache of losing his young friend was weighing heavily on his heart. He was confident that Buckie was with the Lord, and that eased the pain. His concern now was for Luther and Ruby and the precious child. What would become of Luther now that he was alone? How could he help him? What could he say or do to ease his pain? Caleb felt helpless. "Doc," he asked, "What's going to happen to Luther? You don't think he'll give up on life and do something terrible?"

"You read my mind, son," Doc said. "He's lost everything that means anything to him. After the way he responded to Ruby's return and the child, it might have been better for him if she'd not come back. He's a dejected and defeated man now."

"But, Doc, Ruby wants to come home. Why won't he forgive her? She's so beautiful and kind. I had no idea she would be so attractive. I know she wants to come home."

"I have to admit that I was shocked when I saw her myself. But to answer your question, you have to understand why we are the way we are. By nature, man is a wicked creature. Remember after the fall of man what Cain did to Abel, his brother. Not much has changed since that time. Put two babies in a crib with one toy and watch what happens. It won't take long before they'll be scratching and biting over the toy. Adults are not very different. We scratch and claw to get what we want in life even when it hurts others. Even though the great American conflict ended some ninety years ago, the bitterness and hatred that the war fostered still simmers in the heart of most Southerners. It's hard to imagine the ingrained feelings of prejudice that still exists in the Deep South. From birth, we are taught that some segments of our society are inferior to others. Unfortunately, this opinion is not totally unfounded. Now, before you label me a bigot or racist, let me explain. If you were deprived of an education, lived in a shack with only a lamp to see by at night, had parents or a parent with no education, had to work as a common laborer, or maid or cook, were never exposed to culture or the finer things in life, and treated like an animal when you made a mistake or broke the law, would you be inferior? Yes, you would be inferior intellectually and socially. But whose fault would that be? If I'm deprived of an education, is it my fault that I can't read or write or can't speak correctly and sound ignorant when I speak? Times will change and are already changing. We as Southerners don't like to admit it but we've enjoyed it this way. Who doesn't like to be served by others, and we've enjoyed cheap labor. What woman doesn't want someone to clean her house and prepare meals and tend her children? It's our nature to feel that we're a little better or smarter than those less fortunate. It's the way life is and that fact will never change. Luther is the perfect example of being deprived of an education and culture. If you ask him why he's prejudiced, he couldn't answer the question. He has no idea. It's just the way it's been for a hundred years. I don't know what's going to happen to him. I can only pray that the Lord will watch over him as he grieves and tries to find some reason to go on living.

Providence and Hard Work Series
You Shall Know the Truth

I've been planning to talk to you, Caleb. I suppose this is as good a time as any. What I'm going to say has nothing to do with the fact that my son and your father probably died side by side at Normandy in 1944. You should know by now that Edith and I feel as though God has given us another son. You know that I'm not in the best health. I've had some heart problems in the past, and I battle high blood pressure every day. What I'm saying is that I won't be around forever. I see in you the same good qualities that I saw in my son. I've given my life to that hospital, my clinic, and the college. I fear that when I'm gone, there'll be no one here to carry on my work and look after the poor people who desperately need health care. I have no heir to leave my assets to. I have no son to carry on my work at the hospital and clinic. I'm asking you to be that person."

"Oh! Doc, please don't ask me to do that. I'm a dumb country boy. I couldn't wear your shoes in a million years. If Emil hadn't helped me, I couldn't have passed algebra."

"I checked your grades. You have perfect marks thus far." Doc remarked.

"Doc, do you actually think I could cut someone open? I'd faint when I saw the blood gushing out. Or worse, I'd start throwing up all over everyone."

"Did you faint when Emil's intestines were hanging out in your hands? No, you didn't, and you won't faint when your skills stand between life and death."

"Doc, I know I'd die for you, but don't ask me to take on a responsibility that I'm not qualified to handle."

"Caleb, you have no idea how gifted you are or what you're capable of handling. You've underestimated your gifts and God given talents. I won't ask you to give me an answer now. We have a great deal of time before you have to decide. I've told you this so you can have as much time as you need to make the right decision."

"You know how I feel about money, Doc. I think the love of money is the root of all evil and it corrupts decent people. I'd be afraid to be responsible for a fortune."

"Do you think I'm corrupt, Caleb?"

"You know I don't."

"Son, I have no idea how much I'm worth, and it's not important. I put twenty thousand dollars in the bank every January, and we never spend all of it. I have CPA's and attorneys that tend to my holdings. I give quite generously to dozens of charities each year. I'm simply a steward of what the Lord's blessed me with, and I pray that I've been a responsible steward."

"I know Angelle and I appreciate what you've done for us," Caleb said.

"She's a precious child, and I love her as much as I could love a daughter. I plan to see that she'll never want for anything," Doc said, smiling. "You two have become very close through all this adversity, haven't you, son?"

"Yes, sir, we have Doc, and I won't deceive you any longer. I have to tell you how I feel, and you may not like what I'm going to say."

"Oh," Doc said, looking curiously at Caleb.

"I'm in love with Angelle. I've been in love with her from the first day we met. She was the first person I met when I arrived here. I know you cautioned me to stay away from her because she has emotional problems. I swear to you I tried. I really tried, but she's everywhere. She wants to be with me as much as I want to be with her. Doc, I can't help loving her. You might as well ask me to quit breathing. That would've been easier."

"Does she love you, son?"

"I think she does. She said she does, but she's not ready to take off the ring."

"Son, I had no idea your feelings were so strong for her. My concern is only for her emotional stability. She's very special to me. I don't know if you realize how fragile her condition is. My fear is still that you may be adding to her emotional instability. Do you love her enough to give her up for her well-being, if it comes to that?"

"Yes, Doc. I'd do anything to see her happy and well again."

"She's in treatment now with one of the most renowned psychiatrist in this country. My hope and prayer is that she'll respond to therapy very quickly. Then she'll be able to make a decision about whom she truly loves. With God's help, Wellington has been able to accomplish miracles with some patients that others gave up on. Wellington is a Christian psychiatrist. He'll make her face the demons that have been tormenting her. You need to understand that the treatment could take years. Her illness didn't just appear. I won't ask you to stop seeing her again, but please, don't put any added pressure on her while she's in treatment. Be her friend and not her lover. The wrong kind of relationship at present could destroy her."

"I'll wait forever for her, Doc. There could never be anyone for me except her now that I've fallen in love with her. And as far as being her lover, I feel that love making should be reserved for the marriage bed. You'll never have to worry about that."

They drove through Grenada and continued south on US 51 for a few miles. Doc said, "There's the road over there on the right." They turned down the clay road and drove another five miles or so. The small white frame church appeared on the left a few hundred yards away. Caleb's heart jumped into his throat as they neared the church. Dozens of cars and pickups were parked in the small parking area by the church, and some were parked along the side of the road.

Doc glanced at his watch. "It's still thirty minutes before the service. I'm pleased to see that a nice crowd has gathered to support Luther in his time of bereavement."

"How could you not love Luther and Buckie?" Caleb said. "Can you believe that the first time I met Luther and drove him to the hospital, he pulled out his old ragged wallet and took out all his money except five dollars and tried to give it to me? He said he wanted to 'vest in my education.'"

Doc slowed the car to a crawl, put a hand to his mouth, and fought the tears. Then in a broken voice he said, "I don't question the wisdom of God, but I'll never understand short of glory why he chose to take Buckie at such a young age." They drove by the church a short way and found a place to turn around and drove back and parked on the side of the road next to the cemetery. They looked outside the window at the freshly dug grave. Each took a deep breath and let out long sighs. Doc managed a smile as he said, "I see they were able to get the headstone carved and delivered in time. There's something about a headstone that comforts a love one. Are you ready?"

Caleb wiped his nose and eyes and said, "Yes sir," as he nodded.

They walked somberly through the grassy churchyard and up the wooden steps into the small church. The organist was playing softly. Luther was standing by the small white casket. His face distorted almost beyond recognition. Ruby was nowhere to be seen. A dozen young boys were seated on the second pew, most of them with their heads down. A few were weeping. Caleb and Doc walked up beside Luther and embraced him.

"Thank you fer a'comin,'" he murmured. "I feels like I'm 'bout to lose my mind. Brother Branch taken me home last night. I looked around, and I got a feelin' likin' I ain't nary had 'fore. Them walls was a closin' in on me. I ran outside and down the road to Mrs. Mattie's house. We sat on the porch fer most o' the night, and we cried til we ain't had no more tears. Now I can't cry no more."

The door opened behind the podium and Brother Branch walked out of the small office and rushed over to them. "I'm so glad you came, Dr. Marston. I know it was a sacrifice."

"On the contrary, Brother Branch, this was my boy for the last few years. I had to be here for my friend Luther. I'd like you to meet Caleb Morgan. He and Buckie were about as close to brothers as any two could have ever been."

Brother Branch smiled and said, "I wouldn't have been surprised if Caleb had flown in here after listening to Buckie talk about him."

"Look at my boy," Luther said. "He looks like he did 'fore he got sick." Luther's face wrinkled and he put his arms around Caleb. "Tell me he's all right, Caleb."

"Mr. Luther, the angels are watching over your son today. Your boy has looked into the face of God. Jesus Christ has held out his nail-scarred hands and taken him into his bosom. There is no pain, no suffering, just beauty and love through all eternity. In his last days, his concern was only for you, and his mother, Mr. Luther, never for himself."

Luther tightened his grip on Caleb and said, "Thank you, Caleb, for them kind words. I'm a gonna be okay. It ain't gonna be easy, but I'm gonna be gest fine. My boy loved you so much and you done so much fer him. You made him so happy."

The noise of automobiles bouncing down the rough road could be heard outside. In minutes the small church began to fill. Brother Branch said, "Y'all sit here on the first pew by Luther and Mrs. Mattie. You two are the closest thing to family that he has."

"I got more family," Luther said. "Mrs. Gladys and Miss Angelle ur liken family to me and Buckie." They took a long look at Buckie's face, and then Caleb bent over and kissed his forehead. He observed a peace on the sweet child's face that had not been there for a long time.

They took a seat and Caleb whispered to Doc, "Where's Ruby? Did you see her?"

"No. She may have decided that it was best not to come to spare Luther any additional pain."

Caleb shook his head, and said, "No. She has to come."

"I know what you're thinking son," Doc said. "Life is not a fairy tale. Things don't always have happy endings. This is life, and it's not always beautiful."

Luther's face brightened and he said, "Look a here. It be Mrs. Gladys and Angelle." He wiped his eyes and stood up and embraced them. They stood in front of the casket and wept together, embracing for a while. Angelle reached down and straightened a few wisps of Buckie's hair that were out of place. Then she and Gladys kissed him on the cheek and took their seats. Angelle sat close to Caleb and put her arm around his, fighting the tears.

Brother Branch looked at his watch and said, "It's about time, Luther. Are you ready to close the casket?"

Luther sniffled and nodded. They all stood up and walked by the casket to take a final look at the precious child that that they all loved so dearly. They fought the tears as they walked back to their seats. Brother Branch closed the casket and walked to the podium. Before he could speak, a loud blasting sound of air brakes was heard. Brother Branch saw a large Greyhound bus pull to a stop outside the small church. In seconds, the entire football team, followed by the coaches, were marching two by two into the small crowded church. The team members were dressed in blue trousers and bright orange blazers, a sight like most of those country folk had never witnessed. The two lines split as they entered the door and marched down the outside aisles and stood at attention. Luther jumped up and rushed to the front door to greet the coaches and to bring them up to the front pew. He looked out the front door and he saw Ruby sitting on the steps with the child in her arms. He was startled for a second. He ignored her, but turned to Coach Shook and said, "Thank you fer comin' and bringin' them boys. I know if'n the Lord's a lettin' Buckie look down on us, he's 'bout the happiest boy in heaven seein' what you done. Come and sits with us up front."

Coach Shook put his arm around Luther and they walked to the front pew and sat down. Doc reached over and took Coach Shook's hand and said, "Your stock just went through the roof in my book, Coach."

Coach Shook whispered, "If the most powerful and influential man in Mississippi can find time to honor a small child, how could we do any less?"

Brother Branch stood up and walked to the podium again. He saw a car out of the side windows of the church flying down the road. It skidded to a stop behind the bus. A huge young man jumped out of the car, opened the back door, and grabbed a dozen long stem yellow roses off the seat. He ran toward the entrance. Brother Branch waited at the podium. Will burst through the door with the yellow roses in his hand. Brother Branch motioned for him to bring them down.

Everyone turned to see who had delayed the start of services again. A few gasps could be heard because some recognized Will, while others marveled at his size and stature. He was dressed in a beautiful blue silk suit, white shirt, and orange tie, wearing his ostrich cowboy boots. He appeared to be seven feet tall. He walked to the casket and placed the roses on the end of it.

Luther stood up, walked over by Will, and whispered something in his ear. Will nodded and Luther lifted the lid of the casket. Will looked at Buckie's lifeless face and he shook his head almost in disbelief. He was experiencing the reality of death for the first time in his life, and he wasn't handling it very well. He gazed at the two footballs at Buckie's side and the beautiful blue and orange jersey that Buckie had refused to take off. He tried to fight the tears. He reached down and ran his fingers over Buckie's sandy, thinning hair and whispered, "Goodbye, my little buddy. I love you, and I'm going to miss you."

Luther reached down and took the teddy bear from Buckie's arm. He had forgotten that one of Buckie's last requests was that Angelle take care of his most prized possession. Will's eyes filled with tears as he and Luther walked over and sat down on the bench.

Luther handed Angelle the teddy bear and said, "He wanted you to take care of it."

"I know," Angelle said. "I promised him I would."

Luther's head hung low, and he mumbled in an almost inaudible voice, "Why'd she come? Ain't she brung nuf shame on herself?"

Caleb looked at Doc. Doc returned the stare. Caleb gestured toward the front entrance. Doc nodded in agreement.

Brother Branch stood up for the third time and said, "We have gathered here today to celebrate the life of Buckie Cummings. Let's all stand and sing Hymn # 345, 'Shall We Gather At The River.'"

Doc stood up and whispered to Luther, "I'll be back in a few seconds." He walked to the door and down the steps. Ruby was sitting there, head hung low, with Lucky on her lap. "Get up, Ruby. This is no place for the boy's mother at a time like this."

She shook her head and said, "Buckie's gone. I brought enough shame to Luther already. I don't want to hurt him no more."

"If this hurts Luther, he may need to be hurt. It's time for him to grow up and realize that you're a human being and deserve to be treated with some respect. Now, do I have to drag you down that aisle, or will you cooperate?"

"They ain't gonna let me come in, Doc. These country folk are set in their ways, and they ain't scared of you."

"They may not be afraid of me, Ruby, but most of them fear the Lord. Now, get up and show some courage. I'll be with you every step of the way." Ruby stood up with the child. She was so shaky that she almost fell. Doc grabbed her arm and steadied her and they walked inside.

Everyone turned to see who was coming in. There were some gasps, then the ooo's, and more gasps. Then the mumbling could be heard over the singing. The singing almost stopped. Doc marched her down the aisle to the front pew and sat her down by Will.

Will stood up and said, "Take my seat, Mrs. Ruby," and he walked to the outside aisle and stood with the team.

When the song ended, the whispers became very loud and distracting. Brother Branch, with his bugle-like voice, said, "This is the house of the Lord. We are not here to pass judgment on others. If the Lord didn't judge, who do you think you are? We're here to remember and praise the Lord for the life of Buckie, a beloved child of the Lord." The mumbles quieted somewhat, but a few people were still enraged. "Do I need to repeat myself?" Brother Branch said in a louder and more threatening tone. "Anyone who can't respect the house of the Lord and respect the dead will need to leave this sanctuary—now. We'll not continue this service until we have reverent silence." The assembly quieted. Brother Branch read the twenty-third Psalm. Then he prayed a beautiful and comforting prayer. He asked the congregation to stand and sing the beautiful hymn, *Someday*.

After the hymn was over, Brother Branch said a few words of comfort to the family and read a few more appropriate scriptures. He announced, "The boys in Buckie's Sunday school class would like to sing Buckie's favorite song. Come up and sing for us, boys." The twelve young boys, dressed in their Sunday best, walked out in front of the casket, turned and faced the congregation. The organist hit the first note, and the boys began to sing *Jesus Loves Me* slowly and fervently. Their voices blended so beautifully that there was not a dry eye when they finished and took their seats.

Brother Branch said, "It is so easy to question God's motives, but actually who are we to question the author of creation, the Ancient of Days, the Master, our Lord and Savior? We are mere clay. Dust, if you will, molded from the very earth on which we stand and from which we get our sustenance. Man makes his plans, but God orders his steps. God makes no mistakes. Who are we to question his wisdom and motives?" Brother Branch motioned for Caleb to come up to the podium. "Before we proceed to the cemetery, Buckie requested that his brother in spirit say a few words. Caleb Morgan, come and tell us what's on your heart."

Caleb walked up to the podium slowly and began to speak. "I have no idea why my little brother asked me to do this. He knew how timid I am. I imagine he's looking down and smiling and enjoying watching me squirm. I stayed up most of the night trying to decide what not to say about my little brother because there are a million wonderful things I could say about him. Almost every time I went to visit him during the last few weeks, he wanted to talk about heaven. That brought joy to my heart. I'm sure that losing a child is the most difficult thing that a parent could ever experience. I know that the pain Luther and Ruby are feeling now is greater than mine, which is almost unbearable. At times like these, all we have to hold on to is our faith, our family, and our friends. There are dozens of scriptures that I could read that gives hope and confidence of the resurrection. But I want to talk about the spirit of a person, namely, our friend Buckie Cummings. I was not privileged to know him as long as most of you. In the short time I knew him, he taught me more about life and love and faith under the most trying conditions a person will ever face. He smiled when his entire body was racked with pain. He clung to life for months when all medical science said it was impossible. I believe he held on for so long because he loved his father and mother so much the thought of grieving them wouldn't allow him to give up. I believe, in spite of the pain and nausea that he experienced constantly, the last week he spent with his family was the most joyful of his life. Buckie didn't fear death because he was confident that his faith would take him to the other side of the river where he would feel no pain or sorrow. He loved his father and mother, and I know they loved him. God blessed him by allowing him to be with both of them the last week of his life. I want to quote only a few verses of scripture. They apply to Buckie and every one of us that has placed our confidence in the resurrected Christ. A godly old lady who taught me in the eighth grade and has now passed on to glory gave extra credit if we memorized scriptures. God bless her. This is still my favorite scripture. 'Let not your heart be troubled: Ye believe in God, believe also in Me. In my Father's house are many mansions: If it were not so, I would have told you. I go to prepare a place for you. And if I go and prepare a place for you, I will come again, and receive you unto myself; that where I am, there ye may be also.' You remember that Thomas always asked a

Providence and Hard Work Series
You Shall Know the Truth

lot of questions of Jesus, but Jesus told him this. 'I am the Way, the Truth, and the Life: no man cometh unto the Father but by Me.' And the other scripture that I love so dearly is this one. It gives hope at a time like this. 'Eyes have not seen, nor ears heard, or the mind conceived, all the wonderful things God has in store for those who love him.' My little brother, Buckie, did love our Lord, and he's now experiences thing so wonderful that our human minds could hardly believe.

"My concern is not for my little friend any more. I know where he is, and his joy is complete. My good, good friend, Mr. Luther, and Mrs. Ruby will be going through some difficult days for a while. My prayer is that all of you who are truly Christian brothers and sisters will be there to encourage and look after them through this difficult time. That's what Christians do at a time like this. I know Mrs. Mattie will," Caleb said, looking at her and smiling. Mrs. Mattie smiled and nodded.

Caleb walked somberly back to the bench. Luther reached out and clasped Caleb's hands, with tear-filled eyes, and said, "That's why my boy asked you to talk."

Brother Branch motioned for the deacons to come to the front as pallbearers. "We will meet at the gravesite outside," he said. Everyone stood. Luther stumbled as he stood. Coach Shook grabbed his arm and steadied him. He was weary beyond exhaustion, and his legs barely responded. Will rushed to him and put his arm around his waist. They followed the beautiful white casket carried by the deacons out of the entrance of the church to the gravesite. Ruby followed at a distance.

Everyone congregated around the open grave. Brother Branch prayed again. He opened his Bible to 1 Corinthians 15 and read verses 50-58. When he came to the final four verses, his voice bellowed out like a trumpet, his way of emphasizing the importance of that scripture. He read the following words: 'For this corruption must put on incorruption, and this mortal must put on immortality. Then shall be brought to pass the saying that is written, Death is swallowed up in victory. O death, where is thy sting? O grave, where is thy victory? The sting of death is sin; and the strength of sin is the law. But thanks be to God which giveth us the victory through our Lord Jesus Christ. Therefore, my beloved brethren, be ye steadfast, unmovable, always abounding in the work of the Lord, forasmuch as ye know that your labor is not in vain in the Lord.' He closed the Bible, walked over to Luther, putting his arms around him, and said, "Take courage my friend. The Lord will get you through this. I'll be here for you, and I'll be out to see you later."

Luther's friends crowded around him and hugged him and encouraged him. Ruby and the child stood silently a few steps behind Luther. A few of the congregation, who felt shame at their earlier actions, walked over to Ruby and hugged her and begged her forgiveness, as did Brother Branch.

Every team member, including Will, walked up to Luther to give words of consolation and encouragement. Then they loaded up on the bus and pulled away. The small cemetery began to empty. In a few minutes, there were only Doc, Caleb, Angelle, Gladys, Ruby, Lucky, and Luther standing by the grave. They all stood near Luther, trying to console him with words of love and comfort. Ruby and Lucky stood there silently holding hands.

Ruby, void of expression, was silent with tear stains down her cheeks. "Where Buttie?" Lucky continued to ask. Ruby put her finger to her lips and hushed him. Caleb and Doc turned to Ruby and embraced her. They whispered words of encouragement.

Angelle and Mrs. Gladys embraced Luther and whispered words of encouragement in his ears. Luther kissed them and thanked them for all they had done for Buckie. They had a good cry in his arms and then they embraced Ruby and whispered words of encouragement in her ears. They walked to Gladys' Car and drove away.

"We hate to leave you, Luther," Doc said, "but we must. I have a clinic full of sick people patiently waiting."

Luther walked over by Doc and Ruby. He said, "Doc, you knows I canst say what I'm a feelin' inside 'bout what you done fer Buckie and me but …"

"You don't need to say a single word, Luther. Your gratitude is in your eyes. Remember this, my good friend. When you feel like the world is caving in on you and life isn't worth living, get up, and have a smoke. Take a stroll and imagine all the wonderful things that God has in store for your boy. Remember the good years, how happy you were, how much love you two had for each other. You take it one day at a time and remember this, the sun will continue to rise, and with each rising sun, the pain will lessen and the sun will become brighter. Do you want us to give you a ride home?" Doc asked.

"I gest lives around that there curve, 'bout a mile. I'll walk a little later. I ain't ready to leave my boy gest yet." Caleb and Doc gave Luther and Ruby a final hug and eased toward Doc's automobiles. Luther stood by the headstone, heart-broken, feeling as if his world had been buried in the grave before him. Ruby stood close by his side with Lucky standing between them.

As Angelle and Gladys drove away, Angelle turned and looked back at the heartrending sight behind them. A flood of emotions surged through her mind. "I will marry Caleb Morgan some day," she said prophetically.

"I never doubted it," Gladys said. I've never known two people more suited for each other than you two, or more in love. And furthermore there is no fiancé, is there?"

"How could you know that," Angelle said in amazement. "Do you know about my past?"

"I know you've been hurt badly in the past, and the ring is your security blanket. People in love can't stop talking about their betrothed. You've never once mentioned his name. You could do a lot worse," Gladys said softly. "He's one in a million. He reminds me of June. That was Doc's son. The only difference in the two is the color of their hair."

"You are right," Angelle said, lowering her head. "I'm not engaged. Maurice was my father, and this is my mother's ring. I wear this ring so ..."

"So you won't have to make excuses when you're asked for a date?" Gladys said. "You don't have to tell me anymore. I've learned a few things about people behavior in my thirty years of nursing."

"Such as?" Angelle said, surprised by Gladys's comment.

"Such as, you won't shake anyone's hand. I've observed sadness and even panic in your eyes. I know someone hurt you very badly once. What's different about Caleb that makes you think you could marry him?"

"I'm going to get well someday. I believe he'll wait for me."

"Does he know that there is no Maurice? That he was your father?" Gladys asked.

"No—and I'll never tell him until I'm sure I can make love to him and have his children, and we can have a normal marriage. I'm in treatment now. I'm encouraged for the first time since..."

"Since what? Do you want to talk about it?" Gladys asked.

"No. No. I'm not ready for that yet."

"I think you are playing with fire, Angelle. I think he needs to know everything. You need his support through this if he truly loves you and is willing to wait for you."

Angelle shook her head and said, "I can't do that to him. If I don't get well, I'm going to tell him that I'm planning to marry Maurice. I'll leave, and he'll be free to find someone who'll love him in a way that I will never be able to love him."

"I still think you are making a mistake. He might be the one who helps you get through this. But it is your life and you're decision, and your secret is safe with me," Gladys assured her.

Doc took the key out of his pocket to start the engine. Caleb reached over and put his hand on Doc's hand and said, "Not yet,

Doc. Wait just another minute." Doc looked at Caleb and nodded. They sat, watched, waited, and prayed.

There was silence by the gravesite for a long time as Luther and Ruby stood with their heads down gazing at the grave.

"It's time to go Caleb," Doc said. "It's not going to happen because you want it to happen." Doc took the key and started to crank the car and Caleb grabbed his hand again and said. "Look Doc."

Lucky looked up at Luther and reached for his hand. Luther looked down at the beautiful child and didn't snatch it away. The child asked, "Are you my Poppa?"

Tears began to stream down Luther's cheeks. Ruby eased over in front of Luther and buried her face in his chest and wept. Luther put his arms around her and embraced her for a few seconds. Then he reached down and picked up the child and held him close to his heart and whispered, "I reckon I am, son. I reckon I am." The three embraced for a long time. Luther looked at the casket and said, "I reckon things are goin' to be all right, son. I love you, and I'm gonna take care of your brother and your mother... Let's go home, Ruby."

Tears streamed from Doc's and Caleb's eyes, and they were filled with such joyful emotion that they could hardly speak. Doc cranked the car and said, "Let's go home, son. We're not needed here anymore."

As they pulled away, Caleb placed his hand on Doc's arm and said, "Love does truly cover a multitude of sins."

Doc answered back, "'For His anger endureth, but a moment; in His favor is life: Weeping may endure for a night, but joy cometh in the morning.'" They drove over the clay hills and through the dusty valleys. Their joy was inexpressible. After a short while, Caleb began to snicker. He tried to restrain it; however, Doc, as usual, was way ahead of him. Finally Doc said, "All right, out with it."

"It's too embarrassing Doc. I'd rather not."

"I'd rather you did," Doc said, already knowing what Caleb was thinking.

"Yes sir, Doc. I was thinking—joy might come before morning," and he broke out laughing. Doc joined him and they had a good long laugh. When they finally stopped, Caleb said, "It feels so good to laugh again."

The end of book two. Book three coming soon.

ABOUT THE AUTHOR

James F. Hunt holds a Masters Plus Thirty in education administration and supervision from SLU, in Hammond, Louisiana. James coached football and taught in high school thirteen years, served as a high school principal ten years, and was appointed personnel director and supervisor of instruction seventeen years. Additionally he was elected to the parish governing body for twenty- four consecutive years serving as president the last sixteen years. He taught Bible study and counseled parish and state prisoners on Sunday for thirty years.

James was an outstanding high school football player receiving All-State honors. He was recruited by Tulane, and many other colleges, however, he chose LSU and tried out for football and received a scholarship. James never played at LSU because he married his high school sweetheart and dropped out of school. A year later he enrolled at Louisiana College and played on the golf team for three years and received his BS Degree.

Upon retirement from the school board, James built his own golf course near Clinton, Louisiana, and he manages the course while continuing to write novels about his vast experiences. He is currently working on his fifth novel.

James F. Hunt

James and his wife, Ginger, of fifty- two years live near Clinton, Louisiana with Buster, his two-hundred-thirty pound English Mastff, and his second son, Harvey Dan Hunt, a Chihuahua/ terrier cross.

Made in the USA
San Bernardino, CA
05 February 2016